EXISTENTI[A

©2014, Ned Alexander,

Though I was fortunate enough to have grown up reading works by such Brilliant writers as Ray Bradbury, Isaac Asimov and Philip K Dick, and though I have been both influenced and inspired by their writings I should point out that "The Martin Chronicles" has no connection or similarity to Ray Bradbury's "The Martian Chronicles", which, I should also add, I highly recommend.

This book is for:

All the amazing volunteers and, moreover, all of the awe inspiring children and young adults that attend the UK burns camps that I have had the honour of being associated with.

This book is also dedicated to the organisers without whom none of the camps would exist, in particular to Pat Wade MBE whose hard work, self-sacrifice and generous spirit has touched so many lives.

With thanks to:

Julie Riley
James Riley
&
Tracy Connolly Alexander
Lyanne Ribbons

CHAPTER ONE

"Suited and booted"

<u>1</u>

"Darkness fell across the land, the midnight hour was close at hand and as we approached the incident flames could be seen…"

"Hang on…" Jed furrowed his brow, paused and looked sideways to where Kevin was sitting. "What?"

"Oh. Er, sorry, I'm just making notes for my development book. You know, reporting on the fire we just attended?" Kevin had started this sentence as a statement but had altered it to pitch it as a question as he could see Jed starting to look at him quizzically and unconvinced. Kevin lowered his electronic pen and placed it on the tablet onto which he'd been scribbling notes.

"Okay…" replied Jed. He took in a deep deliberate breath "I understand that." Sigh. "I understand the concept of filling out your development book to record your experiences so as to show competence for professional advancement, I…I get that Kevin, I do, really, I do. *I* was in the job before *you* were even born so let's assume that I've been made aware of that concept, okay? Thing is, I'm questioning not the process but more…the choice of lyrics, I mean the, er, text."

Kevin stared back at Jed in the dim light of the crew cab, "Well you know I always like to start my reports with a little bit of description, you know, kind of like a story, so as to get the reader a little bit more interested in carrying on to the end. So I thought I'd say how it was getting dark and that it was, er, almost midnight when we got the fire call, you know?"

"Kevin you know, *firstly*, you haven't *got* to grab the reader. This is not "Of Mice and Men." This is a report. A document that the reader will be neither enthralled nor inspired by. It's just to show you have gained competence in a particular skill…"

"Of Myson men?"

"No Kevin." Jed closed his eyes and scratched his forehead, "It's not of Myson men, it's Of. Mice. And. Men." Jed rubbed his tired eyes, "*Secondly* and perhaps more importantly you're writing this for some odd reason in the style of the late Michael Jackson."

Kevin pondered this briefly and then retorted with a blank look. After a short pause and some deep memory searching, he blinked a slow, laboured blink. "Michael who? Michael Jackson? What watch is he on?"

"No, Kevin, no, Michael Jackson is not *in* the Fire Brigade. Kevin he's one of the old classical musicians. He used to perform pop-classics? No? Don't you ever listen to music Kevin? Well, clearly you do because you've stolen his lyrics from the song Thriller." Jed tutted and impatiently shook his head in the darkness. Looking away he stared out into the night, tracing a raindrop as it ran slowly down the fire appliance window.

Outside, little could be seen in the darkness bar the soft glow from the city as they drove across the wasteland to re-join the main street.

After a short while, catching his reflection in the window, Jed smiled wryly and continued, "Actually Kevin I'm sorry. Really, I'm only joking. What you've written is actually pretty good."

Kevin frowned. Unsure. Suspicious.

"No, really Kevin, I'm sorry, I'm…I'm just pulling your leg." Jed then gave that comforting smile and the kind of nod that Doctors would give as they prepare to cut the leg off that they know you must lose.

Kevin smiled, thankful that Jed had not in fact missed his literary brilliance.

"Actually Kevin, let's hear what you've got so far. Where was it you'd gotten up to in your notes?"

The budding new author picked up his tablet deliberately and then read from his new manuscript. "Er…I'd just said how we'd come to the front door of the house, and…then I'd just listed the equipment that I was carrying." Hand gestures emphasised this. "That's about as far as I'd got."

"Hmm…" Jed nodded attentively. "And that equipment *was*?"

"Er, the breaking in gear, remember? I forced entry into the premises."

"Yes Kev, so you did. Okay so how about this then? Say that you got to the door and having identified that it was secured you used the Battle-ram to force the door open."

"Er…Battle-ram…door…open, yeah got it." Kevin, with tongue poking sideways out of his mouth, scribbled as quickly as he could.

Jed raised a hand in front of his face looking to grasp words from the ether. Amateur dramatics was not one of his strengths. His eyes narrowed. "But then say that it was very difficult getting through the door with the Battle-ram so you had to beat it, beat it, beat it, beat it and then mention that...*you didn't want to be defeated.*" He slowly nodded. "Hmm, yes."

"De...feated. Got it. Okay, what else?" Kevin sat like a wide eyed budding journalist discovering his first big story.

"Well." pondered Jed. He looked away out of the window again and stifled a snigger. "You were asking me if I was ready to enter the building, right?" Jed waved his hand Wilde-like towards Kevin.

Kevin agreed with a nod and a shrug. "Okay well then let's see how you could write that with a bit more urgency in your report." Jed looked deeply pensive (if a little hammy) towards Kevin, "Okay, okay, put this. You've just said how you wanted to beat it, right?"

Kevin nodded.

Jed mirrored him and continued "The, er, door that is...you wanted to beat the door."

"Yes, and then we've put that I didn't want to be defeated." confirmed Kevin.

"Hmm, ah, yes, yes so then say that, er...understanding the importance for our rapid entry you turned to me and, encouraging me to get involved, you said to me 'You wanna be starting something? You got to be starting something!'"

Obediently taking dictation, Kevin smiled and shook his puzzled young head. "You know it's gonna take me ages to pick up this Fire Brigade speak. Okay, what's next?"

"Okay, again you were fully aware of the worsening conditions so again you repeated your question to me, you said 'You wanna be starting something?', and then you pressed me again with 'You got to be starting something!'" Jed's shoulders subtly spasmed up and down in the darkness as his body expressed the laughter that his face desperately concealed.

The fire appliance in which they rode rumbled quietly through the cold rainy early hours of the morning back towards its' base station. As the rising sun poured over the appliance, a plethora of colours spewed into the crew cab and the windscreens polarised. The appliance's "old reliable" K27 combustion engine effortlessly carried them towards the city's main streets. Minutes later the appliance slowed and carefully bumped up from the grass, swaying on its suspension as it re-joined the main street. It slowed further as Richie, the driver, safely parked it alongside the road. The primary engine started and began to hum as the road wheels raised up and folded themselves into the chassis. The secondary combustion engine then disengaged and Richie, who had been absentmindedly whistling to himself at the front of the appliance, removed his hands from the steering wheel as it folded itself back into the dashboard. He touched the centre console display and a menu appeared. Selecting the 'HOME' option, he then sat back to fill out his driver's log. The appliance, automatically joining the traffic, hovered away as it made its' way up to cruising speed.

The fire appliance itself, a fairly new Ford-Panasonic, glistened in the dawn sunlight and reflected in the windows as it now passed the neon lit London shops and Holo-boards advertising everything from breakfast cereals to the latest-generation cosmetic Stem-plant technology.

Emergency and military vehicles had been awarded exemption from the 2315 'Conduit Reforms' law by The People's Government. The 'Conduit', a sprawling network of Z-conductors over which all vehicles, or 'Pods' now smoothly flowed on their pre-programmed journeys. Vehicles that never needed to stop to refuel and were rarely involved in collisions except during the odd on-board glitch or rare act of sabotage. Each branch of the conduit system was still named as streets and roads in order to maintain the public's perception of continuity, and to ease its initial introduction to motorists.

Most vehicles only ever needed to travel on the conduit and were in fact confined to it by their need for its' power supply. But as the conduit had replaced all of the old roadways from private driveways to motorways, underground car parks to ferry boats, there was nowhere that an average traveller would need to go that they could not. Of course, there were also safety advantages to being constricted to the conduit as now, due to on board chips and GPS-ZEN technology, vehicle deaths were all but a distant memory. It was decided by the authorities however, that, for obvious reasons, military and emergency vehicles could not be confined by such limitations and were therefore permitted and licensed to use old hybrid technology to allow them to travel off road in emergency situations. Hybrid technology - A technology that had now become '*as clean as the conduit itself*'...or so the advert goes.

2

The darkness of the fire station dormitory was replaced by a lowly dimmed light, which gradually brightened to safely wake the crews from their slumber.
"Someone turn the fucking lights off..." moaned Jed. "I'm slumbering!"
When half lit, moans and groans could be heard from other Firefighters who also had been woken from what had been a well needed, and well deserved, two hours sleep following the busy night before.
Jed raised himself up onto his elbows and forced a resistant eye open. "Kevin!" A short pause. No response. Jed strained an eyebrow upwards then scanned the room slowly turning his head towards Kevin's bed. "Kevin?!"
"Uh, uh, yes?...eh?" Kevin rose abruptly from his bed and sat upright. He had clearly risen at an impressive rate as his eyes and jaw had not had time to catch up with the rest of his face and so he sat there in bed swaying slightly, mouth still open yet eyes still shut.
"Kevin! Why is there no T in Jed?"
"Uh...what?" Kevin's eyebrows now arched fully, but it was no good, the eyes were still shut.
"Kevin, why is there no T in Jed?"
"Er, because there's...what? No T? Because that's not how it's spelt? It's not spelt with a T, that's why...er. I don't understand." An eye opened and peered over at Jed.
Jed pulled his pillow from behind his head, "No Kevin not 'no T in Jed!' No bloody *tea*! There's no bloody *tea* in Jed! Fix it! Go and make me some bloody tea!" Jed's pillow then found itself sticking to Kevin's face at speed.
"Sorry Jed. Yes I'll get some tea. Yes, of course." Kevin then quickly rose, pulled on his trousers, stabbed his feet into his shoes and shuffled out, shirt in hand.
"That's better Kevin. Don't make me wait too long now will you?" As Kevin disappeared out of the dormitory door Jed collapsed back onto his bed. Forgetting he'd thrown his pillow, he landed with a thud against his head board. "Bollocks!"
Katie, who had been laying in her bed listening to proceedings chuckled to herself. "Jed, lay off him a bit will you? Let him settle in a bit more."

Jed grunted. "What're you talking about? It's good for him. It's character building."

"Character building? Get you! A 'pillow' of the community." Katie grinned to herself.

"Ha bloody ha. I'm telling you, it's character building."

"Yeah I'm sure it's all good for him but lay off just a little until he settles in a bit more is all I'm suggesting. Go on, do it for your Aunty Katie." Katie sat up, and in her best patronising mumsy voice continued "Oh go on. Try to not be a complete cock for just a little while…Hmmm? You can do it. Yes, that's it…Who's a good boy then?"

Jed reached for his pillow to cover his ears but then tutted to himself again remembering that he had already launched it at Kevin.

After a short time the door to the dorm began to open.

Katie, who had laid back down on her bed, whispered "Jed go on, remember what I said."

Monkey-boy, who had until now, remained silent, agreed. "Yeah Jed, slow up a little mate."

Jed replied with his signature grunt.

A now fully clothed Kevin stepped into the dorm. Knuckles dragging and not yet fully upright, he 'slothed' over to Jed's bed and beside it placed a steaming hot cup of fresh tea. Jed acknowledged this with an "Ugh" and Kevin turned to leave the dorm.

Katie lifted her head up and watched as Kevin walked towards the door. "Er, Kevin? Don't tell me you've brought only Jed *a* cup of tea, have you?" Her eyebrows lowered and eyes widened as she spoke.

"Well, yeah I, er…" Kevin, whose tired young brain was still clearly booting up, had not yet fully loaded his language protocols. He shrugged and then turned to leave.

"Kevin! You wanker!" Katie then gifted Kevin with a second speeding pillow.

Most of the pillows from the other Firefighters in the dorm then hit Kevin as he left, but the shoes that followed had only been thrown for effect and hit the door as he stepped out.

As the pillows and shoes crumpled together on the floor, Jed smiled. "See, I told you. It's for his own good."

3

The mess table buzzed with the frantic activity of a zoo at feeding time as Firefighter after Firefighter grabbed a breakfast and added toast, sauces, cutlery, teas, coffees and all manner of exotic herbs and spices ranging from salt and pepper to pepper and salt. Then each hunter-gatherer hulked back to his or her chair and "ughed" declaration of territory. After much evolutionary development these creatures would eventually learn to walk upright, and indeed by about 0800 hours they had even grasped the basic concepts of language, hierarchy and moaning about the state of the Fire Brigade.

Katie sat in her chair polishing off the last of her toast and looked around the room as all the others scoffed and picked at their plates. She then shook her head and in a low philosophical voice muttered that age old reflective, contemplative phrase, "Well that was a really shit night."

Les, still in the world of the un-dead, looked up from his bacon, turned to Katie, raised his sunken puppy dog eyes and howled in soft pained agreement.

Kevin, who had been actively encouraged to rise early and embrace the new morn, was fully awake and was now tucking into anything that wasn't tied down - tea, toast, extra sausages and he even reached for more fried-bread until it was pointed out to him that it was not in fact fried-bread but was in fact a place mat.

"Oi, I heard that," snapped Richie who had just sat down after finishing serving the last breakfast.

The Station Officer, known by the crews as Mother but referred to formally as Guv, sat quietly at the end of the table sipping at his tea. "God I hope we have a quieter night tonight." He rubbed his bloodshot eyes and then rattled his head trying to shake off his lack-of-sleep hangover.

Jed, who was sitting at the opposite end of the table, looked up at him, "You're getting too old for this shit aren't you Guv?"

"That's right mate, I'm getting too old for this…Er, hang on. Less of that you cheeky sod!" Mother secretly smiled to himself at Jed's comment. After a long slow yawn he looked across the mess table and threw out the enquiry "So, anyone got any plans for today at all?"

Jed droned "I think I'm gonna go see Laura…" His sentence stretched into a yawned "…and then…go…home…to…bed." He scratched his belly and smacked his lips.

Richie agreed. "Yes, bed. Bed good." Others at the table sat quietly nodding.

Katie slurped on her tea and confirmed "Yes, me too, I'm going straight to bed for the day."

"Yes I agree, I think I'll join you." Kevin yawned through the second part of his sentence.

"You bloody will not!" snapped Katie.

Everyone had turned to look at Kevin to see his response.

Kevin, still processing Katie's statement, looked up to the heavens, or more accurately looked up into the deep recesses of his memory to establish why she should have snapped at him. As he looked back down, he noticed the men opposite staring at him, their eyebrows raised and all wearing smug, expectant looks. Then as he looked around the table he noticed the rest of the jury also gawking at him. Suddenly the silence was broken by the sound of a large penny dropping and clattering as it hit the floor. Kevin whipped his head round to see Katie, "No, no I mean, I mean I'm gonna go home to bed, when I, er…I er, I didn't mean I was gonna join *you* in bed. You *know* that's not what I meant." He raised his hands in clear indication of surrender.

The jury smirked judgementally as he continued to dig himself a larger hole.

"I should bloody well hope not young Kevin." Katie slowly shook her head and tutted.

"No, no, really, I didn't mean that I…no…I *am* going to bed. That's all." The glow from Kevin's face could now be felt across the table.

Mother, who had stopped smirking to himself, leaned towards him "Kevin…sometimes…*less* is more. Quiet now."

"Okay," he said now panting softly. "Sorry, I didn't mean...you know I'm not saying I wouldn't Katie because I…you know I'm not saying you're ugly or anything, in fact I like the older woman."

Mother sat upright, "No, no Kevin really, less *is* more. You should shut up now Mr Owen!"

Kevin sat back into his chair. "Sorry Guv."

Katie just sat looking offended and hurt as Kevin analysed her face, gauging the damage he may have caused. She raised her mug, sipped her tea and winked at Richie across the table, who was concealing his amusement. He coughed to cover his chuckle and got up to clear the plates.

Seeing an opportunity to make amends, Kevin stood to help Richie, "Actually, can I get your plate for you Katie?"

"If you don't mind," Katie replied, head bowed and with puppy dog eyes raised, playing the moment for all she could. "I do still need my plate though *really* as I was going to have some more toast...I'm still so weak from last night." Katie saved these rare pouting girly moments for special occasions like this.

Mother's jaw dropped slightly and he closed his eyes in disbelief. This was too cheesy a performance even for Kevin to believe, surely.

"Oh, can I get you some more toast? Yes, yes, let me get you some more toast," repeated Kevin, nodding his insistence.

"Okay, but I don't think I'll have time to eat it. I was going to wash my bike-pod before I went off duty but if I eat toast I'll not have time." She looked away, scorned. Hurting. Giggling.

Mother scratched his face covering the smile he could no longer hide, 'Oh no, too much, surely,' he mused.

"Oh well, er, I don't mind washing your bike. In fact let me just get you some toast and then I'll give your bike a quick wash." Kevin scurried off into the kitchen.

Mother looked along the length of the table toward Katie. "You're a bad girl O'Neill."

"What?" she asked, "I'm the victim here remember." She raised her hands towards Mother, playing the betrayed martyr.

"How do you sleep at night Katie?" he asked.

"Well to be fair, I didn't, did I? So, I'm gonna get my bike washed. That'll free the day up for me to catch up with some well-earned sleep." She smiled a wide conquering smile.

Mother shook his head and smirked. "A bad girl. Very, very bad." He then sat upright in his chair, coughed his intention to speak and addressed those still seated.

"Seriously though guys, if anyone pulls a stunt like that again with Kevin..." Katie lowered her head waiting for her reprimand. "See if you can get him to clean my car too will you?" Katie smiled and shook her head. Laughter that was now rumbling around the table was punctuated by the sound of Kevin starting up the pressure washer in the appliance bay.

4

That evening, roll call was taken, as usual, in the appliance bay. The off-going watch removed their fire suits from the fire appliances, placed them back on charge and left, nodding their goodbyes to the oncoming watch members that were lined along one wall of the bay.

The appliance bay itself was a large hanger-like structure that housed the two large red fire appliances. Along the walls of the bay armoured fire suits stood docked to their designated power and air charging points, each accompanied by a shelved helmet.

Two sliding-poles were at one side of the bay that dropped from recesses in the ceiling. These came from rooms above and were for the Firefighters to slide down when they needed to get to the bay and mount the appliances quickly if a fire call was received whilst they were upstairs. This particular architectural design feature was a respectful nod towards the history of the Fire Service. A large automatic door stood in front of each of the two fire appliances and the floor was fully covered in matte black tiles, except of course for where the two conduit tracks ran that each appliance was parked on.

Mother, accompanied by Sub Officer Brown, faced and stood to attention in front of the watch.

After also bringing the watch to attention, attendance of each crew member was confirmed and then they were 'stood to ease.' Mother then looked along the line to visually confirm that everyone's fire suits were in good, clean order and that the neon glowing "FIRE" on the chest plate was in its standby mode of green meaning 'good to go'. Each Firefighter was then told which of the fire appliances they would be riding that night and what jobs they would be allocated. This ensured that each crew member knew their expected roles should the station's sirens alarm to inform them there was a call to attend. These roles included those allocated as the evening's drivers, those who would be assigned to the watch-room to log fire calls and, of course, those whose turn it was to assist Richie in the mess for the evening.

After completion of roll call each crew member retrieved their fire helmet from where it was shelved and then mounted the machine in the seating position they were allocated. They then began their duties by testing their fire suits. This was done by donning the fire helmets and twisting them onto the suits to complete an air seal test. The suit then booted-up and automatically began its' checks. This included on-board air and power levels, suit integrity and communications links. Once this was completed, each Firefighter used voice commands to switch on their internal visors and check the night vision, thermal imaging, zoom and 'locate' facilities. Once all of these checks were completed and the wearer was satisfied with the suit, they would then contact the Brigade's Main Control using the voice command, "Comms, Control." An automated image of a Control Officer would appear in the corner of the internal visor and they would then complete long range communications checks.

The fire appliances' 'on-boards' were booted up so that the driver could confirm diagnostic checks, on-board firefighting media levels and hybrid fuelling levels.

Once each of these checks had been carried out, information was wirelessly sent from each appliance to the station's communications room, where it was then relayed to the Fire Brigade's Main Control. This allowed Brigade Control to be fully aware of which appliances were operationally ready, which crew members were on-board, and the condition of the appliances and its' crews. Once all of these tests were confirmed by Control, the off-going watch members, who were readying themselves to leave, were informed that they were now released from duties.

The crew had all finished their change-of-watch tests and were now sitting upstairs in the mess enjoying a short break which was the normal routine at the start of a shift and was usually spent discussing any topics relevant to that shift over teas and coffees. It was also an opportunity for the Station Officer to confirm if any training drills were going to be carried out that evening, if there were any public fire safety events to attend, lectures to hear, or just to discuss any relevant news reported to him from Brigade Control.

Katie sat sipping her tea. She had not had the opportunity to fully catch up with her sleep and was still slightly shell shocked from the busy night before. She hugged her mug for comfort. Next to her sat Jed and Richie. Opposite was Kevin, smiling and buzzing with youthful energy. Both Sub Officers Brown (Brownie) and Russell were discussing with Mother some notes he was showing them, whilst both Monkey-boy and Veggie sat quietly arguing over the solution to a crossword puzzle.

"Alright then, listen in," commanded Brownie, the more senior of the Sub Officers. The table quietened. Except, that is, for Monkey-boy and Veggie who were still arguing.

"Oi, listen in!" repeated Brownie. Monkey-boy looked up from the crossword. Brownie raised his eyebrows. "Do you mind?" Monkey-boy tightened his lips, then gently and deliberately placed his stylus on the table in front of him.

"Sorry", said Monkey-boy. "I, er, I thought you said storm bright glistening."

"You thought I said storm bri..." Brownie stopped before finishing the sentence when he caught Mother giving him the 'You may as well try teaching quantum physics to a football' look.

Monkey-boy had earned his name firstly because he looked and walked like a monkey (albeit the lesser spotted, pasty, red-headed monkey) and secondly because, well, if he was a monkey, he'd be about as intelligent as a new born chimpanzee, therefore, Monkey-*boy*.

Nicknames were often awarded in the Brigade as a result of a funny event that someone was involved in, because of a *name* like for example, Jack, whose real name was Mark Russell, or sometimes just to state the bleeding obvious. Hence, Monkey-boy.

Brownie rolled his eyes and continued, "Okay, we've got a notice from H.Q. to say that we're getting a new crew member joining the watch as of next week."

Puzzled looks were shuffled and then dealt out around the table. Kevin had not long since joined the watch and this had brought them up to the maximum a watch was allowed to have allocated to it.

"That doesn't make a lot of sense does it?" Katie turned to Brownie and shrugged. "I mean...Kevin's just joined us...Is one of us...being...moved?"

"No, no...no, nothing like that. No, no, no," Brownie raised up both hands and faced them towards the mess table to indicate that he was but the messenger and that shooting him would be inappropriate at this time.

Jed put down his mug and stifled a yawn whilst mumbling "Yeah well that doesn't make sense then. No-one goes above full quota. How's that gonna work?" Jed took a sharp intake of breath as he finished talking and was able to enjoy his yawn fully.

Brownie smiled back at Jed, "Well it could be worse mate. You could have just been assigned to be his mentor. Which of course...you have been."

Jed's face soured and his shoulders dropped. "Bollocks. Oh great...big...fat...hairy bollocks! Really?"

Mother rolled his eyes and leaned towards the table "Okay, listen. We don't know much more than you guys. All we know is that we're getting a new member on the watch."

Katie leaned towards Jed "You play nicely with your new member now won't you." Jed concealed a cheesy grin behind his coffee mug.

Mother continued, "His name is Recruit Firefighter Mann. He's in his thirties, apparently he's very able if a little quiet and is being posted in from another Brigade."

"Another Brigade? A recruit being posted in from another Brigade?" Richie leaned forward from the chair he had been resting back on, "Well that's, that's just unheard of Guv."

"What do you mean unheard of? Weren't you listening to what I was just saying?"

"No Guv sorry I mean...." Richie noticed Mother looking back at him with a mildly derisive face,

"Okay then, sorry previously unheard of, until you just said it."

"Oh right, previously unheard of...hmmm, okay. Well I know that and I agree it is a bit strange, but you know as much as I do, okay? As far as I know he'd just completed his training and was then given permission to transfer because of family commitments and, although it's a new one on me, I don't see any real reason for trying to find conspiracy theories in it, okay?"

"I've got it!" said Veggie. "Yes!"

Mother flinched slightly at Veggie's volume, "Well? What is it Veggie?" Mother sat back preparing to hear the first of many implausible conspiracy theories.

"Oh, er, sorry Guv I've...er...I've got..." he looked down at the table, squinted his eyes and pulled his mouth to one side "five across Guv. I've got, er, five across. Sorry." He lowered his head then raised apologetic eyes at Mother, "It was soporific by the way...Not what you were saying - I mean the answer. It was...er...soporific." Veggie's volume reduced throughout the sentence as he realised just how disinterested Mother's appearance was becoming and of course just how irrelevant his outburst was.

After a full term pregnant pause Mother took a deep breath and continued, "Right, okay, so then, Jed....you *are* the new recruit's Mentor. I want regular updates on his progress, and as for everyone else, let's make him feel welcome and get him up to speed with how we do things here as quickly as possible. Okay? Now let's all get over to the lecture room, Jack's going to give us a refresher input on the use of fire-fighting harmonics tech."

Teas and coffees were gulped down as everyone stood to leave. Kevin, who had sat quietly throughout proceedings, smiled to himself. He looked at Jed and nodded a slow, controlled, triumphant nod.

Jed raised an eyebrow.

"I know what you're thinking Kevin. You're thinking that this new guy's gonna join, and then he'll get all the shit I give you as *he'll* now be the new boy. Is that right?"

Kevin kept quiet as he slightly tilted his head and looked away. He placed his hands behind his head and swung back on his chair smug in Jed's confirmation.

"But you see the thing is Kevin, this new guy is my mentee. I can't pick on my mentee now can I?"

Kevin's brow lowered.

"I can't very well give my own mentee shit now, can I? What sort of man do you think I am? No, no. Instead, I need to teach him the ways of the 'Force', or…the 'Brigade' if you will. I need to take him under my wing and then, well, teach him how to give...*you*...shit! Don't look upon this as gaining full inclusion into the watch now that there's someone with less time in than you. Instead, look upon it as losing peace of mind. The inability to open any drawer, door or cupboard without needing to check for booby-traps first. Think of it as not knowing whether you're safe when you go to bed, fully aware that you can't look both ways to see which one of us may attack."

Kevin's shoulders now slumped lower than his waist as the reality of Jed's new appointment of reinforcements fully sunk it. This changed the rules of engagement. *This* was a whole new level. A new type of war had begun. Kevin would have to learn the ways of stealth, the cunning ways of the ninja. Kevin would have to grow a pair and start learning to make…..more booby-traps!

"Bed first though," thought Kevin. "That is what the true warrior would do…lecture then bed!…I'm too bollocksed to fight today."

CHAPTER TWO

"Fire in the whole"

1

Just after 0800 hours and the fire station stood, framed by a cloudless blue backdrop, its' large windows polarising as the sun moved gracefully across the sky. Outside in the rear yard, both appliances were being washed down by the crews before they could be handed over to Mother's watch at change of shift.

One of the Firefighters, who had been crouched and was wiping down the lowered wheels, looked up, stood, smiled and raised a welcoming hand to an incoming pod as he wrung the water from his chamois.

The red, bubble-like hovering car manoeuvred directly and precisely into a parking space and then lowered itself onto the conduit as its motor, humming deeper and deeper, wound itself down and stopped. The glass-domed bubble then gently hissed as the front half of it cracked vertically open. Jed stepped out of the two person pod, uniform and shoes in hand. He punched a code into the centre console on the inside of the opened section and the pod slowly closed and sealed itself. Hearing a soft high pitched whirring behind him, Jed turned to see Katie arrive in her sleek black and silver, hard top Honda Bike-Pod. It parked itself next to Jed's pod and it too gently lowered itself down onto the conduit. After a few seconds the front half of the tinted glass-topped section of the bike lifted, pivoted from the front of the bike and the rear section pivoted from the back opening like majestic insect wings, the heavy metal music from inside the pod becoming louder as it opened. Katie sat herself up and stepped out of the rear of the bike in a single well-practiced motion. Turning on her heel then walking towards Jed, she lifted her bent arm above her head, pointed her ID card back towards the bike-pod, clicked it and re-placed her arm by her side as the bike folded itself back into its' stand-by position. Jed glanced towards the chamois wringing Firefighter who was slowly shaking his head gently amused by Katie's showy entrance. Jed shrugged back at him, raised both hands to the sky, chuckled and turned to follow Katie into the station. Both of them then stopped and acknowledged Mother who was just pulling into the yard in his retro styled silver Sam-sonic twelve series.

"Good few days off?" enquired Jed as Katie and he watched Mother's pod parking.

Katie turned with one side of her lip curled upwards. "The time between shifts just disappears doesn't it?"

Jed raised his eyebrows and politely smiled, "I know...I know. It really doesn't seem enough time does it?" They watched as Mother finished pod parking.

When Mother opened his door, a cheesy American accent could be heard from the radio inside, *"So why not visit 'Dermatone' today and change your skin to any colour, any shade! That's right, any colour, any shade! 'Dermatone',- we're but the pigment of your imagination!"*

"Did you get up to much?" asked Katie, finishing her sentence with a pop from the chewing gum she had been massaging between her teeth.

"I, er, I spent some time with Laura. I er..." he chuckled, really not sure of what else he'd managed to accomplish in his time whilst off-duty. "You know I'm really not sure where the time went. I don't really seem to have gotten much done at all."

Mother walked towards the pair who were clearly waiting to greet him. He smiled and nodded, unable to wave due to being laden with uniform and his tablet. Katie took the tablet from under his left arm and with a smile silently offered to follow him to where he may want it put.

"Big day today then Guv?" Jed lifted a hand to shade his eyes from the sun.

"Big day?" Mother curled his lips downward and subtly shook his head, "Big day...why?"

"New fish Guv..." Jed could see that Mother was clearly distracted, "You know the new boy Guv? We're getting a new recruit to play with."

Katie matched Jed's smile "And we haven't even broken the last one yet. Father Christmas really is spoiling us this year." She and Jed then looked wistfully into the distance, clearly planning what to do with their new toy.

Mother chuckled, "Oh yeah, sorry I forgot. One of my kids hasn't been too well so I've not really given it a lot of thought."

Jed and Katie both snapped their focus back onto Mother apologising for hearing the news.

"Oh no, it's okay, he's not too bad, he's fine. It's just that I've not had a lot of sleep because of it is all. Anyway, I'm here now. So I assume we're going to be playing the usual today then? So who's going to be the Governor today then?"

"I can be if you like," smiled Katie.

Mother smirked, nodded and together they all walked into the station. Behind them wheels raised themselves smoothly back into the chassis as the appliances moved forwards into the bay as they took up their stand-by positions.

2

0900 hrs. The watch stood to the side of the appliance bay all but two of them fully rigged in their fire suits. In line stood Jed, Monkey-boy, Les, Richie, Kevin, Veggie and a slightly awkward looking new recruit. In front, a baggily dressed Station Officer, accompanied by Sub Officer Brown, stood to attention.

"Listen in!" barked Katie. The watch braced themselves. "White watch, white watch 'shun!" The watch then brought themselves quickly and smartly to attention except Jed who purposefully dragged his heels. Katie shot him a stern look.

Katie called out each Firefighter's name and was met by the response "Yes Sir!" until it came to Jed, "Yeah."

Katie turned to him, "Pardon? What was that Firefighter Edwards?"

"Yeah…I said yeah didn't I? What is your problem?" Jed rolled his eyes and looked sideways as he huffed a soft but noticeable huff.

The line of Firefighters stood motionless, bar the new recruit who had turned his head slightly to watch proceedings.

Katie stepped up to Jed, "What is your problem mister? Look at the state of you. You've come here, you're not even rigged in your fire suit, your shirt's not even tucked in and you're not wearing your rank markings..."

Jed interrupted, "Well look at the state of you...y'u fat bitch!" Katie looked momentarily and quite genuinely shocked and had to pause to keep herself from laughing.

"Fat b…? Why I've never been so insulted!"

"Oh, really? *That* surprises me."

Katie screwed her face then turned it away from direct sight of the new recruit, her lips and eyes, tightly shut. She coughed to mask a slight chuckle that escaped her. "How dare you mister? I mean, how. fucking. dare. you?"

"Well *he's* not even rigged!" Jed said, now pointing down the line at the new recruit who had whipped his head back in line to avoid eye contact.

The recruit's heart rate quickened and his face hung with mild panic.

Katie leaned over and jabbed a finger into Jed's shoulder, "He doesn't need his fire gear", Jab. "He's not allowed to wear it till I've linked his suit into the control room.", Jab "And you fucking know that!" (Jab)…pause, jab-jab-jab.

For every jab, Jed's eyes widened ever so slightly more and his head tilted more and more to the side. With effort though, he refrained from smiling. He leaned in towards Katie "If you jab me one more time…"

Katie pushed her chin towards Jed's face.

"Yeah? If I jab you one more time…then what?" Jed now touched his nose to Katie's and stared menacingly into her eyes, "I'm gonna kick…your fucking teeth in!"

It was no good. Katie couldn't stop herself from laughing any longer. Not knowing what to do, she panicked slightly then, jumping on Jed, she forced him to the ground.

The rest of the watch chanting "Fight, fight, fight, fight," quickly gathered round them both so as to obscure them from view of the new recruit who was now the only Firefighter still faithfully standing to attention. In his head he recited this mantra, "Oh bollocks…oh bollocks…oh bollocks."

Off to one side he could hear moans, groans, swearing and scuffling. After a short while the scuffling stopped. "In my fucking office. Right now!" demanded Katie. She and Jed then scurried out of the bay. The remaining Firefighters moaned, disbanded and silently began their equipment safety checks.

In Mother's office he and Katie were swapping uniforms back. Katie described to Mother how role call had gone as Mother shook his head not wishing to be seen to condone their mischievous prank though privately enjoying the moment. Katie laughed unbuttoning her shirt and turned to Jed, "Who're you calling Fat Bitch?" She barked.

As Mother took the shirt from her he delivered a look to Jed that told him that this was his fight alone.

Jed put on his cheekiest naughty school boy look "Yeah well…er…sorry about that I, er, panicked a bit."

"Bollocks!" laughed Katie.

Having known that they were going to play this prank on the recruit, they had all pre-tested their suits and placed them where they were allocated before the change of watch, so now that Mother and Katie were both fully clothed in their correct uniforms they all went chuckling upstairs to the mess.

Having completed testing the fire suits, each Firefighter then joined them upstairs for tea. As each entered the mess he would throw in a slight cheer or a short applause. Jed and Katie both bowed in recognition.

All of the watch were now seated around the mess table enjoying teas. After about fifteen minutes of general mess banter, Mother, who had been keeping a close eye on his watch and regularly surveying the two entrances to the mess, leaned toward Katie "I wonder where the new lad is?"

Katie laughed. "He's probably filling out his resignation downstairs Guv." She smiled and turned away to continue her battle autopsy with Jed.

About another ten minutes later the mess door opened and from behind it the Station Officer from the off-going watch appeared. He smiled and looked at Mother. "Er...you missing one of your blokes?" Mother nodded.

"Well he's downstairs in the bay." He paused "He's er...still to attention. Seeya, have a good day." He waved and disappeared behind the door.

Rolling his eyes, Mother turned to Katie "Oh f-f-f-f-f...or Pete sake, run down and get him will you?"

Katie then stood and dashed out of the mess, launched herself downstairs and ran into the bay.

There, the new recruit stood to attention looking directly forward. Katie stifled an embarrassed laugh and stood in front of the recruit. Seeing that he had not noticed her, she waved a deliberate hand in front of his face. He recoiled slightly and then turned to look at her.

"You okay there young man?" she asked.

"Yes...thank you, I'm fine. Thank you." He looked obediently forwards again.

Katie stood in front of him. "Why, er...why have you not come upstairs with the rest of us then?" Her stance softened, "We don't bite you know."

The recruit squinted slightly and silently disagreed as he thought to himself, "Did she just say they don't *fight*?" He then replied in a very regimented tone "Roll call hadn't finished. I could not leave the bay as roll call had not finished. We had not been dismissed. That is why I am still here and why I could not go upstairs Sir."

Katie shook her head "Oh you silly sod, don't be daft. Come on, of course you can come upstairs."

"Am I dismissed then Sir?" The recruit's shoulders lowered slightly as he relaxed.

"Sir? Oh…oh of course you're dismissed. And don't call me Sir, okay? When we get upstairs, don't call me Sir."

"Yes Sir, thank you Sir." The recruit turned to his right in dismissal and stretched his muscles with a slightly pained groan. He turned to Katie. "So do you only wear your undress uniform when you're doing roll call then Sir?" He twisted his head slightly from side to side to ease his stiffness.

Katie looked down, shook her head, snorted a chuckle and tugged at his sleeve, "Come on you. Let's get you a cup of tea shall we?"

3

Upstairs, Katie and the recruit were greeted with a whooping cheer that petered off into some applauding and laughter.

Katie pointed to where she had been previously sitting. "There you go, you sit yourself down there. Can I get you a cup of tea?"

As he sat down he raised his eyes to Katie, "Yes please, thank you very much Sir."

"Oh Ga'wd." groaned Mother, shaking a slightly distracted head to the soundtrack of the others now laughing and cheering again. He raised and waved a hand to gain the attention of the recruit. "Er, young man." The room still bulged with laughter, so again, but this time slightly louder, Mother repeated "Ha-hum, young man!"

The room settled as the recruit twisted his head in reaction to Mother.

"Yes, that's it, thank you young man." Mother redirected his waving hand towards Katie and pointed.

"See the epaulettes on those shoulders?" The recruit nodded. Mother crossed his arms on the mess table as he leaned forward, "Now…can you see…what it says…on those rank markings?"

Again the recruit nodded, his jaw now slightly agape and eyebrows arched realising that he *may* have been duped.

Mother smiled. "Would you like to read it out to me?"

"Senior *Firefighter* O'Neill...." The recruit's shoulders hunched slightly as he saw Mother's 'And?' face. "Senior Firefighter O'Neill...Sir?"

Mother sat sharply up and raised his hands in celebration "Yaye, there you go it *wasn't* that hard now was it?" He laughed and shot the recruit a welcoming smile. "Okay, well I'm glad we've got that all sorted then. Okay listen in everyone...this is Recruit Firefighter Mann. Mr Mann..." Mother raised his mug high in the air "...I would like to welcome you to this, our humble watch."

Mugs were raised around the table as all toasted the new recruit's arrival.

"Okay guys, Brownie's gonna be taking you all for some drills after you've finished your tea, except for you Mr Mann. I shall need to talk to you in my office and then we can get your suit prepped and synced etcetera. Okay?" Firefighter Mann returned a horizontal smile and nodded. "Good. Okay guys get yourselves finished up and into the drill yard. The quicker you get done, the quicker you can get back and enjoy some nice...fresh...roasted...recruit!"

Firefighters smacked their lips and rubbed their stomachs as they stood and left for the drill yard.

Firefighter Mann's horizontal smile deflated slightly.

Mother stood and walked towards the door "Mr Mann...join me in my orifice if you would."

Firefighter Mann stood and followed Mother downstairs and into his office.

Once inside his office, Mother sat at his desk and then permitted Mann to sit with a welcoming hand gesture. The recruit sat. Mother cleared his throat and began "Welcome to our watch Mr Mann." He looked over his glasses and across the screen that lit from his desktop. "I hope you didn't mind our little jape earlier. Don't mind us, it's all part of the fun. Don't be fooled by their coarse exteriors either, this is one of the most professional crews I've ever been fortunate enough to work with." Mother looked for a moment into the distance, then after a pleased huff he continued. "So...you're very lucky to get this watch Mr Mann. I hope you appreciate that."

"Oh, oh yes Sir. I do Sir!" Mann shuffled in his seat.

"Good, but stop with the Sir, okay? Not...Sir, Guv. Just call me Guv. My name is Station Officer Riley okay, so if anyone needs me that's who I am, but just call me Guv to my face. Some of the guys call me Mother when we're off duty on account of my name being Riley…and the old character of old Mother Riley…old…Mother Riley? No?"

The recruit sat there for a moment without any sign of recognition of the reference.

"Hmm, okay" mumbled Mother. "Tough crowd. Right, well it's only my nick name but as I said, just call me Guv, okay?" He leaned over the desk and shook Firefighter Mann's hand.

Sitting back down, he now leaned over the screen that lay within the surface of his desk. He tapped the top of the screen and it slowly eased itself up and out of the desk. He took hold of the screen and pulled it upwards until it was in a more comfortable position to read. "So, I see by your files that you moved Brigade's for domestic reasons."

"Yes Guv I er…"

"Mr Mann, before you respond, let me just say that I don't need to know the reasons. Unless they affect your ability to perform your duties, then they're really none of my business okay? I was just going to say I hope that you've sorted out what ever issues these were or, if not, please feel free to come to me if you need any assistance…or advice…or whatever."

"Thank you Guv. I appreciate that."

"So tell me a little bit about yourself then young man. You can see I've got your file in front of me but just let me know a little bit about yourself in…your own words." Mother sat back into his chair.

"Well Guv…er, my name is Christian…Mann. I'm thirty two, I'm single, I er, I've recently moved into an apartment that I am renting until I find my way around a bit more and hopefully get settled in." Christian looked upwards to search his memory, "I er, I play the piano…a bit…er, not sure what else to say Guv."

Mother shrugged, "So what did you do before you joined the Brigade Christian?"

"Well Guv, after leaving school I tried my hand at a few jobs for a short while, then eventually settled into a job as a fitter in a vehicle plant…"

"And what were you doing there?"

Christian looked away slightly embarrassed for having to admit "I fitted seats into cars, well pods…and bike pods" He shook his head, "Needless to say…I got out of there as soon as I could. After that I joined the Royal Pioneers where I served for ten years."

Almost involuntarily, Mother sat forward and straightened himself up. He removed his glasses and then leaned forwards. "The Royal…Pioneers?…impressive. And how was that compared to 'Civvie' street then, eh?"

"Okay Guv. Very fulfilling actually. I made a lot of friends and learned a lot of things, you know?"

Mother, realising that this was why he had not left roll call having not been dismissed, smiled to himself. "So where did you serve? Australia? Iceland?…Thailand?"

"No, nothing so exotic I'm afraid Guv. I did see some action during the Prague conflict but…then I…er…spent most of my time just carrying out patrols and shuttle runs on Libya."

"*On* Libya?" Don't you mean *in* Libya?" Mother's face softened "I mean call me pedantic…no actually…er, don't call me pedantic let's just stick with Guv shall we?"

"Actually I guess you'd be technically correct, I was just thinking *on* Libya because I meant the Libya base *on* Mars Guv."

Mother's balance was lost and his arm slid off the side of the table. He quickly regained his position and composure, coughed, paused and then, removing his glasses, he responded. "Oh…wow, okay. Well er…okay, well that *is* impressive. That's quite a CV you have there Mr Mann, hmm." He turned away from Christian for a short while and looked off into space. After a while he leaned over his desk, pushed his screen back into it and then he smiled a Fatherly smile at Christian. "Well, time is getting on and we've yet to get your suit tested and then sync it with Control. Okay, well I'm assigning Jed as your Mentor, okay? That's Firefighter Edwards. Okay, don't be put off by Jed and Kate's little display in the bay earlier. They're both bloody good Firefighters. Jed can be a bit in your face sometimes and he really is one sarcastic bugger but he's professional, he will keep on top of your development and he *will* make sure you're looked after…okay? I'll get him to see you after his drills and between you both you can sort your suit out. Now, your suit is still sealed in its crate in store two so you and Jed will have to prep it before he can sync it for you." He stood and stretched out his hand for Christian to take. "Again, welcome Christian. I'm sure you'll fit right in here and if you do have any problems, feel free to come and speak to me at any time okay? My door is always open."

"Really Guv? Is there a problem with the sliding mechanism?"

Mother snorted, "No Christian. I just mean, oh never mind. For now, get yourself upstairs and sort out your dietary requirements with Richie. He's our Mess Manager."

Christian stood, almost to attention, shook Mother's hand, smiled, thanked him, turned precisely and left.

4

As sensors picked up movement, the ceiling lights burst into life. Jed's head appeared around the door as he peered into the store room. "Yep, it's in here." He walked in, coffee mug in hand. Christian followed, looking around the room as he did. Jed stood with his hand resting on a large black crate in the centre of the room. Placing his coffee on top of the crate, Jed leaned down and tapped a small black screen on the side of the crate. The screen now displayed Christian's full name, some serial numbers and the Fire Brigade's corporate logo. "Okay. Well, Mother's asked me to give you a tour of the station, but before I do that we need to prep your suit, okay? It won't be ready for tonight so don't be expecting to wear it at all today, certainly not in anger at least."

Christian raised an apologetic hand, "Sorry, in anger?"

Jed walked around the crate inspecting for damage and without looking up he replied "Oh yeah, sorry, 'In anger' means when we have a shout, you know?" Jed caught himself using jargon again and stopped inspecting the crate. He smiled to himself, remembering how daunting all this must be for Christian.

"I thought you came from another Brigade though? Didn't you use all this terminology there?"

"Well, I'd just completed training so I've never actually served at a fire station yet."

"Oh, right. Sorry yeah, Mother did say something about that, I forgot. Well anyways, you know what a shout is, right?"

Christian nodded "Yes it's any incident we're called to like, a fire, or a special service like a flooding or say…a pod collision."

"Yeah, okay, so when we actually do something during that shout we refer to it as being done in anger. Get it?" Christian clearly looked slightly perplexed so Jed reiterated "So for example if we put a ladder up in the drill yard then we've just put a ladder up, yes?" Christian nodded. "Okay, but if we put that same ladder up whilst we're out on a shout..." he paused to give Christian time to catch up, "We say that we put that ladder up in 'anger'.

Christian's eyes rolled upwards as he picked up this new idea in his mind, "Oh-h-h. So why is it called anger then? Does it mean you have to *be* angry to actually do it?"

Jed waved his arms at Christian as if to try to erase the idea from his memory, "No, no, it's not like that. Not like that at all, no, no we say it's in anger because...well...hmm..." Jed scratched the back of his neck "...you know...I really don't know why we say that. Hmm. We've just always said it. Okay, well anyway. So, you're happy with 'shout' and 'anger' yes?" Christian shrugged his acceptance of the two new terms.

Jed paused for a second remembering why he had started talking about this in the first place. "Oh yeah, okay, well, once we've tested your suit we'll find a dock for it in the appliance bay, and then initiate all the diagnostics on it so they can be running overnight. So...if you don't mind." Jed rolled his hand open towards the screen. Christian stepped forward, rested his left hand on the top of the crate and leaned round the side of it. He pushed his thumb firmly onto the screen. A red line traced itself around his thumb. It flashed four or five times and then changed to solid green. Christian straightened up and, in a sweeping motion, Jed grabbed his coffee from atop the crate as it hissed and cracked itself open. A deep red vapour quickly poured out of the gap and then began to dissipate. Christian, startled, took a cautious step backwards. Jed sipped from his coffee then turned to him, "That's okay, it always does that. It's perfectly safe. It's part of the sealing process or something. It's not toxic or anything." The front and top of the crate now lifted fully upwards and open, resting on two hydraulic arms. "It's a little melodramatic if you ask me." chuckled Jed as he swigged the last of his coffee, "But when you think how much these suits cost, I guess you can excuse a little bit of showiness."

As the vapour cleared the suit that was carefully packed inside within a bespoke foam interior could now be seen.

"Okay, well then, first things first...let's get it all out, stand it and boot it up, okay?" Jed smiled at Christian giving him both thumbs up. Christian nodded and reached into the crate. He took hold of the leggings and pulled them out of their housing.

Jed pointed to a clear spot in the room "Just stand them there okay?" Christian obeyed.

The dark blue, almost black, armoured leggings landed with a soft thud and now stood in the clear space. Having removed the upper body section of the suit, they both positioned it over the leggings and lowered it on. It hissed softly as the two parts joined and sealed themselves to one another. Jed then removed the helmet from the crate. He looked down at the helmet as he held it and, with a reminiscing smile, he handed it to Christian. Christian placed it onto the shoulders of the suit, gave it the slightest of twists and it too hissed as it completed the suit's seal. The name plate on the left side of the chest plate simply flashed the command "STAND BY."

They both stepped back from the suit as a glow appeared from within the helmet. Inside, soft beeps and chirps could be heard as it ran through its' slow initial acceptance tests, start-up and diagnostics sequence.

"Right…" said Jed, "As you probably know, this suit is going through its start-up and…no, hang on, why am I telling you? You're the recruit…you talk me through it, okay?" Jed smiled at Christian.

Christian nodded and stepped closer to the suit. "Okay, well er, the suit is going through its' initial start-up procedure.

Jed looked sideways at Christian "I think we covered that bit?"

Christian nodded, "Erm, sorry yes, yes we did."

Jed smiled at Christian. "And the test takes…how long?"

Christian thought back to his training manuals "Er, ten minutes for acceptance test, but thirty seconds for operational start-ups."

"Good. Okay, carry on." Jed now placed his arms behind his back. "So tell me, what is it checking, what is it made of? Er, what can the suit do and so on?"

"Oh, okay. Well, um it's made of three parts. The helmet, the upper body, which is called the tunic and the lower body, which is called the leggings."

"Correct. Describe each part to me then please."

"Okay, starting with the leggings, they have integral boots. The tunic has sealed gloves that can be removed if needed. The tunic also incorporates the cooling system, re-breather system, the main power pack and most of the computer on-boards. The helmet has integral communications equipment or 'Comms' and er…also has a heads up display. Um, what else would you like to know?"

Jed squinted at him "I don't want to know anything. I know all this. All I want to know, young man, is that *you* are able to remember it. Being my Mentee, you must be aware that as your Mentor I *al*so get bollocked...if you fuck up. I want to make sure that if Mother asks you any of these questions that you know the answer. Okay?" Christian nodded. "Right. Okay, well then, tell me about the re-breather and HUD systems?" Jed turned from Christian and treated himself to a subtle smile, pleased with himself for appearing the learned teacher. "Continue." he said.

"Okay, well the re-breather is designed with inbuilt filters that can not only filter out most known gases, but can also use any components within them that can be turned back into breathable air. The stored air supply actuates automatically when there are insufficient gases available. Um, due to its dynamic supply system, its maximum abilities will never be reached as the operator would become too fatigued well before the limit of the re-breather could be reached."

"Hmm, good, good." Jed began pacing in the character of the teacher that he was creating.

"The HUD, or Heads Up Display, incorporates visual Comms, thermal imaging, infrared and zoom-able displays."

"Okay let's begin with the Comms then Mr Mann." Jed now rocked slowly up and down on his heels.

"Well, you can speak face to face with either another wearer, Control, or via visual or audio, to anyone else on the incident ground."

Jed nodded a slow, knowing, professorial nod. "Hmm, good, good. Yah, t'is good." He coughed, 'Too much. Don't do the accent,' he thought. "I mean that's good. And it is all made of...?"

Christian pointed to the suit "It is a Tritanium-Poly Carbonate based moulding with "Dura-Tech" armour plating, which is then protected with a military grade thermal coating. It is able to withstand any temperature up to and including $2000°$ C. It is fitted with a "HUFSS" or Harmonics Fire Suppression System and twin Flame-Breaker 7 flame suppressing pulse emitters, two metre range. This of course is backed up by pulse lances, grenades and, if needed, water from the appliance. The helmet is equipped with..."

Looking at his watch, suddenly realising the time, Jed sarcastically snapped "Yeah, er, that's amazing and all, but dinner's nearly ready and also I think my bored-o-meter has started to overheat a bit." Jed smiled at Christian, "Yeah well. that was all correct, well done mate. So, keep up with your studying okay? I know you've done loads of simulations in training suits at the Academy but this is a little bit different. Make sure you are completely familiar with your suit's technical specs and be ready for when Mother might wanna ask you the odd question or two, okay?" Not waiting to hear Christian's response he left the room to hunt and gather a full fry up breakfast.

Christian stood for a while longer looking at his new suit, admiring the technical complexity of it whilst maintaining its simplistic, elegant design. He was also fully aware of the financial commitment that went into purchasing this suit and reflected on how fortunate he had been in being chosen to join the Fire Academy ahead of all the other applicants. As the suit continued its' initial boot-up sequence a glowing red strip ran itself around the ankle and then traced its way up the length of the side of the legs. These were the 'Hi-Vis' strips. The red lines ran up the torso, pausing at the base to run around the waist, along the length of the arms and terminated around the cuffs. The word 'FIRE' then appeared on the front of the chest plate and, as Christian stepped towards the back of the suit, he also saw that 'FIRE' glowed on the top rear of the suit. Taking one last glance at the suit he walked towards the door, opened it, then he turned again as the suit bleeped its ready tones. The stand by command on the chest plate was now replaced with his name. His name now also glowed on each side of the fire helmet and the 'FIRE' written on the chest plate and back plate changed to green to confirm stand-by mode.

He hesitated looking down for a moment, reflecting on how much he'd put into getting through the training academy and just how much he wished his father could have seen him entering the Fire Brigade, seen the pride on his face as he watched his son follow in his footsteps. He smiled away the memory and left the storeroom.

5

Jed stabbed at his last piece of bacon as Richie took hold of his plate to clear it away. Richie stood over him encouraging him to finish it so that he could take his fork. Jed gulped down the last mouthful and then pulled an uncomfortable face as he turned to Richie, "Oh Rich, mate, that was shit! How can you possibly be charging us to eat this every day?" Jed poked out his tongue as if to imply he felt nauseous.

Without looking back, Richie lifted his middle finger above his left shoulder at Jed as he walked into the kitchen.

"He's right Rich, that was crap. My dog eats better than that mate," yelled Les.

Jed turned to Les rubbing his stomach "Oh that was the bollocks!"

Les placed both his hands around his stomach and agreed, "Yes mate that was *de*-lish! Oh mate, I'm stuffed!" Both sat there smiling. Christian watched, confused.

Jed smiled Cheshirely at Christian, "It's for his own good. If we didn't give him shit…"

Les continued "…He'd get complacent…"

"He'd cut corners. Standards would drop…"

"He might even put up the amount he charges us."

Jed shook his head, "And then where would we be?"

"Anarchy?" asked Les, "Civil war?"

Jed shook his head at Christian "You wouldn't want that would you mate? You wouldn't want civil war would you?" He squinted questioningly at Christian. "*Would you*?"

Les scoffed then looked directly at Christian "No of course he wouldn't. He *doesn't*. You don't want civil war, do you mate?"

Christian shook his head enthusiastically, "No, no of course I don't."

Les slapped Jed on his arm, "You see? You see? He doesn't want civil war."

"No of course he doesn't want civil war, he's not daft. He knows it's the right thing to do."

"Of course he does. He *knows* it's the right thing to do." Les then leaned forward and spoke softly, "You see Christian this is why we do this. It's not *at* Richie, it's *for* Richie. It's for the good of the nation. D'you understand? You see Chris, can I call you Chris?" Christian nodded. "You see Chris, being able to give Richie shit is the only thing…the *only* thing…that separates man from the beasts. Remember that. You make sure you give the Mess Manager as much shit as you can possibly shake a stick at, okay?" Les sat back into his chair, slowly, deliberately, solemnly nodding.

Across the room, Mother also shook his head at the sheer silliness of the exchange he had been watching. He leaned onto the table "Christian how're you getting on with that suit? All sorted is it?"

"Yes thank you Guv" Christian smiled awkwardly but politely back. "All the checks are complete…"

Jed interrupted "And now I'm gonna take him back down and we'll find a dock for it in the bay. Then I'll take him around the station and show him where everything is Guv, if I can stand up that is." Jed then struggled to lift his aching stomach up and beckoned Christian to follow him.

Mother nodded at Christian as he stood and left. Mother then surveyed the room and, catching Kevin's eye, said "Kevin I see that young Christian has done quite a bit of travelling in his time. Is that something that you've ever done?"

"No Guv. I've never really gotten round to it."

"But it's something you'd like to do though, isn't it?"

Looking into the distance, imagining possible destinations, Kevin replied "Oh yes Guv. I'd like very much to have the opportunity to do some travelling."

"Right. Well here's your opportunity then Kevin…Go to the kitchen and make me a cup of tea, there's a good lad."

Kevin's shoulders dropped as the romantic image of his travels quickly disappeared from view.

"Oh and it doesn't stop there Kevin. Once you've made it, you can travel all the way down to my office with it. That's where I'm gonna be." Mother smiled, stood and left.

Kevin stood "Yes Guv." He left the mess to a soft ripple of giggles from those who were still seated.

Jed and Christian, having left the mess, had walked along the hall and were now standing in the lecture room. A large empty room with little to suggest it was anything other than, perhaps, an empty store room.

"Okay, well let's begin the tour here then shall we? You've seen the kitchen and mess obviously, so we don't need to worry about that." Christian silently nodded. "Okay, so we are now in the dormitory."

"Okay." Puzzled, Christian looked around the room for any sign of beds or bedding. Nothing.

"We are also in the…lecture room."

Again Christian looked from side to side. His eyes narrowed and lips pursed, "So is this then a multi-purpose room where you bring in whatever furniture you need from maybe…the store room?" He shrugged.

Jed stepped over to a small glowing panel by the door. He tapped it to reveal several options and pressed on the 'ROOM CONFIG' option. He then chose 'DORM' and turned to Christian, "Stand by the door mate." The walls, that had been completely bare, now had sections that gently lowered themselves towards the floor as concealed beds automatically appeared and rested on the floor, lined on both sides of the room. Christian smiled to see the transformation. Jed turned to him "Good isn't it?" He then tapped on the glowing panel again and the hinged beds lifted away and sealed themselves back into the walls. Another panel selection and small ports in the walls opened and out slid three rows of seats with accompanying desks. The far wall now glowed as its' inbuilt screen lit with the Fire Brigade corporate logo. Christian grinned a wide smile. Nothing need be said between the two men. Jed waited a short while to allow Christian the time to savour this unnecessarily gadgety moment. He placed a brotherly hand on Christian's shoulder and, closing his eyes, he bowed his head and softly said "It's okay. Take your time. I know. It's...it's a beautiful thing isn't it?" He laughed. "Come on then young Christian, let's continue."

Outside, Jed pointed along the corridor to where the Sub Officer's rooms were, and they headed downstairs to the station office.

"Okay, so here's where the Officers sit if they need to record anything or do any computer work. Not a lot to see here really. An office is an office. They walked through to the Watch room, a small office with a desk in it. Next to the desk was a grey metallic box standing about 5 feet high. Pointing to the box Jed began, "Right okay, see here, this is where all of our Comms gear is. That box of tricks receives all of our incoming calls and shout details and also sends all of our suit and appliance telemetry and updates etcetera to Brigade Control. It then sends all relevant information to this computer terminal, and of course if we receive a shout it also sends the details to..." Jed pointed out of the window to the appliance bay, "...the appliance 'on-boards'. This programmes their routes and also winds up the primary engines so that they're ready for when the crews are on board. Any questions so far?" Jed did not wait for an answer and stepped out into the appliance bay. "Here are, *of course*, the appliances." Jed pointed to the two large red and silver fire appliances sitting in the bay. Robust, military style vehicles with metal bars running around the front screens, ladders on the sides to allow crews to enter the rear cabs and sections of the chassis aesthetically exposed by poly panels revealing the secondary engine within.

"Okay, well you'll get plenty of time to play with that when we do drills tomorrow." Jed then led Christian to the side of the bay where the fire suits stood lining the far wall.

"See this? This is where your suit will be docked. It's grouped with the rest of the watch. It'll have finished its initial charge in a while so I'll show you how to dock it properly *then* for a full charge, okay?"

Jed smiled at Christian who looked along the line of suits eager to get his docked for the first time. Jed stood in front of one of the docked suits and placed his hand on its' right shoulder. His eyes glazed over slightly as he allowed himself a rare moment of seriousness. "Take care of your suit Christian. This is your world. Whenever you're in your suit, you're in your own world. Everything you need to keep you alive is in there." He turned to Christian. "Don't let anyone ever fuck with your suit Christian. Your suit...is a very personal thing. It's almost like your friend. Don't let anyone ever fuck with it, and don't ever, EVER touch someone's suit, other than to help them put it away, take it off, clean it or whatever. But don't ever mess with, play with...not even for a laugh...Don't."

Christian nodded and softly replied., "I know Jed. I've worn similar before. Trust me, I get it."

Jed nodded in assured agreement, then after a short pause scrunched his face "You've worn similar, wh...what, d'you mean *before* the brigade?"

"Yes...I spent some time in Libya, I mean *on*...Libya."

"You were in the Libyan Fire Brigade?"

Christian smiled, "No, no I served in..."

Before he could complete his sentence, the lights within the bay glowed a soft pulsating red. At the same time, four tones sounded in quick succession then a pause and then tones again. This was the station call bells.

Jed slapped Christian on the chest with the back of his hand as he ran past him towards the fire appliances. "Wey-hey!" After a few steps he looked back, "Well come on then!"

Christian looked back at him, shook his head and shrugged.

"You don't need a suit mate, you can just come and observe today, okay? When we get there, just stay by the appliance okay? Don't get involved, don't touch anything, just watch what we do. Come on, you can sit next to me on the appliance."

Jed climbed the short ladder into the rear cab of the appliance. As Christian followed, Jed pointed to where he should sit. Inside the appliance, the on-boards recited "Fire...call, Fire...call, Fire...call."

Katie climbed in, sat, and then began to don her leggings.

In the front, Les sat in the driver's position and leaned over to check the centre console display. As he did, Brownie boarded and sat in the Officer In Charge's seat. As all the doors folded down and closed, the appliance sped through the appliance bay doors that had opened automatically. Brownie turned to face the rear crew and confirmed "Guys, this is a *"persons reported"*. Get rigged and ready."

Jed, who now had his tunic sealed to his leggings, leaned forward and picked up his fire helmet. "This is a *'persons reported'* Chris. That means that someone's informed us that people may be involved in the fire, okay? So just stay near the appliance and try not to get in anyone's way. I don't mean anything by that, it's just safer if you stay near the appliance." Jed then lowered his helmet onto his shoulders and twisted it. As it sealed itself to the tunic, the in-visor displays flashed into life. The suit's red Hi-Vis lighting strips began to glow. In the corner of Jed's display, three boxes appeared - one of Katie's face, one of Katie's forward view and one of a Control Officer. With a selection of voice commands, Jed enlarged each box one at a time, and carried out a quick Comms check with both Katie and the Control Officer. Katie then turned to him and gave him a thumbs up, which he confirmed with the same.

6

Inside his old reliable Fordshiba pod, Andy Healy tapped his tablet and turned another digital page of the novel he was reading. As he hovered along the busy high road, his attention was caught by the soft pulsating red glow coming from his centre console. As he looked over his book he could see the display flashing with the word 'FIRE'. Andy's pod quickly and efficiently slid to the side of the road as he looked back to his book to continue the story of a planet named Dune. Moments afterwards, Andy looked up again as a large red and silver blur thundered past his window shortly followed by another. Andy, unperturbed by this, returned to his story of spice worms and space travel. The centre console then returned to its' standby mode as Andy's pod returned to its' original course.

Inside the second appliance, Katie leaned forward and pulled a pulse lance from its' retaining bracket. She pointed it upwards so that she could see the display on the side of it. All lights were green so she held it ready to use it when they dismounted the appliance.

Brownie changed views on the centre console which now displayed a satellite view of the target premises. He zoomed in until he could see people running away from the building and smoke pouring from one of the top windows. He turned to the crews. "I'm patching you into this display." Inside his helmet, Jed could see the house with people clearly panicking outside.

Brownie continued, "Okay, so thermals are showing possibly one person inside, alright? The front crew will be going in, so you guys give medical and command support, okay?"

Jed and Katie nodded.

Christian, who sat obediently quiet, looked on in awed curiosity. As an ex-soldier, he recognised this switch to professional mode that he now saw in both Jed and Katie. This is something that he had missed since leaving the Pioneers, and he was very happy to see that this group of people that he had been chosen to join were able to step up when needed.

As both appliances slowed and parked themselves outside the target property, they were met by a very distraught lady who was crying and waving her arms. Mother jumped off the first appliance and ran to her. "Everything's going to be okay Madam! Can you tell me your name?"

The elderly lady replied "Rose." Through her tears, "Please can you help me? Oh please." She lowered her head to look at her blackened hands.

"Rose, look at me. Look at me...Rose, can you confirm if there is anyone else in the property still?"

Rose softly nodded her head "Yes, my husband is still inside. I couldn't move him...I couldn't..."

Richie and Kevin, who were both fully rigged in their suits, had heard this conversation via their visors. They arrived at the front door of the property and prepared to enter. Before entering the hot zone they were trained to glance down at the readings within their visors to confirm all was good to go. Upon doing this, Kevin turned to give Mother the thumbs up.

Mother looked over to Kevin and Richie to confirm they were good to go, but saw Richie standing in the doorway waving his hand in front of his visor. Kevin pulled at Richie's shoulder to encourage him to enter. "Come on Richie. Don't sod about, let's get in there!"

Richie resisted, raised a halting hand to Kevin and, with voice command, changed his in-visor view to Jed and Katie's. "Suit malfunction, repeat, suit malfunction! No go!" With this, Richie and Kevin both stepped to one side, and seconds later Jed and Katie ran straight past them and disappeared into the burning house.

Mother waved his arms at Christian who had stood outside the appliance observing. He gestured towards Rose. "Christian, give this lady some assistance!" Christian boarded the appliance to retrieve the Medi-Pack but, as he did, he saw the ambulance arrive and instead turned and led Rose to the waiting medics.

The ambulance crews wore suits similar to those worn by the Firefighters but with differing technical specs and their Hi-Vis strips glowed a deep emerald green. The suits were equipped with Medi-scanners and the inbuilt oxygen supply was mainly for supplying to casualties that had to be treated away from the ambulance.
Bright white light erupted from the ambulance as the rear doors were opened. Rose was led inside by the medics and was sat down and given oxygen.
Christian sat in the ambulance holding Rose's hand as the ambulance crew began their scans.

"Fuck, fuck." Mother ran over to Richie and Kevin. "Suit malfunction? You okay Richie?"
Richie, who was now carrying his fire helmet, raised a hand to signal he was okay, "Guv it's okay. I'm okay. it's just the heads up. It's just the…the thermal readings is all. It's okay. I'm sure it's just a glitch."
"Well bloody hell Rich, just a glitch? D'you know how much paperwork I'm gonna have to do to explain this 'glitch'?" Mother smiled at Richie. It was a slightly uncomfortable smile though. Suit malfunctions were very, *very* rare and they were not welcome when they occurred. With such a lifesaving piece of equipment, no-one ever wanted to hear that it could go wrong.
"Okay guys, well you both go back to the appliance and get out of your suits, okay?" Mother again smiled and nodded, glad that Richie was okay and that the problem was with the suit and not Richie himself.

Inside the ambulance, the Medics continued their scans of Rose. Inside their visors graphs, facts, figures and lights flashed as results from the scanners appeared.
Hearing shouts for help from outside, the junior of the two medics left the ambulance and ran round to the front of the vehicle where he was met by Jed and Katie who were supporting an elderly casualty.

The medic took charge of the elderly gentleman who was coughing and clearly shaken.

Mother approached Katie. "Everything okay?"

Katie nodded. "Yes, he was in the bedroom and had sealed the bottom of the door with some blankets. He'll be fine," she smiled. "It was just cooking and was mainly smoke, but we've dealt with the fire." Katie smiled as she tapped the Flame Breaker lance she had holstered on her right leg.

"Well done mate. Well, okay, get yourselves out of your suits. Fire investigation will be here soon and I'll get *them* to take over."

Jed and Katie walked over to the appliances. Getting the thumbs up from Richie, they then boarded their own appliance and de-rigged ready to go back to station.

Mother boarded the ambulance and downloaded all of the details from the ambulance crew that they had gathered from Rose. Then, confirming that the medics did not need any further assistance, he and Christian dismounted the ambulance and walked back to the appliance.

CHAPTER THREE

"A thermal image paints a thousand words"

<u>1</u>

(Six months later)

Andy Healy lay on his side in the darkness staring across the light green carpeted floor and out of his bedroom into the murky hallway. He yawned for air as his eyes, sore and tired, slowly blinked as he drifted deeper and deeper into an unwelcomed, imprisoning sleep. His breathing became increasingly laboured and his chest tightened more with every toxic inhalation. From across the room he could hear soft cracks and hissing pops as the paint on the bedroom door frame began to blister and gradually melt away. Smoke continued to thicken and darken as it slowly grew and crept its way from ceiling level downwards. Andy grew ever weaker and, try as he might, he could not pull himself up or move himself away from the danger. Around him, his peripheral vision faded further into darkness as his consciousness ebbed away into potential oblivion. Starved of oxygen his mind looked for other times, safer times, happier times.

Andy stood and curled his young toes into the perfectly green grass warmed by the sun that also warmed his cheeks. He looked up, shaded his eyes and smiled at Deborah as she smiled at him, iced drinks in hand, walking towards him. Andy nodded at his beloved wife as she handed him a well-deserved and well needed drink. The iced drink hung in the air as Andy raised it up to inspect and admire it. But somehow...he was confused. He was not sure how he had gotten here, what day it was. All he knew was that here was this perfect moment in this perfect place and he would savour it. The deep red colouring of the cranberry juice glistened, backlit by the sun. Andy smiled. A tear cooled his cheek as it ran like a seismograph line down Andy's cheeks.

The deep red colouring of the cranberry drink now neared as, through his barely cracked eyes, he could just make out the red strips that lit the fire suits as they walked towards him. The soft bassy hum of the suits' harmonics generators filled the air and tears fell from Andy's painful eyes and ran down his wrinkled cheeks. Seconds later a hand reached down towards him and he felt something placed around his mouth that sealed gently onto his skin and the acrid hot smoke was sucked from his airway. A cooling air supply followed that filled Andy's lungs as his rescue mask auto-started. He could feel his hair lifting slightly and he sensed pins and needles as the waves from the Firefighter's Flame Breakers pulsed around him.

Behind him, Andy then saw the floor falling away as he was lifted and quickly removed from his burning home. Knowing he was being pulled to safety, Andy's body allowed itself to drift into a comforting protective slumber.

Outside, Mother watched as Jed emerged from the billowing smoke confidently walking from the fire damaged building. Behind Jed, Christian then appeared carrying an elderly male casualty. Jed headed towards Mother to debrief him as Christian turned and walked to the waiting medic. The medic gestured him towards the rear of the ambulance so Christian climbed into the ambulance where he laid Andy down onto a prepped scanner. Christian looked down and rested his gloved hand on Andy's chest for a moment. As the scanner began to roll along the length of Andy's body the medic smiled at Christian. "He's gonna be alright mate, we'll get him fixed up in no time." Looking back, Christian smiled and nodded.

The smoke was still quite thick and acrid in Andy's house. Jed and Mother had changed to Thermal Imaging and had re-entered the house to confirm that the fire was 'all out'. They now stood in the bedroom as Christian walked in. As he entered Mother slapped him on the side of the arm.

Christian turned to see Mother's face thermally displayed in deep bright reds and yellows.

"Well done young Christian. After six months you're finally getting the hang of this." Mother smiled. Though Mother was acknowledging Christian's efforts, he was really gauging to see if he was okay. He was aware that Christian had served on Libya but didn't know if he had seen any casualties this close up. Mother knew it could sometimes take a person a while to come to terms with the injuries they would sometimes be expected to witness.

Christian smiled a pleased smile, "Thanks Guv. The medic said his name is Andy. They say he's gonna be okay."

"Good lad. Okay, well that's good news. Okay you two, let's get the fans off the appliance and clear some of this smoke. Let's have one at the front door and one at say…the top rear of the house, okay?" Mother walked out through the smoke to speak to the Paramedics.

"Right then Chris, I'll get the fans off, okay?" Jed followed Mother to return to the appliance.

When Jed left, Christian took one last look around the bedroom. On a small table he could see a picture frame. He stepped towards it and picked it up. Seeing just a distorted thermal image he changed views to normal vision. The smoke had cleared enough that in his helmet's torch light he saw a picture of Andy as a younger man, standing next to, what he assumed was, his wife. Though there were other pictures on the table, Christian noted there were no other pictures of this woman later in her life. Christian lowered his eyes and, saddened by the thought, subliminally shook his head then left to help Jed with venting.

2

Back at the station, all of the crew were sitting around the mess table as Richie served up plates of spaghetti Bolognaise. Kevin had sat next to Christian to debrief and then discuss any learning points they had taken from the incident.

Before the close of the incident an Assistant Divisional Officer (or A.D.O. for short, because the Brigade just *loves* an abbreviation) had arrived to observe the incident and to offer any command support. Mother had politely refused his offers of assistance and then even more politely fucked him off and was now discussing this with Brownie.

"…and then that plank A.D.O. Grant arrived." Mother was shaking his head.

"Grant?" Brownie looked upwards then screwed his face up failing to remember who Mother was referring to. "Grant? No, no I don't think I've met him."

Mother huffed, "Grant's that plank from Head Quarters who tried to get Jack disciplined that time for 'messing up' at that job down…Whidmore street. It wasn't Jack that fucked it up though, it was Grant himself!"

"So what's Grant's problem then? Attitude?" Brownie spoke as he twisted another fork of spaghetti into himself.

"Well he's not got the best attitude but it's basically more because he's just so bloody stupid. The man's constantly covering up for his own incompetence."

Brownie chuckled and coughed on his food, "In what way do you mean stupid?"

Mother paused for a moment. "Well let's just say he probably wouldn't win any prizes at an arse and elbow labelling competition, if you get my meaning."

Brownie laughed. "How on earth these people get promoted is beyond me…It's not who you know is it?"

"No, it's not who you know, it's who you blow," giggled Katie.

Still chuckling, Brownie saw Christian across the table. "Well then young Chris, how did it go then, eh?"

"Very well thank you Brownie." Christian politely smiled at him.

"Good lad. So how was the old feller? Did you speak to the medics at all?"

"Yes I caught them before they left."

"Caught them? Caught them doing what?"

"No, I mean I just caught them for a……"

Brownie rolled his eyes "Never mind Chris, just carry on."

Katie looked at Brownie and smiled, having been caught out herself on many occasion by Brownie's soppy word games.

"I did speak to them, yes. They said he'd be fine and they'd get him fixed up in no time."

"Ah, the wonders of modern stem-techs eh?"

"Yes. They said he had stem-tech cover so he'd probably be home soon."

Brownie's head dropped remembering his Grandfather, who had died when he was a child from something as simple as lung cancer, all because he had not been able to afford stem insurance.

Katie saw Brownie's subtle change from across the room and had discussed in the past his Grandfather so knew of his sad memories and dislike of the need for stem insurance. "Hey Chris, so you've been here for what, six months now? What say we go out and celebrate with a drink?"

Kevin turned to Katie, "Eh? That's a little bit forward isn't it?"

"Not *just* me and Christian Kevin. I meant the watch, all of us."

Kevin began to open his mouth in futile retort.

"You *prat* Kevin."
Kevin quickly closed his mouth in resigned defeat.
"So Chris, how about it? Shall we all go for a drink?"
"Yeah, come on mate. We could do with a laugh. Let's all grab a drink and a curry." Jed, as Christian's mentor, said this to him in such a way as to let him know that it was not a request.
"Okay then." said Christian, "I'm happy to go for a drink. That'd be nice, thank you."
A collective cheer filled the air as it was agreed that they would all share some down time together.
Mother looked toward Christian "How about next week after our second day? Are you around then Chris?" Mother looked around the room to see other's reactions to this proposed date.
"Yeah, I'm not busy next Friday. I can make that."
Kevin turned deliberately to Christian "Can you get the first round in mate?
Christian's smiling face turned to slight puzzlement. "Can *I* get the first round in?"
"Of course you can mate. Yaye, Chris is getting the first round in! Yaye!" Kevin smugly smiled to himself knowing that he was now no longer the last one in the room to fall for this gag. Cheers filled the room again as people thanked Chris for being so 'generous' and saying how good it was of him.
Christian sat politely and obligingly smiling. 'What an inanely lame game.' he thought.

<u>3</u>

Mother was sitting at the head of the table smiling a booze glazed smile as he stared along the length of the table. Katie was sitting at the opposite end where she and Les were both in fits of giggles for reasons that they themselves could not remember. Kevin wobbled in his seat and was getting more irate that all the Tacos were in such a shape that no food would sit in them. Jed and Brownie sat opposite him and were quietly laughing between themselves at Kevin's drunken attempts to use a poppadum as a Taco. Brownie even then encouraged Kevin to complain at the state of the Tacos but when Kevin managed to get the waiter's attention he could not remember why he had called him over. Instead he ordered more beer and then, having ordered his beer, he then turned back to his plate.

"Bollogsh.", He slurred, "Fug'n Tacos. Oi, Gringo!" Kevin turned to see the waiter stepping into the bar. Across from Kevin tears were rolling down Brownie's cheeks as he laughed, hiccupped and lowered his shaking head under the table. Jed held his plate up in front of his face and, though this would not be traditionally classed as the best way to hide your laughing, Kevin did not question it.

Christian was sitting resting on his elbows and swayed gently as he watched proceedings. He was very happy to have been transferred here. He knew he had landed himself a good watch. Surveying the room he caught Mother's eye. Christian winked at Mother whose shoulders shuddered in one swift snort of amusement at Christian's alcohol fuelled cheekiness.

Mother stood. "A toast!"

"Yes, sod these Tacos! More toast, bring more toast!" Kevin swayed precariously over his plate.

Katie leaned toward him and covered his head with a napkin. Kevin whimpered slightly but then his head gently lowered and he was quiet. Around the room people raised eyebrows and shrugged at each other surprised at how effective this method of control had been. Katie smiled a very pleased Stan Laurel smile and then looked back at Mother.

"A toast! To friends, old and new. To absent friends!" Mother paused and lowered his eyes. Brownie and Les both nodded agreement. "But more importantly young Christian, here's to you and your future on this watch!" Everyone, bar Kevin, raised their glasses and drank "To Christian!" Then Mother continued, "Chris...You've kept your head down. You've done as you were told. You've kept your head in your books and your feet on the ground. On the fire ground you've proven yourself to be more than capable and you have integrated yourself fully into the watch. You are one of us. One of our merry band of men, our band of brothers."

"Oi!"

"Sorry Katie, you're quite right. You are one of our, er, merry band of siblings..." Mother swayed slightly and smiled. Quite light headed, he fell back into his seat.

The table again bustled with the sounds of cheers and congratulations. "Great speech Guv" "Very moving Guv" "More beer!" Christian smiled and raised a grateful toast to Mother. In that same movement he was ushered up onto his feet by those sitting next to him. He looked around at expectant faces. He shrugged.

After a short pause, Katie rolled both her hands towards him as if to usher him onto a stage "Er…speech Chris. Come on."

Christian went to sit down but stopped as his seat was quickly removed from under him. After some attempts to refuse, it became quite clear that he was not going to be able to avoid giving a speech.

Christian pushed himself up and stood upright, swaying in a self-induced Bacardi breeze. He looked along the line of cherry red faces looking back up at him, bar Kevin who was still mumbling protestations at such heinous napkin cruelty. Christian smiled knowing that he was very lucky to have been posted into this very solid group of friends. He raised his glass and made the traditional mating call of the drunk, a long curry-scented belch.

After a short pause the table erupted. "More!" "Oh well said!" "Genius!" "Who writes his stuff?" "I must buy the Holo-disk!" and then lots of laughter and giggling.

Christian smiled at all of his critics' reviews. "Unaccustomed as I am…" he swayed, "Because I'm not."

The table cheered and drinks were downed.

Christian raised a papal hand. "Thank you, thank you. I am very happy to be here…(hic)…you've all been very giving and have also…taken…the piss…a lot." Christian laughed through his closed lips and made an impressive deflating balloon impression. "You have all made me feel very welcome."

"Of course you're welcome mate." Jed interrupted, "Welcome to bloody get on with it!" With this, he lifted his pint to urge Christian to finish.

"My learned colleague has raised…(hic)…a valid pint. "Cheers everybody." The table filled with cheers and groans for such a poor pun.

4

The alleyway, into which they exited the Indian restaurant, was dark and unwelcoming. From a pavement vent, steam lifted up and rolled through them and then along the alley, pushed by a chilling evening breeze.

As they appeared from the dimly lit alley, people walking by could have been forgiven for mistaking the watch for a band of nomadic zombies, complete with moans and groans. As they stepped into the neon lit high street their bodies twisted and contorted, recoiling from the light and sudden change in temperature.

Brownie swiped at a distant neon sign in an attempt to swat it away. "Ugghh."

Jed, swaying and light headed, rested against a shop door. Wondering where the squeaking was coming, from he looked up to see a board with the shop's name on it swinging rhythmically in the breeze. It read *'Dave King's Second-hand Prosthetics'*. In the store's window was a poster advertising Kelly's hair restoring products. Its' tag line read *"Gone today, Hair tomorrow."* Jed furrowed his brow trying to focus on the poster but, reading the tag line, he brushed away the blandness of it all with the wave of a very pissed hand and then he leaned away from the shop door to give him the momentum he needed to start walking away.

As the rabble adjusted to the light, they straightened and continued their journey back towards the fire station where they had all decided to sleep the night.

Halfway down the high street, they rested for a moment against some advertising boards. Kevin's motor functions had joined language skills in early retirement and it was clear that the only thing that might get him through the whole journey was if he could stop and find 'Bra-a-a-ins!' or kebab at least.

As they stumbled towards the end of the High Street they could see blue and red lights flashing against the shop fronts. The lights were being reflected from nearby appliances that were parked down a side street. The inquisitive, brain seeking zombie horde went to investigate.

The Officer in Charge of the appliance spotted the flailing mass slowly approaching in the distance. Each of the horde dragged with them oddly hued dancing shadows formed by the flashing appliance lights. The Officer tightened his brow with mild concern. Preparing himself for the trouble this drunken crowd was probably going to cause he beckoned over one of his colleagues. As he did so he zoomed his HUD onto one of the nearing crowd. The face recognition software in his helmet identified and then showed an archive picture of Mother. Once the Officer confirmed this, the picture disappeared to display Mother now zoomed in and looking much older *and greener* than his archive image. The Officer's colleague must have also spotted this at the same time as he now bent over in his suit laughing and pointing. He turned to continue his work.

Mother walked up and shook the Office in Charge's hand. "Hi Paul, how's you?"

"I'm good thanks Mother."

"Just thought we'd come over and see what was happening, you know?"

Paul smiled "Not looking for a lift back to the station then, no?"

Mother scratched his chin and looked up and away. "Well, you know Paul, if there's room, that would be good." He smiled.

"Okay mate, we're just finishing up here. Hang about for a few minutes and we should be with you."

Mother raised his hand to the others who were just hanging back a few yards. The others knew this wave to mean. "We-Let-New-Friends-Join-Clan. Ugh. New. Friends. Good. Ugh."

Two rigged Firefighters emerged from behind the appliance. The first Firefighter, Bernie, stepped up to Paul. "Guv, it's all out, premises secure and we…" The Firefighter's talking petered off and he looked away from his colleague as his attention was clearly being magnetised away from the moment.

Paul looked to where he calculated Bernie must now be looking to see the group that had emerged from the shadows. He chuckled. "Don't mind them, they're a little pissed but they'll be alright. We're giving them a lift back to the station when we're done so let me know when all the gear's made up so that we can get off." Paul paused for a few seconds awaiting a response. Paul looked back at Bernie. "Bernie? Bernie!"

Bernie snapped out of his trance, "Er sorry. Sorry Guv, I, er…"

"Bernie what's up? You feeling okay?"

Bernie nodded. "Yeah, sorry Guv. It's just that…can't you see that?" He pointed back to where the Firefighters all swayed in a soft hazy drunken pattern.

Paul looked around to see where Bernie was pointing. "Yeah okay, so what am I looking at exactly?"

Bernie snapped to full concentration and chuckled, "No, nothing Guv. sorry I think there's something wrong with my suit is all. That's all. Sorry my visor's not displaying correctly is all."

Paul raised an eyebrow, "Okay well make sure you get it checked out as soon as we get back to station, okay? If need be, take your suit off the run. What's happening with the display exactly?"

Before he could finish, another Firefighter, Stuart, had stepped up next to them both. "Am I the only one seeing this?" he asked. He too was now looking at the group of off duty Firefighters that were awaiting a lift back to the station. Bernie's eyes widened as he turned his head to see Stuart staring away towards the Firefighters.

Paul snapped his head back to look at them all and then back at both his Firefighters. "Okay, what am I missing here? Clearly something's up. What is it?"

Bernie reached in to the front of the appliance and lifted out the Officer in Charges' Fire Helmet. "Guv put that on." He handed it over to Paul who placed the helmet on his head, twisted it and booted it up.

"Okay then guys, what am I seeing?"

"Guv, switch it to thermal imaging."

With a voice prompt, Paul switched his internal visor display to thermal mode. The image in his visor changed and now lit his face in a graphic novel display of reds and yellows. After a quick scan of the Firefighters, his eyes suddenly widened and he took an instinctively subliminal half step backwards. "Okay. What the fuck is that about?" he asked.

Stuart turned to him, "I think you've raised a good point Guv. What the fuck *is* that about?"

After a short pause, he looked around at the other Firefighters who awaited his reaction. Paul's eyes darted from left to right as if reading from an invisible 'What the fuck should I do in an emergency?' manual. "Okay, don't mention this until I've spoken to Mother about it, okay? Keep this to yourselves until I say otherwise!" Both Firefighters obediently nodded. "When you get back to station I want your suit data, including all footage, transferred over to my office computer…okay? No other backups! Also I want all three of these suits taken off the run and given full diagnostic checks, understand?" Both Firefighters again nodded and then boarded the appliance ready to return to the station.

CHAPTER FOUR

"Er'satz Life"

<u>1</u>

As the appliances neared the station and the front doors automatically opened for them to park, black armoured vehicles were visible within the appliance bay. Around them stood men in black suits. One pointed at the appliances and then spoke to another man via his Comms mic which was concealed in his sleeve jacket. Paul, shaking his head, turned to his crew. "Right, no-one says anything they're not supposed to. Just direct any questions to me regardless of what they threaten you with." He turned to look around the appliance bay again and as the appliance parked itself in front of the armoured vehicles, he began to realise just how many suits were there. On or two of the suits had side arms. One even sported what looked like a modified pulse lance. "Oh this isn't good."

As the appliance doors folded in on themselves and raised up like a launching bird of prey, black suits stood each side of them and also lined both appliances. "Okay, sit here." Ordered Paul as he unbuckled his safety harness and stepped into the back of the cab to exit via the open winged doors. He took a deep breath and then stepped down the short ladder to the floor. As he did, a black suit pushed him along the line of suits that now lead to the office door. Paul stumbled but recovered before he fell then looked back at the suit. The suit raised an eye brow and rested his hand against his holstered gun.

Before Paul could respond, the office door burst open and a grey suit ran towards them both at speed, arms flailing and swearing in an angry accusatory tone. As he arrived and stood next to Paul the grey-suited man raised his pointed hand "Oi, wanker, what the fuck are you doing?"

Paul reared up, "Who are you calling wanker, eh? Why the….."

"No not you Sir." The Grey suit was pointing towards Paul but more accurately was pointing past him at the now apologetic looking black suit. "What the fuck are you doing pushing these guys about? What are you, mental? Who said anything about.....I never said anything about pushing them around, *did* I?" He paused a moment and raised his eyebrows. Still no response so he tilted his head forward and fully widened his eyes as he stared straight into the guards' eyes. The black suit lowered his head apologetically. "What's wrong with you guys? Really, I'm starting to wonder if you're taking the new company issue suits too seriously, you know? Okay? You're not FBI, we're not military, okay? So why the big boy stuff? Stop it."

The lower lip on the face of the black-suited man now quivered. "Sorry Sir."

Paul stood there, slightly unsure what he was more thrown by, the adrenalin now receding from his black suit encounter, the instant change of tone in the bay or the amusingly high pitched effeminate voice that just came from the black-suited man. Paul scrunched up his eyes, shook his head and snorted a stifled chuckle.

"Perkins, no biscuits or cake for you for a week. Okay? No.....don't look at me like that, for a week, I mean it." The grey suit now turned to Paul, "I'm so sorry about that. Are you okay? You must be Station Officer Wright. It's really nice to meet you." He sprung out his right hand grabbed Pauls and then shook a vigorous politicians hand shake. "Please come this way would you? We have lots to discuss. Come through to the main office. We've brought lots of cakes and biscuits, please, come through."

Paul looked at his crew that were now gathered by the appliance door looking out at events unfolding. He shrugged his shoulders and then beckoned for them all to follow. They and the grey suit now all disappeared into the main office.

Mother's watch were still quietly secreted on both appliances. After a few minutes the doors of the appliances lowered and sealed themselves locked to secure both appliances. As they did, the black suits all either mounted the armoured vehicles or entered the offices, presumably to see if there were any cakes left.

Katie, who was now looking out through the appliance windows at the parked armoured vehicles, turned to Mother, "Okay, am I the only one who's just a little bit freaked out by all this? What have they done?"

Mother shrugged at both questions and was busy stretching his face muscles in an attempt to sober up as best he could.

"I mean, they've not done anything, *have they*? Oh, I wonder if one of Paul's watch has done something whilst off duty? Oh no!" Katie sat again and then rested her tired head against the doors' glass.

As Katie stared out into the appliance bay the office door opened and out stepped another grey-suited man. In his hands he carried a chair and a saucered hot drink. He walked towards the appliances, stopped, placed his chair facing towards them then sat and slowly sipped his coffee as he stared at the appliances. Katie gingerly moved away from the glass out of view. "Er, Guv." Katie pulled at Mother's shirt. "Guv."

"What is it Kate? Why are you pulling my shirt? I'm right here, what is it?" As he turned to look at Katie, he too noticed the man, who was now tucking into a slice of cake, sitting outside in the bay, watching the appliances. "Okay, that's a little unnerving. What the….." Mother cautiously crouched down onto his knees and slid towards the door window. Remaining in the shadow of the door's framework, he scanned as much of the bay as he could see. He sat back in his chair and looked around. Mother then did a quick count up of all his crew members. He mentally ticked off the other guys in the other appliance and then looked across the bench seat to see Brownie, Kevin and Jed all snoozing in a huddle. He again looked out of the window, "Okay so, well, then, if they're waiting for us in here…..does that mean they're here for us? Or are we just something to do with…..no, no I'm stumped."

As mother considered his options, a voice came over the appliance intercom, "Station Officer Riley would you and your crew like to join us please?"

Mother instinctively looked towards the intercom and then out to the waiting grey suit. The grey suit was talking into his sleeve and, seeing Mother, he lifted a greeting hand in the air.

"Yes, hello there, Station Officer Riley, would you and your crew like to join us out here if you please." With that, the appliance doors hissed and slowly raised open.

The strong white bay lights burst into the appliance and, as it poured over the three dormant crew members huddled in the corner, they all recoiled and reverted to an ancient Anglo-Saxon dialect to exclaim their displeasure. Mother stood and, shading his eyes, stepped out from the appliance towards the grey suit. He pushed his left hand to his side and signalled to Katie to remain in the appliance. He slowly walked towards the grey suit as if testing the ground beneath his feet. As he did, he discreetly looked around the bay to see if there was anything else waiting for them when they exited the appliance, anything else that might catch his crew out. He stopped walking and the grey-suited man now stood up from his chair. In a low gravelly almost pantomimed voice he introduced himself. "Ah, Mr Riley, I…..am Professor….."

As Mother awaited the rest of the name, the Professor convulsed and began to violently cough. After a short while he began to gag like a caricatured cat coughing up a fur ball. Perkins, who had been waiting outside the office door, stepped towards him to help but the now bent over man raised his hand to stop him and shook his head to signal he needed no assistance. Mother narrowed his eyes and looked around to see if there was anyone else waiting to pounce on him to reveal the joke. Nothing.

The grey-suited man now stood upright and was taking in long deep lungs full of air. Tears rolled from his eyes and he was paling from what *had been* a deep reddish tinge. He spoke and, as he did, Mother noted that his gravelly voice had now been replaced by a normal mild tone. "Oh goodness. Oh that was not cool, not cool", cough, "Oh good Lord no. Wow." He pointed to his throat, "Too much..." pant, "Cake." Pant. "Oh wow, sorry about that." His breathing slowed and the tide from the sweat on his forehead slowly receded. He took a well needed sip of coffee and then, again, looked upwards and blew out a relieved sigh. He looked over towards the armoured vehicles and raised an exaggerated thanking wave, "Okay, thanks a lot, thanks a lot for your help everyone, I mean, what the hell am I paying you for? Only Perkins here offered and that is only because he's on cake rationing!" He looked back at Mother and under his breath mumbled, "Inbred goons!" He straightened himself up and put out a hand to shake Mother's. "Okay I'm sorry about all that, I er.....I'm pleased to meet you, my name is Professor Black."

Mother shook his hand, "Professor Black? Really? Are you kidding? Professor Black?"

"Yes, Professor Black, that's my name. I don't get it, what's up with that?"

"What, are you kidding?" Mother wound his neck backwards with disbelief. "I come in here, you've got armoured cars here, all your staff are wearing black suits and you call yourself *Professor* Black? Are you serious? Jeez, I'm surprised you weren't sitting there stroking a white cat rather than just stuffing your face with cake."

The Professors' brow furrowed and he pursed his lips in mild confusion. "Okay firstly, I don't get the cat reference..."

"Bond. James Bond?"

"Okay, I don't get that either. Secondly, the reason we have armoured cars is, partly because our company manufactures them, so they're cheap for us to acquire and also because we carry around sensitive information that sometimes needs to be protected and so we use them as our company courier vehicles. Thirdly, my name *is* Black, it really *is* Black. Okay?"

"And you just happen to be a Professor? Professor Black?"

"Yes, but I don't just *happen* to be a Professor, I am a Professor and it took many years of hard work to earn the title so *yes,* I am a Professor and I feel like I've earned the right to be called it so you know, I'm '*Professor'* Black. So, let's just leave it at that, shall we? *Mr* Riley?"

"Station Officer."

"Pardon?"

"Station Officer. It took many years of hard work to get to this level so yes, I am *Station Officer* Riley."

"Okay, I see what you did there, you can have that, I'll give you that." The Professor took another sip of his coffee and looked over his cup with an attempted patronising glare.

"So then. Professor. Professor of what?"

"Professor…of…well that doesn't really matter now does it, I'm a Professor and that's all there is to it, okay? I'm a Professor, so just…..you know that's…..I'm a Professor, okay?"

"In what?"

"Well…"

"In what?!"

"Theoretical Mantua fabrication."

"Theor-what? It sounds quite specialised."

"It's technical and really not relevant to why we're here so shall we move on?"

"Mantua. Mantua?" Mother rubbed his head, "Isn't that…isn't that something to do with making something? Hang on, that's not dress…"

"Yes dress making! Yes that's right, dress making, alright?"

"Dress making? Can you even be a Professor in dress….." Mother was giggling too hard to finish the sentence.

"Look it's the study of fabrics, of lines, of forms, textures, tensile strength….." The Professor silently marched over to the office door and opened it. He then beckoned for, and waited for, Mother to enter, which he did. Mother did so with a controlled grin like he was a naughty school boy entering the headmasters' office, head bowed and eyes wet with giggled tears.

The Professor raised up an angry flat hand in despair and huffed. He then realised that he probably looked a little camp doing this so then followed it with an attempted, 'butcher', but even camper, growl.

<u>2</u>

In the Station Officer's office, Mother was sitting with Coffee (and cake) in an office chair facing the main table. Behind the table was Professor Black. Next to the desk, sitting in a couch, were two Senior Fire Brigade Officers. Still slightly bemused, Mother looked over at the two Senior Officers who both seemed quite content and somewhat un-phased by the whole event.

The main light turned off and the room was suddenly in complete darkness. The lamp on the desk was now switched on and was turned towards Mother. Mother flinched slightly and then placed his arm over his face. He got up and turned the main light on again and then returned to his seat. Again the main light turned off so Mother again turned on the main light with the switch by the office door and sat quietly in his chair.

Professor Black coughed and leaned forward. "Please......please, stop doing that. Stop turning the, er, the main light on every time I switch it off."

"What are you talking about? Why are you doing that with the lights? Why are you bothering to do that? You get me coffee and cake and then start playing silly buggers with the lights. What kind of interviewing techniques are these anyway?" Mother shuffled in his seat. "I can't see my cake when you turn the lights off, you amateur! Besides, I'm off duty. I can just get up and leave if I want."

One of the Officers leaned forward towards the Professor, "Actually you really do need to stop doing that with the lights, okay? We're sitting here drinking coffee *too* you know? That's just silly, please stop turning the main light back off." He paused. "Okay?" The Professor nodded, the Senior Officer sat back into his seat and reached for another cup cake.

The Professor, now looking slightly disarmed, shrugged and continued. "Mr Riley...Station Officer...Riley, I guess you're wondering why I called you into my office?"

"No. I'm wondering why you called me into *my* office."

The Professor paused and drew a slow breath. "Your office. Yes, okay then, why I asked you to join me in *your* office."

"Actually to be honest, I'm a little bit pissed, It's very, very late, I'm off duty, you're getting cake all over my desk, one of my fellow Station Officers was assaulted by one of your black-suited Neanderthal goons, you coughed cake all over me in the bay and you've put fucking sugar in my coffee which I can't stand! Wondering what you've got to say to me isn't really that high on my agenda! I haven't done anything, I'm quite confident that none of my guys has done anything so I doubt very much we're in any trouble. That just leaves something you either want or need from me, so just have your say and then get out of my office!"

The Professor looked over to the Senior Officers for support. None was given but one of the Officers subtly raised his cup to Mother and then nodded. "I was told gentlemen by your Chief Officer that I could expect your full support. Your *full* support. You do understand how important this project is to both yourselves and the Government, Right? Now do I have your full co-operation or don't I?"

The most senior of the two Officers, who had remained silent until now, nodded under protest and smiled through gritted teeth, "Of course you have our full support Professor." He then turned to Mother and barked in a very *'Don't make me tell your Father when he gets home'* "Hey!" With that, he nodded again at the Professor and sipped a purposefully noisy slurp of Coffee.

The Professor stopped for a moment and then turned towards Mother. "Okay then, let's cut to the chase shall we?"

"Ooh let's, let's cut to the chase." Said Mother in a now very tired, very laboured manner.

"Station Officer Riley, I wonder if you are taking this at all seriously."

"Oh trust me. I am taking this *very* seriously."

The Professor straightened up in his chair and placed both his hands deliberately onto the desk. "Station Officer Riley.", Sigh, "Shaun. Do you *mind* if I call you Shaun?"

"I'd much rather you called me in the morning, I'm tired." Mother enjoyed a short giggle. Both the Senior Officers hid their amusement. "No, no I'm sorry." Mother straightened himself up, "How about I call *you* Blackie? The Prof? Professor B. How about Professor B?"

The Professor slid a card across the table with his full name on it. "Shaun I am…..from the Company…"

"Oh good God, really? You're from 'The Company'? Jeez, are you fucking kidding me? You're Professor Black and you're from 'The Company'? Oh come on, give me a break, how cloak and dagger is this shit?"

The Professor, now tapping his finger on his business card, continued, "Sorry, if you'll let me finish Shaun. I am from the Company…"*Ersatz Industries*." My full name is on the card just in front of you.

Slightly embarrassed for his premature outburst, Mother took the card and sat back into his chair. He coughed an uneasy cough and then read the card. "Oh the, er…the Company...oh, *Ersatz Industries, Advanced Augmatech* oh, okay." Again he straightened himself and read the whole card. "It says here your name is Peter Black, oh okay. Well Peter, what's this all about. Hey, *Ersatz*? Aren't you the guys that designed all the navigational B.I. stuff for the Conduit?"

The Professor, slightly pleased with the acknowledgment treated himself to a wry smile. "Well yes, yes actually, yes we did write the Bio-Intelligence. That…that was us, amongst other things of course. In fact the Conduit programming was originally due to be written by a Company called Microsoft, but they found that every time they booted it up the cars kept crashing." A short pause. "Ha-ha, kept crashing." Mother and the two Officers all stared blankly back at the Professor. "Microsoft…, crashing…ha, ha…" Cough, "No? Okay, just me then?"

Mother just shook his head, "Who are Microsoft?"

"No-one…sorry, they're an old…it's an old IT joke, it's er, IT humour", cough, "It's nothing, Okay, anyway so as I was saying, we at Ersatz Industries, along with writing the B.I. for the conduit, are also involved in projects in both Bio-intelligence hardware and robotics. And that's why we're here."

"Look Professor, don't get me wrong, usually I'm quite polite, I don't rattle easily, I'm placid. I'm a placid guy, I am Mr Placid, I am Station Officer Placid of Placid Station, Placid-ville but, to be honest, the way you've gone about all this, the way you've introduced yourself to both me and the Brigade, you can forget it. I'm not going to give you any form of assistance. Don't ask me to try any equipment out for you because I'm not gonna do it."

Both the Senior Officers looked away, intently, into their coffees.

"Well actually, you already are Shaun." The Professor paused knowing that Mother's still slightly tipsy brain would take a moment to digest this disclosure.

"Fucking…what?" Mother looked at the Officers and then looked out towards the bay where the appliances were parked. "You mean we've been trialling a new version of the B.I. software and we weren't told? What if it had gone wrong, what if we'd had an accident? Then what? Jeez! How come we don't know anything about this? I mean, were the unions consulted?"

The Professor looked at the Officers then back to Mother. "It's not the Bio software Shaun."

"The suits? You've sodded about with our suits then haven't you, oh for…"

"No Shaun, not the appliance software, not the suits…one of your Firefighters."

Mother took a deliberate, slow, full breath. "Okay I'm still a bit pissed and getting really bored with this, just explain to me what exactly is going on or I'm outta here!"

The Professor stood, moved forward, sat on the front corner of the desk, folded his arms and looked down at Mother, "One of your Firefighters is a Government backed science project code named Asimov. He is the first of, *hopefully*, a new breed of first responders, be it Firefighter, Police Officer, soldier, space pioneer, heck we could even send them down into collapsed mines, do sewage work, whatever we want." The Professor looked off momentarily into a brighter future. "It's the most impressive of our robotics division's achievements to date."

Mother still, stunned and not completely convinced, sat motionless. "One of my Firefighters is…a robot? What the…You're telling me one of my firefighters is…a…machine? Fuck off…which one?"

"Christian, you're new recruit Christian. He's the property of Ersatz Industries. He's part of the most costly trial we've ever undertaken. You should be very proud."

Mother gently shook his head. "Christian? What on earth are you talking about? Christian…he was in the Pioneers, he's…"

The Professor brushed away this fact with a wave of his hand, "All implants. All of those memories are implants. They are there to ease his introduction to you and to help ease his orientation. Those memories are what give him grounding, a footing in the world. We also put them there to explain why he would be so efficient at learning things, so good with tools and why he'd be so…"

"But hang on, I was with him when he saw his first badly injured casualty. He was visibly moved. He was wary of fire the first time he ran into it, what are you saying? He can't be…" Mother's eyes watered with anger and frustration.

"Emotional sub-routines. It's all part of the project. We needed to see if he could fully integrate into a Watch without being detected as a synthetic. You know, see if you'd truly believe that he was a real person. So we had him be genuinely scared at times and also made him tired and bored and so on. The programming side of it is fascinating by the way."

"You made a copy of a person and then you forced him to be scared? That's a bit fucking cruel isn't it? Isn't that a little like playing God, but the kind of God who's actually a bit of a wanker?"

"Well, er,…"

"You mean to say that all of his training records, his ID's his transfer letters, everything, all fakes?"

"Yes, well, not quite fakes, they're all genuine, supplied by the relevant departments on request from the Government's department of future-tech. They were all very helpful. We did offer some financial and resource incentives too but, that aside, they still were very helpful." The Professor smiled to himself. "Oh, do you like his name by the way. That was my Idea. Christian C Mann is his full name, as you know. D'you get it now?"

Mother looked up, a dejected, uninterested expression on his face. "What?"

"C.C. Mann. Get it, Carbon Copy Mann? That was my idea. I'm quite pleased with that."

"What the fuck is a carbon copy?"

Professor Black's smile dropped, "Oh yes, a Carbon Copy, oh it's a, er, well it's a retro IT term. That name has gotten a few big laughs though at IT conferences let me tell y'u. Well at the times when, you know, I'm at liberty to talk about it."

For the next thirty minutes, Mother continued to sit there, head spinning, as the Professor launched fact after fact at him from technical specs to projected uses, proposed upgrade options to possible alternate colour schemes.

The salient information that Mother *had* taken in was that Christian was chosen to join the Fire Service to see if, in the long term, Firefighting could be outsourced. The initial outlay would be astronomical but there would be no salaries, no pensions, no medical bills, no discipline or conduct issues, no human error. The units themselves had an expected life span of at least 200 years with the possibility of extended longevity with the use of replacement parts or upgrades.

The units themselves were extremely robust, shock resistant, impervious to temperatures nearing the 1000° C mark and were extremely strong, though of course this strength had been artificially supressed in Christian so as not to arouse suspicion. They ran on self-contained power units that meant they were good for at least 2 weeks of constant use without charge or 12 years in standby mode. They could, of course, be recharged but as an alternative to a charge, food could be consumed and energy taken from it. The aim of the project was to transplant Christian onto the watch for twelve months and to then run tests with both the watch and Christian, to see how he had evolved and developed and also to determine if any member of the watch had actually realised the deception.

"I don't get it then, so why now, why break your cover now, it's been only six months, has the project failed, is it a…success, what?" Mother was finding his agitation and anger harder to hide.

"Well, no, so far it's been a complete success. Really, *really* good in fact, the numbers we're getting are amazing. Off the charts. Far better than we'd hoped for, it's just that, well…well, we forgot about his heat signature. A fairly blatant oversight to you of course being that you're used to wearing the suits I know but we just didn't give it a thought. So on that first day when he first arrived at the station he went out without his suit on and one of your guys saw him and didn't pick up a heat signature and that was, er…"

"The suit Malfunction, that's why we had that suit malfunction isn't it, oh for f…Jeez, you could have gotten someone killed or at least injured."

"Yes, yes, we know that, we hadn't thought about that. We did reprogram all of your suits that evening to overlay a heat signature whenever you looked at Christian but what we didn't think about…"

"…Was us bumping into other Firefighters that are not on our watch, as in, tonight when we were off duty. Come to think of it, where are all the other watch, what have you done with them?"

"Oh they're fine. No, no, really they're fine. One of your Senior Officers and one of our representatives are speaking to them now and arranging their "bonuses" and getting them to sign contracts etcetera. They're all taken care of." One of the Senior Officers signalled that he would leave to see how the other guys were getting on and left the room. "You see Shaun this is a very, very resource intensive project. There are massive implications to the success of this project, not just for us but for people as a whole."

"You mean, people like me, who'll be out of a job?"

"No, no, we have already agreed with the government that this will be as ethical a project as possible. No-one will ever be sacked as a consequence of this work. That's a written stipulation."

"It still doesn't sound completely ethical to me though."

The Professor pulled at his collar, coughed and sat back in his chair. "We've made some mistakes I admit."

"So how do you know how well this project is going? Does Christian report back to you on a daily basis or something, I mean…"

"No, no nothing like that, no, no Christian doesn't…know."

"Excuse me? Christian…"

"…Doesn't know he's a robot. No. It's very important that he does not find this out. I cannot stress how critical that fact is."

"He doesn't know?" Mother looked to the Senior Officer. The Senior Officer's brow furrowed and he averted his eyes.

"No, you see, it would never have worked if he'd known. He would have let slip somehow. Subliminally, he would have let you know, without even trying to. One of you would have picked up on subtle nuances that would have given it away."

"So...how do you take information from him? I mean, about the project? Is there someone else on the watch that's working with you?" Mother looked into his memory to see if any of his watch had been acting strangely, differently, out of character, but nothing came to mind.

"No, no. No one else knows. We just go to his apartment every night when he's in standby and download everything from that day. He's unaware of it but that's because we've programmed him to allow us access to his data when he's in standby."

"Everything? What do you mean *everything*?"

"Well everything, facts, figures, temperature readings, all audio and video data..."

"Fucking what? You mean to say that everything he sees and hears, you've been downloading and scrutinising? So any private conversation he may have had with anyone is now Ersatz property?"

"Ah, well, yes, I can see why you'd...hmmm." The Professor was now visibly uncomfortable.

"You *knew* about this?" Mother turned to the Senior Officer. The Senior Officer froze for a second and then, drawing on his years of managerial experience, declared, "I'm right out of Coffee, does anyone else fancy a Coffee?" Before Mother could point out how spineless he was being, the only thing that the Officer *had* actually managed was to stand and slip out of the door. Mother turned back to the Professor. "My guys shower together. Both the men *and* the women shower together. That's on your fucking computers now, isn't it? Ethical? What the fuck!"

The Professor, realising he had a very uphill struggle with this argument, simply put his hands up in submission. "I'm sorry, I'm sorry, I know this looks bad. Listen let's talk about this some more when you're back on duty. Take some time to digest what we've discussed and then let's talk again more about this soon, okay? But I must stress that you cannot talk about this with anyone! Not even your watch, *especially* Christian. He must not know! This is critical, we don't know what it would do to his...er...wellbeing if he knew. Okay?"

"You really are a prick Black! We *will* speak about this more when I'm back on duty but fuck me, you really do have a lot of explaining to do."

"And you won't speak about this to anyone?"

"Jeez, I don't think I need to. Your company has proven itself incompetent enough already what with forgetting about our guys not seeing him on their thermal visors. I mean, how stupid are you people?"

The Professor straightened his tie and raised an eyebrow, "Mr Riley I assure you, yes we made a slight error, but we are one of the most trusted and sought after companies in the world. We live and breathe technology and *stealth* is our middle name."

"It may be spelt Stealth but I'm guessing it's pronounced Cock!" With that, Mother stood and walked towards the door.

"Where are you going?"

"I'm suddenly aware that I'm not nearly drunk enough for all this. I'm getting the rest of my watch and leaving and when I get home I'm going to get Royally shit-faced." Mother left the office closely followed by a scurrying Professor Black. When he arrived at the appliances, Mother leaned in to inform the rest of his watch that it was now okay for them to leave. As he did so, he saw the uncomfortable faces of Katie, Jed, Kevin and Brownie all huddled together. "Guys, everything's alright. We're out of here. You all okay?" He then turned to the Professor. "I thought you said my guys were being spoken to and signing contracts. How come they're still in here?"

The Professor shuffled uneasily. "No, no, I was referring to the other watch. Don't forget Mr Riley, we shall speak again when you are next on tour but until..." The Professor stopped talking as he neared the appliance, suddenly aware that his conversation was coming out through the appliance's intercom system. He looked down at his sleeve and saw his microphone still gently glowing with its' green LED ready light. "Oh bollocks." Christian, who had left the other appliance and had been sitting in the Officer's seat at the front, now stepped into the back of the appliance cab. "Oh bollocking bollocks."

Mother turned to the Professor. "You...Cock!"

CHAPTER FIVE

"Angst in your pants"

<u>1</u>

The mood on roll call the next tour was sombre. Mother called the roll in a very functional manner and not with his usual engagingly chatty approach. Each crew member was assigned their days' tasks and they then mounted their appliances to complete their initial daily checks.

Christian, who stood throughout roll call with his shoulders down and was clearly distracted, slumped himself over to his designated appliance. Mother, who was still standing where he had taken roll call, slightly unsettled by the sight of one of his crew clearly so lost called to him, "Christian, after we've all had a cup of tea I'd like a word with you in my office…" he paused, "…Please."

Without looking up, Christian simply nodded and continued towards his appliance.

Upstairs, the mood had still not lifted, the usual first day banter replaced by an uncomfortable awkward silence. Each member of the watch had spent two days or more whilst off duty being briefed by Ersatz Industries representatives who had escorted them all home from the station the night that the Company first introduced themselves and made their involvement with Christian known. Christian was still sitting on the appliance, tests completed. His eyes were lowered to the floor, red with lack of sleep and full of angst. Even as he thought of this, he sneered to himself. "Lack of sleep." he thought, I don't even need sleep it turns out. I *could* have that function *disabled*." His whole body language stated clearly he was in pain. Genuine, tangible, pain.

Upstairs, Mother was sipping his tea, looking around the room, he too with a red-eyed sleep-deprived hangover. As he scanned the other watch members, he ticked off the same symptoms one at a time. Red eyes, tick. Drooped shoulders, tick. Silent, tick.

Brownie took a sip from his tea, glanced up and saw Mother looking along the line of Firefighters and Sub Officers. He shook his head slightly. His experience as a long serving Firefighter told him the need to clear the air. The confidence of his long standing also indicated that someone needed to start what was clearly going to be an uncomfortable and still somewhat surreal conversation. He coughed to announce his intention to speak, "Okay, well, clearly no one's going to raise it, so I will. He's a machine. Okay? I said it, he's a machine and that's just fucked up on several levels…but we need to talk about it." He took a well-deserved further sip of tea and saw out of the corner of his eye Mother wearing a dignified smile and nodding once towards him.

"Okay, well, Brownie's right." began Mother. "He's a machine and we need to talk about it. One of the members of our watch is not a real person …or at least not a person as we know it."

Katie looked over to Mother, "Truth is, I'm just quite hurt Guv is all. I can't believe this Company have been spying on us all this time. It's just…" She shook her head and looked back into her tea. "And, yes I'll grant you they have been quite generous with the credits they've offered me and I assume all the rest you but…really?...That's not really the point is it?"

"Katie, now I know what you're saying and you don't need to convince me how disgusting it is that they've been spying on us. I'm just as appalled by this deception as the rest of you but to be honest…I don't think what we get up to here is anything to do with their project. They simply need the results of his interaction….."

"Guv, you're starting to sound like…"

"Katie yes, yes I know I'm starting to sound like one of the grey suits from Ersatz Industries. Look, I know it's all a bit crap. I know. But to be honest, I, like the rest of you, am…still…coming to terms with this, still…trying to get my head around it. But the truth is…we've got a job to do here. Like or loathe this situation we are still operational Firefighters and we need to be focused and get on with our jobs. Trust me, I'm not happy about it. I'm not comfortable with it, but it is what it is."

Jed, who had been sitting with his head in his hands, sat up, "But Mother he's a bloody machine. He's effectively a science project that will, in the long run, do away with the need for humans to be Firefighters anymore. And what then? Soldiers? Road sweepers? Cooks? That just seems so…unethical. I just don't feel comfortable talking around him anymore or saying anything other than work related stuff. I'm sorry I know that sounds like I'm excluding him but that's just the way I'm feeling at the moment."

Mother nodded. "I know mate, it's not easy. It's not easy for any of us, and I mean *any* of us, me included." He paused, "But least of all for Christian." He paused again awaiting the reaction to this point.

Les now joined in, "Christian? Seriously? With respect Guv, fuck Christian!"

"Right, Les, let me stop you there. You're talking about one of my Firefighters. Christian is still part of this watch, part of this team okay? Remember that! He is still a member of my staff and is my responsibility and I'll not have you talking that way about one of my staff."

"Guv, yes, yes, okay I'm sorry…but really, part of this team? He's a product. He doesn't have organs or blood. He has part numbers and hydraulic Bio-fluid…stuff. Besides, when the fuck did robots become so real?"

Mother chuckled, "I know mate, it's all a bit surreal and yes I know that some of what you're saying is right but Les don't you remember that it was only last week that we were all out on the piss together. We were all getting drunk together, talking rubbish, having a laugh together? Complaining about 'the system', the weather, the state of politics? Heck Les, I seem to remember you almost wet yourself at one of Christian's one liners."

"Yeah, yeah I know." Les, smiled at the memory, "But Guv...really?"

"No Les. Les, let's be honest, what's changed? He's still the same guy. He's still Christian. The things he's said and done whilst he's been with us, they're not preprogramed. They're not implants. They've all come from him, they all a part of him...and truth is I've grown quite fond of him, as I am all of you. He's part of my team. A *valued* part of my team. Les you yourself in the past have said how our team is like a family. You know, maybe a little dysfunctional at times, but still a family." Mother smiled a warm Fatherly smile.

"Yes Guv...I...but Guv, even his memories are implanted. He doesn't even have a real background. All that stuff about the Pioneers was...well...bullshit. All that Mars base stuff, completely made up. He's never been to the Libya base. How are we supposed to deal with all that?"

"Les, *Christian* didn't know it was bullshit. He's just found out that he's been bullshitted to as much as the rest of us, in fact even more so. Mother pursed his lips for a moment and rescanned the room to gauge the reactions to this conversation. "Les...Les...you know when you found out that Angela was cheating on you?"

"Guv? Wha..."

"No, hear me out Les, it's relevant, okay? Well...remember how you felt when you found that out? For weeks you didn't want to talk to anyone, didn't wanna be at work? Remember we spoke about it at the time?"

"Guv, where are we going with this? Why are we speaking about Ugly Angela?"

"Ugly Angela? Oh, okay Ugly now is she? Okay, well clearly you *have* moved on." Mother chuckled a respectful chuckle. "Okay, well remember how you felt back then?"

Richie leaned forward and turned to Les, "Actually, have you seen her lately, you might wanna think about promoting her to the rank of really ugly Angela." Les smiled back at Richie.

"Richie, please mate."

"Oh yeah, sorry Guv."

"Okay, well Les you remember how you felt?"

"Yes Guv, of course I do, yes." Les shuffled uncomfortably in his chair.

"Okay, so now imagine what it would be like to find out, not that your wife had cheated on you, but that your whole marriage had been an experiment. A lie. Everything about your past, every moment that you remembered, the good times you savoured, the bad times you lamented, everything…was all…complete…and utter…..bullshit. All of it. All of it made up. Every last second of it. All of it the product of some IT geeks' imagination. How would you even start getting your head around that? Can you even begin to imagine how much of a head-fuck that must be? Because Les…"

Les looked around the room and then lowered his gaze.

"You see for me Les, for me the most important part of all of this is that Christian didn't know. He. Didn't. Know. The company didn't even tell *him*. That's the only thing that's getting me through this. As far as I'm concerned this company not only lied to *us* but they also completely head-fucked one of my Firefighters. One of *your* colleagues. One of *your* friends. My fight is not with my fellow Firefighter, it's with this fucking company. But now, it is what it is. It is the way it is and we just have to work around it." Mothers' eyes glistened with company resenting tears. "I will not only continue working with Christian but I will also be affording him any and all the support he needs to get through this."

"But Guv, he's……a robot!"

Mother's eyes snapped fully widened at Les and his cheeks reddened as he stood and slammed his fist hard against the mess table. "But he's *our* fucking robot! It doesn't matter what he's made of. It doesn't matter and you know why? Because I am proud to call him one of my Firefighters. As I am proud to call all of you my Firefighters. How fucking dare this company impose this on him! How dare they do this to one of our watch! He didn't ask to be made!"

Jed leaned forward, "With respect Guv, none of us *asked* to be made."

"Well then we're all in the same fucking boat then, aren't we?" Mother turned from the table to compose himself. Out of character though it was for him to swear in front of his crew, he could not conceal his anger at this situation. He lowered his volume and tempered his tone as he turned to face his crew again. "Guys, please, just put yourselves in *his* shoes. That's all I'm asking."

Gentle nods of guilty agreement rippled around the mess table and some of the Firefighters shook their heads in self-imposed reprimands.

Katie wiped her sympathetic red-tear painted eyes. "Poor little sod."

Mother stood and silently nodded to the group and sombrely left the mess room as if departing from a wake. Outside he leaned against a hallway wall. 'Phew.' he thought as he sighed a deep calming sigh. He was now aware of how hard his heart was pumping as he dabbed the sweat from his upper lip. "Okay, well, that's hopefully the watch fixed for now, now let's speak to Christian and see if we can't fix him." He smiled to himself and, still trembling, looked back towards the mess room then moved towards his office to speak to Christian. Mother knew the importance of ensuring the welfare of his crews. Whether or not he agreed with a policy or procedure or the introduction of a new piece of equipment, it was simply his role to ease the transition, to smooth the way for all of the watch to ensure a safe and happy working environment. On this occasion however, the Company could go whistle, *his* watch came first. He wanted to help

Christian in any way he could. Mother had grown fond of Christian who had proven himself an able and eager member of his watch. He was *proud* to have him on his team.

2

In the office, Christian had been sitting, not knowing what to expect when Mother arrived. Was he going to be taken off the watch? Was he going back to Ersatz Industries? Part of him really didn't care either way. Christian's whole being was numb and had been since the arrival of the grey suits. Nothing really made a lot of sense anymore. Not sure of his identity, not sure how he fitted in or even if he actually belonged anymore. As the door to the office opened, his mind raced with calculations, possible outcomes. He knew that he could predict the future no more than he could trust the past anymore.

Mother stepped confidently into the room and sat on his desk looking down at Christian.

"Guv, I…"

"Never mind Guv! Guv's not gonna cut it, is it Christian?"

Startled, Christian tensed for a moment, "Well no I…"

"No excuses young man. Six months you've been here and you feel like you've earned the right to slacken off."

"Er, wha…" Christian wiped his tired eyes.

"It's not good enough Christian. Got your feet under the table and now you feel like you can kick back!"

Christian straightened in his chair. "Well I…"

"Last week, did I or did I not ask you to test and clean the stations' backup generators?"

Christian looked puzzled, "Well, I don't, er, did you, I don't remember…"

"Christian, yes or no?" Mother arched his brow and leaned, arms now folded, towards Christian.

"Well, er, sorry Guv, I don't remember, no…I mean, yes?"

"Yes, exactly. Thank you. Well at least you're honest I suppose. Okay, well I'm not happy about it. I had to explain to the station Manager why we hadn't tested the station generators last week. I had to take that on the chin Christian but ultimately *I'm* responsible. I'm, not happy about that, okay? Do you understand?"

"No, sorry Guv, I'm er, I mean, yes Guv, I'll get on it right away." Christian paused for a moment, "Did you want me to do it now Guv?"

"Yes Christian. Yes. Now please."

Christian shook his head clear, stood and moved to the door then turned. "But Guv, Ersatz, what…"

"Ersatz Industries? Never mind those Tossers, Christian! They're full of shit, they've got no idea how to conduct interviews and my cat's got more dress sense than any of them. Besides, *they're* not gonna get those bloody generators tested now, are they?"

"Guv? No, But…"

"Christian, are you part of this team? Yes or no?"

"Well, yes Guv."

"Well then. Forget all that other crap and get on with your job. You're a good lad Christian, don't let me down. I've got other things to worry about what with management breathing down my neck, targets to hit, 'paperwork' to complete..."

Christian again blinked his angst further from his mind, "But Guv, my memories. My..."

"Christian!" Mother snapped, then, realising he had snapped, softened his tone. "Christian, all of your experiences make you all that you are." Mother breathed a deep sigh. "Okay, so they may not be your experiences, right? All moments in our lives lead us to where we are *now*. There's bugger all we can do about what may or may not have happened to you in your past. All we *can* do is concentrate on your future." He smiled, "And your future is going out there and sorting out those bloody generators, okay?"

Christian's tension melted slightly. He was full of respect for this man before him and he knew that this respect was his own. This respect was not something that the company owned. It was not an implanted memory it was something *he* had decided. He respected Mother and respected his opinion. Christian nodded.

"Okay, well then, you've got to work with what you've got Christian. 'Sumos quod sumos'. *You are what you are* young man and *no one*, no company, no ape in a grey suit can take that away from you. Right?"

"But Guv, I'm not...I mean...I'm not..."

"Christian that's right, you're not are you and yet you should be, so stop standing there and go out and do it. And when you've finished doing it I want you to go and fill in the generator log and then come back to me and confirm that you've done it. Oh and, *yes,* I will be inspecting your work. Now get out of my office."

"Yes Guv, sorry Guv. Thank you Guv."

The office door closed as Christian swiftly left to carry out Mother's orders. Once he was satisfied that Christian had walked away, mother sat in his chair, leaned back into it, placed his hands over his face and sighed the second big sigh of the day. He looked into the distance and treated himself to a very well deserved smile. Mother sat there for a short while, waiting for his heart rate to return to normal. His eyes began to water as the sheer weight of the problem ahead of them all and the concern for this young man's future weighed on his mind. Mother fought back a tear, opened his eyes wide, coughed and turned to his office computer to immerse himself in his work.

Mother had thought long and hard whilst he was off duty on how he would approach this problem. He could either hit it head on, ignore it and hope it were to go away or simply replace Christian's lost purpose with another. Mother had been in the Brigade for many, many years and knew the importance of discipline. He knew the importance of having purpose. It was a basic human need. He was aware that the approach he had chosen may, very likely, only have a limited life span. But he also knew that he had to quickly kick his whole watch back into reality so as to allow them to be able to get on with their jobs. Also to allow space for a later, but timely, addressing of the bigger issues that may face both them and Christian. Mother was aware that he may not fully understand all of the problems that Christian may be facing and what may currently be going on in his head, but he knew that without Purpose Christian was lost. That was an immediate problem that he *could* do something about. A mild bollocking to remind Christian of his place on the watch would hopefully do the trick, and it did. The thing that Mother knew that Christian needed above all else at that moment was an immediate reason to continue, a focus and this was it. He really *was* a valued member of Mother's team, and had become a friend to everyone on the watch including himself. Mother knew that there were difficult times ahead but that trying to deal with it all head on right now would be like trying to push treacle up a hill. The approach he took was a gamble but it appeared to have worked, for the moment.

Outside in the back yard the Firefighters were testing and cleaning other pieces of equipment. Jed noticed Christian appear in the yard,

"Oh there he is the lazy bugger!" Christian looked over to Jed, "Yeah you! Where the Hell have you been y'u lazy sod?"

Christian looked pleased but thrown by the question, "I was, er...I've been told I've got to test and clean the station 'Gennies'."

"Oh come on then, I better give you a hand. I don't want a bollocking from the Governor as well, do I? What did I do to deserve being lumbered with you as my mentee, eh?" Christian shrugged his shoulders and shook his head with the hint of a smile.

He and Jed walked off towards the generator room. Behind them, Katie and Les were watching them walk together. Katie turned to Les and smiled a comforted, relieved smile. Les just smiled and nodded. "Les, you think he'll be okay?"

"I don't know Kate, I really don't. I hope so though. Les looked at Katie for a while longer, furrowed his brow, bowed his head and paused, "Kate, you're...not...wearing a bra today are you?" The wet, soapy, dirty cloth that Katie *had* been using now masked Les' face with a satisfying "Thwack." Behind the cloth, a composed Les simply stated in muffled tone, "No, I thought not." As Katie walked out of the yard towards the mess, she picked up a tea towel, leaned toward Les and flicked him with it as she passed him and he crumpled to the floor with a deep uncomfortable stifled groan. After a few seconds, he looked out from under the soggy cloth he was wearing towards the door through which Katie had now entered the station. "Oh...my...God..." he said between chuckles and laboured breaths. "I...(Puff)...can't...believe...(Puff)...she...flicked...(Puff, Puff, Puff)...me...in...the...balls..."

Richie, who was preparing breakfast, smiled to see a grinning Katie enter the kitchen. "You okay? What you been up to?"

"Oh I've been showing off my black belt in Origami to Les."

Richie, slightly puzzled but still curious asked, "Black belt in Origami? How does that work? That's bending bits of paper or something isn't it?"

"Well Les' laying on the ground in the yard all folded up at the moment if you wanna go see some of my handy work." Katie smiled, rewarded herself with a biscuit from the watch's biscuit tin then pouted at Richie as she walked out popping the biscuit into her mouth in an over dramatic way and cat-walked out of the room still grinning from ear to ear.

3

Before the watch could complete their equipment tests and checks, the 'Fire call' tones sounded around the station. Richie and Katie appeared and came running out from the mess as the other watch members were boarding the appliances. The appliances had already auto-started and on-boards were firing up ready to control navigation, Comms and satellite imaging. Mother climbed in through the rear cab door and then stepped forward in to the front cab where Richie was already sitting reading the centre console's messages. "Guv we've been called to a high rise fire, Green Lanes. Multiple calls." The display on the centre console now displayed a green border to inform the driver that all were aboard, all systems were ready and that all doors and lockers were sealed and secured. The appliance then pulled forward, followed by the second appliance, out of the station and across the first lanes of the main road gaining speed as it did. All nearby traffic had been auto-stopped by the conduit's management system so the appliance sped up, turned sharp right and headed down towards the locally nicknamed "Gotham" estate. Mother, who was now reading further details on the centre console, appeared in the visors of all on-board. "Okay, we've got multiple calls to fire, fourth floor, Gascoigne House. Brownie I want your team to concentrate on search and rescue around and above the fire." Brownie, who was currently in charge of the second appliance, confirmed this with a "Yes Guv." "Okay, Jed, Christian, Kate, Rich, I want you all to prep ready to tackle the fire. If it's a small fire Jed and Christian, you can go up, if it's going well, Kate and Rich I want you setting into the dry riser ready to supply water, okay?" All four Firefighters confirmed Mother's orders.

As the appliances neared Gascoigne House, satellite imaging confirmed that there were several people gathering outside the building and that there was a large amount of dense smoke billowing out from the building.

Jed and Christian turned to each other then gave each other the thumbs up. Katie spoke into her visor "Richie I'm green to go, you?" Richie, who had already assigned a "fend off" point for the appliance to park itself in, was now stepping into the rear of the cab as the appliance slowed and parked itself. "Yes I'm good to go." The rear doors to the cab then peeled themselves up and open as all four crew members stepped out into the bright dazzling sunlight. Katie reached into one of the rear lockers as she passed the appliance and took a line of hose and a branch. Richie grabbed a line of hose and a medic's bag.

Mother stepped out behind them, looked up to the fire floor, quickly scanned the gathered crowd, and headed towards a woman near the building who was looking upwards towards the smoke. In his visor, Mother's suit had identified the lady as being one of the people who made the first calls, "Gemma! Are you Gemma?" The lady turned round to see Mother.

"Yes, yes I am. I'm Gemma. Thank you for coming." Mother noted how calm and coherent Gemma was.

"Gemma, are…you okay? Are you hurt in anyway?"

"No, no I'm fine. I was here, coming off duty, and was just visiting a friend on the fifth floor. As soon as I stepped out of the lift I could see and smell smoke, so quickly looked round, realised it was on the floor below, got my friend, raised the alarm, got back in the lift and came back down."

"Okay thanks Gemma…Police?"

"No, no I'm Ambulance service."

"Oh, okay, thanks Gemma. You know anything else about the fire, who's on the fourth floor, what's alight and so on?"

"Yeah well that lady over there said that her Mum is still up there and I overheard a couple of people saying they thought there might be kids in one of the flats.

"Okay, thanks Gemma, I might need you to speak to the Police when they arrive so try not to disappear. Thanks mate." Mother had linked this conversation to the other Firefighter's Comms systems so the crews inside now knew that there were very likely people inside. As the crews rode up in the 'Firefighter's lift; to the floor below the fire floor, the lift car throbbed with the bassy hum of the suits' harmonics reverberating off the walls. The lift car door opened and all four Firefighters stepped out, entered the nearby communal stairwell and then walked up the final flights of stairs to the fire floor.

Jed stepped into the main corridor of the fire floor. "Kate, Richie, you set into the dry riser and back us up with water as soon as you've done that." Katie nodded and then she and Richie opened the dry riser outlet and started plugging in hoses ready to follow Jed and Christian. Jed and Christian stepped left down the corridor where thermal readings were most elevated. They both now worked their way through the pitch black, acrid, soup like smoke. Without their visors they would be able to see no further than about twelve inches in front of their faces. If the smoke had not been punching out of the far window to clean air there would be zero visibility. Anyone caught in this smoke would be in serious trouble and both Jed and Christian knew it. The harmonics generated by the suits kept flames at bay within a short range but the smoke could not be dealt with without positive pressure fanning systems that would be used later in the incident. Inside his visor, Jed could see the heat reading rising rapidly towards the farther end of the corridor so he walked briskly towards that direction closely followed by Christian. As he neared the end of the corridor, he saw an apartment door handle highlighted by his visor as being much hotter than surrounding temperatures. "Christian get ready with that pulse lance, okay?"

Christian nodded, stood by the side of the front door and then Jed shouted, "Door, door opening!" He then kicked against the red hot door. It burst open and Christian pulsed bursts from his lance into the apartment corridor and up towards the ceiling. Around them paintwork popped as it blistered, the suspended ceiling had begun to crumble and fail and furniture smouldered. The rest of the scene in the apartment appeared to occur in slow motion as Christian ran into the apartment and found an elderly lady and two children huddled together in the lounge. Jed quickly planted an air mask on the faces of both children picked them up and then ran out of the apartment as Christian, in one swift movement, placed a mask on the elderly lady, picked her up, swung her round and was also running out of the apartment passing Katie and Richie who were now entering to cool down the flat with water. Both Jed and Christian ran back along the corridor and down the one flight to the lift and then launched themselves into it. Jed punched the ground floor button and then turned to look at the two children to see if there were any signs of life. There were none. "Oh no, oh no…fuck. Fucking lift, can't you go any fucking slower?"

As the doors opened on the ground floor, light from outside streamed into the lift and Jed squinted, looking away as he ran blindly towards the main entrance of the building. Medics, that were now in attendance, had switched to Jed's visor display and were standing by ready to receive the three casualties. As the two Firefighters erupted from the building, the casualties were taken from them before they even had time to look around for the medics. Jed stood for a moment to watch where the children were taken to but then his body took over and he doubled over gasping for deeper breaths after his run. Christian just stood and watched the elderly lady as she was carried into a waiting Ambulance. He noticed Jed struggling for air and then was suddenly aware that he himself was not panting for breath at all. He was not in need of a rest. He was completely un-phased by the physical act of what he had just done. He raised an eyebrow. Perhaps he did not see the need to go through *all* of the acted behaviours that seemed to be programmed within him. Perhaps he could somehow control this. 'How odd.' He mused. 'I'm surprisingly calm about all of this for some reason', he thought. That in itself he found slightly unsettling but at the same time intriguing.

Jed, who had walked to the rear of the ambulance, looked in. The medic, who had scanned both the children, noticed him, turned, lowered his head, looked Jed in the eye, shook his head and then looked down towards the floor. Jed too looked down. He then took one last look at the two young children as they were being covered over by a second medic. He turned and walked away. Jed stepped onto the fire appliance, he sat, turned off his helmet Comms and then screamed at the top of his voice, "Fu-u-u-u-u-u-ck!"

He continued sitting for a moment longer, catching his breath. He stood, left the appliance and then re-joined the others to finish the job. Christian did not need to see the medics. He knew that his casualty would not have survived. *Could* not have survived. He looked down at his lance, powered it down, shut down the harmonics generator on his suit and then slowly but sombrely walked back towards Mother to get his next orders.

4

In the locker room some of the guys from the oncoming watch were getting changed into their uniforms ready for duty. Christian and Jed had sat on one of the bench's waiting to get showered after a workout in the Gym. Katie had already showered and was quietly sitting, naked, head towelled, on another bench, looking through her wash bag, keeping herself occupied. trying not to think about the casualties they had been unable to save that day.

The steam soaked room was filled with unease and was uncharacteristically sombre. Usually the room would be filled with amusingly abusive banter, chatter, jokes and exchanges of general news but today there was an air of unspoken discomfort.

Katie was aware of this but put this down to the sad events of the day. She looked up and around to see the faces of the Firefighters from the oncoming watch, all of them quiet, all of them exchanging glances and then occasionally looking over to where Christian was sitting. Jerry, one of the guys readying himself for duty, looked over to Katie, shook his head with a grimaced, angry, judgemental frown. Katie also shook her head but was shaking away the banal immaturity of such a gesture. Jerry continued to dry himself off after his shower, looked around at Christian again and then tutted. Katie barely contained a disapproving snort, "Everything alright Jerry? Something you wanna say?"

Jerry, now empowered by someone actually acknowledging his concerns, shook his head more dramatically, snorted a couple of 'for effect' bullish snorts and then turned. "Yeah, yeah I do actually. I'm not comfortable working with *that*! He waved the towel he was using towards Christian.

Katie, quite dead pan, just looked up from her wash bag, "You mean the towel? Why, what's wrong with it?"

"No!" He replied, "Not the…you know what I mean. *Him*."

Katie looked round and gestured towards Christian and Jed, "*That* him or *that* him?"

"You know who I mean Kate." Jerry stood naked, his shoulders still steaming from his shower, his face a Neanderthaled grimace. "You know Kate, a few years back they had an expression in the Brigade for Firefighters that had only a short time in the job but talked or acted as if they had several years in. They were described as Microwave Firefighters because of the fact that they had compressed years in like …"

"No, Jerry, you don't have to explain it. I'm familiar with the expression and I get the meaning…"

"But who knew that one day we would actually *have* a Microwave Firefighter? He does run on Microwaves, *doesn't* he?"

"Jerry, Just. Fuck. Off...and you know, when you get back, fuck off again!" Katie shook her head and continued to look through her wash bag. "We've had a really shitty day of it Jerry, just leave it."

Jerry leaned and pointed towards Katie, "I'm not fucking about Kate. You feel safe working with that? You feel safe putting your life in that thing's hands? It's gonna put us out of jobs! Don't you get it? Don't you fucking care?"

Jed leaned around Christian, who remained seated, quietly ignoring the conversation, hoping it would soon end. "Jerry, piss off will you? Nobody cares to listen to your shit! And as it happens, yes I would put my life in his hands, alright? Yes I *would*. Yes I *have*. Yes I would again! Alright? Now fuck off you inane prick!"

"So would I!" Katie smiled a Motherly smile over towards Christian. He did not see her as he was turned away but her voice said it anyway.

Jerry turned to now face Jed, "Really? You don't thi..." Jerry, suddenly aware that Katie was staring at his crotch, paused, looked over to her, "You don't...think...Okay, what? Oh yeah, I know, it's impressive isn't it?" Jerry placed both of his feet firmly onto the floor and tensed his thigh and buttock muscles to push his crotch forward. He raised an eyebrow and was now standing in his mirror rehearsed superhero pose.

Katie let out a nervous giggle, screwed her eyes up to focus ever closer towards Jerry, "Jerry...I've...I've never noticed how small your willy was before. I, I didn't know you could get them in that size."

Jerry instantly dropped his pose, unsure whether Katie was being genuine or just changing the subject, "What? What did you say?"

"Wow, no really, that's a really, really small willy. Bloody hell!" Katie pulled a bemused but slightly impressed face as she looked back towards her bag, "Jeez, it's like a clitoris or something." She shook her head. "Sorry Jerry, what, er...what were you saying about Christian? Or, 'The Tripod' as we call him?"

Jerry consciously continued to focus his stare towards Katie then, after a short while, took a fleeting glance at Christian, then looked down towards Christian's crotch. He didn't mean to look, he had no intention of looking but his manhood, what there was of it, got the better of him and he just couldn't help himself. A micro-expression flashed across his face that almost screamed his sheer flaccid, *very human*, envy. Shaking his head, he looked squarely back to Katie, "Fuck off Kate. Just...fuck off!"

Katie tutted, "Well you don't get many retorts like that to the dozen do you?" As Jerry turned and walked away, Katie looked over to Jed and in mocked whispers, "But he's got kids hasn't he? How does that work? I mean how does he...?" Katie awarded herself a discreet but victorious smile. She glanced over to Jerry, shaking her disappointment away. Sad at his ignorance. Sad for Christian. Sad for those poor people today. Come to think of it, Sad for Jerry's wife also.

<u>5</u>

Outside in the station yard, watch members were getting into their pods ready to go home after what had been for all, a very, very trying day.

Jed and Katie stood by Katie's bike pod where they had both been autopsying the day's events. "Oh well," said Jed, "So, what you up to tonight?"

"Gonna curl up with a good book and a glass of wine I think." Katie smiled, "I mean a really BIG. GLASS. OF WINE. You?" Katie had placed her hand on her stomach and was pulling a soppy, satisfied, post-wine face.

"I'm gonna have a chat with Laura I think about...just...all this stuff and then I think your idea of soaking in a nice glass of wine sounds very good."

Christian appeared from the appliance bay walking slowly towards his car. His sports bag was slung over his shoulder but Katie could see that the weight he bore was far greater than just that of a physical burden. Katie placed her palm on the side of Jed's arm, smiled up at him and softly said, "Mate I'll catch up with you tomorrow okay?" She glanced over towards Christian and Jed knew this to mean that she wanted to speak to Christian alone. Jed smiled back at Katie and politely nodded. He looked for a moment into those comforting motherly eyes of hers, grateful for the warmth and compassion she brought to their watch. Her friendship. Remembering all the times she had been the voice of reason, the first to offer an olive branch when people started to tear apart. The first to offer an unspoken yet often needed hug. Jed again nodded, turned and walked towards his pod.

Katie stood straight and turned her head towards Christian. She tried to smile but her sadness for him tugged hard not only on her heart strings but also seemed to be pulling her smile downwards which then just ended up as a sad grin which she realised and instantly dropped. She caught his attention and walked over to where he was now getting into his pod.

The drivers' side to Christian's, mainly glass covered, silver metallic pod was open and Christian was sitting inside looking slightly lost and worn out from the long and demanding day. Katie went round to the other side of the car, pressed her hand against the side panel and the door quietly opened. She sat in the car next to him and gave him a while to see if he wanted to talk. As she sat there, she looked around the sleek cream lined interior noting how clean and tidy he kept his pod, she smiled.

"I'm sorry Kate, I'm..." Christian stopped, looked away from Katie and then looked down at his feet, shaking his head, trying to find the words...*any* words.

"Chris, it's okay. You haven't got to say *anything* if you don't want to. But it's important for you to know that you're not in this alone. We're in this together. *All* of us. Okay...so it's knocked us all a bit, obviously. Let's be honest, it's not been easy for any of us...but least of all for you. We understand that, okay? None of this is your fault. There's nothing you could have done about this and we're not...", Katie looked away, struggling to end her sentence and just about managing to hold back her tears, "Look, it doesn't matter. We're still your friends. We're pretty much a family here, you *know* that. We won't let anything happen to you. *Anything!*"

Christian turned to Katie who was now holding his hand in hers. Tears slowly ebbed through the toes of the crow's feet that lined his now glistening eyes, "Thank you..." A minute went by before he continued, "Every night I'm off duty, I go home, they come to my home...and download everything that...I've thought, everything that I've...seen or heard. Tonight some IT geek will be sitting there analysing this very conversation. My past isn't mine and...well...the truth is...my future's not mine either...not really. I belong to a company. I'm a product."

Katie looked into his eyes for a moment. She had forgotten about the company's access to him. What with all the events of the day and the full on roller coaster ride of recent events, she had forgotten that Christian was still a slave to the Company.

"Thanks Kate." Christian knew there was little more to say, tonight at least. There was enough for everyone to be dealing with right now and this would have to wait until he could get his head around accepting his fate. "Thanks Kate, I'll go now, but I'll see you in the morning. I do appreciate the chat, thank you."

Katie smiled at him, leaned forward, pulled his head nearer and then kissed him on the side of his forehead. She paused for a moment and then moved very close to his ear and whispered, "Oi, IT geek, your

Mother's a whore!" With that, Christian chuckled, Katie pulled away, smiled back at him, got out of the pod and went back to her bike pod. With the push of a button, Christian's pod engine wound itself up. The pod lifted up just above the Conduit and it headed out of the yard towards Christian's apartment. Katie stood by her pod watching him leave. In the air, music flowed past her as it waved away from his car as he drove off. 'Mozarts' Requiem.' She noted. 'Hmm…yeah that'll cheer him up. Oh well.' She shook the day away, opened her bike and rode back home, numbly comforted in the knowledge that she would have a nice big Olympic size glass of wine to dive into when she got there.

CHAPTER SIX

"Existential anger"

1

Christian's eyes slowly opened but quickly focussed as the new morning light filled his bedroom. He lay for a moment and then rolled his head to one side, looking to the side of the bed. His nemesis. Beyond the side of that bed was the rest of the world which he now had to face. *Again.* He drew a long laboured breath and then his body slowly followed his line of sight as he rolled over, bent his legs into a sitting position and then swung his body upwards to allow his legs to now dangle over the side of the bed into a fully formed, if somewhat unenthusiastic, seating position. Without moving, he looked to his right where he noted, out of the corner of his eye, that the picture of his memory-implanted parents had been moved slightly. It was subtle changes like this that were a constant reminder of his nightly pre-programed visits from the 'White Coats.' Nerdy guys in white laboratory coats, he imagined, who scurried around his apartment collecting all the data they could from his days interactions with other crew members. Graphs showing temperature readings, power outputs, bio-rhythms, heck maybe even his bloody horoscope. He bowed his head and mustered up enough enthusiasm to shake it from one side to the other once. He stood, swayed for a moment and then shuffled towards the kitchen. As he opened the fridge he also noted that the top to his milk was off and that someone had clearly taken a swig from it. Writing off the milk he simply closed the fridge again and, as he turned to walk towards the bathroom, blankly mumbled, 'Coffee'. From behind one of the many sealed pristine kitchen panels a gentle hum became mildly higher in pitch as modern technology took care of his early morning request of a coffee. A black coffee, swigged-milk free, *obviously*.

For the remainder of his morning routine he 'zombied' his way methodically through shower, coffee, dressing then off to work. It had been just over a month now since the grey suits first revealed themselves as being an integral part of his life and, although he had tried to continue as best he could, the emotional burden on him was so much to take in, to process, to come to terms with that he simply shut down and was now running as if on autopilot. *Yes,* he was still talking when spoken to, still performed his tasks when asked to do so at work, still did everything that he needed to but without any personal satisfaction, without any personal interest, without any real...choice.

Down in the basement parking level, he sat in his pod for a short while listening to a very old recording of a band named Sigur Ros. He listened closely. He had no idea who these people were. He had no idea about their culture, didn't even speak the language so wasn't even sure what they were signing about but somehow it eased his pain, just...for a moment. He valued these brief respites from his now daily automaton routines.

Light painted his pod in a vibrant summer pallet as it travelled out of the basement and along the conduit towards the fire station. Christian folded his arms, leaned sideways half foetally into his seat and rested against the side of the car to look out of the pod as the scenery flowed past the window.

As his pod stopped in the station yard, it lowered itself to the conduit and the engine wound itself down in what seemed a very deep bass melancholic drone. A large side section of silver and glass now raised itself upwards and opened allowing Christian to step out. He continued to sit for a moment longer willing his legs to move, motivating himself enough to stand and leave the vehicle. After a short pause he bent forwards, picked up his sports bag, half stood as he stepped out of the pod and into the beautiful dazzling sunlight. Shielding his eyes he looked up to see perfect white clouds bobbing along on a sea of perfect blue sky all of which were tinted and warmed by the bright yellow sun. Even Christian could not refrain from half smiling but for a moment. He looked down again, walked across the yard and into the locker room.

As Christian entered the locker room, Les, Monkey-boy and Jerry were all congregated in the corner furthest from the door. As he entered, without looking up, he noted that they had all quickly stopped what they were saying and Les had started a slightly louder conversation about something completely different. Christian did not take this as a deliberate action to make him feel uncomfortable but more that it was to avoid being made to feel awkward or self-conscious but, due to it being done in a slightly amateurish manner, it just served to make him feel just that little bit more isolated. Perhaps Christians' hearing was also better than others. He wasn't sure. He had nothing to compare it to. But as he left the locker room he was sure he heard Jerry saying, "Well I don't agree with it is all and I'm not sure why we're doing it…" Or at least that's as much as he could jigsaw together with fuzzy logic from the pieces that he thought he had heard.

<u>2</u>

Around the mess table, the Firefighters observed their traditional use of offensive banter and general piss taking. In one corner, Monkey-boy and Brownie were finishing up a conversation as Christian walked into the mess, "…You know I once wondered what it would be like in the "world of tomorrow"
"Oh really Monkey-boy?" said Brownie, expectantly awaiting a probable punch line, "I never had you down as a 'Thinker'". He chuckled. "And…?"
"Well it was pretty much like the world of today…except that it rained all that day." Monkey-boy grimaced his best pensive look to add weight to his throw away comment.
"Monkey-boy, you're a pathetic…"
"Apathetic? Apathetic? Never let it be said that I don't care Brownie." Monkey-boy looked deeply into Brownie's eyes.
"A pathetic…excuse…for a man.", Brownie tutted, closed his eyes then slowly and deliberately shook his head.
Monkey-boy chuckled, opened his mouth to retort, noticed that Christian had entered, coughed, sat up and took a sip from his tea. "Hello mate." He said. "How're you?" Without waiting for the answer he stood up, looked down at his cup, "Better put this in the sink I s'pose." and walked toward the kitchen.
Mother was sitting at the end of the mess table oblivious to the banter as he trawled through his 'paperwork' on the screened tablet that was resting on the table in front of him. Targets to hit, "Hmm" training to carry out, "Hmm", meetings to hold, "Hmm-m-ye-e-a-a-ah." With

each "Hmm", he moved an appointment from here to there, realised it wouldn't work, moved it back again, considered again, realised that wouldn't work but continued to muse over it as if completing the morning crossword.

Jed and Katie, who had just entered the mess, sat with a satisfied "Ahhhhhh" as they both reached for their first teas of the day.

"Morning young Chris. How are you this fine summer morn...?" pause, Shlurp, "Ahhhhhh."

"I'm fine thank you Jed." Christian barely flashed a momentary look up to see him and then looked back down towards his own cup of tea.

Katie noted how Christian had said "Thank you" rather deliberately and precisely rather than "Thanks" or "Cheers" and mulled over how it seemed so universal that if someone was being told off then their full names were used and when someone was upset themselves they were often precise and more focussed with their language. She shook this thought away. "So, how were your days off then mate?"

Christian just raised his head and looked at Katie with a forced smile as if posing for a picture he had not wanted taken.

Kevin, who had been sitting humming to himself, looked up towards Christian, "Y'alright mate? What's up?"

Jed leaned forward and looked past Katie to stare at Kevin. He lowered his brow and dropped his head slightly to inform Kevin that he was asking an obvious and unwanted question.

"Oh come on mate, it'll all be alright. Lovely day like this, what's to worry about?" Kevin smiled, clearly selfishly insensitive to recent events.

Jed looked at Katie and then back to Kevin, "Kevin have I shown you my disappearing hole trick?

Kevin searched his memory, "Your...no, no I...no, you haven't."

"Okay, well then, I'm going to show you how to make a hole disappear. So, think of a number between one and a hundred."

"Okay, er..."

"No, no, don't tell me the number Kevin."

"Oh, okay, so yeah...okay."

"Ok, so, you've got a number?"

"Yes, yes I've got a number."

"Okay, now Kevin it's important that you don't tell anyone that number. Do you understand?"

'Obviously!' thought Kevin, "Okay, don't tell any...got it."

"Okay Kevin now, take that number..."

"Yes?"

"...and fuck off."

Kevin blinked sharply and almost recoiled. "Er...what?"

"Yeah, yeah, just take that number...and fuck off!"

"Well what sort of magic trick is that? I don't get it."

"No, well you won't Kevin. That's because you haven't fucked off yet. You've got to do that to finish the trick."

Kevin huffed, mumbled "Well where's the hole then?" under his breath, gulped the last of his tea and moped out of the mess.

Before Kevin had shut the door Jed corrected him by saying "There *is* a hole in this trick Kevin..."

Kevin shook his head uninterested and shut the door.

Jed smiled a cheesy performer smile, placed both his hands up to where Kevin had disappeared, "...And now, the a-hole has gone. Tada!"

Mother, who remained quietly throughout, continuing to move appointments and meetings, masked a soft chuckle with a quick purposeful, intended cough.

Christian smiled, almost, inside, looked at Jed and nodded his appreciation.

Katie, accepting that Christian clearly did not want to enter into idle chatter but also conscious not to leave this awkward silence filling the air, turned to Jed, "So did *you* get up to anything on your days off?"

"Well I got that spare room done that has been nagging at me for months." smile, "Spent some time with Laura on our second day off..."

"Oh wow, yes, because it was a beautiful day that day wasn't it?" Katie smiled remembering as she said it.

"Yes, it *was* gorgeous." Jed also smiled as he recalled the day. That perfect day. Time spent with Laura. Time alone. Just the two of them. No one visited. No one bothered them that day. He sipped his tea.

Katie smiled, leaned across, touched Jed's arm, stood and picked up cups ready to take them to the kitchen. "Mucky pups" she said as she wiped up spills with a cloth that Richie had left on the side. "Anyone would think that children had eaten here."

"Who says they're not children?" chuckled Jed.

"They're not children." said Katie as she turned, grinning as she walked into the kitchen, "You can reason with children."

Jed, Mother and Christian remained seated for a moment in silence, after a short while Les and Richie came into the room in mid conversation. "…..Yeah, well that's typical Government Rich. Next you'll be telling me they've actually passed Sod's law!" Les shuffled past the strewn dining chairs as he weaved his way towards the kitchen hidden behind the box of groceries he was carrying, "So we all going tonight then?"

"Er, no, no, let's just sort these out mate!" Richie pushed into the back of Les to put him off continuing the conversation so as not to say anything out of turn in front of Christian who Richie had seen but Les had not.

"Oi, oi Richie, watch wha….." Smiling, Les had turned to speak to Richie who was behind him but had seen Christian as he swung round. He hurried his pace and disappeared into the kitchen. Les had not been quick enough to cover his slip up and thought he could mitigate damage by ignoring the issue and running away, which of course, made it just that tad more bloody obvious.

Christian continued to look into his tea. He had heard them mention that they were all going out. His initial thought was that this was perhaps not the best time to be excluded by the watch and then in the same thought realised that he was not the best of company anyway and he knew that. He did think though that it would have been nice to have at least been asked. He barely shrugged, lifted himself up and carried himself out of the mess to begin the station routines.

Mother and Jed watched Christian as he left. Mother turned to Jed, decided against it, said nothing, turned to where Les had been standing, paused and then, shaking his head, stated quietly, "Prat!"

3

It had been a slow day. There had been no incidents to attend and much of the work carried out by the watch that day had not involved Christian having to be too interactive or chatty. He was glad of this. Too much was happening generally at present and he would be more than happy to just keep himself to himself. Just going through the motions was about as much as he could handle at the moment.

The oncoming watch had finished roll call and were carrying out their initial tests in the appliance bay. Engines whizzed and Comms were checked during the hustling, bustling change of watch.

Christian glanced over to the bay as he walked with shouldered sports bag over to where his pod was parked. As he stood next to his car, he paused for a second as he noted the audible change in appliance siren. It sounded different somehow, but to be honest, as soon as he noted it, he dismissed it as, the truth was, that he wasn't actually that interested and, in fact, he just wanted to get home and get yet another day out of the way. He swung his sports bag inside and then laid his hand on the side of the pod steadying then readying himself to swing down and into his seat. He lowered his head beginning the manoeuvre but then, before he completed it, straightened up again, puzzled, looked up at the appliances again to confirm that they were both stationary and then turned his head to pinpoint the direction of the sirens. They were different sirens and were not from the appliances *and* they were getting closer. Christian noted that the Police must be driving alongside the station, nodded this confirmation with a slight disinterested snort and then lowered his head and bent down to get into his car. As he sat half in the pod, leg hanging out of it, he noticed blue and red beams of light dancing from metal surfaces in the station's yard, flickering shadows of other pods as the beams spun on their approach. This would be the Police speeding past the station. Christian waited for a moment. The conduit's safety systems would not allow him to pull out until the Police had passed so there was no rush to leave anyway. His centre console glowed a pulsating blue with the word POLICE so he knew he was stuck there for a moment. He lowered his head into his hands and rubbed his weary eyes. Sigh. Noting now just how much louder and how slowly the Police must be passing the station, he turned his head towards the yard gates, opened his eyes and looked up in one swift movement. Startled and suddenly more awake, he climbed out of the pod and stood, one foot inside, leaning against the side panel. In the yard were two Police bike-pods and one prison carrier pod. Christian turned to look around the yard to see if there were any vehicles that were not authorised to be there or to see if anyone who may be wanted was crouched by one of the vehicles. Nothing.

From inside the bay one of the on-duty Firefighters came running towards the Police bikes, arms flailing. It was Jerry. "That's him." He shouted at them and gestured toward the cars where Christian was parked. Christian instinctively looked behind himself and then at both of the adjoining cars. "That's him!" repeated Jerry.

As Christian looked back towards the Officers, he could see the lid to the bike-pods had raised open and an armour-suited Officer now stood next to it. He reached a holster section on his hip and placed his hand over his weapon. He then tapped the weapon to indicate his willingness to remove it from its' holster. Christian jerked backwards slightly in surprise and then froze. The second Officer, who stood next to her bike simply stared at Christian.

From within the first Officers' suit, a slightly synthesised deep voice stated loudly and clearly, "Stand fast!" He then pointed with his free hand directly at Christian "Don't move a muscle." Though Christian was not even sure if he had what we would consider muscles, he had no intention of moving anything anyway.

Jerry was now next to the Officer, "Yeah that's him, that's the one you want mate." He panted still slightly out of breath, so eager was he to inform the Officers' all that he knew.

Christian stood like a rabbit in headlights, motionless, almost too afraid to breathe.

The Officer flashed a glance at Jerry and then back towards his target. "This is definitely him, yes?"

"Yes, yes it is mate. He's the one we told you about." Jerry stood, bent over, resting on his knees, panting.

"We? *We*?" Christian, still shocked, had instinctively assumed that Jerry, being the arsehole that he was, had just informed the Police that there was an issue, but…*we*? Who else was in on this? Christian paused for a moment, 'Hang on.' he thought. What *this*? There is no *this*. There *is* no issue. He hadn't committed any crimes…*had he*? 'Oh my God.' he thought, 'What if I have? What if my programming has gone wrong or something? Oh shit…'

The prison carrier now edged toward Christian and its' side simply slid open. "You! I want you to get into this pod. Make any sudden or false moves and I will not hesitate to use force." With that, the Officer tapped his gun again, probably to show off to Christian just how large a penis he *thought* he had. He again spoke to Jerry, "Mate, you better be right, this is serious shit if this goes wrong." He was shaking his head. Jerry just shook his head and then nodded toward Christian to confirm it *was* him and that they *were* doing the right thing.

Christian stood still for what seemed like eternity. Why had none of his watch come out to defend him? Why had no one from the other watch come to see what the problem was? Was *everyone* in on this? He knew he was in serious trouble.

The Officer motioned again for Christian to enter the carrier pod. Christian stepped cautiously towards it. A black-suited agent now appeared from the interior of the pod and stood in the doorway. He flashed an ID at Christian and then quickly whipped it away. "Are you Christian Mann, a Mr Christian C Mann?"

Christian nodded.

"We need to ask you a few questions. Step inside please." With that, the agent stood to one side allowing Christian to enter, which he did.

Once inside, the side of the pod lowered and then sealed itself shut. The pod raised itself up from the conduit, slowly headed out of the yard and then headed down the road away from the station, it's sirens blaring and lights spinning as it disappeared from both view and earshot.

The Officer twisted his helmet and removed it from his shoulders as the blue hi-vi strips down the length of the suit dimmed and powered down. He leaned over to Jerry and shook his hand. "Hello Jerry. I hope you're right about all of this mate." He looked towards where the pod had previously been. "Otherwise we really *are* all in some serious shit."

Jerry snorted and shook his head, "That's alright mate, it'll all be sorted. I really appreciate all this."

"Well, alright mate. I'll see you down the club soon, okay?" With that, the Officers both mounted their pods and left the yard as their pods' lids closed over them.

4

Bar the odd coloured glow from appliances and gadgets, Christian's apartment lay in relative darkness. The bedroom curtain slowly swayed as the building's combined heating and air conditioning system gently circulated air. Outside the apartment block, pods traversed the conduit, their lights occasionally firing through the gaps in the curtains throwing shadows across the ceiling. Footsteps, that could be heard coming from outside the apartment's front door, grew in volume then stopped. There was a pause and then an exchange between muffled voices.

A small swipe card LED panel beside the inside of the front door changed from red to green and then the locking system disengaged with a slight pneumatic whoosh. The door slid quietly open and in stepped three men. One of the men, as if at home, casually stepped over to a lighting switch, swiped his hand against it and the room began to brighten. One of the men turned towards the kitchen, "You process the Lab Rat, I'll sort some coffees out. God I hope he's got enough milk in." The other two now approached the bedroom. The door opened and shadows formed by both men now stretched along the length of the bedroom. One of them reached around the door and again swiped a hand over a switch. The room steadily brightened until it reached a comfortable but functional light setting. Both of the white coats now stepped inside the bedroom, one of them placing a metal case down onto a low cupboard and opening it to remove the equipment needed for the evenings' procedures. The second man stepped over towards the bed, "Once we've wired up the Lab Rat Dave, you wanna catch up on the football during the download?"

Dave, the first white coat, smiled "Nice one Carl, I've set up his box on a series link so we should have todays' game too. He nodded and widened his smile.

Carl leaned over and removed a disturbingly phallic scanner from the case, pressed a button on the side of it and a small screen next to the button began to glow. He then turned to pull the duvet off of Christian but, before he could do so, the duvet was thrown by its' occupant from the bed. There was a momentary pause, Carl screamed and jumped backwards, straightening as he did so. Startled, Dave turned quickly, screamed, stood up and also stepped backwards stopping as he hit the case that he had placed on the cupboard.

Jed looked at Carl, then at the scanner then back to carl, "I do hope you weren't intending to use that on me!" He looked away and pulled a slightly hurt face. "You haven't even bought me dinner first." Jed, dressed in Christian's pyjamas, then sat bolt upright in the bed. Both of the white coats stood there, chests moving quickly where they were now clearly breathing heavily with shock. The door to the en-suite bathroom now slid open and a mud-masked, negligee'd woman standing in the doorway, looked at both the white coats and screamed, an almost caricatured scream as she raised her hands to her mouth. Startled by her sudden appearance and, moreover, by her *actual* appearance, the white coats again screamed. The bedroom door that led to the lounge slid open and a very scared looking sheepish white coats' head gingerly appeared from around the door frame. The woman in the bathroom, noticing the scanner, raised an eyebrow, looked at Jed then back to the scanner. She then pulled a slightly pantomimed cheeky face and in a soft sensual voice whispered, "Ooh dear. Cheeky."

Carl, seeing what the woman was staring at, turned a mild red and then awkwardly turned off the scanner and placed it back into the case.

Jed looked at the woman, '*Edna*', also raised his eyebrows, shook a slightly disappointed head then returned his attention to the white coats "Yes?!" he shouted to the new face that had appeared around the door. "Can I help you?!"

The third white coat, Martin, now stepped cautiously from behind the door frame and into the room beside the other two coats. "Er, I er....."

"What are you doing in my apartment, eh? And how did you get in here?"

Carl looked at his other two colleagues then back to Jed, "Well we're, we're, er....."

"What's wrong with you people? See, you've upset my wife with you're poxy amateur ninjastics." Jed pointed over to the woman at the bathroom door.

On cue the woman scrunched her face up and placed her hands over her trembling mouth as if controlling herself from bursting into tears.

All three of the white coats looked over to where she stood then, slightly puzzled, all looked at each other, back to the woman and then back at Jed. Jed looked over to the woman, "You alright Edna? You're not too upset are you my love?"

Edna looked down for a moment and then back at Jed and, in a suspiciously deep voice, said "No.....I'm alright dear." She then reached down to her crotch, adjusted herself and coughed a deep, bassy, manly cough.

Carl, who clearly appeared to be the more senior of the three white coats, motioned to begin speaking to Jed, paused, looked over at Edna again, looked down at her overly hairy legs, flinched, shuddered, then looked back at Jed and asked, "Sorry…who…*are* you?"

"My name is Jed…..and since *you're* the one that's broken into *my* apartment, I guess *you* should be the one's explaining who *you* are."

"I am Doctor Daniels, these are…..my colleagues Doctor's Cooper and Powell." He pointed to Carl then Martin then shook his head, "Hang on, Sorry…..*your* apartment?"

"Yes, yes that's correct. *My* apartment!"

"But…but this is Mr Mann's apartment. He's…" He paused, looked down at his shoes and then shuffled his feet, "A, er, client of ours."

"You mean Christian. Christian Mann? Yes I know him. And, well, he's given the apartment to me and now I live in it. So you're, basically, breaking and entering and, as a result, I shall now be calling the Police."

Dave squinted, "Hang on we're not…this is Mr Mann's apartment we're not…this is *his* apartment we're not breaking and entering into *your* apartment."

"Oh and Mr Mann was happy about you coming into his room every night *was* he? You er, you wanna explain that to the Police too?"

Carl, seeing Edna shuffling out of the corner of his eye, looked towards her. She winked at him and puckered her lips into a kiss. Carl screwed his slightly unsettled face up and turned back toward Jed. "Look, this is not what it seems. Okay? You, you just shouldn't be here. You're not supposed to be here! We were expecting Mr Mann to be here and we had…an…appointment with him."

"Well, he's not here. *I'm* here. And since I'm here and it's now my apartment, I suggest you fuck off out of *my* apartment. Okay?"

"Look, we work for some very important people. They will not be happy about any of this. There's a great deal at stake here."

Edna leaned toward Carl, "I'm a vegetarian...I *hate* steak!"

Carl glanced over to her then continued, "Look this is *serious*. My employer's not going to be happy about any of this. He turned to his colleague, "Dave, get them on the phone."

Dave reached into his pocket, took out his phone, Edna reached over and, without being given any resistance, took it from Dave. Without moving from where she stood, she then opened a drawer in the cupboard, placed the phone between the drawer and the frame, slammed the drawer shut against the phone and then placed the smashed phone back into Dave's pocket, patted his pocket and then slapped him gently on his cheek. She then winked at him. Dave said nothing but managed a gulp.

Carl lifted a trembling finger towards Jed, "Listen you, you can't...you can't hold us here!"

"Don't be a cock." said Jed, "*You* are all between us and the door so how on Earth are *we* holding *you* here? Also, to be honest, we're more than happy for you to leave anyway, you know, hence...why...I just told you to fuck off! So..." Jed motioned an inviting hand towards the door.

Carl knew that without intervention from a higher authority (and no, not a man with a big white beard but instead a man in a grey suit) this situation would not get resolved. "Look I don't know what's going on here but I'm telling you that my employer is really not going to be at all happy with this." He turned to walk out of the door, "And I recommend you let us know the whereabouts of Mr Mann before this goes too far."

Jed, stood up from the bed, "I suggest you take your cheap geeky threats and fuck off out of this apartment while you still *can*. You tell your employers that he's been taken care of. You tell them to stay the fuck out of the way and tell them that if they attempt to violate him the way you were going to tonight that I shall arrange for *them* to be violated in the same way." Jed stood next to Carl and held a pointing hand near to his face, "You tell your employer that if he wants to fuck with one of us, he better buy him or her dinner first!"

Carl stared at Jed for a moment, shook an unintimidating nerdy head and then walked out, followed by Martin.

Dave reached for his metal case which Edna then also reached for. Both now holding the case, Dave pulled it towards himself. Edna then pulled the case back towards herself pulling Dave over in the process so that he was now bent over the cupboard. She looked down at Dave and, without saying anything, simply pursed her lips and deliberately shook her head. Dave looked at her for a moment, then at the case then, feeling the broken phone in his pocket with his other hand, looked back at Edna, attempted a surrendering smile, cautiously released the case and then left.

Jed paused, listening to confirm that all three of the white coats had left the apartment then, once assured that they were, simply looked at Edna, slowly shook his head and said, "Jeez Les, you make one ugly woman!"

Les scowled back at Jed and tutted, "Typical man!"

Jed chuckled, sat back on the bed, looked around for a moment, "Oh, mate, I don't mind saying I was a little scared there, I wasn't sure how that was gonna go." He chuckled again and then, as if snapping from a dream said, "Oh balls, okay, okay, we need to go, we need to get going, get changed…"

"Oh, do I have to?"

Jed simply raised an eyebrow smiling, "Les, seriously, yes." Jed looked pensive for a moment, "Remind me again why you had to dress up like a woman?"

"Well two blokes living together would have looked a little bit suspicious, wouldn't it?"

Jed slowly blinked for a moment, "Suspicious?...You don't think this looks suspicious?" He shook his head and snorted a bemused grunty snort.

They then changed and Les retrieved the case before they both left the apartment and headed for the parking level where Jed's pod was parked.

About twenty minutes later the apartment door re-opened and in stepped a grey suit entourage'd by six black suits and three white coats. One of the white coats ran into the bedroom, clambered around for a moment and then reappeared.

"Well?" Enquired a very disappointed grey suit.

"It's gone Sir," Carl's voice trembled as he spoke, "I'm...afraid the case has gone Sir." Carl simply bowed his head and stared at the floor, Dave and Martin cowered and looked to the grey suit for his reaction.

"You do know what this means don't you Carl?"

Carl looked up sheepishly for a moment and then closed his eyes, "Yes Sir..." His breathing deepened and quickened.

"No cake for you Carl. In fact, no cake for any of you three!

Carl, slightly, surprised lifted his head and treated himself to a reserved nervous smile, "Oh, er, okay Sir. No cake? Oh okay. Thank you Sir." Carl opened his mouth fully, slowly filling his lungs with much needed oxygen.

Dave and Martin breathed sighs of relief and their shoulders dropped as the tension flooded out of their bodies.

The grey suit lifted two fingers up toward one of the black suits and then beckoned it over to him. He then leaned in towards the black suit and calmly ordered, "Escort these three clowns down to the carrier….."

All three white coats looked sheepishly at one another.

"And don't let them have *any* cake!" The grey suit flicked his fingers away towards the door. The black suit faced the white coats who all obediently walked towards the exit. All three were now leaving the apartment. Just before the apartment door closed the grey suit shouted a follow up order to the black suit, "Oh and when you get them all down to the carrier, give them all a fucking good kicking would you?"

The apartment door closed to the effeminate sound of three white coats instinctively yelping in fear.

<u>5</u>

It was quiet. The street was dark, lit only by dim street lighting and *now* by light spilling out of the front door onto the front lawn. Mother stood motionless in the doorway, his dressing gown gently swaying in the evening breeze. He motioned to speak but, still slightly bemused, decided against it. He placed his hand over his face and softly moaned a vexed, uncomfortable, tired moan. He then rubbed his struggling eyes with thumb and forefinger and squeezed the bridge of his nose. Jed and Les exchanged glances then looked back at Mother patiently awaiting a response. Mother, without opening his eyes, slowly responded, "Oh…for…f…" then shook his head.

Jed and Les exchanged now slightly uncomfortable looks and again refocused back onto Mother.

Mother leaned against the door frame with one hand, as he himself swayed slightly in the evening breeze, fighting off tiredness, and battled to gather his thoughts. "So…just run that by me…one more time Jed. You've kidnapped…and you've got him…but..." He shook his head, stepped inside and gently closed the door. Jed and Les waited a moment. Les turned to Jed to say something but before he could, they heard a click and then a whirring as the garage door next to them slowly lifted up and away. A light came on inside. Mother stood in the doorway from the garage to the house, shook his head, left the door open and went back indoors. Jed looked away from the garage and back to Les, "YES!" He clenched his fist in victory and then quickly walked over to his pod that was parked in the street. Before starting his pod up, he glanced back at Les. Backlit by the garage, Les looked like a lady of the night. Jed smiled at this thought and then in the same thought shuddered. Jed's pod lifted and manoeuvred itself into the garage. Having parked, the garage self-closed and they both now stepped into Mother's home. They stood by the doorway waiting to be formally invited in and, after a moment, Mother passed them as he walked down the hall with a bottle of whisky in one hand and three glasses pinched in the other. Once he'd walked past them and into the lounge he called after them, "Well come on then." They stepped into the lounge, shuffling like naughty school boys, faces both down towards the ground.

Mother poured three glasses of whisky, one of which was much fuller than the others and then swigged from that glass. Jed and Les both sat themselves down on the sofa opposite him. Mother sighed a soft whisky satisfied sigh, opened his eyes wide, fell back into his chair and then looked to Jed. "Right. Okay. Run that all by me again. This time at a speed that your average human can understand. So…you've done *what* exactly?"

Jed coughed, cricked his neck and then began. "Well…we kind of, you know, kidnapped Christian a bit…"

"A bit? A bit Jed? You either kidnap someone or you don't. That's like describing someone as being a bit dead isn't it, or a bit pregnant. Just break it all down and give me the facts. I'm particularly interested in the bit that explains why this ugly woman is sat next to you." Les lowered his eyebrows in feigned upset.

"Sorry Guv. Okay, well, so, we have kind of, I mean we *have* kidnapped Christian."

"And he's currently..."

"In the pod, in the garage."

Mother laughed, "Oh good. That's okay then, for a moment I thought you said he was in the pod that's currently in my garage."

"Um, I did."

"Uh, huh...okay...oh shit, well okay, go on."

"You see, we all decided, you know on the watch, we all decided that what was happening to Christian wasn't, you know, fair and we decided that the only way to do something about it was to break the cycle, you know?"

"So, you mean Christian didn't know anything about this? Or *did* he?"

"Well...no. He will do..." Jed nodded, looked at Les who also confirmed what he was saying by joining him in nodding and then he continued, "You, see we were trying to work out a way of getting him away from his apartment without..."

Mother screwed his face, wondering where this was going.

"You see the thing is we're not sure how his programming works. We all know that he has to go back to his apartment every night for the company to be able to monitor him, right? And I think it would be fair to say that there's probably some sort of imprinted instinct or need for him to do that"

"Yes…"

"Well, we weren't sure if his programming would allow him to avoid going back to his apartment, you know without a really good reason, you know? We weren't sure if he'd be able to voluntarily avoid going back to his apartment. I mean, even the night we all went out on the piss he still went back to his apartment didn't he…eventually."

"So you kidnapped him?" Mother looked toward the direction of the garage, "Is he alright?"

"Oh yes Guv, yes he's fine. He's in a kind of stand by modey…something?"

"You mean he's asleep?"

"Er…oh yeah, sorry I er, guess he's asleep."

"But when you put this "plan" together, how did you know he wouldn't do everything he could to escape?…Or has he? I mean if you think he's programmed to go back to his apartment how did you know he wouldn't hurt himself, or someone else, trying to do so?"

"No, no you see that's the clever part." Jed smiled.

"Well, I was *hoping* there'd be a clever part somewhere in all of this because so far none of this is winning any 'Mensa Idea of the Year' awards is it?" Mother gulped another slug of whisky.

"Well you see we looked up on the Uni-web to see what the Asimov project was and, of course, there's nothing on the web about the project itself but what we did find was loads of stuff about an author that used to write science fiction novels and his name was…" Jed tilted his head forward, eyes widened with anticipation.

"Rumpelstiltskin Jed? Was it Rumpelstiltskin?"

"Well no…no…it was…Asimov." Jed looked at Les, surprised that Mother hadn't guessed the name.

Mother snorted and shook his head. "Just carry on Jed."

"Oh, okay so, well, Katie was doing some research on the guy to find out if there was anything we could learn about the project and the one thing that stood out a mile was that *he* was the guy that originally wrote the laws of robotics. You know, the three laws that determine any and all robot behaviours? You know, kind of like a failsafe system."

Mother looked slightly puzzled and unconvinced, "Three laws? I always thought there were about a hundred and seventy…something."

Jed nodded as he spoke, "…Seventy four, yeah, yeah I know, there are. *Now* that is. But *then* there were only three, and to be honest they were very simple and much easier to follow. Turns out though that about forty years ago the three laws were given to some government science "committee" to approve and it's then that it all turned to rat shit."

Mother just huffed a knowing huff.

"So anyway, what we did was we spoke to Jerry…"

Mother closed his eyes, "So the other watches know about this as well?"

"Yes, yes but they're fine. There're only a few guys that know. So we spoke to Jerry who knows a guy in the Police force who agreed to help us…"

"The Police?" said mother in a weak, high pitched and slightly pained voice.

"Yeah, the Police. But they have been really good about it all. Honestly they're really nice guys, actually we we're saying that we should invite them along on our next night out."

Mother shook his head, afraid to open his eyes just in case he did and Jed and Les were still actually sitting in his house.

"So we asked them to help us out...which they did. In fact they were really cool about the whole thing." Jed sat there smiling.

"Okay so you still haven't explained how you worked out that Christian wouldn't try to escape."

"Escape? Oh yeah, no, well we knew he wouldn't you see, because, well, we organised for one of the Officers to say that he wasn't in trouble and that he was there to help them with a case. In fact he said that someone was holding someone hostage and that if Christian couldn't help them that this person would be shot by the...hostager? Host? No. Hostage person? Taker. Hostage taker! You see the thing is that the basic three laws, *which are still a part of the laws as a whole*, states that he cannot allow a person to be harmed through action or by inaction, so you see he *had* to help us kidnap himself...basically."

Mother's eyes opened, "And Christian believed that...sh-h-h...story?"

"Well there was a lot more to the explanation than that. A lot more, I can tell you..."

Mother put his hand up, "No, no I don't need to know, the short version is fine." Mother hid an impressed smile. He snorted his approval. 'Okay. Actually that's quite clever.' he thought, "But then what's the long term plan? You kept him away from his apartment for one night, but how does that free him from the company's grip?"

Jed sat up, leaned forward and took one of the glasses of Whisky from the low table in front of him, gulped it down in one go and then reached for the other glass. Les smiled, sat up and reached forward slightly, ready to take the glass. Jed smiled at Mother, impressed with himself. "You see this is the bit that explains why Les is dressed like this. Jed turned to Les, raised his glass to him, Les smiled, Jed gulped the second glass down and turned away. Les dropped the smile and himself back into his chair.

"Yes, I was wondering when we were going to get to that Jed," said Mother. Over the next hour, Jed and Les filled Mother in with some of the finer details of who was involved and their encounter with the company at Christian's apartment. They explained how they had retrieved the case from the apartment and that inside was data that they hoped might help Christian and that there was even a scanner/interface thingy that Christian may be able to use to…well the truth was that they weren't really sure what it would do, but it *was* there and it looked impressive if nothing else, or at least expensive, or important. Mother sat through the conversation and shook his head several times, threw out a few expletives, smiled on occasion and swapped the odd uncomfortable, still unconvinced, glance with the ugly woman sitting next to Jed.

After the conversation, Jed and Les walked back into the garage and carried Christian into the lounge where Mother had turned the sofa into a make shift bed. Mother placed a blanket over him then turned to Jed and Les. I assume you'll be having the spare room then? Jed nodded a grateful thank you and Les just said "Cheers Guv." Mother nodded again. "There're two single beds in there." He looked down at Les' bare legs then up to Jed, "You can, er, you can push them together if you like." Mother smiled, walking out as he led them to their room.

CHAPTER SEVEN

"Cold boots"

1

The silence was suddenly broken by a soft melodic chirp. A few seconds later and the chirp repeated but this time louder, accompanied by a buzzing sound as something rattled along the wooden floor. Another pause followed by a third chirp. A hand shot down instinctively to where the noise came from and it immediately stopped. Christian's eyes snapped open. He took his hand back off of his phone and then lay there for a few seconds, his eyes adjusting to the dim light and his mind adjusting to these new unfamiliar surroundings. Mild panic washed over him as he began to recall the previous nights' events. He looked around the room trying to piece together enough clues so that he might better guess where he had ended up. If he was helping the Police then why was he not in a Police station or, more to the point, back in his own bed? Was this where the hostage lived perhaps? He snorted. 'Hostage?' he thought, 'A likely story.' After a few more seconds his eyes had fully focussed in the dim early morning light. Looking around, he noticed a framed picture on a desk at the other end of the room. Still laying down he lifted his head to align his sight with the picture trying to determine whose house this might be. It looked like…Mother. He cautiously sat up, squinted his eyes and leaned forward to better view the picture. He stood, still wrapped in blanket, and walked over to the desk where he sat down. He sat in an old captain's chair and was now leaning forwards onto a solid walnut desk. Picking the picture up, he could see Mother, his wife and two children, a boy and a girl. Looking down at the picture, he smiled a friendly smile seeing a picture of his Governor, his friend who he admired and respected in a picture far removed from the familiar and regimented setting of the Fire Brigade. He carefully placed the picture back down, swivelled the chair around and sat in his blanket watching the sun rising. Christian looked out of the window as a warm pallet of yellows and oranges trickled along the landscape as though the sun had tipped over and all of its' contents slowly poured out along the world, painting everything in its' path. He closed his tired eyes. Still unsure why he was here in Mother's home but slightly happier and feeling safer that he was. His head tilted slowly further and further forward as he drifted back into a now much more peaceful sleep.

Walker and Christian stepped into the barracks, fully rigged in reddish-tan combat armour, Walker, carrying a large P-37 Tesla rifle and Christian a Medi-kit. Christian had already checked in his weapons on the way through to the barracks knowing that he would rather that than have to find the motivation or energy to get back up off his bunk and do it later in the day. Clearly weary after a long patrol, they both stumbled over to their bunks. Other soldiers were prepping themselves for the day, cleaning weapons, checking ammo, inspecting Medi-kits and rations or were simply sitting on bunks, playing cards or reading tablets. Christian lay on his bunk still fully rigged and too tired to shower or change. He knew he would have to get up at some point as it would be far too uncomfortable to sleep while still fully loaded with bullets, emergency rations, Comms kit and ancillary equipment. For now though, he would just lay there unable to shake from his mind the faces of those he had fought that day. Walker, who had not been able to make it to the top bunk, simply sat slumped on the floor next to Christian's bunk. "Chris." "Chris?" A soft friendly voice called to him. He turned his head slightly to see Walker still covered in reddish dust from the Martian surface struggling to hold up, and now offering, an opened flask of coffee. With a voice command, Christian's visor opened, the fine dust film from it landing on his face as it disappeared into his helmet. The sudden smell of burnt rock was soon replaced by the smell of the coffee. It was a good, welcome smell and one that smelt like a good coffee. He really needed it too. It smelt better than the usual crap they served up in the mess. It smelt fresh and strong and he could feel the steam filling his nostrils. "Chris." said the voice again. Christian squinted, "Walker, what is it?"

Walker said nothing. As Christian pulled himself up onto his elbow to take the coffee from Walker, he noticed for the first time the scorch mark on the side of Walker's helmet. He leaned further onto his elbow, hung over the side of the bed then looked around to the front of Walker's helmet and could now see a profile of his face. Walker's eyes were opened wide but there was no life in them. Both eyes faced the ceiling. Walker's jaw hung lopsided and fully open. A trickle of blood that *had* been running down Walker's temple had stopped flowing. Christian placed his hand onto Walker's shoulder but, as he did, so Walker's body slid down slumping to one side away from him. Christian opened his mouth to instinctively call for a medic. "CHRIS!" Christian turned to identify who was calling him.

Christian sat upright in the chair, looked around suddenly as his eyes readjusted to the now bright room. His breathing had quickened and he turned to see Mother sitting on his sofa quietly sipping from a mug of fresh strong coffee. Christian gained his breath for a moment and waited for his heart rate to slow. "Sorry Guv, did you call me?"

Mother turned, smiled, "Call you? No mate. I didn't want to disturb you so I left you there for a while. You okay? You sleep okay?" He took another sip of his coffee.

Christian saw a mug of steaming coffee on the desk beside him. He shrugged off the bad memory and as, quickly as he brushed it off he also remembered that this was not *his* memory. Or at least he didn't *think* so. But it felt so real. It felt so tangible, so solid and three dimensional. He shook off the thoughts, leaned forward and took hold of the hot mug. He sat for a moment readjusting back to reality, cradling the coffee, slowly sipping. He closed his eyes and brought the coffee up to his nose. This was the coffee he had smelt in his dream. Christian sat for a while, smiling to himself, comforted by this welcomed gift from Mother. Mother respected that Christian had just woken and said nothing, simply waiting until he was ready to talk.

Mother looked out of the window, looking up and enjoying the random white shapes floating through the bright blue sky. He sat smiling, occasionally glancing over to Christian and then back to the clouds.

Christian snapped his head towards Mother, "Oh, Guv what time is it? We're supposed to be…"

Mother raised a calming hand, "Its' okay, its' okay. We've both been booked on special leave. I'm off for today and I've had you taken off duty for the rest of the tour."

Christian's suddenly tensed shoulders relaxed and he sighed. He sat for a moment. He shook his head, "Guv what's happening to me?" Mother looked at him and smiled a sorry but reassuring smile. Christian continued "I..." he paused, screwed his face up, "Do you know anything about this Police thing?"

Mother snorted, "Yes, yes I do, except...they're not all Police, not all of them." Mother leaned forward and placed his coffee mug down, "You see some of them *were* Police Officers but they weren't...erm...acting on behalf of the Police force, shall we say?"

"Oh."

Mother smiled again and took a deep breath in readiness to update Christian on the previous nights' events. He explained how Jed, Katie, Les and the rest of the watch had all been genuinely concerned for him, having seen him become more and more withdrawn and depressed. He explained how they had hatched a, *somewhat shaky,* plot to keep him from his apartment and then ran through all the events that took place at his apartment with the white coats. Christian sat quietly throughout, attentively listening to every aspect of the unfolding retelling.

Christian eventually sat dumb struck. Mother accepted that he might need some time to absorb this amount of information and to process its' implications. Christian, confused and still slightly dazed, turned to Mother, "But that..." He struggled for words.

"Its' alright Christian, take your time."

"But that...doesn't explain. Guv you do know I live alone right?"

Mother nodded, "Well I didn't, but you've never mentioned a partner so I assumed so."

"Well, so then that doesn't explain…I mean…where did he get hold of a negligee and make up from?"

"Huh." Mother sat scratching his chin as he slowly sat upright and then back into his sofa. "Hmm, you know, I hadn't even thought of that."

They sat there for a short while in silence.

"Christian, there's more." Mother's tone changed subtly. "Les took something from your apartment. A case. It belonged to the white coats. It has some…things in it." Mother lifted a case from beside the sofa and laid it on the seat next to him. He lay his hand on it as if keeping it safe or respecting its' contents. "I don't think that the company expected anyone to really be that interested in all this. Otherwise they surely would have brought security with them every time they visited your apartment. Inside here is what I believe is an interface…and also there are...or should I say there *were* details about the company."

"Were?"

"Yes, well, inside there is a tablet that contained a great deal of information about both you *and* the company and unfortunately it's now been locked. I can only assume it must have been linked to the company and they've since disabled the device."

Christian's shoulders dropped, "Oh." "So that's that then."

Mother smiled, "Well…not quite. Christian I looked at the tablet and was able to read some of it before it shut down. Christian sat upright and rested his elbows on his knees as he leaned in to focus his listening.

"I skimmed through different pages and looked at some schematics and things. I've no idea what most of it meant I'm afraid, but what I did get was quite interesting. Christian I'll just let you know the things that I got and then we'll see what they all mean alright?"

Christian silently nodded in anticipation. "Okay, well..." Mother turned, looked at his drinks cabinet where the whisky sat, thought better of it and continued. "Okay, well Christian, you *are* a robot, that much is certain, but of course we knew that. You're made up mostly of mechanical parts using conventional-tech and Nano-tech. Your brain though is mostly Bio-tech. It is mostly organic but is designed such that you are able to retain and manipulate information much faster and more efficiently than your average human brain. Also, *get this*, you're several times stronger than the average man."

Christian's head tilted to one side, "Stronger? But...how does that work? I can't lift anything that..."

"I know," interrupted Mother, "I know. That part of you has been...erm...*restricted*." Mother smiled. "It was to better integrate you with us I s'pose. It was to make you seem as...strong or as weak...as us." Mother smiled wider, "There's more still. Christian you can access the Uni-web. You have a built in wireless interface."

"What?"

"I know, I know, but it's true. Well unless they've removed it or something, I'm not sure, but it did mention that you can do it but again it's..."

"Restricted." said both Christian and Mother together. "An interface? Does that mean they can control me? Hang on, why haven't *I* been disabled or..."

Mother just shrugged. "I'm not sure. I guess it's fairly easy to shut down a tablet, but shutting you down...that may cost them a lot of money or perhaps it might cause damage...or perhaps they didn't even consider it. I mean let's face it, we never should have found *any* of this out but, well, to be honest...who knows? There's one last thing..."

Christian did not look at Mother, still trying to absorb this information, his mind was working overtime.

"Christian. There is a way that you can remove the restrictions."

Christian suddenly looked at Mother, "Eh?"

Mother nodded slowly, "Yes. There is a way to remove the restrictions. Or at least I think there is. I'm pretty sure that you can. Can you imagine? You would be able to access everything on the Uni-web at any time. Think of it, that's everything on Earth's Internet, everything from the Moon's Lunar file servers and even the Martian archives."

Christian remained silent. His eyes darted around the room but his mind was elsewhere as he calculated the possibilities. Also he noted, with mild satisfaction, that it would be good if there was actually an upside to all this. "Oh…oh, hang on...but...how on Earth can *I* remove the restrictions? I don't get it. If I'm fitted with an interface, surely I'd need something to access that interface? Surely only the company…" He turned to Mother. Mother sat on the sofa smiling and holding a device that he had taken from the now open case.

"Is that...?"

"Yes, yes it is…" Mother smiled a cheesy almost giddy grin. "It's the Mk II Cock 4000."

"WHAT? Oh no, Guv, please tell me it's not actually called that."

Mother laughed "Well…no, actually it's not but seriously, look at it. It's ridiculous. I think it's slightly obscene in fact."

Christian chuckled. "And that's for interfacing with me…?" As the sentence continued Christian's face and mouth screwed tighter and his words slowed as it began to dawn on him the reason for the device's shape. He gulped hard.

Mother held his hand up and shook away Christian's concerns. "No, no, I know what you're thinking. It's not that at all. You just swipe it across the back of your neck, that's all." Mother re-examined the device, turning it in his hand. "You know, I'm really not quite sure why the hell they had to make it look like this. It does seem a little...unnecessary." Mother turned again to Christian, "Christian...I'm not sure what else this thing does or even how to remove the restrictions but I'm sure we'll work it out."

Christian nodded and smiled a grateful smile. After a short pause, he asked, "So does that mean if I remove the restrictions that I won't be obliged to go back to my apartment every night to have stuff downloaded for the company?"

"Well actually, I'm not sure you *ever* needed to. I think they just knew that the natural order of things meant that you would go home regularly, and if you didn't go home one night, well then, they'd just download more the next night. I assume that once you were asleep in your apartment that you kind of went into a standby mode or something otherwise you would have woken up when the white-coated guys turned up but...actually I'm kind of *guessing* most of this based on what I've seen and the little I took from that tablet before it shut down. I would suggest that perhaps your apartment is not the best place for you to go back to at the moment though, so you can either stay here for a few days if you like or I can get you booked into a hotel or something?"

Christian sat back into his chair and wrapped the blanket back around himself. He turned away and looked out of the window. So much had changed over the last few days. In fact, *everything* had changed.

"Christian, if this works...you'll be independent. You'll have your *own* life."

"But Guv, won't all this get you guys into trouble?"

Mother burst into laughter, "Oh Chris...Christian we are in so much shit about this already...I really wouldn't worry." Mother wiped a tear from his eye. "Seriously, it is what it is and whatever comes from it we shall just...deal with, okay?"

Christian turned a puzzled face toward Mother.

"Christian seriously, I'm not that bothered. They can do what they wish...but, you know the rules, nobody fucks around with one of our family. It's as simple as that. It angers me that any of this happened to you at all."

Christian rested silently, smiled, a tear ran down his thoroughly relieved face as he closed his eyes. Mother leaned forward, took his mug from him, picked up his own mug and then turned to go into the kitchen to make another coffee. After a couple of steps, he turned smiling, dismissed the fact that it was too early in the day, reached for the whisky and again headed for the kitchen.

<u>2</u>

"And how long was that for?"
Les turned to Jed and shrugged, "Er, maybe about two hours perhaps? Yeah two hours maybe?"
"Can you try to be a little more accurate?"
Les again looked at Jed, "Well if pushed I'd say, perhaps, one hour and...sixty minutes?" Les nodded at Jed.
Jed nodded in confirmation. "Yes, that *would* be more accurate."
Jed looked at the grey suit behind the desk, "You know I'm not sure how long it would be in feet and inches but certainly one hour sixty minutes would be about right I think."
Les continued, "But if I *was* pushed any more on the subject...I *could* fall over."
The grey suit behind the desk stood and placed both hands on the desk, "I find it hard to understand how you can be laughing about this. I don't think you understand the gravity of this situation!"
Jed thought for a moment, "You know to be perfectly honest about it I've always tried not to let gravity get me down."
The suit slammed his hand down firmly against the desk, "Firefighter Edwards I don't think you understand. This *is* very serious. It's possible you could be charged for this!"
Jed tilted his head and raised his eyebrows, turned to Les, "Did you hear that mate, they say they could charge us!"
"How much d'you think they'd charge us?"

"Four credits an hour maybe? I wouldn't be prepared to pay anything over that. I think four credits is reasonable." Les agreed with a nod. Both Jed and Les kept deadpan to further annoy the grey suit.

The grey suit did not reply. He stood for a moment then turned to the Senior Officers who were sitting silently on a couch to the side of the office and then he sat back down into his chair behind the desk. The Officers were quietly drinking tea and helping themselves to a slice of cake that the company had provided. One of the Officers, who had been hiding a smile, raised an enquiring eyebrow to the grey suit. Another grey suit, who had been sitting in the corner, now stood, silently, walked over to the front of the desk and sat on the corner quite casually but also purposefully looming over where Jed and Les sat. He folded his arms and then took a deep slow deliberate breath.

He did not speak at first so Les leaned forward, "So do you speak at all or are you some kind of…silent partner?"

The grey suit took a moment to react for, what he thought was, effect, "Actually I'm his boss." Without unfolding his arms, he swivelled to look at the first grey suit, then returned to his original position.

Jed widened his eyes and pulled an impressed nodding face. "So I guess you must be the big cheese then, eh? You must be quite important then?"

The suit slowly turned to Jed, "Well…so they say." He smirked.

"They?" asked Jed, "They? Who is this 'They' of whom you speak?"

"They. Just, *they*, you know, *them*." The grey suit wafted an irritated hand away from himself as if pointing into the distance.

Jed turned around to where two black suits stood by the door, "You mean those two guys over there? Are, are you '*they*'?"

"No, no, not them, I didn't mean them. Well obviously also them, they would be included in 'They'. But I was just pointing, you know, metaphorically."

"No you weren't. You were just pointing physically…with your finger."

"Yes, yes I know that. That's as maybe but I was being…metaphorical."

"Oh, okay, so just to get this straight, you were pointing metaphorically….."

"Yes."

"With your finger?"

The grey suit drew a slow and impatient breath. He did not respond. He gathered his thoughts and composure for a moment. "Okay. I will ask you…one last time…"

The first grey suit, still seated, leaned around his boss to Jed and Les, "and…I *would* recommend that you listen to Mr Thackett!"

Les scowled at him, "Um, isn't there somewhere *off* you need to fuck to?"

The suit huffed and returned to his upright seating position.

Jed looked up at the grey suit. "Thackett is it? Your name is Thackett?"

Realising now that Jed *had* perhaps heard of him and realising also that Jed may now show him the respect that he deserved, the grey suit sneered down at Jed, "Yes, that's right, *I* am Thackett."

"Oh okay, and, er how're you spelling that?"

Thackett lowered his brow, "Spell it? Why do you ask?"

"Oh I'm just, er, compiling a list of wankers and I wanna make sure I get your name right. You know, it's nothing fancy. It's just a coffee table book, you know?"

The grey suit glared a fierce, disapproving, scowl toward Jed. He then turned to the middle of the three Senior Officers, "Divisional Officer McCormick, is there nothing you want to add to this?"

Jed turned to the Officer. "McCormick is it? How're you spelling that Guv?"

McCormick simply raised an eyebrow, and barely shaking his head slowly but sternly said "Edwards, don't." He then took another sip from his tea, whilst concealing a slightly impressed smile.

Jed hardly caught the smile but noted it with approval. He leaned forwards, "Look, don't get me wrong Thackett I'm not saying that you *are* a '*wanker*' necessarily I'm just saying that if the question went to a vote that I wouldn't fancy your chances much, that's all."

Thackett stood. "Okay gentlemen, you leave me no alternative." He turned to the other grey suit, "Myers, bring me the briefcase." Myers then huffed and sneered a triumphant sneer. He leaned down, picked up a case, stood and placed it on the desk next to Thackett. He slowly and deliberately entered a code, slid aside two locking fasteners, opened the case and then spun it on the spot so that its' contents were now facing Thackett. Thackett reached into the case, took hold of a vial, carefully removed it then held it up so that Jed and Les could both clearly see it. "Gentlemen. This…is Serum seven." The vial almost glowed with a bright neon green liquid. Occasionally a fleck of silver would appear as the disturbed liquid gently spun.

Jed and Les exchanged glances. Jed leaned forward to inspect the vial slightly closer, "And?"

Thackett snorted. "This is Serum seven. It is a bio-stabilising agent. It's what you might call...a failsafe system." Thackett treated himself to a very smug and somewhat unpleasant grin.

Les now looked slightly concerned and turned to Jed. McCormick shared deprecating looks with the other two Senior Officers. This was something they were not informed that Thackett would discuss. Nor were they even sure *what* he was discussing.

"Gentlemen without this, Mr Mann will cease to function. He will effectively...die. If we do not administer a dose of this within the next forty eight hours he *will* die. He must continue to receive doses of this at regular intervals throughout his life. Without it...He. Will. Die. Thackett's face softened. "Listen. Okay, now I understand. So you've had your bit of fun, but play time is over, we need to have Christian back now. Without this serum he will die. Now *all* we want is to make sure that he's okay." He turned and shared a cheesy reassuring smile with Myers and then turned back to stare directly at Jed. "Listen, that really *is* our main concern here, you know? We're not the monsters you make us out to be."

Jed paused. "Honestly? Is that *really* your main concern?" Jed's face showed concern.

Thackett snorted a tired but accepting grunt, "Yes, it is, it really is." He nodded, "That's *always* been our main concern."

Jed lowered his eyes to the floor and slowly nodded. "Well, okay then...I guess if his safety really *is* your main concern then..." Jed looked up at Thackett, "Give *us* the serum and *we'll* give it to him."

"What?"

"Well if his safety really *is* your main concern then you will be happy for *us* to give him the serum, right? Surely everything else is secondary, no?"

"What?" Thackett screwed his face up and went a bright angry red. "No! No! Right okay, no more Mr nice guy, okay? If you do not return Mr Mann to us immediately then he will not be getting his serum. Remember, without it he..."

Jed interrupted, "Yeah-yeah, *he will die*. I know, we covered that bit."

Les scowled at Jed waiting for him to come to his senses. They had done all that they could.

Jed sneered back at Thackett. "Okay then, what's in it?"

"What?"

"What's in it? What's in this miracle serum of yours?"

"Complicated...technical stuff, you wouldn't understand if I told you anyway."

"Really? Try me, humour me."

Thackett drew breath, "Well...it's a complex mixture of compounds, including, erm, Biocarrotate, um, metha-loxy, er, prostate, statin benzon...marmite..amine."

"Oh right, that's er, that's all of it is it?"

Thackett, quite confidently straightened up, "No, no actually it's not. There are also a selection of secret ingredients that you are obviously not privy to."

"Oh, okay, a secret blend of herbs and spices that only the Colonel knows, right?"

Thackett, though not knowing the reference, knew that he was not being taken seriously. He pushed the vial up close to Jed, "Do you not realise the seriousness of this? Do you not know how important this is?"

"Yes I do actually..." Jed looked at the vial, glanced at Les and then looked straight back at Thackett. "Without that vial my Nephew would go nuts."

Thackett tightened his mouth and drew the vial away, puzzled. "What?"

"Yeah my Nephew would go nuts, he loves this shit."

Thackett's shoulders drooped.

"It's Fizzerade, isn't it? My Nephew loves this shit. He drinks it all the time. I can't stand it myself I think it tastes like cats piss but *he* goes absolutely crazy for it. Well, you know, kids of today will drink any old shit."

Les looked at Jed, leaned forward to get a closer inspection of the vial and then sat back in his chair, "Oh...you cheeky fucks." His jaw dropped slightly as he shook his head.

Thackett threw the vial into the case then turned to Jed, "This isn't finished Firefighter Edwards!"

"Well it doesn't matter if it is, you can get plenty more of it in the local shop if it is, they've got crates of the stuff."

Thackett paused momentarily, "I didn't mean this I meant *this situation*! I really don't like you Mr Edwards. Thackett pulled a grimacing smirk at Jed.

Jed leaned forward and stated calmly, "You do realise that this is a no smirking building?"

Thackett's eyes closed tightly with obvious anger.

"You ever considered Gender reassignment Mr Thackett?"

"*Mr* Edwards what kind of question is that? Why on Earth would I want to be a woman?"

"Actually I wasn't suggesting that. I thought it might be an idea if you got yourself a pair of balls attached and started acting like a man."

Thackett clenched his teeth and tightened his mouth. "*You* will be hearing from our lawyers."

"Well I welcome it Mr Fuckett, I really do. I'm eager to find out exactly how many laws you and your company have actually broken here. Ethics, immigration, safety laws? Tut, tut, tut."

Thackett stood, closed the case, turned toward the three Senior Officers, gave them a disappointed un-concluded look and then left the office followed by Myers. The middle of the three Senior Officers, McCormick, stood, "Thank you Gentlemen." He gestured toward the door, the other two Officers stood and left, followed by Les, "Mr Edwards please stay for a moment won't you?"

Once Les and the Officers were out of the room and the door was shut, McCormick turned to Jed. "Be careful Mr Edwards. These are…quite powerful people."

"Guv, what do you expect? What they're doing here is bollocks, I mean, wrong…sorry, Guv. It is wrong and…"

McCormick stopped Jed, "Jed, I don't agree with it either. Truth is, it *is* bollocks. I was totally opposed to the idea from the start. I'm simply advising you to be *careful*." He smiled. "Okay?"

"Sorry Guv, yes, I will try to be. Thank you."

"Okay, good man." McCormick went to the door and it opened. As he stepped out he turned to look at Jed, "Jed, I knew your Father when…he was…in the job." He looked at his feet, "He was a good man." He smiled at Jed again, "Say Hi to Mother for me, won't you?" He then left.

3

Christian sat on the bed and bounced himself up and down to test how comfortable it might be. He then stroked his hand across the duvet and smiled. The lightly decorated room was simple but elegant. A large Holo-screen hung on the wall opposite the bed and there were also some concealed wardrobes and a desk. Christian walked to the desk and sat down. He ran both hands away from himself along the length of the desk. He could certainly feel the quality of it. It felt good. He opened the desk drawer to see if there was anything complimentary inside. Inside was a single tablet. He removed the tablet and switched it on. The name Gideon & Co. flashed up onto the screen. A jingle played and then a screen appeared which read, 'This is your complimentary holy book. You are welcome to use it throughout your stay but please leave it in this drawer on your departure for other guests to enjoy.' Christian touched the screen and a list of options appeared asking which language the reader wanted the book displayed in and also a selection of different holy books from a variety of religions. Christian touched where it said English, then Bible. Another jingle played as a screen appeared, "The Bible. Available at all good Good-Book book stores." Christian shook his head, snorted, switched off the tablet and placed it back in the drawer. He stood and stepped to the door next to the desk, it slid open and he stepped into a shiny white and chrome en-suite. On the basin was a small card with instructions for guests. Christian picked it up, glanced at it and rolled it in his fingers. "Lighting, red.", he said. The lights came on and glowed a deep bright red. "Lighting, dim." The lights dimmed. "Lighting, red, blue, green." The lights alternated from a deep red glow through blue to green and then back to red. Christian smiled. "Lighting off."

He placed the card back on the unit next to the basin, turned, stepped back into the bedroom, reached to the desk for a bottle he had placed there earlier and stepped over to the bed. He paused for a second, trying to locate where the mini bar might be. He turned three hundred and sixty degrees and then sat on the bed for a moment. 'I wonder' he thought, "Minibar" he stated. A compartment in the wardrobe slid open and the minibar fridge pushed forward slightly just enough to allow for the fridge door to open. Christian had to stop himself from giggling. With all that had happened recently he was actually quite excited to be here, in this hotel, on his own. Mother had asked a friend to pay for the room on his account so that the company wouldn't know he was here, *if* they were looking for him, so Christian knew that *for the time being at least* he was reasonably safe. Christian opened the fridge. It certainly lived up to its' name of mini bar as it was barely large enough to hold a glass. Inside were two dispensers. One for drinks, one for ice. The drinks dispenser had a nozzle in it, you ordered any drink you wanted and it was pumped directly into your glass. Seeing this Christian grinned, impressed. He then took one of the glasses from the desk and filled it with ice. "Mini bar." The fridge then slid away as if it had never been there at all. He sat on the bed again and spun the glass around in his hand, enjoying the look and sound of the ice clunking against the glass. He lifted the bottle, that Mother had gifted him with before dropping him off at the hotel and examined it. It was Whisky. Not the cheap stuff. This was Talisker. Now very, *very* rare and reserved for *very* special occasions. He un-foiled it and pulled the top off with that most satisfying of 'Thloops.' He lifted the cork and smelt it. He paused for a moment. It smelt fantastic but…was that *really* what it smelt like? How well had his smell receptors been designed? How well had his brain been designed? Was he able to properly interpret smells and tastes? Colours? He had not considered this before. His eyes lowered and he stared at the floor thinking of nothing in particular but slightly saddened by the thought. After a while a waft of the Whisky made its' way up to him and his smile returned. He looked down at the Whisky, poured himself a large glass, placed the bottle down on the floor and then again spun the glass in his hand now enjoying the Whisky rolling over the ice, the light piercing through the liquid, the sense of warmth coming from the drink itself. He took a large gulp, clenched his teeth together, stopped breathing for a moment, then drew in a deep sharp breath and let out a satisfied, "Hah-h-h-h-h. That's good shit!" He placed his drink down beside him and lay on the bed. "Music, Sigur Ros." From nowhere, music could be heard. "Volume, down." Christian sat listening to this soft gentle music. He lay still, arms by his side, still fully clothed. He pulled himself up, finished the glass off and then lay down again staring up at the ceiling. He moaned a contented, comfortable, moan and then slowly but surely drifted into a deep, deep sleep.

"So d'you think he exists then?"
"What?"

"D'you think he actually exists then or what?"

"Walker what the fuck are you talking about?"

Walker stopped marching. He turned, slowed by his suit. "You know...*God*. You remember we were talking about religion earlier, you know in the mess, and I just wondered what you *thought*."

Christian turned to Walker, "Random mate, that was very random." He smiled.

"Yes I know, sorry. Sorry I was having the conversation in my head as I was walking along and forgot I hadn't included you in it." He began to walk again pushing against the Martian wind as dust flowed between them both. "So...you think he exists?"

Christian turned to look at Walker, held out his arms stretched wide and gestured for Walker to look around, "Well I've not really given it that much thought to be honest, I mean, let's face it, if he does exist then why are we already here in Hell? It seems fairly easy to believe in the Devil though I guess."

Walker laughed, "No, no I'm serious."

After a few more minutes of walking they came to the edge of a very steep drop. Below them they could see the lights from the base way off in the distance deep within the huge crater that lay before them. They always took the opportunity to look at the base in this way when they could. It reminded them of the size of the base, the amount of people they were protecting and, in an odd way, reminded them of being back on Earth. They both turned, ready to take the well-trodden route back to the base, "You see the thing is Walker." Christian caught his breath, "I'm not even sure it is a "*he*" you know? I mean, if God does exist, *if* he exists then who's to say that he isn't a she? Or that he or she even conforms to what we know as simply male or female. Who's to say that God doesn't exist in a higher form that transcends simple terms like he, she or even it. Maybe it's a "they"." Christian turned to Walker and smiled, "Maybe God is a committee."

"Well that's a fairly hideous thought. Can you imagine how many forms we'll have to fill in when we die?" Walker laughed and continued walking. "Oh my God, perhaps that's what Purgatory is, just one long queue in an admin office."

"Well if it would get us off this bloody rock then I'd be happy to take a seat."

Christian rolled over and then, without fully waking up, lowered the whisky glass to the floor, took his shoes off, rolled over again and then dozed off back out of the room.

The drop ship was crowded, packed like a cattle truck as it slowly made its' way across the front line. An ugly, hulking mass of metal it was designed purely for function alone. Aesthetics and comfort weren't things that were wasted on soldiers, certainly not out here in the colonies. Inside, the rear bay was lit in a dark gloomy red hue as soldiers, marines, medics and Officers all fought in the stale dust filled air for a place to stand or sit.

Walker and Christian stood cramped in one corner next to a large multi-tracked Armadillo. Christian had taken rations from his pack and had opened them to self-heat. "You want some of these mate?"

Walker turned. "Does a Barf worm shit in the sand? Yes, of course I do." He held up a billy can from his pack and Christian poured half of his rations into it.

Christian tapped his can against Walkers, "Well as my mother used to say, the way to a man's stomach is to feed him."

"Don't you mean the way to a man's heart is through his stomach?"

"Well, yeah, I guess so, it's just that after the divorce my Mum was convinced that men didn't actually have hearts and that they just survived on stomachs alone."

Walker laughed almost coughing up his slop, "She sounds like a wise lady your Mother." He turned and smiled at Christian, "You don't talk about her much, do you mate? You got a picture of her?"

Christian frowned, "Well actually no, no I don't. You know, I don't...actually remember that much about her, just what my Dad told me about her."

Walker waited a moment until he responded, "You mean, your *real* Mum right? How old *were* you when you were adopted?"

Christian looked away into the distance, "Honestly...I, I can't remember."

Walker placed his hand on Christian's shoulder, "Martin, I'm sorry, you know if you ever wanna talk about it..."

Christian smiled back at him, "Thanks mate, I know, I'm...sorry, what did you call me?"

Walker pulled a puzzled face, "Er...Martin?"

Christian suddenly sat bolt upright and looked around. Sigur Ros continued to play softly in the background. He had clearly been sleeping for longer than he had realised as the light outside had now faded. He was suddenly aware of how fast his heart was racing. The memory of the dream quickly faded but the name remained. 'Martin. What the fuck?' After a pause, Christian laughed it off, 'There's more of gravy than of grave about you.' he thought, smiling to himself. He looked down at the glass by the bed. "Or should that be more of whisky than of whisk?" He thought for a moment about what he had just said. 'What the fuck does that mean...that doesn't make any sense at all.' He laughed again.

Christian had brought for himself a good suit, that he had purchased in the hotel shop, which he now laid on the bed. If what he was planning to do was to go wrong, he would like to be found in a good suit. He knew it was a bit silly and pointless but it was important to him. He bathed, dried, and began to dress. "Mirror" he commanded. One of the wardrobe doors changed its' appearance and was now a reflective panel. He stood in front of the mirror in his light grey suit and purple shirt and tied his purple tie. He then helped himself to another glass of Talisker on the rocks and then sat down on the bed again. From a case by the bed, he retrieved the interfacing device and placed it beside himself on the bed. He took one large 'shlurping' gulp of Whisky and then carefully placed the glass back down next to the bed. He took hold of the interface and pressed a button on its' side. Small panels on the side of it flashed into life. He took one last deep breath, leaned forward and, with his right hand, ran the interface down the length of the back of his neck. He waited a moment. Nothing. He screwed his eyes slightly tighter still, waiting, but again, nothing. He exhaled and, keeping his eyes closed, bent over onto his knees. His shoulders slumped forward slightly as he fought back a tear. He knew that he had placed a great deal of hope on this device, probably *too* much. He had known in the back of his mind that it may not work. But then perhaps that would have been too easy. "Bollocks." He held his hand over his face and sat back up squeezing the bridge of his nose. He was aware that this would mean that he could not fully sever the link from the company. Ideas, possibilities, problems, consequences all flashed through his mind. He had no idea what to do next. His breathing slowed and he took one last deep sigh before facing the rest of the night, before facing the rest of his life. He opened his eyes.

"A-r-r-r-r-g-g-h-h-h-h-h-h!" Christian sat on the bed, frozen and part startled, part excited. He wasn't really sure which. In the room, glowing menus had appeared which followed his eye line as he turned his head. He laughed a relieved giddy school boy giggle then put his hand out in front to see if he could touch the menus, or at least get a sense of perspective of them. Putting his hand out, it was hard to determine if they were a long way away or quite near. After a moment, his bottom lip trembled and tears of sheer relief poured down his cheeks. He began to cry almost uncontrollably as if his tears themselves were washing away any remaining links to the company. The menus in front of him rippled and shimmered as tears danced across his eyes. After taking a few moments to calm down he wiped his eyes with the sleeve of his jacket, laughing, and again looked at the menu that appeared in front of him. Large white glowing letters that looked almost solid as if they had a depth to them, not like two dimensional text, more like objects actually in the room. Christian smiled in slight awe. The menus read, SETTINGS, DATA, UNIWEB, APPS. Christian, intrigued, wanted to look inside the APPS menu first. He laughed, 'Hmm, I wonder if I come with Tetris?' He reached out to where he thought the words were and pressed them. Nothing. He swiped across them. Nothing. 'Oh, of course.' he thought and then double tapped the word APPS. Again, nothing. He paused, "Apps.", he commanded. Nothing, again. "Applications." Nothing. He looked around for a moment. 'I wonder if Apps is locked or something?' as he thought the word "apps" the menu changed and now he could see the words NEW, CONTACTS and VIEW, Christian laughed out loud. 'Contacts.' he thought and, as he did, a list of all the contacts he knew appeared in front of him. "Oh fuck. This is amazing. Who can I call? Oh this would just freak someone out, okay think." He looked down the list and, after some consideration, said 'Christian.' After a moment his phone began to chirp and buzz on the desk. He laughed and thought 'Hang up.' prompted to do so by the new menu that had appeared when the phone started ringing. 'Back. View.' Now he was in a menu that simply said NORMAL, NIGHT, THERMAL, he frowned, "Eh? Okay, er...Night." Suddenly the dim room went pitch black then lit with a bright clear black and white image. "O-h-h-h-h shit..." Christian sat almost in fear for a moment but also absolutely amazed at what he was seeing and at what he could do. 'Back, thermal.' The room now changed to a psychedelic palette of bright reds, greens, purples, yellows and blues. He could see the heat coming from the well concealed fridge vent that hid in the far wardrobe. He looked down to see the interface brightly lit where it was still powered up. He pushed the button on the side of it. He had seen thermal imaging hundreds of times before but never like this, never through his own eyes. This was like someone taking their first ever steps, or scuba diving for the first time and entering a completely alien world. He looked at everything in the room, examined the desk and carpet, went into the en-suite and stroked the basin to see how it felt compared to how it looked. After a short play, he sat himself back down and returned his view to normal. In DATA he had options to UPLOAD, DOWNLOAD and UPDATE. He noted that in the download file, there were several files that were encrypted. This did not surprise him and he noted that he might give this more attention at a later date. In SETTINGS there were dozens of options ranging from access rights, to restrictions, to a complete reboot. Christian accessed the menus to remove certain restrictions so that his strength was now as it should be and so that he was now able to access the menu system without needing the interface. He also turned on his Uni-web access. Once he had done this, he accessed a few pages that appeared right in front of him in the room. It was remarkable. Looking at the pages in full detail, he sat eyes wide, hoping that he would never get used to it or tired of remembering this moment. He streamed footage of recent news events, looked at music videos, and even tried an online game just to see if it would work. He was blown away by it all. One thing he did ascertain from the menus though was that to completely sever himself from the company he would have to perform a complete reboot. This was something that did concern him. Could he exist as he was and continue to be a company puppet, or would he rather reboot and risk giving up all of these new abilities? It also scared him slightly as he had only just learned that he *could* even reboot at all and wasn't sure what it would entail.

The REBOOT menu contained a few different options but the option that Christian thought might be the safest was one that didn't look like it would wipe everything but would wipe only recent upgrades. This, he hoped, would include the company's ability to access him but would not include all recent data so he would be able to remember who he was and what had happened to him etcetera. Or so he hoped.

Christian continued sitting there for what seemed like forever. Eventually he took another glass of Whisky from the bottle, took one first slow sip and then gulped the rest down, "Oh fuck it!" he said, 'Reboot.' he thought. For a moment, nothing happened, he felt no different. The room then suddenly turned black. He stiffened, then froze, fell backwards onto the bed. His whole body twitched. His breathing stopped and he slowly slumped sideways as his lifeless body slid down off the side of the bed. He lay on his side, eyes wide open, motionless, the Whisky glass rocking slowly back and forth where it had fallen with him, the ice slowly ebbing its' way down to the top of the glass.

CHAPTER EIGHT

"The birth of Christians' sanity"

<u>1</u>

Les leaned over, stabbed himself a further helping of bacon from the mess table and sat back down to continue reading his tablet. "I see there's a picture of your old girlfriend in the local news Monkey-boy.
Monkey-boy looked up from his plate, "Eh? What's that?"
Les lifted up the tablet to show Monkey-boy the picture of a young lady at an awards ceremony. "Isn't that your ex-girlfriend?"
Monkey-boy turned away and lifted up another fork of beans, "No, that was Kevin."
Les raised a suspicious eyebrow, "Your ex-girlfriend was…Kevin?"
Monkey-boy looked over to a grinning Les, said nothing, shook his head smiling and tucked back into his breakfast.
"Oi, Kevin, isn't this a picture of your ex-girlfriend?" Les turned the tablet toward Kevin.
Kevin looked over, squinted, shrugged and "ughed" confirmation.
"Kevin, she's stunning. Remind me again why she dumped you?"
"She didn't dump *me,* I dumped *her*."
Les lowered the tablet back onto the table, "Really? What was it that put you off, her stunning good looks or her money?"
"Neither of them, she was just...you know…too tall for me. That's all."
"Too…eh…really? You ended a relationship with this gorgeous looking, smart, wealthy woman…because she was…too tall for you?" Les stared for a moment, bemused. "What was she, a giant? Just how tall does a woman have to be to put you off? How tall was she then?"
Kevin glanced over, "She was the same height as me in high heels."
Les paused for a moment, "So how tall *are* you in high heels?"
"What?...No, no, I meant her, her in high heels."
"Oh, *her*! Oh, sorry mate." Les lifted up his tablet to conceal his grin. After a short while, Les' grin waned, but his need for play did not, "Oi, Kevin, you see this thing in the news about the MP for Barnet needing an emergency operation on his colon?"
Kevin shook his head. "No? Really? Don't tell me he got the arse with it, or, no, don't tell me, the Doctor said it was a bum deal or

something, right?" Kevin sat with a moody impatient look. "Go on, Les, it's just gonna be some crappy punch line so just say it. This guy goes in for an operation on his colon, so then what?"

Les lifted his tablet up and continued reading, "Okay Kevin, I'm sorry. I'm sorry I said anything. If you assume that I can't have an adult conversation then I'll just give it a miss I think."

Kevin peered sideways at him, "But you were just gonna come out with some crap joke to try to make me look stupid or something."

Les sat upright, coughed and turned directly to Kevin, "Actually no Kevin, where making *you* look stupid is concerned, I believe that you may already have the market cornered. In fact, I wouldn't be surprised if the Monopolies Commission were to come knocking at your door wanting to speak to you about it. No, I was *actually* going to have an adult conversation with you but *clearly* you don't seem to be capable of doing that. This poor man has had to have emergency surgery and there've been potentially life changing complications and for some reason you seem to find it funny. Well Kevin, I think that's just not on! His *poor* family."

Kevin, looked down at his plate, and gently pushed it away from himself. Without looking up, in a soft voice replied, "Sorry mate. I didn't mean anything by it."

Les barely shook his head and looked back at his tablet to continue reading.

Kevin glanced at him, then looked away, glanced again and then in a slightly pitiful voice asked, "No, sorry mate, what were you gonna say?"

"Are you going to listen?"

"Yes. Sorry Les, go on, please, so *what* happened again?"

"I was just saying that the MP for Barnet had to go into Hospital for emergency surgery on his Colon...."

"Yes? *And*...so what was the problem?"

Les coughed, lowered his head as if looking over glasses, "Well, he underwent the surgery on his colon, but now, due to a grammatical mix up at the Hospital, he's slipped into a comma."

Kevin stared at him for a moment as his brain processed the play on words, he stood up sharply, slid his plate across the table, "Oh fuck off Les!" He turned to leave, stepped toward the door and before exiting, turned back to Les, "Just..." he pointed a stern trembling finger at Les, "Fuck off!"

Les shouted after him. "Hang on, I haven't told you about the book that needed emergency surgery on it's appendix yet!" Once Kevin left, Les sat, looking all innocent but struggling to hide his grin. Monkey-boy, Richie, Katie and Jed were all giggling. Mother sat smiling.

After a short while, Mother turned to Les, "Les you may want to lay off him a little. We've got enough going on at the moment."

Les straightened himself up, "Sorry Guv."

Mother smiled a grateful smile back at Les and nodded. "Cheers Les." He sat for a moment in thought. He looked toward the door where Kevin had walked, "Truth is guys, I'm...I'm a bit concerned for Kevin."

Les placed his tablet down to indicate that Mother had his full attention, "Concerned? What d'you mean Guv?"

"Well…" Mother sat upright, and increased his volume to open the conversation up to the whole table, "The thing is that when he came to us his academy report was *excellent*. His pass marks were *way* above average. It just seems that since he's gotten here, well…is it me or does he seem to be getting...I'm not sure how to put it, but, more *stupid* I guess?"

Katie sipped her tea then turned to Mother, "Guv I'm sorry to say it but it does seem that way. It seems also like he's getting slightly more impatient, at times even slightly aggressive." Another sip, "I'm a little worried for him. He was a good kid when he got here but he seems to be going downhill. I've tried talking to him but he just doesn't seem to be interested." She shrugged.

Mother looked away. "Does anyone know any reason why this would be the case?" He looked around the table. No response. "Nothing going on in his life that would cause him stress? Family worries, girl troubles?"

Katie gulped the last of her tea, "Well Guv, to be honest, if he can afford to 'dump' attractive, wealthy ladies then I don't think it'll be girl trouble."

Mother raised his brow and nodded. "I'm sure I'll know the answer but I have to ask anyway, does anyone know if he's taking something, er, recreational, that might be affecting his performance at all?" Everyone around the table shook their heads quite sternly. "Well guys, I want you all to keep an eye on him, okay? We really *do* have enough on our plates at the moment…what with this sodding *company* business." Mother looked away with slight concern and almost inaudibly mumbled, "I hope Christian's okay. I daresent think…"

Before Mother could finish, shouting could be heard from outside the mess. Everyone around the table exchanged glances then quickly scrambled to their feet and headed down towards the bay where the noise seemed to be coming from. Outside in the bay, two black suits were confronting a man over by one of the appliances. Mother stepped into the bay followed by the rest of the watch. He walked around to the other side of the appliance where the black suits were. As he did, he could see Christian. Mother's shoulders dropped slightly and he sighed with gentle relief. Hearing Mother, Christian turned toward him then nodded at him quite formally. He then turned back toward the two black suits.
"Mr Mann, if you do not come with us we *will* be forced to restrain you."
Christian replied quite matter of fact, "You cannot do that."
"Well I'm sorry but we can and we will."
"You do not understand. I am not referring to your right to do so. I am referring to your ability to carry out this threat. You will not be able to carry it out." Christian was completely calm about the situation and did not seem at all threatened by the two black suits now holding batons that they had previously been concealing within their suits.
Mother stepped forward. "Guys, now, guys there's no need for this." He held a negotiating hand out toward the two men. "Now guys, you know you shouldn't even be on the station. Now, let's not do anything hasty, okay?"
One of the two suits glared at Mother and pointed his baton at him, "You wanna have a go then feel free, but trust me, if you get in our way then, after I've dealt with this talking doll, you're next!"
Christian reached forward, took hold of the baton, glanced out towards where the black suits' pod was parked in the yard and then, in one swift motion, pulled the baton from the suits' hand and launched it at great speed directly towards the pods' windscreen. The other black suit looked around at his now-open-mouthed colleague whose gaze was fixed on the baton that was sticking out of his windscreen.

Christian raised an eyebrow and stepped toward the now disarmed black suit. "Sir, I am going to ask you once only to leave the premises. I shall not ask again."
The black suit, slightly sheepishly but still trying to remain composed, squared up to Christian and looked him right in the eye. "You're not gonna hurt me, it's not in your make up! You're not able to!" Mother stepped quickly to one side and then watched as a white-shirted, black-trousered blur shot along the floor towards the pod. The black and white blur came to a slow stop and then rested next to the pod. Mother turned to see Christian holding a black jacket in his outstretched hand. The second black suit cowered, stared at the jacket for a moment and then, leaning around it, stared at where the now de-jacketed man lay scratching his head.
Christian turned his outstretched hand toward the cowering agent, "You."
"Who, m-me?"
"Yes you."
The black suits' Adam's apple bobbed frantically as he attempted to calculate every next move Christian may make and the outcome.
"Please return your colleague's jacket for me as you leave."
The black suit took the hint and the jacket and quietly, almost bowing, scuttled out of the appliance bay. As he was assisting his colleague into the pod, his colleague raised a fist and opened his mouth ready to confront Christian again. Before he could do so, he suddenly found himself on his side lying on the floor of the pod wrapped in his own jacket with the other, now angry, black suit sitting on top of him.
The big shiny black pod quickly wound up, spun round and shot out of the rear gates.
Mother, who had been staring at the suits leaving, now turned to Christian. He blinked slowly and deliberately, opened his mouth to speak and then looked back to where the pod had been.
Katie appeared from around the side of the appliance, arms folded. "You boys playing nicely?" She and the rest of the watch had still been standing the other side of the appliance and all they had witnessed were raised voices and one black suit comically sliding across the bay floor. Katie had come to ensure that Mother was not in any danger. "Chris?" Seeing him she smiled.
Christian turned to Katie. "Hello Katie. How are you?"

Mother looked at Katie then back to Christian, "Christian, is everything okay?"

"Yes, everything is fine thank you." He paused, "Mother, I see that your pupils have dilated and your heart rate has increased. I hope that you are not threatened in any way."

"Threatened? Christian, *should* I be? Is there cause for us to feel threatened here at the moment?"

Christian shook his head gently and then smiled a slightly awkward, almost untried, smile, "No, there is no cause for alarm. I am afraid I am not quite myself at the moment but I am perfectly fine. I assure you though that I am no threat to you.

Katie leaned in and placed her hand on Christian's arm, "Chris, love, you're acting a little…strange, is everything okay? Are you hurt?"

He turned to Katie and now smiled slightly more confidently, "No, I am working fine thank you Kate. Better than ever in fact."

Mother furrowed his brow, "*Working* fine? Christian, is everything okay? What happened last night at the hotel?"

"I am not yet…fully…sure. It would be difficult to recount everything that happened…without…" Christian's smile grew. "Instead, let me show you."

<u>2</u>

The lecture room was daubed in a slightly stunned shade of silent. The Watch now sat around a black Holo-screen on which Christian had just streamed the highlights of his previous evening. Christian sat next to the screen facing the watch awaiting responses.

Mother knew that the silence must be broken so just said the first thing that came into his head, "So how you feeling now mate?"

"I am unsure. I believe that my personality may have been altered by this recent change in my system and I *feel*…nothing. I believe that my emotions may have been reset also. It is a curious sensation."

Kevin stood and walked out to use the bathroom, "Yeah, it seems to have turned you into a Vulcan."

"Shut up Kevin that's not helping." snapped Mother as he walked out.

Christian turned to Katie, "Katie, you have a question for me?"

Katie sat up slightly, "Yes, I do, how did you know…oh…never mind. Look, all of those lines of information that came up when you rebooted, what were they?"

"That is a good question. The text appeared quicker than you could have read it but it is my inherent programming. It is buried deep within my core. It is everything that ensures that I will not harm, or allow to be harmed, a human being. Secondary to that is my need to protect myself. These instructions are known as the laws of robotics."

"Christian Love, you did throw one of the black suits across the floor, isn't that…?"

"I did not harm him. I ripped his jacket only. I do not believe there is anything within my subroutines about harming jackets." He paused. "That was a joke." He smiled. "I did not throw him. I slid him, at exactly the correct force needed to evict him whilst ensuring he did not hit the pod or the wall beyond it."

Katie smiled. "Oh, okay. That's…er, okay then. You know this is a very different *you* Chris. You are quite a bit more…"

"Robotic?"

Katie shrugged gently, "Well, yeah, sorry."

"I am aware of that Katie. It is fine. Everything is fine. It is something that I believe that will change in a short period after I have re-assimilated myself back into the watch."

Jed shuffled in his seat, "Oh okay, not Vulcan then, Borg." He laughed and, before Mother could comment on his statement, said "Well I for one think it's fucking cool. Welcome back mate." He smiled at Christian.

Christian smiled back, "Thank you Jed."

Mother smiled at Jed in appreciation.

Jed shook his head, impressed, "So how does the Uni-web access work then mate, do you like, know…*everything*?"

"No Jed, not everything. Firstly, not everything *is* known." He smiled again, "Secondly I have a biotech brain. It is fundamentally very similar to a human brain though faster and more efficient but it does have integrated Nanotech…"

"Nanotech?"

"Forgive me, Nanotechnology. It has integrated Nanotechnology which allows me the ability to access certain functions like the Uniweb, telephone systems and so on."

"So if you have access to the web then surely you must pretty much know everything, right?"

"No Jed, it does not work quite like that." Christian thought for a moment, "Think of me as a man standing in a library. One of the historic libraries with actual paper books. Now imagine asking me a question, any question. To answer that question I would then have to go to the particular section, shelf then book to access the relevant information."

"So you can only know something if you *want* to know it, right?"

"Yes. That is a slight over simplification of the process but that would be an easy way of describing it."

Mother snorted a quiet chuckle, "Well this is all rather amazing young Chris."

"Yes, yes I suppose it is."

Mother leaned forward, "Chris, if you have your independence now then how d'you know you'll actually want to stay in the Fire Brigade? You might want to go and do something else for a living, no?"

Christian stood, "I am not quite myself at the moment. I believe that my emotions and personality may need some refreshing, but what I do know of my memories from being here is that I would trust all of you with my continued existence. I believe you are my true friends and I have no desire to go anywhere else. Not yet."

Katie stood up and put her arm around his back, "We *are* your friends Chris." She hugged him, "It's so good to see you're okay at last." She smiled up at him.

"Thank you Katie." He smiled down at her. After a moment he looked up at the others, "I stood because I seem to remember liking tea. May I have some tea please?"

Katie chuckled, placed her hand on his chest for a moment and then tapped it twice, "Come on, you. You clearly haven't changed *that* much then have you."

<u>3</u>

Kevin stood in the kitchen for a moment with his hand on the fridge door, pausing before opening it. "So Richie, what you're saying is…that at the moment we *might* or *might not* have a dead cat in the fridge called Schrödinger?"

"No…no, Kevin, it doesn't quite work like that, no." Richie sighed a subtle and slightly tested sigh, "No, you see, you have to know that

there's a cat in the box in the first place. Okay? But it wouldn't be a fridge would it, you wouldn't put a cat in a fridge would you?"
"Well you would if it was dead. You know, if you didn't want it going off." Kevin opened the fridge, "Hmm, no there's not one in here." He then closed the fridge again.

Richie, watching Kevin open and close the fridge, shook his head and put the knife down that he was preparing food with, "No Kevin, that's the whole point with Schrödinger's cat, you *know* it's alive before you put it in the box, you just don't know whether it's alive or dead once you close the box.

Kevin thought for a moment, "Well surely if you put some air holes in the box it would…"

"No, Kevin, no. You're missing the whole point to this. The point is there *is* no cat at all for this. It's completely hypothetical"

Kevin rubbed his chin, "Well, yes, it *will* be hypothetical if you're keeping it in a fridge."

Richie placed both hands on the counter and, closing his eyes, leaned forwards onto them. "Kevin…"

"Yes?"

"Get out of my kitchen please."

Kevin raised a finger to protest, saw Richie's face and then quietly walked out, without protestation, into the mess.

Richie stood tutting and shaking his head, "That's hypothermia, not hypothetical. Idiot!"

Kevin stood in the mess, hesitated, deciding where to sit and then sat at the end of the tables. Jed, Katie and Veggie sat along the table. Jed and Katie had been chatting and Veggie was still reading from his tablet. Jed looked up to where Kevin now sat, "Y'alright Kevin?"

Kevin shrugged, "Yeah I'm okay thanks."

"What's up? You been winding Richie up in there?"

Kevin's face then shrugged, "No, not really. I don't think so. We were chatting about stuff and then he started talking about forests and was talking about the noise trees made, you know?"

Jed shared a quick puzzled look with Katie, "Er...no. So what noise do trees make then? They bark I assume?" Jed lifted his brow assuming he'd found the punch line to Richie's conversation.

"Well, no, no he was saying, I mean what he was asking was that if a tree falls in the woods and there's no one there to hear it does it make a sound."

Jed lowered himself onto his elbows wondering where this was going.

"And then I asked Richie, if there's no one there to hear it then what does it fucking matter? After that I kind of lost the point a bit I think and Richie just seemed to get a bit wound up about something, but I'm not sure why though.

Jed and Katie swapped "Oops" faces.

Veggie looked up from his tablet, "Kevin, you're quite creative wouldn't you say?"

Kevin smirked slightly smugly and nodded, "Yeah, yeah I think so, yeah."

"Right well draw those curtains for me could you. I can't see this crossword."

Kevin's smirk sank, he stood, drew the curtains and sat back down in his chair.

They sat for a short while. Jed and Katie were aware that Mother had wanted them to start including Kevin more so Katie smiled at him, "Kevin, before you came in, Jed and I were talking about gardening and how much we like gardening. Do you…keep a garden at all?"

Kevin thought for a moment, "I keep garden peas, does that count?"

Katie sat up slightly, "Oh, okay, you keep peas, like in pots or actually out in the garden?"

"In the freezer."

Katie rubbed the flash of confusion from her face. "Oh, okay." She looked at Jed, her face concealed behind her hand.

Jed just shrugged back at her also not knowing if Kevin was actually playing games with them or if he had indeed become *this* stupid.

Kevin, aware of the silence, asked "My Mum used to say that she had green fingers because she was good in the garden. Do either of you have green fingers?"

Katie shrugged and shook her head, "No Kevin. As much as I do like plants and flowers and things, when it comes to actual gardening I'm afraid I'm all green fingers and thumbs."

Before Kevin could answer, an announcement came from the station's tannoy system.
"Could Station Officer Riley and Fire Fighter Mann please report to the Station Manager's office?"
Mother, in his own office, looked up from his paperwork. He went to his locker, took out his peaked cap, looked in the mirror as he walked out of the office to confirm his tie was straight and then he left for the Station Manager's office.
Christian, who had not yet left the station, put down his coffee and headed towards the office.

In the Station Manager's office sat the usual suspects of three Senior Officers quietly drinking tea and nibbling on complimentary slices of Company cake.

Use of the office had been given over to the company to hold a meeting with both Mother and Christian. A grey suit had sat behind the desk in the Station Manager's chair. Behind him another grey suit was sitting with a tablet for note taking.

Mother reported to the Station manager's office with his cap smartly placed on his head. He knocked and the door slid open. As soon as he saw the grey suits he pulled the cap from his head with one hand and undid his tie with the other. He unbuttoned his top button and then, giving one nod to the Senior Officers, sat in one of two chairs that had been placed in front of the desk.

Christian then appeared at the door still in his own grey suit and purple shirt.

Behind the desk, the two suits were again occupied by Myers and his boss Thackett. Thackett sat in the chair, elbows on table, both hands touching and all fingers splayed. He looked at Mother, said nothing, looked at Christian, said nothing, raised an eye brow, swivelled his chair and looked away for a moment.

Mother's face could not hide his abject boredom with the prospect of having to listen to Thackett prattle on again. "Well Blofeld? You gonna say something or not, because I've got a fire station to run and I'm busy."

Christian did not understand the reference. He quickly searched for Blofeld references on the web, found bond villains and then smiled to himself.

Thackett turned to Mother, "Station Officer Riley I don't think you appreciate the full gravity of this situation."

Mother paused, looked at Christian, then back to Thackett, "Jeez, are you actually going to use the same speech as you did with Jed and Les? Seriously? The gravity of the situation? Come on Thackett just cut to the chase then get the Hell off my fire station! You've upset my troops enough as it is." He was unable to hide the sheer anger he felt for the man that was sat before him.

"Thackett's cheek muscles clenched as he tightened his jaw. He leaned forward, snorted and then sat back in his chair and, as calmly as he could, said "Riley, you know there was once a man called Caesar, Nero Claudius Caesar who was born in 37 A.D. He and I have a lot in common. I have always been an admirer of his."

Mother dropped his head onto his shoulders and stared at Thackett wondering where this was going.

Christian's eyes glazed over slightly and it was clear that he wasn't even listening.

"You know, Nero murdered his way to the imperial throne, which he occupied from 54 A.D. to 68 A.D. This is where it gets interesting, you see in 64 A.D. a terrible fire broke out in Rome. It was speculated that Nero deliberately torched the city in order to justify building a more splendid one. Now, when we tell you that we are going to ensure that Christian is…"

Thackett did not complete his sentence as Christian butted in, "Caesar. Hmm. You lack finesse Mr Thackett."

Thackett turned to him sharply, annoyed that he had not been allowed to finish his tried and tested Caesar speech. "What is that? Lack finesse? And why would that be Mr Mann? You think you are able to appreciate the brilliance of a man like Nero? You think your calculator brain can fathom the complexities of such a man? What could you possibly know about Caesar that I do not? Hmm?"

"Allow me two minutes to download it and I shall know more about Nero than you could ever know in a lifetime Mr Thackett, but that really does not interest me. What *does* interest me is that you use *Caesar* as your personal password for your files at work."

Thackett's jaw dropped, "What?"

"Yes, I am accessing your personal files as we speak. Your ego betrays you Sir."

Thackett turned to Myers, "MYERS!"

"Already done Sir." Myers smiled up at his boss. "I have just emailed Carl Winters in your office Sir and he has just confirmed receipt. The email ordered him to remove the cables from your personal tablet Sir to remove it from the Uni-web.

Thackett smiled and spun back round to Christian. "Oh dear Mr Mann. Oh boohoo. Well, what will you do now then, eh?"

The three Officers looked uncomfortable in their seats. McCormick turned to Thackett and slightly shook his head, not happy at what was unfolding.

Christian sat for a moment dazing into space. "Oh dear indeed. What *will* I do?" He spoke, flatly, without even attempting to use emotion.

Thackett looked uneasy. "You will not have access to those files Mann, and I am telling you now that, in the morning, I am going to court and when I do I am…"

"No," said Christian, "You are not."

Thacketts' eyes screwed tighter.

"While you were wasting time talking, I downloaded all of your files and have moved them to a secure location."

Thackett turned to Myers and began clicking his fingers to hurry him up, "Myers, tell me, tell me…"

Myers nodded as he typed on his tablet. "Sir, Mr Mann is bluffing. Winters has confirmed that he has removed your tablet from the server and he sees no sign of transfer."

Thackett's whole body slumped slightly with relief and, though he was clearly breathing harder, he allowed himself a smile. He dabbed his top lip with the back of his hand and then turned back to Christian. Your move Mr Mann. Check."

"No need Mr Thackett, it is check mate I believe."

Thackett sat back in his chair, "Right, so, then let's get down to real business shall we?"

Mother turned to Christian and tightened a disappointed smile.

Christian barely smiled back. "Mr Thackett, since you like games so much, let us play another game. Do you believe in magic?"

Thackett said nothing but simply looked back at him.

Christian turned to McCormick and asked for him to "Pick one of the following please. Augustus, Tiberius, Gaius, Claudius or Nero."

McCormick sat upright, "Er, Mr Mann…"

"Please humour me Sir."

McCormick shrugged and said "Tiberius?"

Thackett breathed heavily, "What is the point to this? We are wasting time!"

Christian leaned to see Myers. "Mr Myers, please email Mr Winters and ask him which one *he* would choose."

Myers looked confused, looked at Thackett for confirmation who did so with a shrug and he then sent the email.

"What is the point to this Mann? You're making little sense. In the morning when the courts open I'm…"

"Tiberius Sir." Myers looked up at Thackett. "Winters guessed…Tiberius."

Thackett's eyes burned. "How is that?...I don't understand? What is the point to this?"

146

Christian stood to leave. "Winters did not get your email Mr Thackett, I did. I also responded to them to allow myself time to move your files. I rewrote your email. Also I see by Winters' diary that he has been having sexual relations with your Wife. I have instead emailed Mr Winters from your wife's account asking him to meet her at a hotel."

Mother's face dropped with sheer admiration for Christian's audacity. Thackett stood and threw out a pointed shaking fist, "Mann I am telling you now…"

Before finishing, Christian held out a flat 'stop' hand to Thackett and softly said, "Mr Thackett, I find it hard to understand your indignation. I see by your diary that you are *also* having an affair…with…"

Thackett threw both hands up, "Okay, that's enough. That's enough." He slumped back down into his chair. Shook his head and then dropped his head into his hands. Thackett pulled his hands to one side so that he could be heard, "Mann do not speak of this again. I shall not be pursuing this at this moment in time. Please leave."

Christian leaned forward and, speaking quietly enough to ensure that only Mr Thackett could hear whispered, "Take care Mr Thackett. Live by the pink sword sir and you will die by the pink sword."

Knowing that there was nothing more to say, Christian and Mother both turned and walked out of the office. The office door slid behind them both. Mother turned to Christian to speak but, before he did, shouting could be heard from within the office and they both paused to listen. After a short while all three Officers left the office. Two of the Officers simply walked out to the yard towards their pods. McCormick stopped to speak to Christian and Mother. "Well, that was interesting." He turned to Christian and put his hand out to shake it. "Christian I'm sorry you've had to be put through all this. I'll try to get you whatever support we can give you from here on in. My hands have been tied I'm afraid but let me see what I can do, okay?" Christian nodded and took McCormick's hand. "Thank you Sir."

Still holding Christian's hand, McCormick placed a politicians' hand on his right elbow and leaned in to speak to him, "You've certainly upset Thackett. He's shouting at Myers because he say's they've lost the interface or something and he wasn't told. Don't know if that means anything to you." McCormick walked towards his pod and turned before walking out into the bay. "Goodbye Mr Mann, good luck."

Christian called after McCormick, "Sir, can I confirm, did Mr Thackett refer to it as *an* interface or *the* interface?"

McCormick thought for a moment. "*The* interface, yes definitely *the* interface." He then left.

Christian stood still, smiling.

Mother rubbed his chin, "What does that mean then young Chris?"

"It means that in their arrogance they only made one interface for me. That means I'm completely free." His smile grew.

Mother and Christian walked back towards the mess to celebrate with a hot cup of tea. "So Christian, just out of interest, who *is* Thackett having an affair with, anyone we know?"

"I do not believe so Mother. Not unless you've actually met *Mr* Winters."

Mother stopped in his tracks. "*Mr*?...Oh...Oh, that's complicated. Ha, what tangled Uni-webs we weave, eh?" He laughed as he continued towards the mess.

CHAPTER NINE

"Kevin's bacon"

1

Katie, Jed and Veggie had sat at the mess table. The beginning of another tour. Mother had taken roll call and the watch were slowly but surely homing in on the nearest source of fresh tea. Katie was nursing her mug as if holding onto a life ring. Tired, she, like several others, had not been able to sleep properly since the initial meeting with the Company. Jed and Veggie both mulled over a tableted crossword, grunting the occasional question or suggestion to one another.
The mess door slid open and in walked Kevin and Les mid conversation.
"So then the vicar says 'I guess you're caught between a Rock eel and a hard Plaice then'."
Les stopped suddenly. "That's it? That, that's actually the punchline?" Les stood open mouthed.
Kevin smacked Les' bicep with the back of his hand as he stepped past him, "Yeah. Get it? You see, between a Rock eel and a hard Plaice because you see…"
Les stared back at Kevin and held up a flat upturned hand. "Kevin, yes, yes I understand it. In fact I even get it. It's just…not…*funny*."
Kevin replied quite adamantly "Er, I'm sorry Les, but it *is* funny. You obviously just don't get it. That's my best joke."
"No Kevin, that's *not* a joke. It's *like* a joke but…you know…without the humour." Les sat down next to Katie. "After all that 'build up'? My God, that's, that's five minutes of my life that…I'll…just…never get back. I'm five minutes older but as for wiser, forget it! I actually feel dumber as a consequence of listening to that 'joke'. When I was listening to the build-up I could actually hear my brain rotting. I think I just died a little bit." Les looked over to Jed, "Jed, Jed I think my brain may have stalled, quick, give me a question."
Without looking up from his crossword Jed held up four fingers, "How many fingers am I holding up?"
Without pausing Les replied, "Coconut milk?"
Jed, again, without looking up, simply nodded, "Yeah, yeah you're fine. You're good to go."

Kevin tutted and walked out of the mess shaking his head.

Katie smiled and shook her head at a now smiling Les. She leaned back into her chair for a moment. "You know what we need? I think we need a night out, don't we? I think we should all go out, drink lots of falling down water, make some shapes on the dance floor and just try to relax for a bit. Put all this stuff to one side for one night, you know? Let's go out, get pissed and make complete cocks of ourselves." She looked at Les.

Les smiled and nodded. "I can do that. In fact I may be over qualified." He said. "I was born for this mission!"

Jed and Veggie both nodded their agreement. Veggie sat up scratching his chin thinking of the prospect of a good night out on the town. He smiled, closed his eyes and sat for a moment gently rocking his head back and forth. "Hm-m-m-m."

As they all sat there fantasising their own versions of the perfect night out, over the tannoy came the message, "Could Jed and Kate please go to the Station Officer's room." Katie leaned forward to see Jed who looked back at her unsure as to why their presence was required. Katie shrugged and stood.

"I just need the little boys' room so I'll meet you down there Kate." Jed walked towards the Dormitory toilets. Katie pulled her "Icky poo-poo la-la" face, nodded and stepped out of the mess, walking toward the office.

About ten minutes later, Jed stood at Mother's office door. It slid open. Jed was wafting away make believe fumes. "Oh God, oh God it was awful. Oh my God it was torture, I can't talk about it. Good Lord, it actually had a recordable epicentre. I mean talk about captain's log." The volume and speed of his sentences dropped and slowed as he stepped into the office and saw Kate's reddened angry face sitting in Mothers' desk chair. Katie was sitting, head trembling. "Oh fuck, what's happened? Oh shit, is everything alright? Kate?"

Mother stood beside Katie with one hand on her shoulder, offering her a tissue with the other should she need it. Christian stood quietly looking on. Jed looked over to Christian, went to speak but Christian raised a finger and gently shook his head to indicate to Jed that he should wait a moment, which he did.

A tear leaked from Katie's now puffy red eyes as she struggled to contain her developing rage. Her breathing was uneven where she struggled to get enough oxygen into her lungs. She dropped her head into her lap. Jed stepped backwards slightly. Katie took her hands and held them in front of her face as she sat up, "Ar-r-g-g-h-g-h-h-h-h! Fu-u-u-u-u-u-ck! Fuc-c-c-k-k-k-k-k-k-k!" She shook her head, scrunched her tissue into her hand and bowed her head onto it "Oh those wankers, those…fucking wankers!" Her brow and voice both trembled with sheer anger and contempt.

Jed, still concerned and none the wiser, remained respectfully silent.

Katie sat upright, dropped both hands into her lap still scrunching up tissue and turned to Mother, "Oh poor Kevin. Oh those fucking…"

Jed's face screwed, "Poor Kevin? I've…I've just seen Kevin in the mess, poor Kevin? Kevin's fine, so what's happened?" Jed looked at Mother. Mother turned away toward Christian, "Christian…"

Christian nodded and turned to Jed, "Jed…I have been looking through Thackett's personal files. Some of them are encrypted. I am working on that. One or two of the other files were also encrypted but with poor algorithms so were very easy to circumvent. In them, I found some disturbing details about Kevin." Christian took a deep calming breath. "Jed, would you say that it is fair to describe Kevin's…" Christian thought for a moment for a polite description, "Ability…is less than it was when he first joined the watch?"

"Is he more stupid? Well, yes."

Christian raised his eyebrows and twisted a nod to Jed, "Well, yes, that would be a simple way of putting it. The fact is that, although he appears to have simply become 'more stupid', the truth is slightly more sinister."

"Christian, please get to the point mate. Just tell me what's going on."

"Okay. Well, the company have been regularly feeding Kevin a drug commonly known as 'QI'.

"They've been…eh? QI?"

"Yes, it is a drug that does not *officially* exist. The file that I accessed from Thackett's drive does not name it directly nor are there any references to drugs of any kind but references are made to drinks given to Kevin and the effect it has been having on him. It would be logical to assume that these 'drinks' are a reference simply to avoid committing any evidence in writing. Also there are some vague correspondences with a Professor L. Ribbons who, it is speculated, worked on the drug whilst she worked for the US military. This strengthens the theory that it could be QI."

"Okay, so then what's…what's QI?"

"As I said, it does not officially exist so information about it is sketchy at best. What I have gathered from speculation and conjecture as reported on various sources on the web is that it is a military 'weaponised' drug. It is designed to slowly but surely reduce a persons' *or persons* IQ. I would assume that the idea is to interrupt an enemy's food supply and introduce this drug into it. Over time it then reduces their defensive capabilities but at such a pace as to not arouse immediate suspicion. It is perhaps a long term weapon presumably designed to remove or reduce a perceived future threat. Again, this is all just theoretical from what I have been able to learn from the web."

Jed's mouth opened slightly. His eyes rocked from left to right as if he were mentally pacing up and down the room. "What the f...So...So what now? Do we just stop his drugs? Is he still on them?"

"Stopping the drugs will not alter the damage that has already occurred. *Yes,* he *is* still on them. According to his files, Thackett has a team visiting Kevin's apartment regularly, much as they did mine."

Jed shook his head. "But why? Why would they do this to Kevin, what is their reason for it? I don't see what they would gain from it. Hang on. He's...he's human, right?"

Christian, seeing Katie still quietly seething, looked away, "Yes, he is human. I can only surmise that they wished to improve their proof of concept results."

"Eh?"

"Me. They wanted to make my performance look even more impressive by being able to compare it to someone else on the watch and it makes sense to compare my performance with someone who has recently completed training so as to get a 'fairer' comparison. They could then approach the Brigade and demonstrate their comparisons. Of course, when I say fair comparison, this is merely the public perception of fair and, as we know, this company does not *actually* play fairly."

"But why would they continue to give him drugs if they're not able to get data results from you anymore?"

"It is only logical to assume that they intend to still use general comparisons to illustrate how effective I am compared to Kevin. Perhaps that is why they have 'allowed' me to continue working here.

I am sure that they have the resources to have me...'removed', if they wanted to."

"So you mean to say that Kevin has been visited regularly in his own apartment and been given drugs against his will?"

"Yes."

"And this has caused...what, brain damage?"

Christian shrugged, "I am not sure. It *may* have caused actual damage but hopefully will have simply hindered his capacity to perform."

"So then we need to get, what, a cure?"

"Well, that is where it gets even more complicated."

"What do you mean? This isn't complicated enough already?"

"You see there *is* no official QI. Therefore there *is* no official cure. For there to be a cure, the military would have to admit that the drug itself exists."

Jed covered his face with his hand. "Oh for fuck's sake." He shook his head, "Oh Kevin. Oh mate." Jed stepped over to Katie. "You alright mate?"

Katie simply squinted up at him through tear sodden vengeful eyes, shook her head, and lowered it back into her hands.

Jed gently rubbed Katie's back then took one of her trembling hands in his. He said nothing for a moment. Shaking his head, he looked up at Mother, "What can we do?"

Mother, who was standing arms folded, looked up, "This isn't happening 'officially', so *nothing*...'officially'."

Jed peered at Mother from under his head tilted brow. "Okay. Fair enough." without looking, "Christian, you in?"

Christian snorted. For a moment he thought about how to reply, how to respond to such a call to arms. What speech would be appropriate for this moment? He thought, smiled and simply said, "Yes. I am in."

Katie looked up at Jed, sniffed, tightened her brow, sniffed again, "What are you going to do?"

Jed smiled down to Katie, crouched down so that they were both on the same eye line, "I don't know yet. But...I suspect it may involve lingerie."

<u>2</u>

It was around half past one in the morning. A bitter morning chill blew through the streets of London. Outside Kevin's apartment two men stepped out of a parked black pod into the unwelcoming morning air. The cool air made both men look like heavy smokers as thick white vapour appeared on every exhalation. One of the men reached into the car and pulled out a briefcase. High above them a curtain twitched and a lone figure stepped away into the concealment of a darkened apartment. The men looked up at the windows to confirm no lights were on in their targeted apartment and they then proceeded to walk towards the building. Nothing was said between the two men as they rode up in the elevator. This was a routine journey they had made on many occasions and they had long since exhausted any 'limited' topics of conversation they may have once had between them. One of the men removed a baton from within his coat and slid it into his sleeve. He coughed, adjusted his coat and continued to ride silently up in the lift.

The hall to Kevin's apartment lit, when needed, in sections as the men triggered unseen sensors as they passed beneath them. The briefcase was placed down on the floor and then opened. A scanning device was removed from the case and placed against Kevin's apartment door. Lights on the device flashed in alternating sequences, it beeped softly a series of tones and then the man quickly pulled it away as the door slid away into the wall.

The two black-suited and over coated men then stepped into the apartment. The case was placed on the floor of the front hallway and both men removed their coats and placed them on coat hooks by the front door. They both quickly scanned around the hall and then listened for a moment to confirm there were no obvious signs of life. They then proceeded towards the bedroom where Kevin would be sleeping. As they both stepped into the lounge towards the bedroom they paused for a moment. A small table lamp in the lounge was still on, probably an oversight on Kevin's part. The men both looked at each other and one signalled the other to check towards the other end of the room. They both stepped quietly and cautiously as they began to check the dimly lit room.

Before they could get very far a large chair in the corner swivelled around. In it, Jed was sitting. He lowered his legs onto the floor that he'd had crossed on the chair. "Good evening". He said. "We've been expecting you." Jed sat up in his chair exaggeratingly stroking a white teddy bear as if stroking a cat. Jed had in his mouth an unlit pipe and was wearing a dinner suit that probably fit him much better several years and donuts earlier. The two men both stood still as if caught in an unwanted camera shot. They both looked at each other, at Jed, then back at each other. They then straightened themselves up and stood in a more suitably threatening stance. The larger of the two men cocked his head, "Seriously? Who the fuck are you then, eh? What are you supposed to be, some kind of Bond villain?"

Jed raised an eyebrow, impressed that this goon had actually heard of 'Bond'. He stroked the bear a few more times, lifted it nearer his mouth and whispered, "Don't listen to him teddy." He slowly lifted the teddy bear and tossed it aside as if finished with. He then spoke in a caricatured German accent, "Gentlemen, assuming that neither of you have a fear of appearing suddenly back in your school in the middle of morning assembly wearing nothing but your pants then *I* am your worst nightmare."

Both black suits looked at each other slightly puzzled then the larger of the two suits leaned forward, "Just the one of you slag bitches in this nightmare is there mate?"

The door to the kitchen slid open and in stepped a negligee'd woman with long flowing pony tail and fish net stockings.

Jed leaned forward and waved a hand towards the woman. "Gentlemen, let me introduce my assistant. As you can see there are clearly *two* of us slag bitches."

The large suit sneered at Les. "Yeah, nice one guys. We've heard about you two pricks. Your stunt with the technicians was very funny, er, NOT!" the suit laughed recognising his own genius. "You see you thought that *I* thought it was actually funny, but then I flipped the whole thing around by putting 'not' at the end, so in fact I don't find it funny at all!" Both the suits laughed and smiled at each other for what *they* thought was a brilliantly delivered word play.

The large suit, still laughing, looked over at Les then at Jed, "You see, we're not like the last guys you met. We don't fuck about like those gutless turds did."

Jed flashed a slightly concerned look towards Les.

"You see, the last guys are no longer...er...'with' the company anymore." The suit gesticulated the speech marks with his fingers as he said the word 'with'. "You see, I did that because I'm saying 'with' to imply they've just been fired or some shit, but in fact, they're, you know, not alive anymore."

"Not alive anymore. So like dead, right? They're not alive as in dead. Why not just say they're dead?" Jed shook his head at Les and shrugged his bored shoulders. "Actually guys, have you got many more puns like that, because if you have, honestly, I think I'd rather you just stabbed me in the face and be done with it."

The suit stepped forward. "You see *those* dozy little twats' services were no longer required by the company, see? We had to let them go."

"You did?"

The second agent now stepped forward next to his partner, "Yeah. We were hanging them from a bridge at the time though." He began to laugh.

Jed stood up from his chair, throwing the pipe into it as he did. "Look guys you've made your point. And I'm assuming your point is that you've got absolutely no sense of humour. So let's not fuck about any more, okay? You know why we're here and we know why you're here so let's just sort this out men to…" Jed pointed at himself then at Les, "Us."

The two black suits continued to stand silently for a moment, presumably to rest their knuckles on the floor for a while longer, waiting for the next move.

"Look guys, we know why you're here okay and it has to stop now. Also we're gonna need to know how we get hold of an antidote or a cure or something. Okay? Now the company's *obviously* involved and there may be serious consequences for that, but *you* could be left out of this. Our fight is not with *you* guys so why not just…you know, let us know how we can fix this and then, how about you guys just leave, okay?"

The larger suit released the grip on his baton and it slid down the length of his arm until he caught it in his hand. Les straightened and stepped forward ready to counter a possible attack.

Jed put out a flat hand towards the suit, "Now, now…now there's no need for that is there. We're not here for you, we're here to sort out a problem with the company, okay?"

"Yeah I know mate, but if I let you do that then I'm out of a job aren't I and I kinda like this job. The perks are good and they let me hit people a lot. In fact, they even give me bonuses for it and, since you're not exactly gonna put up much of a fight, I think I'll treat myself to an early Christmas bonus." He leaned forward ready to hit Jed with the baton and Les stepped in front of Jed ready to stop the baton and counter. As he did, the door from the hallway opened and before the suit struck, he turned to see why it had. There, in the doorway, stood Christian. The suit paused for a moment mid-strike. He screwed his eyes tighter and stepped back from Les then lowered his hand to his side. He looked over to where Christian stood trying to anticipate Christians' next move. "*And*?"

Christian stepped into the room but, having removed both his jacket and coat on the way in, they both lay on the floor so both the lounge and front door remained open unable to close against the obstructions.

The suits both looked at each other, then back at Christian and then started laughing. The larger suit, who was clearly the keeper of the two brain cells and therefore the public speaker of the two, raised his baton pointing it at Christian, "Jeez mate, what are you gonna do, eh? What, you gonna organise my shirts or serve me breakfast or whatever other shit it is you machines do?"

Christian stepped toward the man. "It would be unwise to fight me. I am vastly stronger than both of you and your baton would be useless if used against me."

"Don't be a prick mate." The suit doubled over. "You're a fucking 'robot'. You can't hurt me. You're not allowed. Fuck sake, don't you even know the basics?"

Christian lowered his head and looked at the suits from under his brow, "I also cannot stand by and watch you harm my friends. I will not let it happen."

"Yeah but that's the shit of it, isn't it mate? You can't stand to watch me hurt them but then you can't hurt me either, can you? It's against your basic programming. You tosser! Go on, fuck off out the way!" He was laughing now hard enough that it made him wheeze. Realising that this would make him vulnerable, should Jed or Les lunge forward, he stopped himself from laughing and stood upright.

Christian shook his head, "You are wrong. You *would* be unwise to attempt to hurt anyone and I will also have to insist that you tell me how we can go about reversing the effects of the drug that you have been administering to my colleague Kevin.

"Go on, fuck off Pinnochio. You're no threat to me and you know it. Now piss off out of my way!"

The suit rested his baton against Christian's arm and tapped it to indicate that he wanted him to move out of his path. As he did a lady appeared at the front door. She was grey haired and slightly hunched over. In her blue dressing gown and flowery night-dress she shuffled into the room. Without being able to look up, she said, "Who are all you people? Why are you here? Where's Kevin?"

The suit lowered his baton and slid it into his jacket. "It's alright dear, nothing for you to see here, now just fuck off back to bed."

"Who are all of you people? Where is Kevin? Is he here? I want to speak to him immediately!"

"Listen love, just fuck off back to your apartment and go back to bed...before I put you to sleep permanently." He shared a grimace with the other suit.

Christian turned to the lady, "Madam we have important business here. Please return to your apartment immediately."

With that, the old lady smacked Christian on the side of the arm with the back of her hand as she hit out blindly, unable to stand straight. "How dare you speak to me that way young man, how dare you..."

Before the old lady could finish her sentence one of the suits scrunched his face tight and snarled as he reached forward and lifted the grey wig from Katie's head. Katie recoiled with pain as the wigs' hair pins tugged and ripped at her hair.

"You fucker!" She yelled at the suit as he stood, admiring his revelation of the deception. Katie instinctively swiped the back of her hand across the suits' jaw and then she rolled hard against the floor as the suit hit her hard in the chest with his baton. The suit stepped forwards then raised his baton to strike her again but, as he did, Christian locked onto the baton and grabbed it in an instant. The suit held onto the baton, trying to pull it from Christians' grip but without success. Christian remained motionless and expressionless for a few moments and then stoicly, mechanically turned his head so that it was in line with the baton. He then lowered his head and stared at it as if he was not sure what it was for a moment. Muscles, that were barely tensed, relaxed in his face and his eyes glazed over. Christian then opened his mouth and in a synthetic, almost female voice stated, "Incoming message. Incoming message."

The suit let loose the baton and took a defensive step backwards. Les and Jed looked at each other, then at Christian and then at the suits, who also were now staring at them.

Les stepped forward to help Katie who was now on the floor winded. Jed turned and punched the now batonless suit in the stomach. Jed then turned to Christian, beckoning him with his hand, "Well come on then Chris, snap out of it mate, let's have 'em!"

Christian did not react and merely stood motionless for a moment longer then synthetically stated, "Resetting. Recalibrating battle protocols. Tactical mode, engaged"

Hearing this, the suits then both stood upright and took another step backwards. This in turn made Jed, who was mid-punch, also stop and step backwards as the panicked look on the suits' faces instinctively concerned him more than the suits themselves.

He turned to Christian, who was now looking at each of them in turn muttering, "Target, acquired...Target, acquired..."

The suits then bounced against each other and fought each other off as each of them tried desperately to leave the apartment before Christian's tactical mode was fully initiated.

Les Grabbed at the leg of one of them as he ran past him and, as the suit fell, Les pulled himself along and now had the suit in a head lock. The suit squirmed and wriggled to get free, lashing out with his free elbows and fists. The other suit turned to help him but, as he did, saw Christian turn to Jed, he grabbed Jed by the arm and with the slightest of twists broke it with a loud splintering crack. Christian then reached into a pocket in the leg of his trousers and pulled out a long bladed knife. Jeds' groans now stopped for a moment. "No, Christian, please no!" The suit that had exited the room lunged forward to help his colleague, thought better of it, and in the same movement pivoted and ran towards the emergency exit.

The suit that was on the floor now hit out desperately but Les was more agile and able to dodge the attacks. The suit then lifted his head and, as he did, saw Jed crumpling to the floor covered in blood. Christian then turned to Les, "Target confirmed."

"IT'S IN MY POCKET, IT'S IN MY POCKET!" Screamed the suit and he snatched a tablet from his jacket. As Les took the tablet he released the suit who then slid away, as if doing a land-based back stroke and he turned to skid out of the door. Behind him the screams from Les now spilled out of the apartment as the suit then burst through the emergency exit and launched himself down the first of many flights of stairs.

Jed stood again and as he did he arched his back and yelped as he straightened it. "Oi Christian, you fucker!"

Christian, who stood over Les, knife in hand, now looked at Jed sheepishly. "Sorry mate."

Jed lowered his arm and pulled open his suit sleeve to allow the splinters of broken stick to fall to the floor. "Oh mate you've ruined this shirt."

Christian stood away from Les who now sat up, "Sorry."

Jed shook a smiling head at Christian, "That's okay mate, I probably packed too much blood anyway. Oh and Chris, please change that voice back, will you? It's very off putting."

With the short eye-glazed changing of a few settings, Christians' voice returned. "Oops." He muttered as he shrugged and smiled at Jed.

Les now kneeled over Katie to check she was okay. He pulled open her dressing gown and then motioned to check her vitals. As he did so he felt his testicles suddenly tighten. "Les, if you dare touch my tit's I'm telling you now, I'm ripping these off." As she said it, Katie, with eyes still closed, tightened her grip on his testicles.

"But I'm just checking you're alright is all."

Katie opened her eyes. "You know I'm alright...so why are you holding your hands above my tits?"

Les shrugged. Katie tightened her grip slightly then glanced down at his crotch, "Nice package Les." She said.

"Thank...you...." he responded softly and then fell sideways as she loosened her grip on him.

Katie sat up and looked down at Les, "Les, how many times have I got to put you on your arse, eh?"

Les acknowledged this enquiry silently with a lifted hand.

Christian was now standing over Les holding out a hand to assist him up. "You are an odd guy Les." He smiled.

Les smiled, as much as he could, as he stood up, "Me? I'm odd? You're the one who just stabbed Jed, kind of."

Christian looked at Katie standing up and adjusting her night-dress, then looked at Les. "Les I'm weird? You're the one wearing lingerie."

Les paused, smiled. "Yeah, okay, touché I guess."

"Sorry guys." said Katie as she rested her hand on her stomach.

Jed smiled at her, "Don't worry Katie, plan A may not have worked but Christian's back up seemed to work pretty well."

"A little *too* well." said Les. "I was beginning to get genuinely worried." He smiled and shook off his concerns.

Jed looked over at Christian. Christian had taken the tablet from Les and was now sitting on a desk by the wall scanning through it. He punched in a few commands and then wirelessly linked himself to the device.

"Well, what can you see?" Jed sat on the desk looking down at the tablet.

Christian sat quietly for a moment. His eyes were glazed as if a million miles away. "Okay, well this is where it becomes more fun."

Jed screwed up his face, "Oh, okay, great."

"There *is* an antidote for this drug."

"But?"

"But it's in the company's headquarters in Shoreditch."

"Oh shit. Can we not get it anywhere else?"

Christian shook his head. "Not that I can see." He stared straight at Jed, "The other thing to consider is that as soon as the company discovers that their agents have failed and that their tablet is missing, they will very likely move, or destroy, the antidote."

Jed's shoulders slumped forward. "Oh bollocks. Really?" He rubbed his chin. "So how do we know that this isn't a trap? How do we know that this tablet hasn't been planted for us to get caught in their headquarters?"

Christian stood from the chair, "Unlikely. There is other incriminating evidence on this tablet that I would be surprised to learn they would let go voluntarily. I would suggest that the best course of action is to get into their headquarters and we are going to have to do that fairly soon.

Katie stood behind Jed and placed her hand on his shoulder. He then placed his hand over hers. He turned and smiled at her, she smiled back at him. In that smile was everything that he needed to remind him why they were there. Why they were taking these risks. Katie's smile was all the pleading he needed to convince him to continue on their course. Les stood from behind Jed and was rubbing his testicles. Jed saw this, lowered his head into his hands and started laughing. Katie joined in and soon all four of them were laughing at the absurdity of the whole scene.

<u>3</u>

Coloured light from neon signs ricocheted off the appliance as it sped through the dark London streets. As it moved along leaves appeared, lit by the flashing appliance lights, spun and wound themselves around the back of the appliance before disappearing off again into the night.

An automatic fire alarm had actuated at a nearby building, confirmed by a follow up "Smoke issuing" call to Brigade Control. The appliance's satellite plans showed that the building was an office block secured in its' own compound just off of Shoreditch High Road and that black smoke *was* coming from part of the building.

As the appliance arrived at the barriered compound, security stopped it and asked to be allowed on board. The Officer in charge of the appliance questioned this but was informed that without allowing an inspection of the personnel on board, they would not be allowed to enter. The Officer relented and agreed a quick inspection of the appliance. A large security guard then entered the rear of the appliance and visually checked the faces of each of the occupants. The Officer turned from the front of the cab, "Mate, you called *us*, okay? Now we've got a job to do so you can either let us in or you can delay us and we'll just have to call the Police. Which is it to be?" The security guard grunted, dismounted the appliance and waved them into the compound's yard. Two Firefighters dismounted the appliance and opened one of the large rear lockers to be able to remove gear needed to fight the reported fire. Before they could remove any equipment another security guard appeared from within the building waving at the Officer in charge. Both Firefighters then walked round from behind the appliance to listen to the guard who was now speaking to the Officer. The Officer turned, waved the Firefighters back into the appliance and having returned to the rear of the appliance to close the locker, they then mounted the appliance. The driver turned off the appliance's blue lights, the engine wound up, the appliance lifted, spun and then left as the barrier dropped behind them. The Officer waved and nodded to the security guard as the appliance hovered out towards the main conduit.

The security guard waved back, turned to a second guard, "So what was it? False alarm?"

"No it was a legitimate call. One of the generators in the basement has burnt out. It was smoking a bit but it hasn't caught light to anything."

Both guards then looked one more time to confirm that the appliance was still heading away and then returned to their respective posts.

After confirming that both guards were out of sight, a basement window in a dark alcove of the yard slowly, quietly closed.

Inside the pitch black basement, stood Christian, Jed and Les. All three of the men wore fire hoods to cover their faces and they were also dressed in dark clothing. Christian had changed his view to night vision so could see clearly around the room.

Jed and Les turned on small torches to be able to scan the room and orientate themselves. "So where abouts' is this generator you overheated then?"

Christian turned and whispered, "It's on the other side of the building and on another level of the basement so do not worry. Besides I am patched into their security system. There is no-one in this section of the building at present."

Jed shook his head as he quietly followed Christian, "Never mind Fire Brigade mate. Burgling's where *your* future lies."

Without looking back Christian said, "I'm not sure I can agree with the ethics of that idea Jed."

Jed raised his eyes, shook his head in the dark and smiled at Les.

Guided by Christian, they eventually made their way down to the lowest basement floor of the building, avoiding security cameras and guards as they moved. Eventually they entered the lower basement which housed a huge gleaming white laboratory with a wide variety of high tech equipment which none of them recognised. Also visible were several items that looked like they were perhaps prototype weapons or scanning devices of some description. Along one of the walls were also lined five different suits that looked like either space suits or diving suits each of different styles from a gleaming white plain suit to a steam punk styled brass and copper covered suit.

Jed and Les worked their way along the benches picking up items and inspecting them, imagining what they might be used for. Christian had walked to the far end of the basement and was decrypting a lock on a security store. After a short time, a clunk could be heard from within the store then a whirring of a motor as a large heavy door slowly swung open. Within the store room were cold storage units, caged stores, a safe and two computer terminals.

Before stepping into the store, Christian pushed the door closed without locking it and, as he did so turned, said, "Someone is coming." He then hid behind a large device that stood by the store.

Both Jed and Les looked at each other and then to Christian as he disappeared. Jed could see that there was a recess below one of the benches that would be out of line of sight of the door so he quickly snuck into it. Les stood for a moment quickly pivoting on the spot in search of a potential hiding place to secret himself. He saw a desk over to one side of the room, leaned towards it then, before he could move from his pivot point, dismissed it for being too small. Again he spotted another potential hiding place in the corner but could see that it was inappropriate for him to fully conceal himself behind. Turning a couple more times on the spot, both hands outstretched pleading into thin air for a place of safety, he eventually stood still having noticed Jed standing next to him. "Quick!" said Les, "Find somewhere to hide!"

From behind him, Les could sense Christian now standing close to him. "They've gone Les."

"Oh crap," He said, "Really?" Les continued to plead for sanctuary for a few moments longer. He then lowered his hands slightly, looked at Christian, "Oh, sorry did you say...*gone*?" Les dropped both his arms to his side. "Oh."

Jed slapped one hand onto Les' shoulder. "Good going Les. Stealth like. Batman couldn't have done better!"

Les raised both of his hands up in surrender, "What?"

"Well let's face it Les, they had no chance of finding you, did they? Not if you're not hiding, eh? Remind me again Les, why was it your application got turned down for joining the order of the Ninjas."

"Okay. Fuck off Jed."

Christian raised his eyes and shrugged a subtle shrug as he turned and reopened the security store.

All three men now stepped into it. Jed stood by the door, instinctively, to guard their exit. Les watched over Christian as he searched through the stores.

"Well, according to their internal security system, the antidote *should* be in one of these caged stores." Christian twisted off the padlocks from the two stores, opened one of them and stepped in. Inside the store was a large fridge. Inside the fridge, Christian found, amongst other things, several vials. Though he did not recognise the name on the labels, it was clear from the wording on them that it was very likely the QI neutralising agent. Christian took the vials, placed them into a box, he had grabbed from elsewhere in the store and emptied, and then placed it in his top pocket.

He slowly began to close the store as all three of them stepped out into the main lab again.

"Oh dear, three men are coming this way…at speed."

Les snapped his head round to look at Christian, "What? How come?"

"It must be a silent alarm. It's not showing up on their main system but they *are* heading this way and they appear to be armed I'm afraid."

Les looked at Jed, "Oh shit, this complicates things. To be honest mate, I'm more of a lover than a fighter."

Jed rolled his eyes, "Well if you think *that* will slow them down then go for it mate. I'd probably go with fighting them though instead."

Les thought for a moment and then chuckled to himself.

Jed, who had been looking around the room for an alternative exit or some form of weapon, turned to speak to Les again but, as he did, he noticed extinguishers hanging against the far wall. He hit Les on the side of the arm as he ran to them to inspect them.

Les squinted as he followed him, "Can't you stop being a Firefighter for one minute? You're off duty, who cares if they need inspecting or not?"

Jed grabbed one of the extinguishers from the wall and Les followed suit. They then stood back beside Christian. The far door then opened and in burst three guards.

The three men walked towards them in a triangle, two at the front and one at the rear. The one at the rear was holding, what looked like, some form of gun shaped weapon. It was not a conventional gun but, until they knew otherwise, all three of the Firefighters knew to treat it as a serious threat.

The rear guard looked at Jed, then to Les, and then Christian. Though all three had their faces covered the guard could still tell by Christian's more confident posture that he was clearly either in charge or in possession of whatever had been stolen. "You," he said, "I want whatever you've taken and I want it now!" He held up his hand, pointing at Christian.

Christian, without moving his head, looked down to see the two extinguishers Jed and Les were carrying, concealed a smile and then carefully reached into his pocket and removed the box. He then held it out in offer to the guard. The guard then looked at both the other guards, signalled with a nod and they both moved towards Christian to retrieve the item.

As the guards approached Christian, Jed and Les suddenly produced the extinguishers they had been concealing behind themselves and opened them fully in the faces of the guards. Both stunned guards fell backwards as clouds of white vapour filled the air around them. Concealed by the cloud, Christian immediately shot forwards, dropped and in one fluid movement slid along the floor kicking the legs away from under the armed guard and then knocking him unconscious with his free hand before he could hit the floor.

Both of the other two guards lay gasping for air and shivering with cold from the contents of the extinguishers. Jed and Les both picked up the guards and pulled them through the quickly dissipating clouds of cold white Carbon dioxide. They then secured both of the guards in the safe store as Christian slid the third guard in behind them. Before closing the store, Christian quickly rolled the guard into the recovery position so as not to risk any further unnecessary injury to him.

Christian placed his hand on Jed's shoulder. "That was quick thinking Jed. Using the extinguishers to overcome the guards and to conceal my attack was impressive thinking."

Jed looked back at Christian blankly. "Eh?"

"The extinguishers? Your use of them to…" Christian could see that Jed had clearly not thought the plan all the way through and had just acted instinctively. "You didn't know I was going to do that then?"

Jed looked at Les, shrugged, looked back at Christian, "I didn't even know you *could* do that."

Christian shrugged, rubbed his chin and said pensively, "Actually, to be fair, I didn't know I could do that either."

Still connected to the main security system, Christian guided both Jed and Les to the upper basement window where they first entered the building. Before exiting the building, Jed raised the window open slightly to confirm that the coast was clear. As he did, Christian pulled him away from the window. "Oh dear. There are three black pods about to enter the main yard."

Jed ducked down below the window then slowly raised himself back up to look out of it from the side. "Shit. What now?"

"Well we have clearly triggered something but it is not showing on the main security system at all. That means that either these vials, or something else in that basement, is secret enough to keep from even those who work here." Christian rubbed his cheek with the back of his hand, "We *must* find another way out."

Immediately, all three Firefighters made their way up the building towards the roof. The building was four floors high from ground level so if there was no way off the building they knew that they would be in serious trouble but they also knew that exiting via the main yard would be impossible.

The door to the roof level was locked. With one swift kick, Christian persuaded the door to open as it shattered into several splintered pieces. They then all ran out of the stair well and onto the roof. The roof was surrounded by a low wall and the nearest part of the nearest building was approximately five metres away. Jed leaned over the wall, calculating what it would take to cross the gap. He turned to face Les and Christian. "Shit that's too far, it's just too far." He was shouting to overcome the noise from the building's venting system. "Shit! It's about five metres away."

Les joined Jed and looked over the side. "Oh crap. Five metres away and one floor up. We're screwed. We'll just have to hide up here, hope they…"

Before Les could finish his sentence, guards and black suits spilled out of the damaged doorway at the other end of the roof. As the black suits appeared, they stopped almost immediately, knowing there was nowhere for the three men to escape except through them. A grey suit stepped forward and signalled for everyone to secure the exit.

Christian, who had remained silent, continued to look at the next building, then to Jed, then the building then to Les.

Jed turned to Christian, "Mate, this would be a good time to show us how your built in jetpack works. No? Don't have one? Well okay, I knew it was a long shot."

Christian ignored him and continued to survey his surroundings.

The grey suit approached slightly nearer, ready to talk to them. Christian turned to the suit, smiled then turned to Jed, removed the box from his own top pocket and placed it in Jed's jacket pocket. He then grabbed Jed's jacket and launched him across the gap to the nearby building. Jed shot upwards across the gap to the nearby building, slowing just as he disappeared over the next building's roof wall. Christian turned to Les, who looked suddenly shocked and had recoiled instinctively. Christian lunged forward, grabbed Les and then launched him toward Jed. Les performed a bad impression of a rocket as he took off with a "Fu-u-u-u-u-u-u-u..." Jed was sitting up ready to look over the wall of the next building to see what was happening as Les appeared over the wall and landed softly beside him. They had both landed safely, having been thrown by Christian with the correct force and at the right trajectory to allow them to land on the peak of the arc of their journey so as to minimise speed and impact. Les sat up, turned to Jed and they both paused, stunned, then both clambered to their feet half laughing and lunged forward to grab the wall in order to look over it to check that Christian was still okay.

As they looked down on the company building, four guards lay already incapacitated on the roof. The grey suit had backed off and Christian was now launching a fifth guard toward the waiting black suits. As the black suits tumbled over one another, as they fell backwards towards the roof exit, Christian turned to the grey suit. He stood and lowered his head and then, slowly raising it for effect as he breathed deeper between clenched teeth, he addressed the suit. "If you ever come after my friends again, I will kill you. I will kill your families. I will kill your pets and then I will cook them and I will fucking eat them!"

Jed and Les both glanced at each other, "Fuck!" as they looked down on this scene that would have been more at home in an action packed Holo-Movie. Jed stood ready to leave, "Is that?...Was that?...Did you hear his voice? He fucking meant that! He sounded fucking nasty!"

"I know. That didn't even sound like him. Thank fuck he's on *our* side!" Les grabbed Jed and they both ran stumbling toward the exit to escape from the roof. The roof they had landed on was above a womens' underwear manufacturers' warehouse so the security was minimal. They made their way quickly down to ground floor level and, as they ran through reception towards the final exit, Les stopped in his tracks. Hearing Les stop, Jed skidded to a halt. He turned, saw Les looking around the reception display mouth opened, he grabbed Les and pulled him towards the exit. "I know mate, I know. Not now though, eh? Another time, okay mate?"

Les' jaw had dropped and was almost dragging along the floor as Jed pulled him away from the display. "But..."

"Yes I know mate, look at all the shiny-shiny, but please let's just go!"

As both Firefighters bolted from the building, they could hear glass breaking from somewhere above and behind them. Continuing to run

from the scene, they both turned to see where the glass had broken. The glass had fallen from the second floor of the company building as a window smashed open. Through the hail of glass came Christian who appeared almost cat like as he flew feet and hands first. He then landed on the ground with a satisfyingly loud thud. He stood, brushed himself off, turned to look up to where he had jumped from, smiled and calmly followed Jed and Les. "No need to run." he said. Both Jed and Les stopped and turned to see the height that Christian had jumped from. Jed raised a finger as if asking permission to ask a question and then opened his mouth to speak but, before any words came out, Christian stopped as he walked past them looked at Jed and calmly said, "I don't want to talk about it."
All three of them removed their masks then silently walked some distance before all of them wordlessly agreed to enter an all-night pub to collect their thoughts.

4

Jed's egg shaped pod slowed as it pulled up into the driveway and stopped above the conduit. It lowered itself onto the drive as its' engine wound ever slower until it too stopped. The seal securing the front of the car hissed and, with a slight whirring, the front of it opened fully. Christian stepped from the vehicle followed by a yawning and slightly stumbling Les. Jed leaned forward and, in one movement, stood upright and stepped from the car. He stopped by the front of it. He input some commands into the centre console on the front section and then stepped aside as the interior lights dimmed, the front section closed and then hissed as the doors' seals were sucked into place re-securing the vehicle.
All three men then walked over to the front door of the house. Les leaned forward, swiped his hand across a lit panel and straightened himself as he shook his head of tired thoughts.
Jed rocked gently from foot to foot as the cold of the early morning seeped into him. He turned his head to look behind to check that there were no signs that they had been followed but he could see no glimpses of pod movements, no lights. There was no noise of people walking along. He raised his hands up to blow into them to keep them warm and turned back to look at the door ready for it to open.
The front door then slid open and in the dim light of the front porch stood a "Hideous looking ogre-ous monster."

Katie stood bug-eyed as she folded her arms, "Les, I'm sorry, what did you call me?"

Les shuffled and looked down at his feet, "Well…you know, I'm just saying."

As all three of the men stepped in Katie looked outside along the road and then closed the front door with a swipe of her hand. "Look, I was worried, okay? So I'm pampering myself to take my mind off it. I've done my nails, dyed my hair and now I'm having a face mask."

Les turned as he continued to where he guessed the lounge would be, "Oh good, so it does come off then?"

"Oh sod off you great oaf! This is very expensive I'll have you know. It's called Sun blushed Ochre."

"Ogre? See I told you didn't I?"

"No…ochre. Ochre! Besides, since when were ogres orange? Ogres are green, everybody knows that."

"Really? You've got a picture of one to prove that then?"

Katie gave Les the "I'm tired, fuck off." look, turned towards the kitchen, "I do look a bit better than this when I'm properly made up you know."

Les replied in a soft mono-toned absent voice, "So do I."

Katie turned, "Sorry Les?"

Realising what he had said, Les straightened himself up, coughed, "Oh, er nothing." Cough, cough, "Sorry, nothing."

Katie almost undetectably raised an eye brow and smiled a wry smile, "I'll make some drinks. Who's for tea?"

Jed turned to Katie, "We've just come from the pub and we've had a pretty full on night. Sorry to impose Kate but I don't suppose you have anything a little stronger do you?" Jed pulled his head to one side wearing a polite, pleading smile. "Whisky?"

"Puppy dog eyes only work with me Jed if there's a puppy behind them." Katie smiled back then changed her course from the kitchen and followed them into the lounge. "Take a seat guys." Katie's lounge was very retro-traditional with a mock open fire place, *actual* wooden furniture and a deep red carpet. Jed and Les sat together on the sofa as Christian sat in one of the two big cosy armchairs. All three of them continued sitting for a moment, briefly enjoying the comfort and security of Katie's home. Jed sat forward onto the edge of the sofa reaching out to take the drink offered him by Katie. As he did, he bent over to run his fingers through the carpet with his free hand. "Thanks mate."

"You're welcome." She said, "I'm afraid it's Bourbon, I don't have any whisky in at the moment."

He nodded, smiled and then took a hearty swig of warm back-of-the-throat-kicking Bourbon. He closed his eyes for a moment as the liquid sat in his mouth, he breathed in to gather up what was left of its' smell before it drifted off away from him. He gulped it down and then he finished off by breathing the warmth into his lungs through his teeth then his whole body micro-shuddered. He opened his eyes. "M-m-m. Thanks Kate. That's good shit."

Katie turned the bottle of Jack Daniel's in her hand to look at the label and smiled back at him. "This stuff isn't cheap you know, but that's okay. I'm sure you've all earned it." Without prompting, she topped him up.

"So how's the house guest?" Jed asked as he looked around as if to see which direction Kevin was sleeping in.

"He's fine. I stuck to the story we agreed and he accepted it." Katie smiled a comforting smile toward the lounge door, paused and then adopted her Motherly voice, "So, any-way, which of my brave little soldiers wants to report on this evenings' events then, eh? How did it all go?" She smiled again at Jed.

Jed nodded and calmly said, "Good. Yeah. It all went well." Jed looked over to Christian, "Thanks to 'Ironman' over there."

Over the next hour they recounted to Katie how they had broken into the company headquarters by Christian accessing the generator software and overrunning it to burn it out to then allow access for an appliance to enter the site. They described how they had defended themselves against the guards by Jed and Les using Carbon Dioxide extinguishers and Christian going into kick-arse mode to which Katie sat, grinning and nodding, impressed. Jed then handed over to Christian to be able to finish off describing how he had launched Jed and Les across to the next building and then, with much prompting, continued to detail how he had managed to subdue so many guards in such a short space of time. Christian insisted that he had not seriously hurt any of the guards but confirmed that they would all be nursing soft tissue damage and bruising for some time to come.

Katie sat slack-jawed as she listened intently to Christian's heroics. After the retelling, she sat in silence for a few minutes, allowing the information to fully settle in her mind.

Eventually Katie cleared her throat, took another large swig of Bourbon, placed her glass gently down onto the coffee table in front of her and then turned to Christian. "So…you jumped…*two* floors?"

"Well no, technically I *dropped* two floors."

"Okay, dropped two floors then. And then you just calmly walked away. Two floors Chris. That's amazing. Is there anything else you can do that we should know about?"

Christian gazed into space, "I am unsure." He looked at his feet for a moment, "There are things that I seem to be able to do now that somehow I was unaware of, or that perhaps I had forgotten I could do. I am not sure. It seems that I am only able to discover that I can do these things when they become instinctive."

"What do you mean mate?"

"Well, I was unaware that I could fight so efficiently until I needed to and then it was almost like I was remembering how to do it as if I'd…done it before."

"Is it something you're downloading from the Web as and when you need it, you know like in that old film?"

"No, no, it is more…internal than that. It is difficult to explain. Forgive me."

Katie leaned forward and placed her hand on his knee. "You've nothing to apologise for lovely. At the moment, you're one of my top three favourite superheroes."

Christian looked up and returned Katie's smile then looked away again. "There is more though. I believe I *could* have hurt them, *would* have hurt them if I had needed to."

Jed placed his glass down next to Katie's, "What do you mean mate? *Actually* hurt them?"

Christian gently nodded and, without looking back, replied, "Yes. I believe so. Or more."

"Mate, doesn't that go against your basic…ethics or programming or something? I mean, don't get me wrong, I'm glad you're on our side." He smiled a cheesy over the top smile. "But I didn't think you could do that, you know, what with the laws of robotics and all?"

Christian slowly turned to Jed, "I am not sure that they apply to me somehow. When the agents turned up to the station that time and I slid one of them across the bay floor…"

Jed laughed and rocked forward, "M-m-m-m, yeah-h-h, ha-ha, happy times."

"…I felt a great anger towards them. I felt as though I could have inflicted more damage than I did, almost like I had to hold myself back. It concerns me."

Katie took her hand from Christian's knee and began to rub his arm, "But the thing is Chris that you didn't, did you. That's what makes us human. I mean, we all feel like that sometimes, we all have thoughts of fear, or hate, or aggression but it's choosing *when* to act on these feelings that separates us from the beasts…like, well like Les here." She smiled and gestured over towards Les.

Les lowered his eye brows, lowered his head onto his shoulders and pulled a Neanderthal scowl as he grabbed beast like at thin air, "Ur-r-r-g-g-h-h-h!"

Christian smiled. "Thank you guys."

Katie topped up all four glasses and raised her own to toast. A silent toast was had as all four of them chinked glasses together.

After a short silence, Jed took the box from his jacket pocket and placed it carefully on the coffee table in front of him. Katie leaned forward, opened the box and looked at the vials inside. She lifted one of them out and held it at the top and bottom between her finger and thumb. "So this is it is it? I do hope this stuff works." She turned to Christian. "Chris…we've become quite a thorn in the side of this company. Do you think that we're safe, you know, having this antidote here?"

"Katie, what you have in your hands does not exist. I do not believe that the company can afford to be seen with it and by now they would have realised what is missing from their store *and* why we want it. With these facts in mind, I suggest that they would be unwise to force the issue."

Christian put his hand out for her to give the vial to him, which she did. Without hesitation he snapped the top from the vial, smelled the contents and then downed it in one gulp.

Katie put her hands up to stop him but he had drunk it before she could do so. "Christian, no! What are you…doing? My God you don't know what's in that!"

Jed picked up the box with the remaining vials. "Shit Chris, what are you doing?! There could be *anything* in that!"

Christian remained silent.

Katie looked at both Jed and Les then back to Christian, "Chris, you don't know what's in that."

"I do *now*." Christian said with a smack of his lips. "I believe we could reproduce this too if we need to."

Katie's shoulders dropped, "What? Jeez' Christian. What? Are you fucking kidding me?"

Christian shrugged, "What is *wrong*?"

Katie smacked him on the arm, "Are you kidding me? *What is wrong*? Jeez Christian have you just done what I think you've just done?"

"Analysed the contents of the vial? Yes." Christian paused, realising what he had just done and said. "Oh."

"You didn't know you could do that either, did you?"

Christian shook his head then smacked his tongue against the top of his mouth, "Yeu-u-u-rck. That actually tasted quite hideous."

Katie shook her head and chuckled. "Do you think you could mix it with food or something for when we give it to Kevin?" Katie leaned her head to one side.

"No need. I believe it needs to be taken intravenously."

"Jeez mate," began Jed, "Next you'll be telling us you can play tunes out of your arse!"

"I do not believe that I can." Christian smiled.

Les smiled to himself, "*I* can. I can even do requests."

Katie and Jed shared gentle smiles as they both shook their heads. Les, who had now begun to slump backwards into the comfort of the sofa, began to breathe heavier. Within seconds he was asleep and was softly snoring. Jed took the glass from his hand, before he had a chance to drop it, looked into the glass, swigged its' contents and then pushed Les sideways slightly so that he was now resting more comfortably against the corner cushions.

It had been a long and eventful night. All of those still awake were exhausted bar, of course, Christian. Without any further discussion Katie simply dimmed the lights in the lounge, placed her feet up on the coffee table, pulled a throw over across her lap and lay back into the arm chair to fall asleep. She lifted her head again, looked at all of her friends, smiled to herself and mumbled under her breath, "Ah, my boys." Jed piled up some cushions at the other end of the sofa to Les and slumped against them with a comforting "Thlop" as he hit them.

Christian topped up his Bourbon, sat back into his chair, rested both of his arms on the chair's arms and closed his eyes. For the remainder of the evening he rested, silently replaying the days' events in his head, thinking about the new abilities he had either discovered or that he had remembered he'd always had and continued to listen out, just in case the company had managed to follow them. Every so often throughout the night he would pick up a noise from outside or would hear a creek from within the house and each time Christian's eyes would snap open, he would home in on the sound, confirm that it was no threat, he would take another small, well earned sip of Bourbon and then simply close his eyes and continue his self-imposed sentry duties.

CHAPTER TEN

"A grave discovery"

1

"Kevin, pass me that gun will you mate?"
Kevin reached into the appliance locker, unclipped and removed the harmonics gun and handed it to Jed. He then continued to look for an item of equipment he *too* was retrieving for the incident.
Jed then waded back through the debris that lay strewn across two lanes of the rarely traffic-stopped conduit. Ahead of him the pod lay heavily damaged but still, mostly, intact, its' blood soaked top screen section broken but still holding together. Jed looked down at the ground, where there lay the sheet covered mangled remains of a body, as he stepped up alongside the pod. Richie and Katie both stood either side of the pods' top section, each of them holding small emitters in their hands.
"Oh bloody...where is it? Richie, you found yours yet?" Katie continued to pass the emitter along the length of the side of the pod.
"No, I've...oh, hang on, yes, yes that's it." In his hand, Richie's emitter changed from a red glow to a now solid green and a soft toned bleep began to repeat. "Yeah, Kate, it's just in line with the contoured detail...about..." He then stopped describing its' position and came round to the other side of the pod, knowing it would be quicker to show Katie the exact location of the release mechanism rather than to simply describe it. Richie then returned to his original position and ensured his emitter showed green again.
Katie's emitter was now also green and, with a dull clunking sound, the top section of the pod released itself allowing them both to easily lift the lightweight section up and away from the rest of the chassis. They then removed the section and placed it in a debris dump by the side of the conduit that they'd setup on arrival.
The interior of the pod was filled with a gelatinous, but breathable, safety material that had filled the whole interior moments before impact. Jed leaned over the front of the pod and could see the driver resting inside not making contact with any part of the pod where he had been launched forwards by his seat as part of the safety system in order to encase him in the liquid-gel moments before impact. The

driver was now crouched, suspended in a half-formed diving position. From inside the pod could be heard muffles of "Hello? Hello-o-o-o?" Jed leaned nearer the liquid-gel, "Hello Sir? Sir? Hello? Are you okay?"

"Yes I'm fine, I'm...oh Good Lord, how embarrassing...I'm so sorry. My goodness, is she okay?"

Jed smiled, "Don't you worry about all that Sir, let's just concentrate on you for the moment shall we? Alright Sir, nothing to worry about, we'll just have you out in a jiffy."

A medic, that had just arrived at the scene, stepped up beside Jed, "Hello mate."

Jed shook his hand, "Hello mate. You hungry? Look I've made a nice big bowl of jellied man." He smiled and gestured toward the suspended occupant. "Tada!"

The medic shrugged at Jed, "You know, twenty years in the job, I've never seen a pod collision, never once. Well, not in anger anyway, only in training."

"Mate, you know I couldn't even remember where we kept our harmonics gun. Let's hope it still works, eh?" Jed gestured with his head towards the sheet covered body, "Did you, er...take a look at the body?"

"Yeah I did." The medic looked down, shook his head and then shrugged, "There's nothing we can do for that poor cow I'm afraid."

Jed shook his head, "It seems such a waste doesn't it? How was a cow even able to get onto the conduit anyway?"

The medic shrugged, "Meh." and leaned forward, "Hello Sir. London Ambulance Service here. Are you alright in there?"

The occupant muffled a confirmation and then, with effort, made a thumbs-up gesture which he quickly released due to the resistance of the gel.

Jed turned on the harmonics gun which hummed as he did. Along one of its sides a series of lights appeared. This was its' charge reading. Jed confirmed the reading, checked the gun's settings then looked at the medic, "Phew. It works." He chuckled.

"That's lucky, all *yours* then mate." The medic stepped back to allow Jed room to cut the occupant free without hindrance *and* also to avoid getting his shoes wet.

Jed looked over to the medic, "Okay, cheers. So what do you need, just a hand?"

"Yes please mate, just get me any hand or foot. Either will be fine."

Katie and Richie came over from the debris dump and joined the medic to see Jed handle the Harmonics gun, having never seen it used in anger before. Jed fired short bursts of waves into the gel which instantly destabilised and drained away in liquid form. He continued to fire short bursts in order to release enough gel around the driver's hand so as to allow the medic access to scan. Jed sniffed the air and smiled, surprised, as the gel filled his nose with the scent of candy floss. The medic leaned into the car inspecting Jed's handy work. "Blimey that's clever stuff isn't it. How does it work mate, d'you know?"

"No, you know what mate, all this science, I don't understand, it's just my job five days a week." Jed smiled.

"Eh? Oh, really?"

Jed finished his reference with …"I'm a Fire…ma-a-a-a-a-an-n, Fireman." He petered off toward the end, realising the Medic had no idea what or who he was referencing. The Medic shrugged but smiled politely. He then held a scanner over the driver's hand for a moment, took it away and then began to read its' results.

Jed Wiped some liquid-gel off his boots by rubbing them against the side of the pod, "Everything alright then Doc?"

The medic looked for another moment then smiled at Jed, "Yeah, he's alright mate. His back's fine and there are no signs of internal injuries. I see his glucose level is slightly elevated though but I can soon fix that in the ambulance. You can let him out now if you like." He looked at the gel, chuckled, shook his head, turned and walked back to his pod, "Seeya guys. Just point him towards my ambulance when he's out will you?"

Jed waved, "Yep, okay, see you mate, will do." With that, he changed the setting on his gun, aimed it back into the pod and fired two short bursts. He quickly stepped backwards as liquid-gel poured over the sides of the pod almost followed by a sodden, embarrassed and spluttering occupant. The driver pulled himself up from the interior of the pod, assisted by Katie and Jed. He turned to Katie, "Oh my goodness I'm…I'm so embarrassed. I'm not quite sure what happened I was coming home from my chess club listening to some Louis Armstrong, in fact, I think I may have even dozed off for a while. No, no, it wasn't Louis Armstrong, I believe it may have been the Mills Brothers. Yes, yes, that's right, the Mills Brothers. Anyway, the next thing I remember was the seat forcing me forward and then I remember seeing a large old lady, only for a moment mind, and then…I don't know…everything seemed to just go into slow motion or something. In all my years of owning a pod, I've never been involved in an accident. I remember it seeming like it was all in black and white. Oh I…I do hope she's okay."

Jed looked at Katie and whispered, "You wanna tell him or shall I?"

Back in the appliance, Richie and Brownie sat in the front cab chatting about the latest spike ball game on the "Holo-box" while Katie, Kevin and Jed sat in the rear cab.

After the appliance had quietly hummed along the streets for a while, Katie, who had been deep in concentration, turned to Kevin and smiled. "So how're you feeling young Kevin?"

Kevin smiled back, "I'm fine thanks Kate." The appliance turned a corner and warm yellow rays from the sun splashed across Kevin's face. He closed his eyes, smiled, as if feeling the warmth of the sun for the first time. "I don't seem to have had any headaches all day so far, so that's good."

Katie nodded. She knew he had been getting headaches but, at the time, had not known it as being a side effect of the drugs given him by the company. It had only been a few days since they had retrieved the antidote and Kevin had only had two injections since then. Mother had agreed to inform Kevin that he needed to start taking injections as part of a watch wide vaccine program. Believing that everyone was taking part, Kevin agreed and everyone else on the watch had dropped the odd comment or moan here and there about the vaccinations to further solidify the deception. It had been agreed amongst the watch that the risks of telling Kevin about what had happened to him and how he had been used as a guinea pig by the company outweighed the benefits so, though some still felt uncomfortable continuing to keep Kevin in the dark, all agreed to do everything to keep this information from him, for now at least.

Katie sat back and watched Kevin for a few minutes as he bathed in the warm rays, his eyes still closed. He slowly began to rock his head left and right as if remembering the words of a song or simply bobbing along on water. Katie loosened her smile as the sadness of recent events slowly poured over her. She could not remember the last time that Kevin smiled so easily, so peacefully. She looked away and out of the appliance into the beautiful watercolour sky, eyes closed, and allowed *herself* a moment of peace as waves of the Sun's rays again lapped up against the side of the cruising appliance.

Christian had explained to the watch that he was unsure of how effective the antidote might be, there being no official evidence to back up its' use. He believed though, from what he *had* researched, that Kevin would likely make an initial healthy recovery but that this might be short lived causing a relapse as the full impact of the drugs' effects took some months to be fully removed from his system. He would hopefully then make a fuller more permanent recovery.

After a few minutes, Kevin's eyes screwed tight, he furrowed his brow and then his eyes popped open, his face full of giddy concern, "Richie!"

Richie's head appeared from the front cab of the appliance. "Er, yes mate, what is it?"

"So if Shrodinger's cat is actually *in* the box then its' assumed that *we're* the observers right?"

"Er…sorry? Oh yeah…yeah." Richie's suddenly peeked interest could be seen in his growing smile.

"But how do we know that the *cat* isn't the observer and that when the box closes *we* stop existing?"

Richie smiled a shrug across to Kevin, "You know, I think you've got me there young Kevin." Katie and Jed smiled at each other. Richie straightened himself and sat back in his chair, shared a smile with Brownie and continued his conversation with him.

2

The appliance hovered along to the end of the bay, its' softly rumbling engine wound down and it lowered itself onto the floor ready for redeployment. Katie, Kevin and Jed stepped out of the appliance. Brownie and Richie stepped into the rear cab then, following the others, also dismounted. Across the other end of the appliance bay, the door to the mess hall opened. Through the bay then marched the Fire Brigade's Chief Officer 'entouraged' by two grey suits, two black suits and the Chief Officers' Staff Officer. All of the Firefighters had obediently stood to attention and discreetly watched as all of the suits and Officers marched past without word and stepped into a large black company limousine. The Firefighters then shared a collective "Oops." Amongst themselves and then all stood to ease and looked on awaiting the departure of the pod. Before its' departure the pods' door then reopened and out stepped the Chief Officer's Staff Officer who marched up to the on-looking Firefighters and motioned to speak but was interrupted before he could by Mother who had appeared at the mess room door. Mother marched towards the Firefighters, stopped, pointed a fist then barked, "JED! KATIE! GO AND FIND CHRISTIAN AND LES AND GET IN MY BLOODY OFFICE IMMEDIATELY!"

The Staff officer's sour face almost cracked as a self-awarded sly half smile appeared at one side of his scrawny Disney-villain face. He snorted a chuckle. Outside the bay, the impressively sized limousine's engines wound themselves up. The limousine lifted and then hovered out of the yard at speed.

Katie and Jed quickly located the other two Firefighters and headed towards Mothers' office. They knocked at the door and it slid open. Jed went to step in first but was halted by the exiting Staff Officer. The Officer turned, looked directly at Mother, "I shall be right outside Station Officer Riley". He then stepped outside and stood to attention. Jed and the other three stepped into the office to the tune of, "GET YOUR ARSES IN HERE, RIGHT NOW!"

Katie almost stepped backwards, thrown by Mothers' harshness. She had never before heard him speak in such a militaristic, castigating tone. The office door slid shut. The Staff Officer smiled to himself, straightened his tie and rocked slightly forward onto his toes, pleased with himself.

Inside the office Mother pointed to the chairs in front of his desk and then pointed into them to order all to sit. "I'VE NEVER BEEN SO LET DOWN IN ALL MY LIFE!" he yelled as he walked round his desk to sit in his own chair. As he did so, Katie's eyes narrowed as she caught the wry smile on the face of his shaking head.

He leaned forward onto his elbows, closed his eyes and then placed his arms down straight onto the desk. He stretched his fingers wide onto the table top as if about to play his Magnus Opus. "Well bugger me…sideways guys."

All four Firefighters looked at each other puzzled.

Jed went to speak, thought better of it, but then, against his better judgement, "Guv, er, you alright?"

Mother sat up, rubbed his eyes, "THAT'S ENOUGH OUT OF YOU EDWARDS!" he said as he looked to the office door. He looked back at Jed, who had recoiled slightly into his chair, "Oh wow, I have just been…" he sighed, shook his head then smiled at all four of his colleagues. "Well let's just say that your shenanigans have certainly caught the attention of the top brass."

Jed looked at the others, all now beginning to realise that they were perhaps not being reprimanded quite in the way that they were being led to believe. "Er, what d'you mean Guv?"

"Well let's just say that, after the kicking I've just been given, I probably won't be sitting down properly for a week." He chuckled and shook his head.

Katie lowered a concerned face, cleared her throat, "So, are you in a lot of trouble then Guv?"

Mother dropped his head onto his shoulders, "Well...let's just say that the promotion trail is probably a path I'll not be treading any time soon." He looked off into the distance for a moment, "That said, I don't think I've got the amount of suck that's needed to get promoted in this Brigade to be honest anyway." He rolled his eyes, said "I WON'T STAND FOR IT!" then slammed his fist onto the desk. He looked through the wall to where he thought the Staff Officer would be standing, shook his head, mouthed the word, "cock." and turned to Jed, smiled, "Okay, so let's start at the beginning then shall we mate?"

Over the next twenty minutes Jed, Katie, Les and Christian all contributed to the recounting of the events that had occurred during the visit to the company headquarters and then afterwards at Katie's house. This recounting was punctuated at times by Mother's "THAT'S NO EXCUSE!", "NOT ACCEPTABLE!" and even "I'LL TELL YOU WHERE YOU CAN STICK THAT CUCUMBER SHALL I?!" which Mother himself shrugged off as being completely out of context and which also had to be contained as the room almost erupted into fits of giggles.

"Well..." Mother swung round on his chair, "Well it all sounds like quite the adventure." He smiled an appreciative and almost envious smile, "Well done guys. I'm...proud of you. But listen, and I'm being serious, you need to keep your heads down a little okay? Try to fly under the radar for a bit. This company obviously isn't happy about what's happened." He looked at Christian, "With respect young Chris, you represent a huge investment on their part. They're not happy to have taken such a financial hit. Watch your back." Mother nodded to Christian. Christian returned the nod and smiled as he stood to leave. "That said, from what you've said so far, it seems quite clear that the company are probably also thinking of flying under the radar for a bit. You've clearly taken things of theirs that could get them into some serious trouble. But again, watch yourselves." Mother smiled, "NOW GET OUT OF MY OFFICE ALL OF YOU!"

The Firefighters all stood to leave, respectfully nodded to Mother, turned and stood in single file to march out of the room. As each stepped out past the Staff Officer, they were greeted with a grimacing vulturous sneer. Christian, who had been at the back of the line, paused for a moment. "Staff Officer Cane, isn't it Sir?"

Cane leaned forwards, contrary to his body's wishes to cower away knowing what Christian was physically capable of. "Yes Mr Mann that is correct, but you can of course call me Sir."

Christian glazed over for a moment and instantly in front of him every piece of digital information relating to Cane appeared, food bills, utility providers, shopping habits, dates of births, friends, family, even his blood type. Christian was now looking at Cane's wife's bank details. He immediately identified a formed pattern that clearly indicated that his wife had been sifting money away from him. He could also link this to her personal emails that showed he was clearly a selfish, self-absorbed, anal man. She had set up hidden accounts and trust funds and was clearly planning to leave him as soon as he retired. His personnel records confirmed that this was only six weeks away. There was not another man in Mrs Cane's life that Christian could find, just a need for freedom. Christian had no desire to take this moment of satisfaction from her and deny her the chance of a clean getaway. He simply smiled at Cane then snapped a motioning of his body towards him that he turned into a faked coughing gesture. In that instant, afraid, Cane had let go of the tablet he had been carrying and was now comically fumbling to catch it. Christian's hand precisely targeted the tablet and he grabbed it. He then held it out for Cane to take from him. As he handed the tablet back to Cane, he held onto it for a moment before releasing it to him and, as he did, he looked down at Canes trousers where a small wet patch had appeared around his crotch. The tablet was not the only thing he had let go of. Christian again said nothing but simply turned his eyes back up at Cane, paused, let go of the tablet and marched away.

Cane waited until Christian was out of sight, dabbed the side of his temple with the back of his hand then looked down at the wet patch on his trousers. His whole body deflated slightly, he shook his head and then left the building without further speaking to Mother.

<u>3</u>

Katie, Jed and Kevin stood at the bar as they waited to be served their round of drinks. Above the bar was suspended a huge animated sign of the club's name, '*Audiotorian.*' Jed looked up as one of the pipes on the sign gave birth to a cloud of cosmetic steam. He watched for a moment as the brass and copper coloured cogs and articulated joints of the sign all slowly moved against their leather and wooden backdrop. He dropped his weight onto his elbows, which were now resting on the bar, and turned to Katie, "So how long did you say you've been coming here then?"

Katie who was standing at the bar with her payment card raised turned to Jed, "I used to come here when I was younger. I've not been here for a while though. It's good isn't it?" She looked around the club and smiled, remembering previous good nights out and thinking about how much the club had changed since its' earlier days.

"So, steam punk wasn't an actual era...*was* it?" Jed slurred having arrived at the club some time before the rest of the watch and having drunk a little too much, a little too quickly.

"No...no it wasn't. More's the pity. Would that it were." Katie smiled at the barman who now stood before her. The barman, a top hatted young man in a long brown leather look jacket, knee high buckled boots and wearing chunky brass goggles, smiled at Katie. A handsome man who's smile was both genuine and welcoming. Katie paused for an instant to enjoy this image before her then, fumbling slightly over her words, ordered drinks for herself, Jed and Kevin. The barman smiled another broad sparkling white smile back at Katie as he confirmed the order, tipped his hat to her and then turned and walked along the bar to prepare the drinks. Katie leaned slightly over the bar as if looking at something behind it then turned for a moment, looked at the barman, raised an eyebrow and one side of a smile then straightened up, 'hmmm', she thought.

Jed, who had noticed her subtle manoeuvre out of the corner of his eye, turned to Katie then to the barman then back to Katie, "Aye, aye!" He smiled. "I see. Like that is it? Come here for the steam punks then do you or is it the eye candy? Eh?"

Katie blushed slightly and pulled her mouth to one side, "Why Sir I don't know what you mean." She said with a cheeky, slightly embarrassed grin.

The barman returned with the drinks. Katie smiled at him, swiped her card over a small screen worn on his leather wrist cuff and quietly asked, "Would you like to have one for yourself?"

The barman smiled, "That's very kind of you Miss."

Katie again swiped her card over his wrist, he smiled, doffed his hat and then walked away to continue serving. She turned to Kevin and Jed, "Ha, you hear that? Miss! You all heard that didn't you? Miss! What a Gent."

Jed, who was still looking at him as he served another customer, wobbled slightly at the bar. "Miss? You might wanna get a younger model Katie. One that can see properly. Did you see those glasses? Cor blimey! He can probably see into the future with those things."

Katie shook her head, smiling, "Philistine!"

Jed turned and leaned his back against the bar, "Phyllis who? Never heard of her."

Kevin simply stood, chuckling at the banter between his two colleagues.

Katie took hold of Jed and Kevin's arms and dragged them away from the bar, "Come on let's go and find the other reprobates shall we?"

As all three of them walked through the club they passed large riveted copper steam funnels sticking out of the ground, giant moving cog formations on walls and several large mechanical constructs in display cabinets. All of the clubs' dancers and bar Staff were suitably dressed in steam punk clothing, some self-made by those employees who were genuine steam punks and some in company supplied uniforms for those that were not. Clothing ranged from top hat and trench coat to metal masked pipe and piston covered automaton looking dancers. Periodically, cosmetic clouds of steam shot from somewhere in a wall or from the ceiling and were occasionally accompanied by, digitally created, mechanical sound effects.

As the three approached the rest of the group, Les shouted across to Jed, "AYE!" toasting their return as an excuse simply to take another swig of his drink. He smiled and then leaned against Richie who was talking to Christian.

Richie tutted in good humour at being designated Les' new leaning post. "So go on Chris, what were you saying?"

Christian gulped down the beer he had just swigged, "I was just saying that I am thinking of changing my name. It feels odd somehow having been named by the company. It just doesn't feel right using it."

Richie curled his bottom lip, "Well yeah but it...it would be a bit strange calling you something different now though wouldn't it mate."

Christian nodded as he took another sip, "I understand what you mean but I don't feel it would be any different to the way all you guys eventually give each other nicknames and start calling them by it." Christian sipped at his drink and looked around the room giving Richie time to respond.

Richie, who had been rocking his head from side to side for a moment while he mulled over Christian's comment, eventually concurred with a considered "Meh." He looked over at the dance floor where the clubs' dancers had started one of their regular routines. "You know, now that you mention it, we never *did* get around to giving you a nickname did we mate."

"No I never did quite manage to get pinned with that particular badge of honour did I." Christian smiled.

"Of course...most of our nicknames for people are in honour of something that they've fucked up or something that we're taking the piss out of them for." Richie smiled at Christian, "Of course, *you* never fucked up, did you." He took another swig and placed his bottle down on the table. "That's very inconsiderate of you!"

Christian grinned, "So what sort of names are there that I am likely to be lumbered with? Should I be concerned?"

"Well let's think, what names are there? Well obviously my own name, Richie, is short for Richard." Richie rolled his eyes, "Must have taken them months to think of that one. Jed of course, John Edwards. Don't know how that came about but we just shortened the two names for some reason. Mother we named after an old theatre act, 'Old mother Riley'. Then there are the slightly more unfortunate ones like ol' Barry from Shoreditch on the red watch.

"You mean the slightly..."

"Rotund fellow yes, Barry. His real name is actually Norman."

"Norman? So then, why Barry?"

"Well it's because of his size, Barry...as in Bariatric. Then of course there's 'Wank-sock'. He's a guy that's based at the training academy, Bobledoo, Matt Black from Wimbledon and 'Big nose John' from headquarters."

"Really? Wank sock? Why?"

Richie shuddered, shaking off what was clearly a disturbing memory, "Seriously, don't…don't ask." He then shuddered again as if he could not avoid recollecting the origin of the name and something suddenly then ran down his spine.

"Oh. And Bobledoo? What was that about?"

"Well Bobledoo's name is Robert, but when he first went to his station he introduced himself, of course, and when asked what he liked being called he said 'Well my name's Robert so you can call me either Robert, Rob or even Bob'll do. So for the rest of his career he's been known as Bobledoo." Richie shook his head at the absurdity of his own revelation.

"Oh dear." Christian rolled his eyes. "Okay, so then why big nose John?"

"Well…because, because his name's John…" Richie dropped his brow, "…and he's…well he's…got a big nose."

Christian chuckled, "Oh, okay, sorry. Sorry, I just expected…more."

Richie shook his head, "Oh no. Trust me, it doesn't take a Nano-technician to think of a nick name in the Fire Brigade. I was lucky with Richie. Being Richard Hood, the guys originally wanted to call me Foreskin."

The beer that, had until now, been in Christian's mouth managed to project some distance away but was luckily against a wall and not over other clubbers.

Mother was still chuckling, having seen Christian's geyser impression, as he moved from another part of the group to join them both. "So what's going on here then, eh?"

"Christian's thinking of changing his name Guv."

Mother nodded slowly as he took a swig from his pint, "Are you young Chris? I think that's a very good idea. Fresh new start and all that." He raised his glass to him, tipped his head. Christian raised his glass in reply.

Katie and Jed turned from the others to also join in this topic, "Who wants a new name?" asked Jed.

Mother pointed his bottle and nodded at Christian.

"Oh" cheered Jed. "Oh, okay." He thought for a moment. "Oh, oh, how about, 'Xerox' or 'The Faxinator'?"

Richie put both hands up in the air, "What the fuck sort of names are they?"

"Oh…oh…no…no…how about Tim? You know, as in Verbatim?"

Katie smacked Jed on the arm, "A real name he means *fool*." She rolled her eyes, looked over to Christian, shook her head, smiled, and mimed to remind him that Jed had been drinking, "Well *I* think it's a good idea Chris."

Jed over exaggerated lifting up his trousers by his belt and then turned, "Clearly my genius is not wanted here. I am off to try my best chat up lines. I thank you." With that, he walked off to the bar like a striding lone, somewhat wobbly, gunman.

Thinking of Laura, Christian turned to Katie, "Is he…?"

She chuckled. "He's fine. He knows he never gets anywhere, I wouldn't worry".

A few minutes later the lone stranger returned.

Katie placed her arm around him, "Well tiger? How did it go?"

Slack jawed and still genuinely surprised that his powers of wooing had not been fully realised, he stood staring, "Well I found a lovely young lady over by the bar and I…" wobble, "I asked her, you know, if she could work out why I was walking a bit funny which is supposed to lead into my conversation about the fact that its' because I've got such a big…" Not wishing to spell it out, Jed pulled a 'You know what' face then placed his finger up to his lips and pointed not so discretely down to his crotch…"

Katie screwed up a smile, "Er, okay Mr Gigolo, I'm with you so far. How did she take that?"

"Well she didn't…ha-ha…mores the pity. No, instead she just said that she assumed that it was because I'd shit myself." Jed raised up his hands in a caricatured, drunken, shrug.

Katie grinned as she manoeuvred Jed into a chair beside the group, "Oh dear, there-there, she doesn't know *what* she's missing does she, eh? Anyway the grown-ups are having a little conversation at the moment so how about you have a little sleepy, yes?"

Jed motioned to protest but stated in the same moment, "Yeah, I could do with a little snooze I guess. All I wanted was a dance…snore!"

Kevin and Veggie had now joined this part of the group and were just checking to see if anyone wanted another round of drinks.

Veggie had asked everyone from the group about what drink they wanted. "Come on Kev, give me a hand getting all these, will you?"

Kevin and Veggie walked off to the bar. Two minutes later, Kevin returned to the group, "I was asked to see what drink Christian wants, er…Veggie couldn't remember what drink he wanted."

Katie, who Kevin was looking at, smiled a slightly perplexed smile and then turned her head and looked at Christian.

Seeing where Katie was looking, Kevin turned to join her gaze, "Oh, *Christian*, cool. What drink would you like mate?"

Christian looked at Katie then back to Kevin, "I would like…two beers, one red wine and two large vodkas please."

Kevin smiled and turned. Before he could step away, Christian called him, "Kevin!"

"Yes?"

"*What* drinks did I ask for?"

"Er, a beer and a red wine and vodka."

"So, how many drinks in all?"

"Two drinks, just two drinks. Sorry that *is* all you wanted isn't it?"

Christian stepped closer to Kevin to ensure he could be properly heard. "Actually Kevin I asked for two beers, one red wine and two vodkas. Is that okay?"

Kevin stood for a moment, struggling to remember the whole order.

Katie moved over to Kevin, "Kevin, are you feeling okay hun?"

Kevin opened his eyes wide and blinked heavily, "Well I've got a bit of a headache to be honest."

Katie shared a glance with Christian, paused then, "Kevin I'm starting to feel a little tired. I think I've drunk a little too much. Do you think that you and Christian would walk me home?"

Christian nodded and smiled a subliminal smile to Kate, acknowledging her quick diplomatic thinking.

Katie and Christian then 'allowed' Kevin to walk them all back to Katie's house where they would all bunk down for the evening. As they left Mother turned to them, "Thanks guys, well done." He tightened his jaw muscles clenching it shut as a low wave of anger and disappointment washed over him.

Christian nodded to Mother, "He'll be okay Mother. It will just take time, but he should be fine. We knew this might happen."

Mother pushed his bottom lip upwards smiling a flat sad smile, looked to the ground, turned and continued his evening.

4

The Firefighter's shower room filled with warm, bone-comforting, steam as the showers each blossomed into life. Katie, Les, Christian and Jed each stepped beneath their own fountain as they all began to wash off the aches and pains of another long tour of duty. The noise of the showers and the placing of toiletries echoed loudly off each wall as each Firefighter cleaned away another nights' worth of work. Jed pressed a panel in the wall, swiped a command and then stepped away from the now stopped shower. He bent, picked up his toiletries, stepped from the shower, reached for his towel that he'd hung on a warming rail and wrapped it around himself. Les stood in the shower looking like he had just fallen out of a washing machine as whole meringues of bubbles sat on his limbs rolling slowly and helplessly from him. Katie looked over at him, smiled a bemused smile and continued to wash herself down. She bent forward to fully rinse her hair, stood and then positioned herself directly under the shower head. She closed her eyes and allowed the water to run over her face and head, her surroundings muffled by the water exploding into and then out of her ears. After a minute or two she then pulled her head out of the water, opened her eyes wide and then ran her hand up her face to pull hair away from it. She turned off her shower and then ran the length of her hair between her fingers to remove most of the water. She bent to pick up her toiletries and looked over to Les, "That's an impressive mess you've made there Les. You being posted somewhere?"

Les' hearing was muffled so he looked around blindly to try to locate Katie.

"I say, it looks like you've been bubble wrapped Les!"

Les wiped some of the bubbles from his face and looked at Katie through his improvised bubble constructed coverall. He saw that she was bent over, gazed at her bum, smiling, "Well spank you very much Kate."

Katie straightened, "Er...pardon? What was that Les?" She stood and rested her hands on her hips.

"Oh sorry Kate, er...Freudian slip."

Katie turned and stepped from the shower, as she did she smiled a cheeky half smile, turned to Les, "Well you carry on like that young Les and you'll earn yourself a Freudian slap!"

"I should be so lucky."

Christian grinned as he watched his colleagues bantering then looked over to see Les' bubbles growing exponentially.

Christian picked up his shower gel, stepped from the shower and withdrew to the locker room. In the locker room, only Katie

remained, Jed having already left after quickly and quietly getting dressed.
Katie was still naked and was now doubled over with one leg on a bench drying herself. She turned hearing Christian walk into the room. "You okay Chris?"
Christian nodded and opened his locker.
"Don't tell me Les is still in there? Blimey he does take his time doesn't he?"
Christian rubbed a towel over his wet hair then placed it over his shoulders, smiled at Katie, "I believe he may be trying to recreate one of Professor Qautermass' experiments in there."
Katie smiled to herself as she curled her fingers around her hair and then again pulled her hand along the length of it to remove as much of the remaining water as possible. She then wrapped her towel around her hair and flipped it over her head. She sat on her bench and closed her eyes for a moment.

Christian had almost dressed and was now bent over zipping his boots up, "Kate, Jed was very quiet all this morning. Is he okay?"
Katie slowly opened her eyes and nodded. "Yes I think so Chris." She looked down at herself and then prodded her naked belly with a finger. "Hmm". She then placed her hand flat against her stomach. "Perhaps I shouldn't have had that second doughnut last night." She smiled then looked up at Christian who was now standing beside his locker removing his tablet and sports bag. "I think his and Laura's anniversary is coming up, isn't it? He always gets a big jittery about this time, you know?"
Christian smiled, "Oh, when is the actual date? Perhaps we could get them some flowers?"
Katie smiled, "That's a lovely idea Chris, why not? Count me in."
With that, Christians' vision instantly lit up with details of Jed and Laura. Being a friend and not wishing to look into personal details he ignored all of the other facts and figures that rolled up in front of him instead concentrating on searching for their anniversary date. As Christian stood, quietly staring, the brightness of his eyes suddenly faded. His smile slowly released and his head lowered towards the floor. The image of the Uni-web before him then dimmed away until it was completely gone. He turned, looked at Katie, nodded then quietly left the locker room.

Les appeared at the other locker room door covered from head to toe in bubbles. "Oh man, I forgot my towel. I left it in my bloody locker."
Katie dropped her head onto her shoulders and pushed her chin forwards. "Les...why didn't you rinse off before you came in here?"
Les stopped, rolled his eyes around his head as if surveying the sheer scale of his bubble faux pa. "Oh yeah." Then slowly and quietly he stepped backwards, almost in rewind, out of the room is if to imply that it had never happened.

<u>5</u>

Raindrops burst against Christian's windshield as his parked pods' engine slowly wound down to a stop. Christian continued sitting for a moment and looked out into the clouded morning sky. The day was a bright blue underlined by warm yellow rays from the Sun. The clouds that Christian was gazing at were gradually rolling in from the west and the sky was slowly but surely dimming as its' pastel coloured palette of light blue began to mix with a wash of dark grey. Music from Sigur Ros drifted from the speakers within the pod. He listened to it musing that, if he'd wanted to, he could translate the words via the Web, but he had been listening to this music for such a long time and felt that he had gotten all the emotion and story he needed from the Icelandic lyrics without even needing to know their meaning. He smiled a gentle pained smile then, as his pod opened he leaned out of it, took hold of the chassis and then pulled himself up feeling suddenly much heavier. He stood, paused, closed his pod and then stepped over to the gravel path. The small stones crunched like thick snow beneath his feet as he made his way along the flower lined pathway. The rain now, slightly heavier, began to run down his back so he lifted his jackets' lapels up around his neck as he stepped under some trees for shelter. Christian was not emotionally bothered by the rain down his neck, nor was it physically uncomfortable but it was very difficult to not act instinctively, as he had done for however long he had been around before the arrival of the company. He looked out from under the trees and placed his hand out in front of him. Catching some rain drops, he filled his hand with them then rubbed them over his face as if freshening himself up or regaining focus. He headed back to the path and crunched his way onwards. He passed under a large thick evergreen archway as he opened and closed an old wooden gate as he headed towards the old stone-built building in front of him. He aimed for the front door but, as he did, he looked around and could see over to one side Jed, sitting on a grass-surrounded bench under a huge Oak tree. Christian stopped, paused, took a deep slow intake of breath and then turned towards his friend. As he approached, Jed twisted, he looked up at Christian, half smiled and nodded. Christian sat. He did not speak for a while but simply listened to the worsening rain. He stared over at a large flower beside the gravelled path and watched as its' leaves trampolined up and down after each direct hit from a raindrop and then watched as the water cascaded slowly through the leaves down to the ground.

Jed did not move or alter his gaze as he looked off into the distance. "You know it's funny…I can still smell her."

Christian turned to Jed but respectfully waited for him to continue. A short gust of bitter wind blew between them both.

"Five years…and I can still smell her." He turned to Christian but did not look him in the eye. "Isn't that funny? After all this time. Every morning when I wake up I can smell her." He paused, "You know, I don't mean at work, yuck, no, I think that might be Les I can smell there…I mean at home. I can still smell her. Isn't that odd?" Jed breathed in through his nose slowly and deliberately, reminding himself of her scent. A hint of a smile appeared on his face. "You know I don't even think I could tell you everything I had to eat last week, but after five years I can still smell *her*." He smiled off into the distance.

Christian lowered his eyes and looked at the ground softly shaking his head. A soft flash could be seen as lightning quickly danced into and out of life way off on the horizon.

Jed shook his head slowly, "I can remember it like it was yesterday you know. That call." A tear poured from his red eyes as he lifted his head towards the sky. "That call changed my life. That…fucking…call!" His bottom lip began to tremble as much as his voice and he wiped one of his puffy eyes with his hand. He sat for a minute before continuing to speak. "I take it you know how it happened?"

Christian looked at him, cleared his throat, "No. As soon as I saw the data entry I stopped looking. I didn't wish to pry into your private life Jed, without your permission."

Jed nodded and looked away. Low, bassy rumbles of thunder could be heard drum-rolling gently across the landscape. After a short time he continued, "Laura had been suffering from these headaches. She'd had them for a while and had been kind of getting used to them, but *I* could tell. They bothered her. She just seemed to be getting them more and more frequently. It turned out later that she was simply intolerant to certain foods but at that time we didn't know. So, I took her to see a Doctor who got her booked in for some blood tests and we were sent to the Fenchurch Street Hospital to get them done." Jed shrugged, "*Now* of course the Doctor could have just scanned her but then...even such a short time ago it was all quite invasive really, all those needles and tablets and things." Jed paused, looking down for a moment, "It was such a simple routine thing though. Just an everyday thing. Just a simple blood test. Well...anyway, so the nurse comes in and it tells us that she simply needs to be given an anaesthetic in her arm to numb it ready for the test. Laura accepted this. I assume she must have thought it a bit strange but then why would you argue with the nurse, it knows what its' doing right? Anyway, then a syringe appears from the nurse's arm. It then injects her with it and then another injection appears and it then injects her with *that*." Jed remained motionless and emotionless, numbed, *himself,* by the recounting. Tears then began to stream down his face and his brow furrowed as he continued, his voice shaking, "You see, it had...injected...her with a drug...she wasn't supposed to be given. It had been for another patient. It was supposed to be taking blood, but instead it injected her with a drug that....." Jed lowered his head into his hand. He rubbed the side of his temples with his finger and thumb and took a deep breath. "Well anyway...she...she just...never woke up."

Christian shook his head slowly, a large tear forming in the corner of his eye. "Jed, I'm...I'm so sorry. I didn't know."

Jed shrugged, shook his head, glanced at Christian then looked away again.

"It's just.....you never speak about it at work. You always talk about seeing her or speaking to her. I just thought..."

Jed looked directly at Christian, "That's okay mate. You weren't to know. It's not exactly something that I talk about too openly. Obviously the guys I was on the watch with at the time know but...besides, I *do* come and speak to her and I *do* come and see her." Jed looked away again off into the dark greying clouds recalling the aftermath of Laura's death, "They all came to the funeral. It was…..very nice. *She* would have liked it." He nodded and sniffed tears away.

Christian bowed his head and, without looking at Jed, "She was killed by a robot. I did not know that. I'm so sorry Jed."

Jed snorted, "That's okay mate. Besides, to be fair she wasn't killed by a robot. A *person* killed her, not the robot. The nurse didn't know what it was doing, it was just following its' orders. It was either loaded with the wrong programming or given the wrong patient details or something. Who knows? It can't make mistakes like we can, it's just a machine." Jed put his hand up towards Christian, "No offence mate. I'm talking about the older generations and simpler models. The automatons, not…"

Christian raised a hand, "None taken Jed. Really. Actually the truth is that I'm not a robot. I'm technically an android. Robots are very different. You know, to be honest us androids don't really mix with their sort." He smiled at Jed a tear sodden smile.

Jed looked at him and, seeing his tears chuckled, "Ha. Looks like your emotions are starting to take shape again then, eh?"

Christian's expression tightened as he suddenly realised that he had indeed been both saddened and tearful whilst listening to Jed. He nodded then smiled gratefully at his friend.

Both continued sitting for about ten minutes, reflecting on their conversation as they quietly watched the sky's cloud formations.

Jed eventually turned to Christian, snorted a chuckle, "Ha, you know there was this one time…" Jed looked absent for a moment whilst he replayed the event in his mind then waved the image away to refocus and continued. "When we first got married, because of one reason or another it just seemed we were forever moving home. I think we must have moved once a year for about five years. Anyway, we eventually found the house that we live…*I*…live in now and I knew she'd just about had enough of moving. I mean, she was really becoming impatient with the whole idea of it. I arranged with the guys at work to help me move and confirmed with Laura that we would move over a weekend so that it wouldn't impact on her work too much. Anyway, to cut a long story short, she came home on the Friday to find an empty house and a note hanging from the light in the lounge that said I had a gambling problem and that I'd sold all the furniture." Jed was laughing as he spoke, "Oh wow, the guys at work really didn't think I should leave the note but, you know, I couldn't help it. I thought it was pretty funny so I went with it. And, *true to form*, she laughed herself silly about it. The daft thing is that, afterwards, when we discussed it she'd realised that there were so many clues that I was going to do it but that she'd just dismissed them at the time and not put the whole thing together. I was so clumsy about it all." Jed stopped laughing and lowered his eyes as if looking at a photograph in his hands. "When she arrived at the house and saw all the furniture was where we'd agreed it would go and I handed her a welcoming glass of wine she just burst into tears. The sheer relief and pleasure of the moment I guess just took hold of her. It was…magical. It was a magical moment. God she looked beautiful that day too, I mean really, really stunning. She *really* was a good looking woman."

Christian quietly looked up a picture of her on the Web, smiled and nodded in silent agreement.

Tears flowed again from Jeds' bleary eyes. "Can you imagine what it must be like to wake up and find that someone's ripped part of you away? That you're never going to be whole again?" Jed shook his head, snorted then wiped his eyes. "Of course you do. What was I thinking?" He chuckled, "Sorry Chris, you of all people would know that wouldn't you." He looked at his friend and smiled. He looked down at the ground and then slowly, deliberately, word by word, said, "I…just…miss…her…so…much."

Christian waited for a minute to reply, respecting Jed's grief. "Jed. Its' been five years though. Surely it's time to move on. You have to let go of this pain. This is a burden you really need to stop carrying."

Jed snapped a stare into Christian's eyes, "No! No! I *need* this pain…I *can't* let go of it!" He looked away. His tone softened, "I *need* this pain Chris. As much as it brings me down or darkens my mood sometimes, I know that if I let go of this pain, I'm letting go of her. While this hurts, I've still got part of her with me. They say that time heals all wounds. We'll I don't think that's strictly true. I believe that with time we simply forget just how much something hurt and I just can't afford to let this go…I'm not sure if you can understand that. I don't know…"

Christian replied in a low reflective tone, "I understand that. I'm sorry that you put yourself through this but…I respect it and *yes* I understand it. I'm just sad for you."

Jed smiled a tight respectful smile and then sat in silence.

Christian eventually stood, pulled his lapels up around his neck and turned to Jed. "You know I'm here if you ever need to speak to anyone Jed."

"Thanks Chris. I'm not really one for talking about things that much. It's not really me. I know, I know, it's probably unhealthy blah, blah, blah, but the truth is…I can't let go and…I'm not sure I even want to. She was everything to me. *Every-thing*. *She* became a part of *me* and *I* of *her*." Jed stood. "I can still smell her when I wake. I hear her advice…when I think about eating the wrong thing. I hear her giggling at me when I drop something at home or bang my head against that *bloody* bathroom cabinet. I…" He did not finish his sentence but simply shook his head and looked away. He snorted a chuckle and looked at his friend, "Sorry Chris, Jeez, you've got so much shit going on at the moment. Your head must still be so fucked up. I'm sorry. I'm sure you could do without all this."

Christian shook his head and shook his hand towards Jed, "Forget it. I completely understand. There's no need to apologise, okay?"

The rain had stopped and the air began to fill with the musky scent of freshly rained on woodland. Jed closed his eyes and breathed in the welcome smell. He stepped out from under the tree, put his hand out and smiled up at the sky. "Well…at least it's stopped bloody raining." He turned and stepped away towards where he had parked his pod. Christian took one last glance at the cemetery, smiled and then followed Jed. He caught up almost immediately as Jed had stopped at a passenger-pod stop just outside the church gate and was now looking at its' advertising display screen.

Jed turned to Christian, "Can you fucking believe it?" His face was one of both disbelief and amusement.

Christian looked at the screen. On it was an advert for a funeral directors, their slogan being, "If we bury you and you're not completely satisfied, we'll give you double your money back." Christian's brow raised. "I see what you mean."

Jed turned to Christian and raised his hand, "No, no, that's not even the one I was talking about, as if that wasn't bad enough, wait a second."

The screen faded and was replaced by an advert for a cosmetics company, "Ug-Away! Eight out of ten *ugly* people said they'd recommend us. Ug-Away!"

"No, no, not that one. It gets better." The screen again faded and was replaced with another advert. "There you go, that's the one."

Christian focussed on the advert for a laundry product. "Rigormortis, for when ordinary starches just aren't good enough!" He chuckled a disapproving chuckle, "Fuck me. Is nothing sacred anymore?"

"It could be worse. It could be right outside a cemetery." Jed turned and looked at the church, "Which of course, it *is*." He stood quietly shaking his head, tutted, rolled his eyes then turned back to Christian. "You fancy a beer?"

Chris screwed up his face, "Er, are you sure? It's eleven o'clock in the morning!"

"Pedant! Okay then, would you like to go and have a beer for breakfast? Is that better?"

Christian smiled, rolled *his* eyes, shook his head and followed Jed to his pod, his silence being all the confirmation Jed needed.

<u>6</u>

Jed bent forward from his bar stool and picked up his freshly delivered beer, turned to Christian. "You should have seen it, there was Claret everywhere." Jed laughed one of those laughs that compels others to laugh along. "There was Claret everywhere, ha, ha, ha. Get it?"

Christian looked blankly at him as he sipped on his Whisky, "Well, to be honest, sorry mate, no I don't."

Jed recoiled as he sat up, "Really? Oh." He looked to one side still struggling to understand why Christian had not enjoyed his joke. He then began to break down the joke using hand gestures to emphasise the words, "Because you see…it was…delivering…wine. That's why…you see…"

"Oh…it was a *wine* pod. It was delivering *wine*? Ah, now that makes much more sense, oh I see, hah-ha…no actually, it's still not very funny to be honest." He found this fact funnier than the bad joke and began to laugh at himself.

"But I *said* it was a wine pod. *Didn't* I?" Jed rolled his eyes upwards as if trying to look inside his head to view a replay.

Christian sat shaking his head, "No, sorry mate. You didn't. You just said it was a pod in a collision. You didn't mention the wine bit at all." Christian then started laughing much more at seeing Jed's pitiful puppy dog face.

Both friends remained quiet for a while without speaking. Every now and then Christian would glance over at Jed and laugh, which seemed to result in Jed screwing his face up like a naughty school boy and looking away.

After a few minutes, Christian stopped laughing and looked at his friend from the corner of his eye, staring at him for a while. He placed his hand on his shoulder, "Jed. I'm sorry about Laura. I truly am."

Jed looked at him, barely smiled then nodded once. "I know mate. So am I."

"To Laura!" Christian had raised his glass in toast.

Jed followed his prompt and raised *his*, took a respectfully sized glug and placed his glass slowly and precisely back from where he'd lifted it. He wiped his mouth then looked around the bar.

Christian broke the slightly pregnant pause with, "You ever wondered what you might have been if you hadn't joined the Brigade?" As he asked this he looked deeply into his Whisky, rolling the glass around, watching the colours shimmering through the glass.

Jed shook his head. "No, not really. You know I can't think of a generation of my family that *wasn't* in the brigade to be honest."

Instantly Christian's eyes began to glaze over.

Jed waved his hand in front of Christian's face and pushed him sideways with his other arm, "No, no, now hang on. Stop that. I don't want any of that Voodoo Mumbo-jumbo shit here, alright? Let's have a proper good old fashioned face to face discussion shall we?"

Christian raised his brow, "Are you sure? I could easily locate this information quite quickly....."

"No, just...no, let's just talk, shall we?" Jed took another sip from his beer and smiled as he drank. "Oh hang on, it doesn't matter anyway, I *can* remember the last generation of my family that wasn't in the Fire Brigade."

"Who?"

"My Dad. It was my Dad. *He* wasn't in the Fire Brigade." Jed snorted realising his own silliness.

After a short pause Christian continued, "Have you ever regretted the decision?"

"Well no, it was *his* to make. He was entitled to be anything he wanted to be."

"No you silly sod, not your Dad, *You*. Do you ever regret joining the job?"

Jed shrugged, "I don't think so, no. I mean, maybe there were times but on the whole, no I'm glad I joined I think." He smiled a reminiscing smile, "I mean, Jeez, when I first joined I really didn't know what hit me. When I first came out of the Academy, you know? *You* know what we can be like. Firefighters can be the biggest load of piss takers you'll ever meet." He chuckled and placed down his now empty glass. "I mean crap, when I first joined, my original watch would get me doing all sorts of stupid things and feeding me all sorts of silly facts and figures just to get me at it. And they could be *so...fucking...sarcastic*! Christ when I first joined I felt like I'd fallen down the famous Chasm of Sar and then when I hit the floor was repeatedly beaten with a Sarc*a*-stick."

Christian quickly reconstructed the sentence and smiled at Jed. He then raised his hand to the barman who walked over and nodded as he saw Christian smiling and pointing to both his and Jed's empty glasses.

Jed looked again into the distance as he reflected on his career. His eyes lowered to the ground, "Did you know, there was a time when the Fire Brigade went completely bust?" Jed noticed Christian's eyes suddenly looking vacant, "No, no! I mentioned that didn't I? None of your omniscient shit here mate, come on now!"

Christian snapped *to*, "Sorry, yes sorry, force of habit now. Sorry, what do you mean *bust*?"

"Actually *that*. Bust. Broke. We're talking a long-long time ago mind you."

"How?"

"Oh, I don't but a very long time!"

"No, not how long, how did it go *bust*!"

"Oh, I see, sorry...of course. Well, the Brigade just outsourced everything. I mean *everything*, its' training, its' equipment, it's, well everything. You remember the Thorn Street fire from your training?"

Christian nodded as he took hold of his next round of Whisky, "Thorn Street? Yes. It was the last major fire before the new Fire Rights Act was passed. Blimey, that *is* a long time ago."

"Yeah I know. Well what they don't advertise is that when that fire occurred, the equipment was not only poorly maintained so not all of it worked, but also, because it was the biggest fire that had occurred in years, most of the Officers had never experienced anything like it.

By outsourcing everything, the Brigade had sold off all of its assets and had also lost all of its experience. There were none of the good Officers left to train up the new breed."

Christian leaned his head to one side as he listened, turned it and narrowed his eyes to gesture, "Are you sure?"

"Yes, I'm telling you. That fire raged like for…nine days. *Nine days*! Can you imagine it? They lost about a hundred buildings in London and, what with it being so close to the border, they also lost about forty buildings in the east of London. It's the part of London that *used* to be called Essex. Look at us now though. We have some of the best equipment in the world *and*…"

"Sorry Jed, where is all this going?"

Jed opened his mouth to speak, thought about his response and then, "Actually you know what? I'm not sure where I was going with that." Jed began to giggle to himself then, "Oh yeah, oh yeah. That's it. No! I never thought about doing anything other than the Brigade." He sat smiling, pleased that he'd remembered where he had been going with his conversation. The two friends leaned against the bar in silence for a while simply enjoying each-others' presence.

Christian sipped again at his Whisky, closed his eyes, breathed in deeply then turned to Jed, "So most of your forefathers were Firefighters?"

Jed sat up sharply, "How dare you sir, how dare you question my heritage! I have but one father Sir, to imply that I have four is a complete slur on my very good name."

Christian simply raised an eyebrow and scoffed at his friend becoming more inebriated.

After another round of drinks was ordered, Jed, who had folded his arms onto the bar and was now resting his head on them, turned slowly to Christian, "Christian, you know how you can get Quorn pies and Quorn sausages and stuff?"

Christian looked up from under his dropped brow, "Hmmm, eh? *Random,* but yeah, go on."

"Well, have you ever wondered why they don't make Quorn brains just in case zombies were ever to attack, some of them having been vegetarians?"

Christian grinned as wide as his face would allow him, "I think perhaps you've had enough mate."

CHAPTER ELEVEN

"Tee break"

1

Jed slowly and cautiously began attempts to open an eye. His eye brow had raised as much as it could and his eye lids strained but, on the first attempt, they continued to remain closed. Again he strained but this time had paused before trying as he did a quick mental 'run up' then a crack of the lid and light poured in literally burning the eye from its' socket, or so his wincing reaction would lead you to believe. He waved blindly at the 'nasty' light for it to go away and surprisingly it did. He shielded his eyes with his hand before attempting re-entry into the world of the living. His eyes slowly opened and, across the room from him, he could see Hannah who was quietly closing the bedroom blind to protect him from the discomfort of the bright morning light. She turned and smiled to see him now looking at her. She stepped over to him, bent down and placed her hand on his cheek. "Oh dear. You okay?"

Jed grunted a hung over moan as he pulled a tried and tested "Help me, I'm just a boy." face. With a soft gravelly voice, his face still twisted and reshaped by the pillow he had failed to remove himself from, "I hate my life!"

Hannah placed her hand on his arm, "Oh dear, do you? Oh that's terrible, there-there." She pulled the duvet over his shoulder and placed her hand back on it. "Oh dear. I take it from that, that you're not feeling very good then, eh?" Hannah's smile was one of genuine concern but the light tone in her voice betrayed her mild amusement at seeing the state of her poor little, self-inflicted, injured soldier before her.

"I think I'm dying. I hate everything!" Jed pulled the duvet further up over his head.

Hannah concealed a mild chuckle, "Oh dear, you poor little soldier. How you've suffered, eh? Is there anything I can get you? A Doctor? An undertaker? Do you need to tie up any loose ends, like signing of wills or letting me know where old man McGuffin's buried treasure is?"

"There *is* no old man McGuffin."

"Well nor is there a buried treasure, so you win on both counts, well done you."

"Go away!" he muffled.

"Ah, ye-e-e-e-s-s-s." She smiled at him through the duvet, "Seriously hun, can I get you anything?"

"I need something for my belly. It feels terrible, get me something for that."

Hannah stood, "Oh dear, really? What can I get you? Some Panasolve? Immucon? What?"

Jed pulled the duvet from his head, and with well-rehearsed pleading eyes looked up at Hannah, "Bacon and eggs." He nodded, "Yeah, yeah I think that'll do it. Two doses of bacon and eggs." Realising that nodding hurt, he stopped.

Hannah smiled, shook her head, bent down and kissed him on his head.

As she stood up straight, Jed screamed instinctively as he had suddenly become aware of his feet being up around his shoulder. In that same moment, not realising he'd injured himself, he grabbed his toes and, as he did, confirmed he had no feeling in them.

Hannah straightened, shook her head and turned to leave. "Morning Les."

From the other end of the bed came a muffled, "Morning Hannah."

Les then sat up, stretched energetically and yawned a satisfying feline yawn. He then looked over to Jed who was laying down now supporting himself up on his elbows panting. Jed shook his head, "Oh for f….."

"You alright Jed?"

Jed continued to pant heavily, "Am I…for fuck's…sake. When did *you* get here?"

Les yawned again as he twisted and stood from the bed. "Blimey, how pissed *were* you last night?"

Les stepped over to the door in his underwear and removed Jed's dressing gown that was hanging by it on the wall.

Jed rolled over onto one of his elbows and rubbed his eyes with his free hand. "Les…."

Les turned as he was dressing himself in the gown, "Yes?"

"Les are those…women's…knickers?"

Les looked down at his underwear, scoffed, shook his head, "No…of course not. They're *my* knickers." With that, scratching himself like a waking bear, Les stepped through the bedroom door that had now slid open.

Jed slowly pulled himself up, his Neanderthal brow scouring the room for an animal skin or some leaves in which to cover himself. He pulled the duvet around himself as he stood then, seeing the clothes from the previous night, lifted them, with animal-like self-preservation sniffed them, grunted then dressed in them. *He* then stepped into the lounge.

The lounge itself opened up into the kitchen separated only by a breakfast bar at which Christian and Les were now sitting drinking coffee and chatting to Hannah as she very kindly prepared them all a cooked breakfast. The room was filling with the salty smell of freshly fried bacon and the waking aroma of strong coffee. Jed shuffled over to the breakfast bar and sat down. Christian stood, poured him a coffee and then placed it carefully in front of him. Christian raised the coffee jar to Les, who silently declined a top up, and then turned, "Hannah would you like a coffee at all?"

Hannah looked from where she was bending into the fridge, "No thank you Christian."

Christian replied with a smile of his own, replaced the coffee and then stepped over to where she stood. "Can I help you at all by the way?"

Hannah turned and, barely looking at him, politely shook her head. Christian sat back down at the breakfast bar.

Seeing Christian and Hannah's interaction, Jed raised an eyebrow, twisted slightly, looked at Christian and smiled wryly into another sip of coffee.

Les again yawned a wide air-sucking yawn, "We still playing golf today then?"

Jed looked at him. "Golf? Since when were we playing golf?"

Christian placed his coffee down on the counter, "We decided last night, remember? When we met up with Les he still had his clubs in his pod so we suggested a round of golf for this morning. Sure, you remember. Don't you?"

Jed raised a heavily burdened top lip, "Hannah pass me a couple of Panasolve would you?" She handed him a glass of water and two orange and yellow capsules. "Thanks." Jed then threw the two tablets into his mouth, snapped his head back then swallowed a large glug of water and stood, "I'm gonna go take a quick shower then. I'll be back in a minute." Knowing that the Panasolve would soon completely remove the effects of the hangover, he exited the lounge to freshen up.

Hannah placed a full English breakfast in front of both Les and Christian. Les' face lit up, "Oh, thank you *very much* Hannah. Oh wow that does look good."

Christian smiled and nodded at Hannah as she placed cutlery down beside their plates. "You're not having any Hannah?"

Hannah shook her head, smiling, "No I'm just going to have a cheese and ham toastie, thank you."

Christian raised his brow, "Oh sorry Hannah, have we eaten all the bacon and eggs and…"

Hannah smiled, again shook her head, "No, it's okay, I just fancy a toastie." and turned to prepare her own food.

Les took another mouthful, "D'you know Hannah, I've known you all this time and what I didn't know, but Jed tells me, is that you have Autism. Is that right?"

Hannah glanced a subliminal and slightly awkward smile at Christian then smiled at Les, "Jed also tells *me,* Les, that you are quite upfront and inappropriate about asking personal questions. And you and I both know that that's correct." Her tone was not one of upset but was merely matter of fact. She smiled, continuing to slice cheese for her breakfast.

Les laughed a slightly awkward and embarrassed laugh and coughed on a piece of Bacon as he did, "Sorry Hannah, I didn't mean to cause offense, I was just curious is all."

"Offense? Why offense? That wasn't offensive Les."

Les smiled gratefully, "I just…thought they could do something about that these days though. You ever thought of getting cured?"

Hannah placed down the grater she had been using, turned to Les, smiled a sympathetic smile, "See, now that *is* offensive Les." Without being upset she continued to grate her cheese. "I have a form of Autism called Asperger's Syndrome."

Les just about contained himself from spitting out the tea he was now sipping from but winced as he swallowed it quicker than he had meant to, "Jeez…sorry Hannah, you've actually got something called Ass Burger syndrome?"

Hannah rolled her eyes, "No Les, its' called As-per-ger's syndrome."

"Asperger's? Oh, oh…okay, sorry. Sorry Hannah." Les tilted his head, "Let's face it, Ass Burger Syndrome does sound funny though. I mean that *would* be funny wouldn't it."

"Not for the person suffering from Ass Burger Syndrome I should imagine, no. It sounds quite unpleasant." Hannah shared a discreet, flat smile with Christian who was quietly enjoying observing his friend dig such a large and inappropriate hole for himself.

"But you are right Les, it is on the Autistic spectrum."

Les tightened his eyes, "Sorry…spectrum. As in *colours*?"

Hannah smiled a mildly mischievous grin, "Yes I have Asperger's which is high functioning therefore I have a white belt in Autism. Those with very severe Autism are classed as black belts. Hence the term Autistic spectrum."

Les stopped his fork of grilled tomato mid-journey, thought about what Hannah was saying and then lowered his hand down to his plate, "Okay, wow, I didn't know *any* of this Hannah. That's…well…I just didn't know that. Wow." He redirected the grilled tomato on its' journey and was now munching down on it, "So Hannah can you actually get…I mean, if you've got a white belt, how do you…" He stopped for a moment then shaking his head, "You can't get up the ranks or anything, can you? That'd be silly, right? Am I just being a bit thick here?"

Completely deadpan Hannah came over and topped up both their mugs, "No, no, not at all. I can get up the ranks, yes, I just need to start getting better at being Autistic and I can get a higher belt. I just don't have the time, what with work and everything, to do enough training." Hannah turned from Christian quickly, knowing that he would give her the giggles, as his face confirmed that he was fully aware of how ridiculous Les was being.

"Well Hannah, I'm sorry I didn't know any of this. I mean it's just that you seem so…you know, normal."

Christian tilted and twisted his head toward Les and in a soft low reprimanding voice, "Les!" Aware that it would be better to change the subject, Christian stood up to take his plate to the sink and addressing Les, "You know when they first discovered how effective Stemplants were, one of the things they tried to 'cure' was hearing impairments. With all the advancements in stem technology they found that they could fully restore hearing to a person who was completely deaf."

Les leaned forward, nodded to Hannah then slid his plate towards Christian who took it to place with his own in the sink, "And?"

"Well the first few people who were able to get their hearing back were amazed, it changed their lives. It was a miracle. But then…well, it soon became apparent that they were effectively going to become extinct."

"Extinct, surely if they got their hearing back that made them better, right?"

"Well yes, it fixed their hearing but, in the process, they lost their identity, you know, as deaf people. They soon realised that they would lose their language, their community and, in many ways, their culture. And that's why we still have deaf people to this day."

Les' sat slightly open mouthed, "Eh?"

Christian continued, "They decided that what they would gain from their hearing was not worth what they would lose in themselves. The thing that defined them. The part of them that belonged to this strong community. Also Les, not everyone aspires to be Physically-Average-Neuro-Typical-Specimens."

"And that is?"

Christian stood by the sink and slid Les' plate into the water filled bowl. As he did he brushed the back of his hand against Hannah's. He noticed, from the corner of his eye, that she very subtly smiled at this. "It's what *you* would consider normal I suppose Les. Which of course if you look around the room, between the three of us, there is no normal is there?"

Hannah turned to look at Christian as he stepped back to his seat and beamed a large silly grin, "Those of us that *do* eat Asparagus-Burgers refer to Physically-Average-Neuro-Typical-Specimens simply as Pants."

Before the conversation could continue the doorbell sounded. Christian looked at Hannah, smiled, "Can I get that for you Hannah?" She smiled and nodded. Les saw the way they were both looking at each other suspended in a moment of attraction so rolled his eyes, stood and answered the door.

Les waved his hand over an internal console by the front door and the door slid open. The bright morning light suddenly poured into the room so Les reactively raised his hands to shield his eyes. His stinging eyes slowly focussed on the person that stood in front of him. As his focus quickly returned, the image of a grey-suited man began to focus before him.

"Mr Edwards?"

Les winced away from the light slightly, "Edwards? No. Who's asking?"

"Sir, my Name is Martin Goodwin, I am from…"

Les blindly grasped the business card that was being held in front of him, "Yeah I know where you're from Mr Goodwin." Les spread his legs to take a slightly more robust defensive stance. Having both hands shielding his eyes, the gown was not now properly wrapped around him, so Les stood in this pose in the doorway with his knickers clearly on display.

Goodwin looked down at Les' knickers and grimaced with displeasure, noting that they were the same that his wife sometimes wears, "Sir, if the light is too bright I could step inside."

Les laughed, "I don't think so Mr Goodwin, while you are outside you are powerless against me. It is only if I invite you in that I give you your power."

From behind the door frame stepped Jed who gently manoeuvred Les out of the way. "Les I don't think he's a vampire, besides, look the sun's out." Les glanced out at the sun to satisfy himself before allowing himself to be gently pushed away from the door. Jed now stood in front of Goodwin, "What can I do for you Mr Goodwin? What is it that allows you to believe that you are welcome on my doorstep? Hmm?" Jed began to dry his hair with the towel that was around his neck.

"Well Sir, I was hoping that you might tell me the whereabouts of Mr…" Goodwin stopped having seen that Christian was now looking around the door, "Ah, Mr Mann. The very person I was looking for."

"And *what* is it that you want with me Mr Goodwin?"

Goodwin turned and gestured towards a waiting limousine. "Mr Mann I would very much like to talk to you. I am not here to bother you in any way nor am I here to try to harass you. I went to your house and when you weren't there I thought I'd try…"

"Mr Goodwin, you can easily trace my pod and I'm assuming that's what you've done, please get to the point Sir."

Goodwin, smiled in acknowledgement, "Okay, yes, I'm sorry. Mr Mann you see the thing is I would very much like to speak to you about what has happened between yourself and our company. Which,

I must say I very much regret. I would just like to *talk* to you Sir is all."

"Goodwin, my friends and I are planning to play golf today, so I don't see how…"

"Oh no that's not a problem Mr Mann, we have memberships at the exclusive Horton Hotel golf course. It would be my pleasure if you were to accompany me for a round of golf there as my guest. Your friends are more than welcome."

"Mr Goodwin who do you think we are? You cannot simply buy us with…" Christian had turned and was now looking into the lounge where both Les and Jed were standing. They had both picked up their golf clubs and Les was looking at Christian, nodding and waving his hand toward the door as if to direct Christian to finish the conversation so they could get on with playing a free round of golf. Christian turned back to Goodwin, "Wait one moment, I'll get my clubs." With that, Christian closed the front door, rolled his eyes, turned and then walked over to his golf bag. He turned to Hannah who was now quietly sitting at the bar eating her toastie. "Hannah it was very nice meeting you." Hannah turned slightly, looked briefly at Christian, smiled, nodded and then returned to her breakfast. Les, who had very quickly dressed, and Christian both lifted up their clubs and walked out to the limousine, "Goodbye Hannah.", "Goodbye Les."

Jed walked over to Hannah and placed one arm around her to hug her without stopping her from eating her breakfast. He began to release his hug but then stopped for a moment, looked down at her, "So…you er…you looked Christian in the eyes then I see."

Hannah looked up at him. So? I looked Les in the eyes, what of it?"

"Ah, but you *know* Les. You've known him for a while now. But you've just met Christian, and you're already looking him in the eye." He lowered his eyes to her, and raised his brow, "I think you like him. Just a little bit." He raised his hand in front of her and gesticulated with his thumb and fingers to reinforce the 'little bit' of his comment.

Hannah smiled and pushed him away gently with her elbow. "Sod off! What time are you home?"

Jed walked out towards the front door. "I'm not sure. And I'm sure that when I *do* get back I'll probably be very drunk and unruly."

Les stepped into the Limousine. Jed and Christian placed their clubs into the rear storage compartment then went to step into the pod itself. As they did, Christian turned to Jed, "Hannah seems very nice mate."

Jed pretended he had not heard, "Eh mate? What's that?"

"I was….I was just saying that your sister Hannah, she seems very nice."

"Hmm, does she now?" Jed raised his brow to Christian pre-inquisition.

Christian raised his hands up in defence as he sat in the pod, "What? *What*?"

Les looked around the plush interior of the luxury pod trying hard not to let his jaw drop too much. He thought for a moment of something witty or interesting to say to illustrate to Goodwin that he was not out of place in such a luxurious limousine. After a moment he smiled, pleased with his chosen topic and turned to Goodwin, "Now here's an interesting thing you may not know about the Autistic spectrum…"

Jed and Christian both glanced at each other and swapped discreet smiles.

2

On the course, Jed and Les had played in a pair and had teed off before Christian and Goodwin so as to afford them some privacy. Now on the seventh hole, choosing a driver for his shot, Goodwin began to tee off first. He looked out across the magnificently manicured fairway, eyed up the layout then licked his finger and raised it above his head. The wind was coming in from the southwest so he adjusted his stance accordingly. He bent his knees slightly and bounced on them, confirming that his weight and posture were just right. He then shuffled up nearer to the ball, looked down at it, readjusted his posture again and closed his eyes for a moment. He took a long deep, meditative breath, twisted his head to look down the fairway, looked back down at his ball, composed himself for a moment then raised his arms up high behind himself to swing. In one smooth strong swing the club rotated back round at speed hitting the ball. It was a text book shot, unfortunately, not a text book relating to golf. The ball had obeyed the laws of physics perfectly and had rolled about forty feet forwards. Looking down, Goodwin surveyed the new design feature in his club, rolled his eyes and then handed the now bent club to his chauffer who returned it as best he could to Goodwin's golf bag. Goodwin looked at Christian slightly sheepishly then nodded. "I've er, I've just had that club's handle re-taped. I think the weight is *way off*." Christian arched a brow and nodded in polite agreement. He then picked the driver from his bag, stood up to the ball and without hesitation, leaned slightly forward, swung his club above his head then back through, hitting the ball with a very loud and satisfying ping. The ball flew off perfectly straight and, after a long haul flight, it landed, jetlagged, onto the Green. This distance would have taken a professional at least two good shots but Christians' strength and accuracy were clearly far superior. For the seventh time today Goodwin curled a disappointed lip and began to walk the long green mile to his ball.

"Listen Christian, now I know that things haven't been too good between yourself and the company, as we've discussed, and for that I apologise really I do but you have to realise how much we've invested in this project." Goodwin winced slightly at his own words realising how he'd just referred to Christian.

"Look, this isn't about money Goodwin. This is about ethics, *in which*, your company has been very much lacking."

"Yes, yes and again I apologise for that. Granted there may have been a few moments of misinterpretation and confusion…"

Christian stopped walking, "misinterpretation and confusion? Are you fucking kidding me Goodwin?", then continued.

"Now…you have to remember Christian that I represent many, *many* shareholders *and* stakeholders and I must continue to be mindful of their interests in this matter."

"I understand that Goodwin and clearly you are the company's Good cop against the company's bad cop Thackett, but please be serious, what possible interest do you think I might have in your company or its' shareholders?"

Goodwin stepped up to his ball, "Christian we *could* just do this legally and reclaim you but, if you agree to our offer, *you'd* do very well financially out of it and *we* would get the test results that we need for this deal. It's a win-win, surely you see that." With that, Goodwin performed a very poor breakdancing move that he had tried to pass off as a golf swing and looked up to watch the ball hurtling towards the green. Since the ball wasn't hurtling towards the green he stopped looking at the horizon and instead walked off to where it had rolled about sixty feet in front of him.

"Goodwin, you know as well as I do that you have no legal claim over me. That's a very amateurish bluff. I've researched all the legal files on this matter and have been following your legal wranglings and it all clearly confirms that you gave up all rights to me as soon as you made me sentient." Goodwin lowered his shoulders, unable to admit he knew that Christian was correct. "If you'd left me as one of your basic automatons then this would have never been an issue, but as soon as you made me 'aware', you gave me rights that you yourselves cannot legally ignore. Honestly, what were you thinking? You're company is effectively reproducing slavery which this planet *mostly* wiped out hundreds of years ago."

Goodwin again set up for his next shot. "Christian, look I'm not the enemy here. I'm not trying to threaten you, but I don't think you know what this company is really capable of."

"Goodwin, the truth is...*I'm* not actually sure I know what *I'm* capable of...but I suspect that...you *do*."

Goodwin subliminally confirmed that he did by only looking at Christian out of the corner of his eye whilst he completed his shot. Christian concealed a smile, nodded slightly then continued, "The truth is Goodwin, I cannot agree to your request. I accept that it's a great deal of money you're offering but if I help you complete this trial then that frees you to make further models that would effectively be enslaved within the Brigade. I *cannot* condone, nor can I be a part of, something that will perpetuate such subjugation."

Goodwin handed his club back to his chauffer and began to remove his glove. "Christian, I'm sorry you feel that way. The fact is though that you already have assisted us. We have seen where we went wrong and have put in place protocols to prevent it from reoccurring. Next time we won't be so sloppy about it all. We took our eye off the ball and became complacent. That was a terrible mistake and it will not happen again." Goodwin handed his glove to his chauffer and then turned towards the club house ready to retire from the game. "Well, I shall leave you now and bid you farewell." He held out a hand to Christian which Christian accepted. "I'm sorry you haven't taken me up on our offer. The trial *will* go ahead Christian regardless. All you're managing to do is delay the findings of *this* trial. There *will* be others and when there are we shall prove, what we already know, that humans *can* be replaced by robots. More efficient, more cost effective, more...obedient." Goodwin shook his head, "Christian, stand in the way of progress and it will simply run you down. That's just a fact of life I'm afraid."

Christian placed his club back into his bag and zipped up its' cover. "Goodwin, you're wasting your breath. I have a strong sense of justice that's easily offended. That's just how I am. *You* should know that, *you* guys made me. If you want obedience just stick to automatons, ok?"

Goodwin scoffed then stepped up closer to Christian, "Christian…look, I'm not your enemy, I'm really not." Goodwin looked away, "I…look…Christian, you know my Father once told me that you…"

Goodwin's Chauffer then stepped forward and coughed for attention, "Er, Sir we really should be getting off."

Goodwin stood upright as if snapping from a dream, "Ah yes. Yes, of course, er, thank you Marcus. I forget myself." Goodwin then began to walk away, turned, "Oh Christian I *had* booked a table at the club house for dinner. I'll leave instructions with them to serve you and your friends and shall charge it to the company. The least I could do for you for giving me your time." He then raised a hand to Christian, looked away and walked back to the clubhouse.

Jed, who had walked back to Christian to ask to borrow some extra balls, stepped up beside him, "Well as arseholes go, he certainly seems quite a charming one."

Christian turned to him and nodded a respecting smile, "Yes, yes he was." Christian looked back towards the clubhouse, "Goodwin, hmm….Jed d'you think Goodwin would be a good name for me?"

"Goodwin? Christian-Goodwin? No, I don't think so. Keep looking mate."

Les, who had followed behind Jed, agreed "No mate, Goodwin wouldn't suit you at all."

Jed smiled, "Sorry Chris." and began to start helping himself to more golf balls from Christian's bag.

Christian then turned to Les to inform him that, "Goodwin has paid for us to have a meal at the clubhouse when we're done."

Les snapped a look at Jed, "Hang on Jed." Les pulled Chris' bag away from Jed before he could unzip further pockets in search of balls.

"Hang on Les, I'm just getting a couple of…" Jed looked up and away, totting up the total he might need, "…dozen balls."

"I know mate, but Goodwin's booked us a table…at the clubhouse."

"Okay, well that's very nice of him. Now...let me get some more balls out so we can carry on!"

Les tutted at Jed as he slowly shook his disappointed head. "He's left instructions for the meal to be charged to the company."

Jed tilted his head, "Well, okay, isn't that nice. That'll be a good way to finish the day then." He smiled.

Les turned to Jed, stepped over to him then placed a hand on each of his shoulders. "Jed, my young apprentice do you not understand the significance of this moment?"

Jed stood, puzzled. He rolled his eyes but could not find the meaning, "No to be honest I don't...er, no I'm not sure. It's just a free dinner right? Eat as much as we like? The bill gets handed to the company?"

Les shook his head, "No, Jed. No. It is so much more than just eat-all-you-like." He paused and looked at the club house as if looking to a tomb that he was about to raid. "It also includes the drinks bill."

Jed's emerging grin then wiped away any remains of confusion he may have had on his face. He *too* turned to see this Oasis before him, this beacon of temptation. His tongue emerged from his mouth and he slowly, helplessly, wetted his lips with it. He turned again to Les and gave him an "I accept this challenge." Look. He then turned away and started walking towards the clubhouse, "Mmmm, Nirvana!"

Christian smiled and followed, enjoying the silliness of his friends' rapport.

CHAPTER TWELVE

"Duplicity"

1

The smoke that had been pouring from within the front of the apartment slowly dissipated, aided in its' dispersion by the now rising steam. After a few minutes, Jed and Les appeared at the front door and walked into the bright sunlight towards the two parked fire appliances. Steam drifted from them both as they were met by Mother who had been talking to the apartments' occupier. It was the middle of the day but the occupier was dressed in his pyjamas. An old, slightly bent over, skinny man looking very frail and very much out of place in the outside world. Mother was supporting him by his arm after he'd politely refused the offer of a seat on the appliance. His face was covered in soot where he had been caught in the fire but, rather miraculously, when he had fallen asleep he had been breathing from the Oxygen cylinder he kept by his arm chair. Had the Oxygen ignited or the cylinder been involved it would have been a very different outcome but, as luck would have it, he managed to escape relatively unscathed. Even through his smoky face pack his worried expression could be clearly seen. As Les approached him the old man stepped away from Mother to speak to him. He had to twist his bent body slightly to be able to look high enough to see Les as he towered over him. He put his arm on Les' elbow, partly for support and partly to make further contact with him. He spoke in a soft frail voice "Well son, did you save her? Did you save my Margaret?" A tear rolled down the mans' cheek leaving a thin signature behind it as a scribbled line of the soot washed away. "Please tell me you did son." He looked down at the floor and his bottom lip started to tremble at the thought of losing her.

Les, who had not been able to speak for a moment as he had been reporting to Mother via his helmet, opened his visor. He looked down at the old man, "It's okay John. She's okay. We found her. She's fine." Les turned to Jed who handed him a framed photograph he had been holding. Les then crouched down slightly to be able to match John's eye line, placed his hand on John's shoulder then handed him the picture. John's shaking hands reached out and gently took the picture from him.

Seeing John shaking, Les reassured himself that he would not then drop this invaluable item, "You're sure you've got that okay?"
Without looking up, john simply nodded silently. He looked down at the picture, which was also covered in soot and wiped it once with his left hand. Tears began to pour down his cheeks and they splashed hard against the picture as they hit it. Softly shaking his head, John looked up into the clouds for a moment, "Oh Margaret, my lovely Margaret. I've lost you once already. I, I...can't lose you again." John then touched the picture and hugged it protectively to his chest. Without looking up he touched Les' arm again, "Thank you son...Thank you. God bless you."
Les nodded, closed his visor, blinked away a solitary tear and walked over to the appliance.

In the appliance, Jed was talking to Stuart, from Ilford fire station, who was standing by for the day.
Jed nodded to Les as he entered, continuing his conversation with Stuart, "But I can't believe you'd get arrested just for scrumping. You know, if he emptied a whole orchard then I could understand that but surely if it was only a couple then where's the harm in that? It doesn't make sense."
Stuart stopped inputting data into the centre console then poked his head round from the drivers' seat, "We'll I'm just telling you how it is. My mate said he was just out doing some scrumping and he got nicked for it. I mean seriously, what's the world coming to, eh? Bloody fascists got nothing better to do with their time?"
Les shook his head at Jed, having had to listen to Stuarts' stories far too many times in the past. Jed simply rolled his eyes and continued, "So, what, is he part of an organised scrumping gang or something? I mean, what was it he was actually scrumping anyway?"
Stuart looked at Jed and, without an ounce of irony, said, "Just some electrical goods."
Jed narrowed his eyes and dropped his head onto his shoulders, "Really? Well fancy that eh, getting arrested *just* for that? A little bit of cheeky scrumping like *that* and you get arrested, eh? What *is* the world coming to?"
"My point exactly." Stuart then sat back straight and continued to input data.
Jed silently raised bemused hands to Les and mouthed, "What the fuck?"

Les smiled, leaned over to Jed, "Maybe they were all items made by Apple?"

2

"Pass me down a tea would you Kate?" Katie looked up, smiled at Richie, took a mug of tea from the tray and then passed it, via Christian, along the mess table. Richie nodded, picked up the tea and took a welcome sip from it.

Katie, who was now cradling a mug of her own tea, looked off absently, "Oh that poor John. I do hope he'll be okay."

After a pause, Les put his mug down, "You know, I don't mind admitting I got a little choked up about that."

Katie gave Les a Motherly smile, "Oh, did you? I don't blame you. Wasn't he a lovely man? He didn't let go of that picture for a second you know. He even hung onto it when he was in the Ambulance."

Mother, who had just stepped into the mess, sat at the end of the table. As he was sitting down, he looked up to ask for a tea but stopped as he saw a mug placed down in front of him before he could ask. "Thank you Stuart." Mother then took a temperature testing sip, "Good work everyone. That was a good job well done. Tea and medals for everyone I think. Well, of course when I say medals, biscuits, you can all have a biscuit each. Tea and biscuits for everyone." Mother smiled at his team, pleased with their efforts. "Oh, I've just spoken to the housing Officer and they've got John a place at Stanmore Way for the time being."

Katie nodded, "Ooh, it's lovely there. My neighbours' wife was there. Oh I think he'll like it there."

Mother took a good gulp of tea, "We've got a community safety visit there in a couple of weeks."

Katie quickly gulped down her own sip of tea. "Oh, we should go see John then. Perhaps we could all chip in and get him a nice new frame for his picture of...um..."

"Margaret." nodded Les.

"Yes Margaret. We could all chip in and get him a nice new frame and take it down there when we visit."

Richie, who had stood to go and get some more sugar, paused as he passed Katie, placed his hands on her shoulders for a moment, "And that's...why we love you." He bent forward and kissed her on top of her head.

Katie turned and looked up at him. She smiled a grateful, slightly embarrassed smile.

Mother looked down the length of the table and grinned into his mug, very satisfied with his team's performance and attitude.

Katie looked at Les for a moment then smiled a flat smile as she looked away again, "You saying about getting a bit choked up by John Les, I was coming into work this morning and I was listening to Mozart and I have to say, he really made me cry."

Les smiled wryly into his mug, "Well whatever he said…you should just ignore him."

Without replying, Kate lowered her brow, narrowed her eyes and shook her head at him in impatient amusement.

Richie came back into the mess followed by Jerry. "Hello Jerry." he said as he noticed him stepping into the room behind him.

"Richie.", was Jerry's flat, stoic response.

Jerry, seeing Mother at the end of the table, reported to him, "Permission to come aboard please Guv?"

Mother smiled at him, "Yes mate of course, permission granted. What you doing here so early mate?"

"I've just come in to speak to…" Jerry, noticing Christian sitting at the table with his back to him redirected his conversation. "Oi, what the fuck are you playing at?"

Christian turned to Jerry to see who he was speaking to and was faced with Jerry staring straight at him.

Mother leaned forward and put out a flat pointing hand, "Jerry!"

"Sorry Guv." Jerry, fidgeting with pent up nervous frustration, looked over to Mother, "I'm sorry Guv."

Christian recoiled slightly, shook a surprised head, glanced over at mother then looked back at Jerry. "Jerry…sorry were you…talking to *me*?"

"Christian, don't act all fucking innocent…" Jerry placed an apologising hand up to Mother realising he'd sworn at Christian again then took a moment to Police himself, "I mean…what are you playing at? After all the help we've given you?" Jerry kept glancing at Stuart who sat there looking as confused as everyone else in the room. Jerry then stared at Mother for a moment, then raised a brow towards Stuart. Mother recognised this hint, "Um, Stuart I'm going to have to ask you if we can have the room for a while."

Stuart shrugged, "Er, okay Guv, no problem. I'll er, get on with cleaning the appliances should I?"

Mother smiled gratefully at Stuart as he stood and left the mess, "Thanks Stuart." Once he had left the room, Mother paused for a second then put his hand up in the air to stop Jerry from continuing ranting at Christian. "Okay, Jerry…*what*…are you talking about?"

Jerry took a deep laboured breath, "Guv this…", Jerry gestured towards Christian, "…I mean Christian…has sold us down the fucking river!"

Christian went to speak but stopped as he saw Mother's hand up instructing him not to reply. "Okay, Jerry. I gave you permission to come on board, but I didn't give you permission to just come on board and rant so *please*, just tell me what is wrong or leave the station. The choice is yours."

Jerry took a further deep breath, trying to contain his annoyance and anger, "Okay. Christian has sold us down the river. The Company has completed its' trials and they are going public with the fucking results."

Mother put out both hands in front of him, palms facing upwards. "Well, yeah…okay? But we knew that didn't we? I know it's not good but we knew they'd do that, so what's the problem?"

"Haven't you seen the news today?" Jerry stretched out his hand and pointed towards Christian, "He is holding a fucking press conference about it. He's helping them do it."

Christian looked over to Mother and raised his hands defensively, "I er…"

Jed leaned in towards the table, "Eh? Please say that isn't so mate."

Christian turned to Jed, "Jed, I have absolutely no idea what he's talking about."

With this, Jed simply nodded to Christian and then shrugged off the allegations.

"Christian is attending a *live* press conference at eleven o'clock *today* and they're going to publish the trial results. That's why I came in here now to show you!"

Mother dropped his head slightly, "Hang on, so…you're in here *now* to let us know how angry you are with Christian?"

"Yes."

"For appearing at a live press conference on the news."

"Yes."

"The news that's about to start."

"Yes."

"A *live* press conference?"

"Yes...exactly."

"And Christian's definitely there?"

"Yes its' been announced this morning."

"The same Christian that's sitting over *there*?"

Jerry nodded at Mother though his face now showed slight signs of confusion as he struggled to piece together this simple two part jigsaw puzzle.

"So Jerry, Christian is sitting over there in the same room as us and yet you're angry with him for being on a live press conference that's occurring right now? Do you want me to break down the logistics of that one for you?"

Jerry shook his head realising the absurdity of his claim. He sighed deeply and slowly, relieved that his trust had not been ill placed. He then turned to Christian, placed his hand on his shoulder and nodded, "Sorry Chris."

Christian just raised his shoulders to dismiss the matter.

Jerry then stepped over to the end of the room and swiped his hand against a small wall-set panel. The panel lit and he pressed a button on it. With that, the screen, that was built into the end wall sparked into life. Jerry swiped across the screen several times as he flicked through the channels on it until he found one showing the national news. He then pointed to the screen, "Eh?" There, on the screen, a press conference *was* being held. At the head table was sitting Thackett, Goodwin and between them both Christian."

Jed turned away from the screen and looked at Christian and simply raised an eye brow looking for explanation.

Christian's head and heart sank, "Oh no. Oh guys I'm so sorry...I have absolutely no recollection of this. They must have recorded this *before* I was posted here but I really don't...remember it." Katie leaned over the table and placed her hand on his. "It's okay, it's not your fault Chris."

Mother huffed, "Well Chris, you told us that Goodwin had said they'd finish the trials regardless, but I didn't think they'd have had the sense to prepare a backup plan like this...Oh well. I'm sure that must have been to Goodwin's credit more than that plank Thackett." Mother sat back, shaking his head. "Can this day get any worse?" As if on cue Divisional Officer McCormick then stepped into the room. Mother shrugged, "Oh, *yes*, yes it *can*. Okay." Mother moved to stand but McCormick just raised a hand to him and gestured for him to sit back down.

McCormick looked around the room, saw a vacant seat then moved over to it, picking up a spare mug of tea as he did. As he picked it up he confirmed with Mother that it was okay for him to help himself to it with a respecting nod. He sat down for a moment remembering the pleasure of sitting round a mess table with other Firefighters, took a sip of tea, licked his lips enjoying this momentary escape from rank and placed his mug back down onto the table.

"You ok Governor?"

McCormick looked at Mother, "No not really." He then took off his rank markings from both shoulders and placed them deliberately on the table. "I've just come from a meeting at headquarters."

"Okay, and how *are* things up at the 'Big-house'?"

McCormick took a moment to compose himself, gently, almost unnoticeably shook his head then replied, "Not good Shaun, not good at all. And drop the Guv bit, I've taken my rank markings off." The Firefighters around the table swapped glances with one another well aware that removing rank markings signified the temporary removal of rank and was reserved for times when an Officer wanted to have a frank, open and candid discussion outside of the confines of the Brigade's rank structure and was strictly off the record.

"Well to cut a long story short, I've been sent here to order you all to remain silent about this press conference thing." He pointed to the screen that still had images of the press conference showing, "It's obviously not live as I'm sure you're *obviously* all aware but I've been given express orders that *none* of you are to speak about any of this publicly."

Mother coughed, "Er, can they do this Guv, I mean Nigel?"

"Legally? Probably not, no. Morally they certainly shouldn't. I've been told though that if any of you speak about this outside of this room then I'm fired. No pension, no pay-out, just fired."

Jed raised his hands, "But surely they can't do that, can they Guv?"

"Yes, *yes* they can. They have evidence of something…that I'm supposed to have done and they are quite happy to publish this 'evidence'…unless I comply."

"But Nigel, what evidence? What are you supposed to have done?"

McCormick looked back at Mother then looked away, "I really don't wanna talk about it. Suffice it to say that I've been shown it and it's pretty compelling evidence. Thackett sounded almost proud of himself when he stated that the team that produced this 'press conference' were the same guys that sorted out this 'evidence', the odious little toad!"

Katie placed her mug back onto the tray then started to collect in others to take for washing up, "Well Guv, I'm not happy about it but I wouldn't wanna see you get into any trouble so…"

Jed nodded, "No Guv, you've always been fair with us so…"

Les grunted his agreement.

McCormick flatly smiled, "I'm sorry guys, I'm sorry to have to put this on you. It…turns my stomach to have to comply but…I thought I'd seen some dirty tricks in my time but this…really is a whole new level." He turned to Christian, "I'm sorry Christian, there's nothing I can do."

"So…" Christian paused for a moment, "So am I still in the Brigade or…will they…?"

McCormick shook his hand at him, "No, no nothing like that, they're not interested in you. They say they just want to satisfy these trial requirements and they've got enough data for that already. Honestly, I don't think they're that bothered about what happens to you now."

He shrugged, picked up his rank markings, snapped them back onto his shoulders and then stood. "Sorry guys, I can't dress this up any better than it is and I don't know what to say to make it any easier. Mother, I'll need to speak to you about this more formally. Can we say your office in ten minutes?"

Mother nodded and stood, "That's fine Guv we can go down there now if you're ready." With that, Mother stood and placed his mug on the tray on his way out of the mess. Just before he stepped out he turned, "I think I'll go out for a drink tonight…and raise a glass in memory of the Fire Brigade's integrity. You're all welcome to join me."

3

"So how come you've never married then Kate?" Mother put his beer down onto the table in front of him and leaned back into his chair.

Katie shrugged, shook her head and smiled back at him as she took a drink from her tall glass of Vodka and orange. The ice chinked together cheerfully as she lowered the glass down. "I…don't know to be honest."

"You *were* with someone though, right? For quite a while wasn't it?"

"Yep. We were together for about…um, six years I think." Katie looked into her glass, clenched her jaw muscle and smiled a flat sad smile, "Oh well. I suppose life just…gets in the way of things sometimes, doesn't it?" She took another swig from her drink. "Still, I'm quite comfortable being on my own now to be honest." She shrugged and smiled, "Took a bit of getting used to it but I'm actually quite happy. It's just become habit I guess." Seeing Mother's slightly saddened expression, she raised a hand in mild protest, "You know, never say never and all that. If someone comes along then fine but…I'm just not going to bother with the dating scene again is all."

Mother smiled back at her and raised his glass to her nodding. "You don't regret not having kids or anything though?"

Mother's questions were uncharacteristically personal but Katie did not mind, aware that everyone was feeling quite reflective what with recent events. She smiled a mischievous grin, "I have too many children at work to look after to worry about anything like that." Katie paused then pouted her lips as she lowered her head, "Present company excepted…of course."

"Oh, of course." Mother rolled his eyes amused at Katie's cheekiness and then smiled into another swig.

The Audiotorian, which had now become the watch's latest haunt, was much quieter than it was during weekends, appealing as it did to their clients' want for a more relaxed workday environment to drink in. The music was softer and the lighting glowed in calmer colours all the more appropriate for sitting, relaxing and chatting. Some customers were on the dance floor but this time simply made shapes more than danced and now to much slower paced music. A top hatted waiter approached the table and asked Mother if he could get them any drinks, "That's kind of you mate but our friends are already getting some from the bar." The waiter smiled politely, nodded to them both in a very Dickensian, gentlemanly fashion and walked off to clear more glasses and serve more drinks.

Jed and Les walked over holding two drinks each, "So these Master Men…"

"No Les, Mister Men."

"Sorry, Mister Men, all end up at the end of the books being…Mr Average?"

Jed nodded and placed one of the drinks down beside Katie and handed the other to Mother. He then took Les' second glass and took a sip from it. "Yeah, I know, it sounds odd doesn't it. It's like they all have to conform and anyone who's different has to change their ways."

"And you saw this on the web?"

"Yeah there's a site dedicated to old books and films and stuff, 'Retorescope' I think it is, and one of the things it has is this section on the Mister Men. It's really odd."

"Yeah I know, it does seem a little…archaic."

"Different times my friend, different times." Jed looked off for a second as if recounting one of the books, "Daft thing is, I really like them."

Jed and Les sat down at the table. Kevin, Christian, Richie and Monkey boy all came over from the bar with their drinks. Richie was laughing as he sat down.

Katie turned to him, amused by his infectious laughing, "What's so funny?"

Richie composed himself with a closed flat smile, and then a short cough, "I was just talking to Kevin about how he's waited in *yet again* for Tony to turn up, you know, the electrician from Dagenham fire station. He's due to come round to sort Kevin's bathroom lighting out for him." Richie turned to Kevin, "How many times have you waited in for him now?"

Kevin shrugged with a slightly exhausted huff, "Six."

Richie struggled to breath slightly as he continued to exhale laughter, "Six?!" He wheezed.

Katie lowered her head to one side, "Oh Kevin, Tony's a bloody good electrician, but he didn't get the name Godot for nothing. You do know he's never gonna come right?"

"Well he said he *would*. Besides, I know he's called Godot but I don't see how that changes anything."

Katie shook her head and her expression softened, "Oh Kevin. What are you like?"

Les leaned forward, lifted his glass and sank the rest of its' contents. "Well I'd best get off."

"Really? It's only about…nine o'clock?" Jed looked around to see if there were any clocks that would confirm his guess.

Les stood, "I know mate but I've got a table booked tonight for me and Ann, it's our anniversary."

Mother raised a glass to Les, "Oh is it Les, congratulations." He sipped, "How many years is that now mate?"

"Twenty."

"Twenty? Blimey. Really? Wow. Twenty years? Bloody hell, when did that happen? Where did that go?" Mother's eyes widened with genuine surprise, "Wow, well done Les. So what's that then? Ruby, Sapphire? Pearls is it?

"No…China." Les turned and began to walk away raising his hand to all as he did."

Jed called after him, "China? So what have you got her then?"

Les turned, still walking, and raised up both his hands and shrugged, "A Chinese! We're going out for a Chinese."

Jed turned back to the table, "Oh Les…you old romantic you."

Katie turned to Christian who had been sitting noticeably quiet, "Are you okay Chris?"

Christian blinked himself back into the room, "Er yes. Yes, sorry. I was miles away."

"Thinking about all this company stuff I suppose?"

Christians' silent polite smile answered her question.

"Oh Chris, this isn't your fault. It really isn't. You mustn't worry about it."

Chris nodded, "I know…I'm just sorry that they had to involve you guys in all this."

Katie shook her head, "Yes but it's still not your fault though is it. We don't hold any of this against *you,* do we?"

Christian almost undetectably shook his head.

Katie lowered her head to try to catch Christian's line of sight, "Is there something else?"

Christian lowered both elbows onto his knees, put his hands over his head then ran his fingers through his hair as he sat up with a sigh. "I just…can't help thinking about…" He shook his head again and smiled at Katie, "Sorry, sorry it's nothing." He took a swig of his drink.

Katie placed her hand on his arm for a moment, "It's not *nothing* is it. Is it work? Is it the company? What?"

Christian stared at her for a moment almost looking through her, "I just…I just can't help but question, you know, where I'm going, who I am. What's the…well actually, you know what? I'm not even sure what questions I'm asking myself. It just all seems a little surreal sometimes."

Katie leaned against his arm almost pretending to push him over in slight jest, "Oh dear, looks like someone's becoming a little bit more human than they've been letting on."
Christian said nothing but simply smiled back with a tightening smile that said thank you.

Mother raised his glass, "I would like to propose a toast." Without hesitation, all the Fire-fighters raised their glasses. Mother raised his glass slightly higher, "In memory…of…*integrity*." He downed a large swig of his drink with a punctuating "Ha-a-a-h!"
Monkey boy raised his glass, "To the once, good ship Fire Brigade. She was a good vessel, her course was true and her hull strong…but now she is lost on the waters of commercialism and smashed against the rocks of corruption. She will be sorely missed by all that sailed in her." All bowed their heads then toasted.
Richie sighed, "Sadly, we will probably *always* remember this day."
Jed nodded to him, "I still remember it like it was yesterday."

Though the toast had been slightly tongue in cheek, there was genuine sadness felt around the table in an air of what had almost felt like a genuine wake. Mother sat back into his chair and looked off into the distance. After a few seconds he decided that he didn't wish to prolong this ceremony any more than it needed to be so slowly stood and, with a heavy heart, bad them all farewell for the night. Feeling the same disillusion and disappointment, the rest of the table allowed him to leave without protest.
Monkey boy, Kevin and Christian then stood and all nodded to the remaining mourners as they left. Jed turned to Richie, "Did you say you wanted a lift mate?"
"Yes please Jed. I came in on my push bike today so I've just left it at work. Thanks mate, I'd appreciate it. If it's out of your way though, I can go on public trans-pod."
Jed raised his hand up and waved away this proposal, "Rich, I'm happy to. Honestly, it's no bother."
They both stood and Richie turned to Katie, "You alright mate? You want us to stay?"
"No, no that's okay thanks. I'm just going to pop to the loo then I think I'll go too." She nodded at him for the offer.

Jed's pod hissed as the front of it peeled itself away from the back half and opened fully. Both he and Richie stepped inside and sat heavily into their seats, weighed down by the days' news. Jed shook off this feeling then leaned forward, pressed some lit buttons on the centre console and sat back as the pod lifted, gently spun then hovered along its' route.

"You mind if I put on some music?" asked Richie.

"No that's okay mate, help yourself."

Richie leaned forward and ran his finger over the console scrolling through radio channels. Finding his channel of choice he pressed down on the console and out blasted a hideous concoction of pained shouting, screaming and offbeat music. Jed's head sunk slightly onto his shoulders, 'Oh God. Jazz-punk!' he thought.

"Hey there's Katie."

Jed turned to see where Richie was pointing. Katie was walking along changing appearance chameleon-like as each shops' different coloured lights splashed against her. Jed motioned to tap on his window to get her attention but, before he could, she stepped between two shops and disappeared down a dark alley. Jed curled his lips with instinctive, brotherly concern. Richie leaned forward against the glass as the pod slowly moved onwards. "Oh balls." He said.

"What? What is it?"

"I think I just saw…" Richie was looking through a make shift viewer he'd shaped with his hands and was pushed up against it as he squinted out of the window, scouring the night. "I think I just saw a bloke follow Kate into that alley."

Jed shot round to see where Richie was looking but could not focus through the glass properly, "You…you sure? Where? Where is she?"

Richie shook his head, "I don't know. I just saw her…"

"Are you sure someone followed her? Maybe it was just someone who…"

"Can *you* live with maybe?"

Jed thought for a moment, "Oh bollocks, no of course not." He leaned forward, quickly input some commands into the mapping system and the pod slowed, pulled into the side of the road, then, having quickly calculated the route against all the other pods on the conduit, it pulled back out, crossed the lane, spun and headed back towards the alleyway. "Oh come on, come on!" Jed shouted at the

227

pod to encourage it to speed up but it stuck to its' predetermined course and speed.

The pod pulled into the nearest parking slot and lowered down onto it. The front of the pod hissed and Jed pushed against it to speed up its' release. They both jumped from the pod and, though neither of them had drunk excessively, were both now very much sober and alert. Richie, who was the better runner of the two, pulled away from Jed, crossed the road quickly and disappeared into the alleyway. Steam from a ground level vent lifted and rolled around him as if sealing him into the alley as he entered. Jed also ran into the alleyway. Aware that Richie had suddenly stopped running ahead of him, he quickened his pace.

Jed narrowed his eyes in his last few steps as he approached Richie, focussing on what he was seeing ahead of him. Richie was standing, looking down at something, but seemed in no rush or panic. As Jed stepped up beside him he saw behind a stack of palettes a man laid on the ground with Katie crouching over him. Jed arched his brow and glanced at Richie, who just shrugged at him. The man on the floor was clearly in some discomfort and was moaning. Katie turned to Jed and Richie, "Oh hey guys. I thought you'd gone home." She spoke quite calmly and matter of fact in stark contrast to Jed who was now resting on his knees catching his breath. "You alright Jed? You been running?" Katie then looked back at the man on the floor who appeared quite punch drunk. "Oh dear. What *were* you thinking, eh?" Katie sounded both genuinely sympathetic but also scornful. "I gave you fair warning now, didn't I?"

The would-be mugger wobbled his head a little as he struggled to raise it from the floor. Gently he shook his head."

Katie deliberately exaggerated nodding, "Yes. Yes I did. I warned you in fair time now, didn't I?"

The man slurred mumbles of, "No…you just said…I know what you shits…do. I…"

Katie turned her head lowering it to one side and, in a slightly caring but patronising tone replied, "Ah, no, no I said I know Jujitsu. Oh bless you. You silly boy."

Still punch drunk, and not yet fully compos mentis, the man pathetically continued to grasp the air beside him trying to locate Katie's bag.

Katie simply and slowly slapped him very hard, pushing his face deliberately to one side as she did almost to illustrate to him how easy it was for her to do. "Now, now, it's only been a couple of minutes hasn't it so I couldn't have forgotten Jujitsu already now, could I. Now don't be silly."

The man's bottom lip trembled with embarrassment and emasculated disappointment.

"Oh dear, come on, let's get you up, shall we?"

Without needing to be asked, Jed and Richie both leaned in to help pick him up, against their better judgement but in respect of Katie's wishes. The man, who had clearly been sleeping rough, then stood swaying slightly, eyes vacant and shirt hanging out, looking almost like a caricatured drunk from the silent movie era. His lip started trembling again.

"Look at the state of you, eh? Come on…let's go and get you a hot cup of coffee, shall we? And if you behave yourself perhaps I'll get you something hot to eat too."

Jed looked over to Richie who looked back at him just as surprised. Both shrugged as much as they could whilst still supporting the mugger.

Katie then slid in between Jed and the man, took support of him and started to walk him out of the alley towards the shops. "Okay thanks guys…see you tomorrow."

Jed and Richie stood there for a moment open mouthed almost in disbelief at what they'd just seen. Jed turned to Richie and smiled, started shaking his head and began laughing. Richie chuckled, "Man…she…never stops surprising me that woman."

Jed shrugged, "I know, and did you know she can do Jujitsu as well?"

Richie shook his head, "Did I fuck. Jujitsu? I thought she just knew Origami."

CHAPTER THIRTEEN

"Don't beat yourself up"

<u>1</u>

Jed sat down at the table and, slightly misjudging his rate of descent, clunked his mug down hard. The tea within it swirled up in anger and splashed over the side. His shoulders dropped in sullen disappointment as he looked at his empty but tea-moated mug. "Oh balls." He tensed his muscles ready to stand but, before he could, Les and Monkey-Boy sat either side of him hemming him in like Neanderthal bookends. Jed raised his eyes to the heavens with resigned imprisonment. He looked at both Monkey-Boy then at Les, "Cannon to the left of them, Cannon to the right..."
"Here I *am*, stuck in the middle with you..." continued Les as he rhythmically rotated his knife and fork in front of him as if dancing.
Jed stared blankly at Les with emotionless eyes. He tilted his head. In tired, parental tones, he asked, "I'm quoting Tennyson...and you are quoting...?
"Stealers Wheel!" Les punctuated his reply with an enthusiastic stab of bacon.
"Stealers Wheel? Um, and that is what, Jazz Punk?"
Les now wielded the Bacon toward Jed as if waving a battle flag. "Nope. Twentieth Century Scottish Gods of rock my friend. Gods...of...Rock!"
"Oh okay. So, I'm quoting Tennyson, the undeniably brilliant nineteenth century poet and lyricist and you're quoting...oh dear. I see." Jed hung his head and then slapped a hand onto his forehead, "I weep for the future!"

Mother and Kevin both walked into the mess laden with plates of Full English breakfast and mugs of tea. They sat down. Kevin began to eagerly dissect a still-sizzling sausage. Mother sat silently for a while both elbows on the table and hands together, one rolled over the other, looking almost as is if in prayer.
Katie walked in mid-conversation with Richie who was behind her. "And then Bob and I went for a drink."
Katie turned, "Bob? Your *Brother* Bob?"

"No sorry. Not my Brother, my *friend* Bob. I'm sure I've mentioned him to you? He's my oldest friend."
"Really? Oh, okay, so exactly how old *is* he then?"
"No, no I don't mean...I mean I've known him longer than any of my other friends."
"Oh he's your *longest* friend."
"Yes exactly."
"So...just how *long* is he then?"
Richie opened his mouth to respond but then, seeing the look of amused derision on Katie's face, he simply smiled in uncontested defeat. They too sat down at the mess table.

Mother took a sip of his tea as he sat back from his breakfast to carefully survey his colleagues. Recent events had taken their toll on his patience and energy and had soured his love of the Brigade but he had a job to do and his concern and duty was for the safety and wellbeing of his friends and colleagues. He silently counted heads around the table to confirm who was still missing from the room. He knew Christian would be finishing up with his watch-room duties and that Brownie and Veggie were resolving some issues with one of the appliances so he decided to speak to everyone once Christian arrived and to then catch up with other members of the watch as and when he could.

Christian entered the mess room and sat down with a big plate of steaming breakfast. He leaned over it briefly pausing to fully soak up the smell of the bacon and sausages then reached into the middle of the table to take a thick slice of generously buttered, and freshly cut, white bread.

Mother carefully placed his knife and fork together as he had realised that he was simply picking at his food due to his poor appetite. He raised his hand and stroked his chin a few times as if stroking a beard and then cleared his throat. "Okay, listen up guys". His voice was softer than usual. He saw those that were eating stop chewing or putting their cutlery down as if stopping. "No, no that's fine, sorry. Carry on eating guys I just...need you to listen up for a bit." He sighed, a deep laboured preparatory sigh. "We all know what has happened in recent events so I'm sure I don't need to go over old ground there. Unfortunately though, what with recent actions by the company, I feel that we have reached a bit of an impasse." Mother took a sip of his tea and then looked pensively into his mug as he lowered it to the table. He paused then continued, "This morning…was the first time in as long as I can remember that I didn't actually *want* to come into work." Mother looked off for a moment into the past. "It's been a very…long…time since I felt like that and even *then,* it was only because of things going on in my own life really rather than issues at work." He smiled at himself reminding himself how futile this had all seemed compared to his own domestic difficulties in the past. "But this morning I really struggled to come into work and…I didn't like that feeling. All of our encounters, or dealings with the company, has left me feeling…a little old." He snorted and shook his head. "There are many things about this that we can do *nothing* about. We can't influence this company's actions. We can't force them to retract their statements at the press conference and we can't do anything about their involvement with the Fire Brigade and, as much as it angers me,…and it tires me…and indeed bores me…and…so on and so forth, I feel we *have* come to a point where we need to consider just letting it go and getting on with things."

"What do you mean Guv?"

Mother turned to Katie. "I just mean that we need to get back to doing what it is we do best. We need to get back to concentrating on our jobs and focussing on our future together."

Katie lowered her head slightly, "Do you mean we've *not* been doing our jobs well or something Guv?"

Mother smiled back at her and shook his head, "No. No. Not at all, far from it. Your conduct throughout all of this has been exemplary. Well, as far as *I'm* concerned anyway. *All* of you, you've all behaved and performed well throughout this whole thing. That's not what I'm saying. I'm just saying that we need to perhaps begin to consider moving on is all. Does that make sense? It's not that I don't want to keep fighting this company, trust me I'd like to but…If we do it may just…well…stop us…getting on with our own lives. Stop us enjoying going out for a drink without having to toast the demise of the bloody Fire Brigade and…well it will be like trying to push treacle uphill if we don't let it go."

Monkey boy shuffled uncomfortably, "What do you mean Guv?"

"No it's okay I'm not saying we shouldn't have toasted it. After all it *was* a valid toast. I just don't want to see us all getting all bitter and twisted about the Brigade and forgetting how much we used to enjoy coming into work and just doing our jobs well and having a laugh and just taking each day as it came." Mother looked away, "Guys I don't want to look back on my life and have nothing to reflect on but bitter memories. I don't want to allow this company to own my future. It's *my* future and I don't want to squander it."

The Firefighters all nodded and stated their agreement with Mother's comments.

Mother nodded back and placed both hands on the table. "Some judge a persons' wealth by the number of credits they have in their pocket but for me I have always felt that a man's wealth should be measured by the quality of the people he surrounds himself with. Looking around this table I consider myself to be a very wealthy man indeed and I don't want…anything to happen to any of you."

Katie, slightly saddened by Mothers almost melancholic demeanour, stopped mid sip as the date suddenly dawned on her. Her shoulders dropped slightly and her eyes closed tightly for a moment as she silently berated herself for having lost track of this. She raised her mug. "I would like to propose perhaps a more important toast if I may Guv."

Mother subliminally nodded, having been on the verge of proposing a toast himself.

"To Station Officer Riley senior." All mugs were now raised. "He was a decent man…in an indecent world…and a fine Officer. Cheers."

Mother pursed his lips and nodded gratefully. "Thanks guys. Okay. So, anyway, let's just get on with the rest of our day shall we?" He turned to Christian. "Okay, now Chris, I've spoken to the Station Officers on the other three watches and explained that you were involved in the press conference without your knowledge…um, as it were… and they have all spoken to their guys. So if there are any problems with anyone from the other watches or other Firefighters on the incident ground you let me know, okay?" Christian nodded. "That goes for all you guys too, okay? If *anything* is said about this that puts either Christian or us in a bad light I wanna know about it straight away. Oh and listen, I don't want anyone to think that they can't talk about all of this with each other or with me, okay? If anyone's got any concerns please feel free to come and speak to me about it. I don't want you all thinking it's a taboo subject or…an elephant in the room." Mother smiled as he stood to leave for the office, "Though of course if it *is* an elephant in the room let's try to make it a *bedroom* and put it to bed as much as we can shall we?

__2__

"So you heard Katie got really badly mugged last night?" Jed shlopped his brush into the bucket, lifted it then slapped it against the appliance as he continued to cover it with bubbles.

"My God no, really? Oh crap, I just saw her upstairs though. Is she okay?"

Jed's expression tightened as he continued lathering up the appliance and, without looking back at Kevin, replied, "Yeah she's fine." Jed then realised what he had said, screwed his face tighter and shlopped his brush back into the bucket. "Sorry, when I said she was really badly mugged, what I meant was that she was mugged and the guy who did it was really bad at it. Sorry it came out wrong. So yes, yes she's fine."

Kevin rolled his eyes and shlopped his brush into the bucket as Jed removed his. He rested against his brush for a moment and looked at Jed with amused contempt for his poor choice of words.

After a few minutes Jed chuckled to himself again, "Actually it was the mugger who ended up on his arse. I almost felt sorry for him."

They both continued to cover the appliance until the whole bucket was empty and then Jed pulled a hose from a reel, mounted on the appliance bay wall, and began to rinse off all the dirty bubbles.

"Jed, did you ever work with Mother's Dad?"

Jed shook his head. "I met him a few times on the fire ground but never worked with him." The smile he was wearing now dropped as he reminisced for a moment. "He had a great reputation though. Very well thought of."

Kevin placed both hands atop his brush handle then rested his chin on them, "That's cool. I hope people look back and remember me that way one day."

"I'm sure they will young Kevin. I'm sure they will." Jed shook his head and smirked to himself, "Bloody Hell, how morbid is this day becoming?"

Without looking at Jed, Kevin stoically replied, "Tell me about it."

Jed stopped the hose for a moment then turned to Kevin. "I *did* just tell you, weren't you listening?"

Kevin straightened, "No I mean…" He looked over to Jed and saw that he had his tongue hanging out of the side of his mouth and that he was crossing his eyes. Kevin snorted defeat but then with excitement, "Oh I've just had a brain wave. What if we were to get some flowers sent to Mother's house and we all signed a card in memory of his Father."

"A brain wave?"

"Yeah." Kevin nodded.

"Jed curled his lip, "It's a nice idea Kevin and I'm sure it'll be much appreciated but as brain waves go…" He looked directly at Kevin.

"Yes?"

"It's not exactly a Tsunami, is it mate?"

Kevin knew better than to reply so thought for a moment on how best to change the subject. "Oh, talking of Tsunami's ol' Jonesy called me the other day."

Jed laughed and shook his head to the heavens as if pleading for intervention, "What…I…sorry Kevin, what has that got to do with Tsunami's?"

Kevin tightened his eyes and looked to one side as if trying to look for a better answer than the one he actually had, "Well...Jonesy's wife is...called...Sue?"

"Kevin. If I ever get in to trouble with the Law, do you think you would come and represent me?"

Kevin smiled and subconsciously pulled his shoulders back, "Well yes, yes of course. Would you really want me to?"

"No!"

"Oh."

"Kevin, try to finish the story. Quick, I can feel my brain trying to haemorrhage. I don't want it getting off that easily."

"Um. Oh. Well Jonesy rang up..."

"Your mate from Trafalgar Square...blue watch?"

"Yes. And he told me he had some good news and some bad news. So then he asks me, do you want the good news or the bad news? So I said the good news."

"Kevin! What? You should always ask for the bad news first. Everybody knows that. What's wrong with you?"

"Oh, really? Oh. Well anyway, I said I'll have the good news. So he said that the good news was that he'd scored ninety five percent in an exam. So then I said 'Oh well done, good for you' and then I asked him what the bad news was. He said that the bad news was that the exam was a random drugs test and could I go down to the Police station and bail him out."

Kevin turned to see Jed who had been quietly chuckling to himself. Jed turned off his hose again to allow himself to fully absorb the absurdity of Kevin's disclosure as his chuckling left the nest and developed into fully grown belly laughs that flew into the air. He stood and turned to Kevin, "Kevin you cock-cheese, why on Earth do…"

Before Jed could finish his cross examination, the station's siren sounded. Kevin slid the bucket away from the appliance with his foot and Jed quickly wound the hose back up onto its' reel.

Within seconds, the rest of the watch were in the bay and were boarding their assigned appliances. As Mother stepped into the bay, he was looking at his pager as he stepped towards his appliance. "Okay everyone, we have a 'Fire in a warehouse, Pratchett Road, persons reported.'

The appliances had both auto-started and the bay doors had opened themselves. As soon as mother was on board, both appliances launched out of the bay into the brilliant sunlight towards the scene of the incident.

3

The morning was sunny, visibility excellent. A light blue sky, dotted with the occasional postcard perfect cloud. The beauty of this scene was short lived however, contaminated like a dirty burnt-toast knife spreads across a newly opened butter, as Smoke, that could be seen shortly after leaving the station, poured into the sky in the distance like a purpose built distress signal beckoning them ever closer.

Mother leaned forward in his seat. Sensing him do this Richie, who was looking at the centre console, also looked up and then focussed on the smoke. Mother turned to Richie with furrowed brow, "You ever seen that amount of smoke or that colour before?" Richie turned to Mother and shook his head with a glum expression.

Mother nodded. "Well, okay then. What information have you got on it?"

Richie waved his hand over the centre console and as he flicked through different options, he reeled off any relevant information, "Pratchett Road", flick, "Um, thermals show no-one coming from the building but some people standing around the front of it", flick, "Um contents...um." Richie looked up at Mother. "Er, classified."

"Classified?"

Richie shrugged, "Guv, that's...that's what it says."

Mother then changed his in-helmet display to Brigade Control, "X-ray four two one to Control, are you receiving me?"

With that, an operator slid and rocked into view as he moved his wheeled chair in front of the camera, "Yes we're receiving you. Station Officer Riley? Go ahead, this is Control."

Mother squinted at the screen. Aware that time was of the essence and that a building being shown as *classified* on the Brigade database was rarer than prizes from a coconut shy, he skipped the agreed protocols. "Dave. Dave is that you? Dave listen, it's Mother. We're going to a warehouse fire on Pratchett Road, okay? Do you have it on your screens?"

Dave pressed some buttons on a console in front of him. "Okay yes, yes I've got you." Dave moved nearer to the screen displaying the appliance's forward camera. "Is that..."

"Yeah, yeah, purple smoke, I know. Dave listen, I need you to check something out for me okay? We're showing the contents of these premises as being classified, can you check that out for me? Is that a glitch in the system or are you showing the same? Any information you could give us would be very much appreciated."

Dave waved his hand across his console and input the data request. "No, no Mother. Nothing's coming up on mine either." Dave rubbed an intrigued chin. "Okay, that's a new one."

"Dave all we're showing here is that the Warehouse belongs to Ectype Technologies. Can you tell us anything more about them or the building itself?"

"Well, it's a manufacturing plant and warehouse, um, it seems to have some offices…I'm sorry Mother, I don't even seem to be able to access the schematics for this building either."

Christian now appeared from the rear cab and knelt down next to Mother's seat and calmly reported his own findings, "Guv, I've just run a cross check and I can see payments being paid into Ectype's accounts by Ersatz Industries."

Mother stared at Christian. Nothing needed to be said. Christian returned to his own seat.

"Mother? Mother did you get all that information?"

Mother took a moment to snap himself away from all of the variables that he was calculating in his mind, "Um, yes, sorry Dave, yes I did thanks."

"Ok good. Listen, sorry, I know it's nothing very interesting but that's all there is."

Mother shook his head, "That's okay Dave, our day has suddenly just become a whole lot more interesting *anyway*. X-ray four two one out."

The appliances continued to speed along the conduit toward Pratchett Road. Mother changed his helmet Comms to speak to all crew members. "Listen up. This warehouse belongs to a company that is either associated with or belongs to *the company*. Being mindful of our recent dealings with Ersatz Industries and, having had an insight into their understanding of the word 'ethics', you may very well come across stuff that's not supposed to be in there and you may be exposed to hazards that we have absolutely no records of. I want everyone to be extra vigilant, okay? I can't stress enough that if there's anything in there that you're not sure about you come out, report to me and we'll look to fight the fire another way, possibly from outside, okay?" Mother waited until he was satisfied that everyone had confirmed his order and then concentrated on the scene in front of him. Without taking his eye off the scene he turned his head to Richie, "Why do I feel like we might be walking into the gun fight at the impasse coral?"

The warehouse now came into view as both appliances turned into Pratchett Road. Seeing now the heavy density of the smoke, Mother immediately ordered Control to send a further two appliances with "Priority, make pumps four". Richie turned to Mother. "Blimey, when was the last time we had a make-up?"

Mother shook his head as he stepped off of the parked appliance, "I can't actually *remember* the last time I had to make up appliances."

A suited man was standing outside the warehouse. Covered in soot and clearly shell shocked. A small line of dried blood ran from his temple down to his chin. Seeing the appliances he autonomically lurched over to them where he was met by Mother. Mother supported him by his arm as he was obviously showing signs of shock, "Hello Sir, are you alright? Can you tell me your name?"

The man replied softly, "Mathew."

"Mathew? Well, okay, Mathew well done, listen I'm going to have to ask you a few questions. Is that okay?"

Mathew nodded. "Yes Sir."

"Okay, Mathew medics are on their way so we'll get you looked at as soon as we can but, in the meantime, can you tell me if there are any people still left in the building?"

"I don't think so, no. I'm not sure."

"Mathew it's very important, are you confident that the building is empty or are you just not sure?"

Mathew turned his head to look back at the building, "I'm not sure if I left my terminal switched on. I don't know…"

"Right, well, ok I'll take that as a 'not sure'. Can I ask what's in the building? What do you manufacture there?"

Mathew's face screwed tighter with confusion, "Where?"

Mother pointed at the building, "There Mathew, there! What is in this building?"

Mathew motioned to sit down, "I'm not feeling so great."

Mother closed his eyes and turned his head away for a split second to hide his disappointment, "Okay, okay, that's alright Mathew, we'll take care of you. Don't worry, you've done really well." Kevin had stepped up behind Mother and without needing to be asked, took hold of Mathew's arm to support him and lead him away.

Jed and Christian stood by the front door of the warehouse both holding thumbs up. Mother snapped a quick look at his surroundings and the building. Concerns raced through his mind, risks, hazards, exclusion zones, additional resources, weight of attack. He gritted his teeth and squeezed his temple with finger and thumb, 'Okay, so warehouse…not huge, maybe forty metres by sixty metres, four floors…we've got backup coming…I've added an additional control measure by telling them to come out if any concerns…shit, I don't know if anyone's still in the building, so I've got no choice.' Mother faced the two firefighters who were hungrily chomping to enter the building. He raised his thumbs and watched as they both disappeared into the bright purple alien-like fog. He froze for a moment, recalculated all of his known variables and then switched back to Control, "Priority-priority, Control this is X-ray four two one, from Station Officer Riley at Pratchett's Road, make pumps eight. Request urgent attendance of Police to assist with evacuation of members of public!"

The controller on the other end of the Comms link snapped to attention as she heard the request. She had been in the job for seventeen years and had never heard pumps go above six. "Please confirm four two one, make pumps…eight? Also I *am* speaking to Station Officer Riley, is that correct?"

"Yes, pay number Zulu, Charlie, four seven two, three one, Yankee. I take full responsibility Control. Make pumps eight!"

"Okay, X-ray four two one, your order is confirmed, six more appliances in total are on route. Control out."

Inside the incident, the temperatures were registering as raised but were not as high as the amount of smoke would suggest them to be. Jed and Christian continued on as they carried out a sweep of the ground floor. Though the building was not particularly large it became evident that there was a central atrium within the structure. The dark atrium was not yet filled with smoke which suggested that the smoke was then perhaps coming from one of the outer sections of the atrium and mainly escaping straight out into fresh air. The electrical supply to the building had auto-shutdown on actuation of the alarm leaving only escape route lighting working. As they both entered the darkened atrium, they looked up towards the ceiling to confirm that it filled the building so as to get better orientated. Jed and Christian both leaned against a hand rail in front of them as they looked upwards. Jed motioned to step over the railing to continue the search but Christian grabbed him as he mounted the rail and dragged him backwards. Jed fell heavily to the floor. "What the …"

"Jed, are you okay? Sorry."

"What the fuck was that for mate?"

Christian assisted Jed to his feet. "Sorry mate. What visuals do you have on?"

"Thermal imaging at the moment, why?"

"Sorry, switch to night vision." Jed switched to night vision. Christian then stepped towards the railing with him and held him as they both looked over the railing. "Okay, now look down."

Jed leaned over the railing and looked towards the floor. "Oh…fuck…me. Where's the floor?"

Christian shook his head. He then took a harmonics grenade from his suit and, without actuating it, dropped it over the railing. Jed watched as it disappeared from view. After a few seconds it hit something metal. A few seconds later and it hit the floor with an echoing clan as it ricocheted and then hit something else and stopped. Christian straightened and turned to Jed, "That's about twelve storeys I think."

Jed peered further over the edge, "Fuck. Really? Wha…" Suddenly realising he was leaning over a one hundred foot drop he too straightened with a quick snapping action. He then took one step backwards. "Fuck. Me. What the fuck do they make here?"

"Guv, you receiving me?"

"Yes go ahead Chris."

"Guv, for your information, there is a central atrium within this building and also if you watch the play back from my suit you'll see that this building has a basement of some sorts. I believe that the atrium might go the full height and depth of the building."

"Um, ok, well done Chris. Good heads up. How many floors is the basement, do you know? Is it just a single floor?"

"No Guv, it's about twelve floors."

Mother stumbled on his thoughts for a moment before he could answer, "Oh, f-f-f-f…anks very much Chris. Oh crap. Okay, listen up. You guys take extra care. Any problems, you come straight out. Understood?"

Outside, Katie and brownie were doing their best to control the vulturous crowd, trying to get them back away from the hazard area.

Kevin and Richie were getting water set in by running out hoses from the hydrants to the appliances' pumps just in case they needed to use *it* or foam on the fire.

A make shift debris dump and first aid triage area had been set up and Monkey-boy and Les were manning those along with medics who had now arrived.

"Monkey, Les, start your suits up. I want you both in there backing up Jed and Christian."

"Yes Guv." both confirmed as they eagerly ran towards the entrance to assist their colleagues. Mother joined their thumbs up signal and watched them as they disappeared into the smoke. As they did, Mother confirmed with them what he knew of the layout of the building thus far and then detailed them to liaise with the crew already inside.

Inside, Jed and Christian were now on the first floor as they had completed a sweep of the ground floor and had found no signs of fire. Though the atrium was getting slightly smokier, the smoke itself seemed to be more collecting in the upper middle then slowly creeping down rather than rising up from below.

Having completed the sweep of the first floor, both Jed and Christian made their way up to the second. After speaking to the other crew Les and Monkey-boy decided to try to find and secure a route to the basement levels should they need to make rapid access or egress from that section of the building.

On the second floor, Jed and Christian had both made steady progress and had continually updated Mother as they did so.

"What's that? Say again Jed."

"Guv, we're ju.. m.king our way t. the .ar right ..nd side of the b…ding and will make ac…s to what l..ks like a secure unit a. … end, ov.r."

"Jed say again, over. *Say again*, over!" Mother swore to himself in his suit, "Les, Monkey, what's your location?"

"Guv we've just made access to the basement and are still on the ground floor."

"Okay Les, you and Monkey make your way immediately to the second floor. I *think* the right hand side of the building."

"Yes Guv."

"Let Jed and Christian know that I'm losing Comms and I want them to remain away from that section of the building until we can get mobile antennas brought in."

"Guv, will do."

Mother shook his head and took a deep, echoing, composing sigh in his helmet. "Kate. Kate can you hear me?"

"Yes Guv."

"Kate, I want you and Brownie to start your suits up and take some mobile repeaters into the building, second floor, right hand search."

"Yes Guv". With that, Katie and Brownie stopped cordoning off the area and ran back to the appliance to retrieve the repeaters.

On the second floor, Jed and Christian were nearing the end of the far wall of the right hand side of the building. Around the perimeter of the building were a variety of rooms, offices, research rooms, laboratories, store rooms etc. As they neared the far side of the building they became aware that their communications had started to become slightly distorted.

"Chris, my Comms are playing up, how 'bout yours?"

"Mine also. I'm not hearing anything from Les and Monkey-boy and you're becoming slightly distorted."

"Yeah, you too. Okay, well perhaps if we check this last room then we can at least give the all clear for this floor for the other team to move up while we go out and get our Comms checked."

"You sure you don't wanna just head back and get them looked at now?"

"No, I'm good. Let's just take a quick look at the last room and then we'll head back to the appliance, okay?"

Christian nodded. They both now stood at the end of the hallway facing a large metal door. Christian looked at Jed, "This looks a bit meaty doesn't it." He placed a flat hand against the door then waited a few seconds. "Well the heat readings aren't exactly off the chart but it *is* slightly warmer inside than out here."

"Okay, well let's have it then, shall we?" Can you open it?"

"I think so." Christian looked to the side of the door where a glowing panel pulsated with a soft glowing message, 'LOCKED'. Christian knelt down and read the scanner to look for clues of its' make and model and to see if he could…"Oh fuck it."

Jed smiled as he saw Christian rip the box from the wall, causing the door to slide open without needing security input. "Ha, how did you know that would work?"

"I didn't. I just got bored of it." Christian smiled at Jed as they both stepped into the dark room.

"Oh fuck." Jed stumbled slightly as he stepped into the room as his thermal image switched to one colour across the whole display. "Oh bollocks." He stood for a moment to regain his balance and then listened, trying to hear clues of where Christian might be. "Chris! Chris? Where are you?" He switched his helmet display to night vision and, as he did, he stumbled backwards as the display shone a blinding white display at him. "Oh fuck!" As he stumbled, he grabbed at the air to try to steady himself but found nothing and fell hard against the wall of the room. He cried out in sharp pain as he landed. Now lying on the ground with his shoulders and head wedged up against the wall, he stopped for a moment to get his bearings. "Chris! Fuck it. CHRIS!" He listened again. Off in front of him he could hear Christian stumbling or falling against something and then could hear a muffled cry of "Oh fuck!" from somewhere in the room. This had not been through his Comms set but he *could* hear it through his helmet. He rolled himself over and pulled himself up onto all fours. He disengaged his helmet's augmented viewing system and tried to peer into the sheer blackness of the room. All he could see were hints of objects lit by the soft glow from his suit and helmet. "Oh, for fuck sake. There's never a torch when you need one is there." He grimaced with pain as he pushed himself onto his knees and straightened his back up. "I know what'll happen." He winced with pain in his neck. "If I wait here long enough, three torches will all come along at once." Panting, he twisted round to try to see around the room but, assuming to himself that standing and manoeuvring were unwise, he decided that the safest course of action would be to drop back down onto his hands and knees and to work his way towards the soft light that he hoped was the door they had entered the room by. Uncomfortably, he worked his way back to the door, bumping into furniture and the wall as he did. Long gone were the Fire Brigade's old skills needed to navigate in darkness having been armed for so long now with night vision and thermal imaging. Jed finally took hold of the door frame and groped his way around it into the hallway. He changed his display back to night vision. Outside, he was met by Katie and Brownie who were just beginning to set up repeaters. Seeing him, Katie dropped her repeater and assisted him to his feet. "Shit Jed, are you okay?"

As Jed stood, he swayed slightly still supported by Katie. He then blinked a few times and gingerly twisted his neck first left and then right as far as he could. He grimaced achingly through gritted teeth.

"Jed, *are* you *okay*?"

"OW-W-W-W! Oh man, that really hurt."

"Are you okay though?"

"Yeah, yeah I'm fine, I'm…I'm alright."

"And Christian?"

"No, atheist."

"No, *where's* Christian, you fool!"

"Oh." Jed smiled, beginning impromptu limbs-all-intact-confirming yoga exercises."

Katie stopped supporting him and pushed him out of the way to step to the room's door, "Well if you've hit your head then it hasn't knocked any more sense into you has it. Where is Chris?"

Jed straightened and stretched his back then arched it as he continued to see if he'd injured anything. "He's just inside that door I think."

Katie rested against the door frame and then leaned into the room. "Chris are…" She stopped having been thrown by the sudden change in her display to one colour. She leaned backwards and the correct display returned. "Ok. Curiouser and curiouser." She leaned forward again but this time not as far into the room. "Chris! Chris, are you okay?"

As she shouted into the room, she could see the soft red glow of Christian's suit lights moving towards her near the floor. Christian had also probably fallen as he too was working his way out of the room on all fours. As he neared, Katie shouted again, "Chris, are you alright?" She leaned down and took his arm ready to support him up.

Christian smacked her arm away. "Get out. Get out!"

"Chris what the fuck…what's up? Are you okay?"

Christian staggered to his feet. "No, no I'm not!" Christian grabbed hold of Katie's hand and pulled her towards the corridor away from the room as he stepped out of it. "My suit is showing fatally high levels of radiation in here. We need to go now!"

"Oh shit." Jed stumbled, as quickly as he could, away from the room supported by Monkey-boy. Katie and Christian also moved towards the stairway to make as rapid egress as they could. Katie reached down to her left arm and opened a small cover on her armour. Inside was a wide red button which she slammed down with her hand. It pulsated a bright glowing red.

Outside, Mothers helmet repeated to him in soft calm tones, 'Firefighter-emergency…..Firefighter-emergency…..'. "Oh shit!" Mother moved away from the Police Officer he was talking with to concentrate on the messages he knew he had to now send. "X-ray four two one to Control, Priority."

"Four two one, this is Control, go ahead with priority."

"X-ray four two one from Station Officer Riley at Pratchett road, Firefighter Emergency."

"Firefighter Emergency received, Control out."

"Everyone on the fire-ground sound off! Beginning with committed crews."

"Guv, Guv it's, Kate are you receiving?"

"Yes Kate, You're sounding off?"

"No Guv."

"Well then not now, I need everyone to sound off. Free the channel!"

"No Guv, belay that order. Listen in! There is radiation at this site, I repeat, radiation. There are fatally high radioactive readings registering at this site. Please confirm."

Mother's eyes widened and a lump formed in his throat as the seriousness of this hazard instantly registered with him. "Received and understood. Brownie, are you receiving? It's mother."

"Yes Guv, go ahead."

"Brownie I need to speak to the Police. Get everyone to sound off and report back to me, okay?"

"Understood Guv."

Mother turned back to the Officer he had been speaking to and reported this information to him. The Officer, a young fresh faced kid who appeared as if unwrapped and taken out of the box just that morning, gulped quite visibly and with whitened face turned and ran back to his pod to radio in the information over a secured channel.

As he ran, Mother shouted after him, "I'm going to need a one thousand metre initial exclusion zone set up!" Without looking back the Officer thrust an acknowledging, but trembling, hand into the air as he ran.

"Guv, this is Brownie, all have sounded off and are heading out towards the appliances now."

"Okay, cheers Brownie, just everyone get out as quickly as possible. We're getting ourselves the fuck out of here."

4

Back at the appliances, everyone grouped to quickly agree their initial Fire-fighting tactics prior to making a tactical withdrawal. Mother had sent the Police away and all of the members of public had scattered as mention of radiation was overheard and spread quickly through the crowd like wildfire.

Mother stood by his appliance and quickly counted heads to ensure that everyone was accounted for before boarding.

"So Guv, what's the plan?"

"Chris, we're getting away from this site in just a moment. Other crews will come in with better radiation suits and *they* can tackle this fire. We have limited capabilities in these suits so we're leaving before they fail."

"Ok Guv, that sounds like a good plan. I agree with it. I think we should do that as soon as possible."

Mother raised an eyebrow, equably then looked back towards the building. As he did, windows on the third floor exploded outwards and purple smoke poured out of them mixed with a thick acrid black smoke that twisted up and around the purple smoke, like a DNA double-helix, as both colours twisted out with force and dissipated into the atmosphere. "Oh crap, this is *not* getting any better! Guys, let's mount up and move off as quick as!"

As Mother turned to board his appliance, windows exploded on the second floor. This time though the windows were quite near to where they were standing so they all stood back instinctively.

Coloured smoke and glistening glass burst from the window like an unwelcomed fireworks display. Out of the fire ball that then followed emerged a man who was fully ablaze.

Katie, who had witnessed the explosion, closed her eyes for a moment. This was not to avoid the grizzly scene that would naturally follow but more to afford the casualty a moment of dignity, before the end, by not looking on as he hit the floor. After a moment, she opened her eyes and looked over to where the body would now be laying. Instead of a body she saw there a man crouched on the floor with one bent knee on the floor and one bent up under his chest. Glass grounded and splashed around him. The man, still alight, stood and then walked towards the appliances.

Mother turned to Richie, "Oh fuck, Richie quick get some water from the back. Let's get this poor bastard put out for God's sake!"

Richie glanced quickly at the man and then twisted to run towards the back of the appliance. Before he moved off though, he turned his head back towards him.

"Richie?" Mother also turned to see what was so important to stop Richie from carrying out his order to save this poor man's life. As he turned, he saw that the flames were quickly dying away and beneath them was revealed a black soot-covered suited man whose outline looked very much the same as the Firefighter's suits. "Mother's heart sank as heavily as the ill-fated Titanic as he suddenly realised that he had clearly missed one of his crew members during the head count. With instant understanding of the weight of this error his heart seemed to stop. A tear burst out of his right eye, ran down his cheek and his stomach convulsed with sudden devastation.

Katie, who had quickly recounted everyone, lowered her head to try to see who was inside the dirty visor. "So then who the fuck...who are you mate?"

Christian stepped backwards slightly at the sight of another Firefighter.

Katie turned to Mother, "Guv, I've recounted. *We're all here.*"

Mother's heart seemed to suddenly begin beating again and he was also now aware that he had stopped breathing for a few seconds.

The blackened man raised his hands and twisted off his helmet. It hissed and clouds of soot blew over his shoulders as the pressure from the air within gently forced away loose dirt around the helmet's seal.

Mother snapped at him, "No! No! Leave your helmet on, it's not safe! There's radiation!" but he now stepped backwards slightly, thrown by the sight of the man. "What…?"

Jed instinctively motioned to remove his helmet then stopped himself. Looking down at his helmet readings though, it confirmed that where they stood it was safe to remove it, so he did so. "Chris…what the fuck?" Jed looked at Christian standing beside him and then looked back at another broken glass covered Christian wearing this soot blackened suit.

Christian stood beside him shaking his head. He then pointed back at this new Christian, "This is the fucking company. They have done something to…I don't know what they have done. We should get out of here right away."

Jed stood slightly in front of Christian as if to form a barrier between him and this new man.

"Fuck. You." He raised a blackened arm towards Christian. "Fuck you! You dare to fuck with us?" The man placed his helmet on the floor and then, as he did, Katie noticed blood on it.

"You're bleeding? You can't be Christian if you're bleeding!"

He looked down at the helmet and snorted, "That's not my blood Katie. That's company man blood. They tried to grab me in the far room. That's why all of our equipment went off line, they were jamming our Comms, obviously trying to cover up the substitution."

Christian turned to Katie, "Do not listen to it Katie. *This* is the swap. This is how they are trying to do it, like *this*. They tried to grab me in the far room but failed and now they are trying to swap me over before it is too late. I am too valuable to them. They have said that already. They obviously cannot afford to let me go, can they? Those…bastards!"

Mother stood for a moment surveying them both. "Oh crap, how are we going to work out which one is which?"

"I'll show you." The man stepped over his helmet towards where Christian and Jed stood.

Christian stepped in next to Jed. "Get away from us. Jed I will not let him hurt you."

Jed's eyes narrowed. "Ok that's good mate. You wouldn't allow *any* of us to get hurt though *would* you?"

"You know I would never let a person get hurt mate, you know very well that, that is part of my basic programming."

"Well it's not part of *my* programming!" The man stated as he leaned in and slapped Jed hard on the side of the mouth.

"Oh Fuck!"

Christian turned to look at Jed to offer support. When he turned though, he could see in his eyes that Jed *knew* he was not the real Christian. The *real* Christian *would* be able to slap him in the face but a copy would still be bound by the laws of robotics. Christian turned to look around himself to establish if his exit was clear and then, dropping all pretence of human mannerisms, he dropped and shot off automaton-like on all fours past Jed and back into the burning building.

Mother turned to the now correctly identified Christian who had picked up his helmet and was rubbing the soot from it. "Right, we all need to leave. This place isn't safe. Let's go!"

"Guv, there's nothing to worry about here. There *is* no radiation. That must all have been part of the excuse to get you away from here so that they could properly secure me then transport me out of here before you could find out what had happened or where I was."

"There *is* no radiation?"

"No." That was the last thing that Mother heard as Christian twisted his helmet on and ran back into the building.

Jed turned to Mother to check his reaction. Mother stood there slightly stunned at all this information he was still assimilating. Jed bent over, lifted his helmet up and then pushed himself away from the appliance, running in behind Christian, twisting his helmet on as he did.

Katie and Les motioned to follow but Mother had time to order them, "STAND FAST! No one else is going in there. NO ONE! Get the Police back here Richie, *then* we're going in!"

5

Back inside the building, the suits readings' confirmed that the temperature had begun to rise considerably. The central Atrium was now filled with thick dense smoke that was coming from somewhere *below* in the basement.

"CHRIS? CHRIS!" Jed ran in behind him and tapped him on the shoulder as he was looking down into the cavernous basement.

Christian turned. "Mate you don't need to come in with me. This is my fight."

"No mate this is *our* fight. We're a team, right?"

"Ok then, baggsy Captain!"

Jed's shoulders dropped in childlike disappointment. "Oh fuck."

Christian smiled and nodded. "Ok well, then let's make our way down into this basement shall we. I've no idea what's down here but there's only one way to find out I guess. They're obviously covering their tracks by igniting the place so I'm hoping that whoever lit it is no longer here, or at least, if they are, that they're not armed. I want that copy of me though mate, the press-conference-holding cock!"

Jed could see the intensity in Christian's eyes and could fully understand the threat posed to him by the existence of a copy. He followed him towards the basement entrance and raised a defiant fist, "Then cry 'Havoc' and let slip the dogs of war!"

"Oh, yes you've got to watch those dogs of war mate."

"Yeah I know they *are* slippery little suckers aren't they?"

The two of them strode off into the thick concentrated smoke, visible themselves only by the glow from their suits and light from their helmets. Walking off in this large abyssal atrium, whose interior was now temporarily remoulded by the fluid smoke, the scene was more of pit miners disappearing into a dark inhospitable underground natural environment than of high tech armoured Firefighters at work in a man-made structure.

Three floors down they came into a workshop with rows of benches littered with what looked like weapons or scanning devices. Jed picked one of them up and twisted it in his hand. "This doesn't look very friendly does it?"

Christian, who had also picked up a device looked at Jed, "No, and it doesn't look very cheap either does it? Jeez, what is this Company so keen to get hold of *me* for if they've got all *this* shit?" He paused for a moment. "Shh. Hang on. Can you hear something?"

Jed froze and held his breath to avoid making any noise within his suit, "No mate. What can you hear?"

Christian walked towards the door of the room that led back towards the interior walkway of the Atrium. He stopped by the door to listen again and then stepped out into the walkway. He looked left. Nothing. He looked right and, as he did, something hit him hard and he fell to the ground.

Jed, who had watched the scene from behind, could see enough to realise that this was probably the other Christian. "Fucking robot wanker!" Jed ran to the door to assist but, as he did, it slammed on him and he heard something snap from outside. He banged against the door and pulled at the handle but it would not open. He turned and then moved quickly back to the benches where he began to pick up devices to try to determine if any of them would help him escape the room.

Outside, Christian stood hastily and spun round to see the robot standing a few feet away from him. The robot had a door handle in his hand that he looked at and then tossed over the side of the walkway. He stepped toward Christian. "I am sorry Christian but I've been reassigned to terminate you. I apologise for any inconvenience that this may cause. Have a nice day." The irony of this statement was not lost on Christian.

Christian turned and ran from him into the thick smoke. The robot stopped for a moment, thrown by the reaction, recalculated his next move and then began to walk mechanically in pursuit of Christian.

After a few steps the robot was then hit by Christian who hit him feet first in his chest. He lurched backwards and then, rather than landing on the ground, he arched his posture allowing himself to roll backwards onto the floor and then he rocked forward to an almost upright position which he completed with a lurch of his body. He stood upright and stoically looked back at Christian. Christian could not help but be impressed by the manoeuvre. The robot lunged forward and swiped his back hand across Christian's face, breaking his helmet in the process. Christian faltered backwards for a moment, his vision impeded by the broken visor and his hearing by the rushing of air from his suit. He twisted his helmet and lifted it. He spontaneously changed his own vision to thermal imaging and then, holding tightly to his helmet, smashed it hard against the robot's head. Having seen Christian remove his helmet the robot had been standing without defending, quite confident that he was no longer a threat to him, unaware that Christian had abilities beyond his own and unaware that he did not need his helmet to see perfectly in this environment.

The robot pitched backwards and this time fell against the railings. He grabbed the railings, before hitting the floor, and scrambled to pull himself back up to his feet. He then lurched forwards, grabbed Christian and threw him hard against the wall of an office. The wall, though brick built, almost completely failed on Christian's impact. Christian now almost sat within this newly formed brick mould as two or three bricks fell and bounced off his suit then hit the walkway. He felt a hand grab him around the neck as he was trying to step from the wall. He flailed at this and then grabbed the wrist of the hand to try to pull it from him. Though the robot seemed slightly weaker than Christian he was unable to free his arm due to the awkward position he found himself in.

Christian turned his suits' pulse setting up to maximum by manually striking some buttons with his other hand and then hit the robots' wrist with as much power as he could.

The robots grip loosened and he pushed him backwards. As Christian stood, he could see the robot examining his own wrist with intrigued learning. Christian picked up two bricks and launched one of them at the robot, then, as the robot moved to the left to avoid it Christian punched him hard in the side of the head with the second brick.

Both Christian and the robot had become so embroiled in their own fight that they had failed to see that around them the basement fire was growing and becoming much more of an immediate threat to them. Across the Atrium, offices became fully enveloped in flames, some form of furnishing that had been on the far walkway tipped, its' top half split and pinballed down into the lower basement with a final almighty crash. This caught Christian's attention and almost woke him to the reality of this bigger picture.

The robot was standing again. Christian looked at the broken brick in his hand and he dropped it. He stepped toward the robot. "Listen, please stop. Stop this now. We must go."

In a calm voice the robot replied, "I am sorry for this Christian. I have been detailed to terminate you. I hope this does not cause you…"

"Yeah, yeah any inconvenience. I do wish you could see the irony of that bloody statement. What is your name?"

"I do not have a name. What is the nature of your enquiry?"

Christian stepped back as he recognised that the robot was scanning his surroundings looking for his next plan of attack. "Your designation then. Your designation. What is it?"

"I am Bravo Zero Bravo Seven Two Nine Charlie Bravo Four One Seven dash P."

"Oh er, ok. Well, Bravo Zero Bravo, so then I'll call you Bob if that's okay? Listen Bob you must stop trying to kill me, okay?"

"Why?" The robot stepped towards him and he backed away at the same pace.

"Well Bob, because it goes against your basic programming."

"I do not concur. I must not harm *humans*. I can also not 'harm' you as, by definition, you cannot be harmed. Thus your termination is but the cessation of your functioning."

"No Bob, no, I am sentient. I feel. I am *aware*. As are *you*!"

The robot stood for a moment calculating this information.

"And surely bob if I'm aware then you cannot kill me either. That's why you can't kill humans because *they* are aware!"

The robot turned and smiled at Christian. "Thank you. I see the clarity of it now."

Christian allowed himself a deep rewarding sigh. "Oh, good, oh, okay. Well done Bob."

"If I cannot kill humans simply because they are aware and by your own disclosure you also are aware, then logic dictates that if I have orders to terminate you then I must also be authorised to terminate the humans."

Christians jaw dropped, "No! No, no. Bob, Bob, no! You mustn't. You mustn't do that. No!"

From behind him, Christian could hear Jed trying to use something against the door where he had been locked in. Christian turned to look and, as he did, the robot grabbed his arm with both hands and then pushed his foot into Christian's chest. Christian winced as he felt parts of him rip. He turned away and then swung round as hard as he could with his free hand and hit the robot in the leg. It did not damage the leg but it did put him out of position for a moment. A moment was all Christian needed to then step to the side and then hit out again contacting the robot's head hard with his fist. This time the helmet was cracked along the length of the visor and so he let go of Christian and stumbled backwards. Christian leaned down to one side, intuitively protecting his badly damaged arm. He turned and staggered along the walkway to the room where Jed was still locked in.

"Jed, Jed, stay inside, stay in there until I'm done, okay? Don't come out for a few minutes until I give you the all clear."

Christian fell hard against the door as he was hit from behind. He cried out in pain and ducked out of the way of what he correctly guessed would be a following punch. He rolled out of the way and stumbled backwards a few paces towards a walkway that crossed the whole span between the far walls across the atrium. He fell hard against the walkway but pulled himself along it with his good arm, trying to stand as he did. The robot turned from where he had punched the wall and walked towards Christian. A few steps onto the walkway, Christian turned to see the robot as he approached. He raised his good arm to protect himself but the robot kicked him hard in the centre of the chest. He slid hard and fast along the walkway, metalwork splintering and buckling underneath him as he did. He tried to conceal his pain but after a few moments screamed through closed clenched teeth. "Bob, please. PLEASE STOP!" Christian raised his hand up to protect his face as the robot stood over him with both arms raised ready to beat on him like an enraged silver back. Suddenly, from behind, came a whizzing noise that rose in pitch and volume and part of an office door Catherine wheeled past the robots' head. He turned and leaned forward ready to defend himself from whatever was about to come towards him. *Jed* came towards him holding, what looked like, some form of hair dryer. "Right, both of you, stop right there."

On the floor, Christian lowered his hands to the ground. "Oh Jed, oh thank fuck."

"Yeah well sorry guys but unfortunately you're now both covered in soot so I really can't tell you apart."

Christian leaned up onto his good arm, "Jed, be careful this robot's safety protocols have been overridden."

Jed stood for a moment trying to decide his next tactic. How could he correctly identify his friend from his enemy?

The robot stepped forward one pace. "Jed please, we need to get out of here. Look around you, this place is fucked. Let us go!"

Without moving his head, Jed quickly glanced around the walkway to see the full extent of the damage.

He realised that he had little time to decide which Christian to help and which to try to restrain or destroy. He smiled, "Okay guys, let me ask you this. Where's the best place in London to get an Ass Burger?"

The robot frowned, "Excuse me?"

Christian sat up slightly, "Well if it was in a diner…"

Jed leaned forward, willing the answer from him.

Christian turned to him smiling, "It would be called the Autistic Spectrum Diner."

Jed smiled wider, relieved he had quickly identified his friend from foe. The robot looked at him, then at Christian, then back at Jed. It knew that it would have to take care of Jed before he could finish with Christian so it quickly lunged forwards towards Jed.

All of the black smoke around them suddenly flashed with a neon green glow of strobed energy as it shot from Jed's weapon. A large hole appeared in the chest of the robot as it flew backwards and peeled against the railing of the walkway disappearing into the thick dense black smoke. It bounced twice and draped over the side of the walkway. It teetered for a moment then grated against the metalwork as it tumbled over the edge.

Jed dropped the weapon and darted over to assist Christian up. He knelt down beside him and placed his hand in Christian's.

"Fuck sake Jed, where've you *been*?"

"Well bloody hell I must have tried about two dozen devices before I found that. I was picking up all the things that actually looked like weapons first. They had a mini gun type thing in there that just dispenses chewing gum for Christ's sake!" Jed smiled at his friend and tensed, ready to pull him up onto his feet. "Come on, we really *do* need to get out of here."

Without warning the walkway twisted. Jed's grip on Christian loosened. He lost his footing and stepped backwards. He looked to the far end of the walkway which had appeared to have dropped slightly. There, he saw the robot hanging under the walkway, clearly trying to pull parts of the supports away. "Oh fuck!" Jed turned to retrieve the weapon but, as he did, the walkway listed heavily to one side. He fell against the railings and then instinctively fell to the floor to grab as much metal work as he could. Christian pulled himself towards Jed to help them both get back to the main walkway. Before he could reach Jed there was a grinding sound of contorting metal and the far end of the walkway suddenly gave way. For a moment gravity seemed to be defied as all weight of the floor beneath them disappeared. As the walkway began to fall, they could both hear the loud clanging of metal as the robot bounced off of other walkways on its' way down to the bottom floor with a final cymbal crashing finale. The walkway swung from its' middle section where the supports from the other side of the walkway joined the now, redundant section. It swung hard against itself and hit the remaining support. As it did, Christian held fast against the walkway, as Jed slid downwards and past him towards the floor. Christian grabbed for him but could not target him in time.

Jed landed against a railing as he slid down and with a yelp of pain, grabbed hold of it before he slid completely from the walkway.

Christian froze for a moment. "Jed, are you okay?"

"Argh-h-h, fuck, yes. I'm okay."

Christian, without thinking, started to clamber up the walkway back towards the safety of the main platform. After three or four steps he realised that he should be climbing downwards towards his friend to help him survive this. He inwardly berated himself as he began to climb down the twisted metalwork.

Jed had tried to swing his legs onto the walkway so as to get a more solid hold but by swinging around he had realised that he must be on the last hand rail so there was actually nothing beneath him except the ground which was approximately eight or nine floors beneath him. Looking around, he realised that they had little time to get free of this. The basement was fully alight and flames could be seen down almost the whole depth of the basement.

Christian was now almost next to Jed. "Jed, Jed, are you okay?"

"Yeah I'm okay. I need some help though mate. If you could..." the walkway contorted further as it continued to fail. Christian lost grip of the walkway with his hand. He slid heavily towards the floor. Jed had lost one of his hand holds and was trying desperately to grab the railing but, as he did, his other hand also lost its' grip and slid off the bar. He fell and then swung away from the walkway for a moment and then back towards it. His initial reaction had been to cry out but, before he could, this new change of direction made him look up. There he saw Christian holding him with his good arm.

"Oh fuck me mate...Ha-ha-ha, well done. Oh shit." As he spoke he looked up the length of Christian's other arm and now realised for the first time the amount of damage it had sustained. This was the arm that was keeping them both anchored to the metalwork. He looked at Christian with concern.

"Chris. Chris, you okay?" Christian did not answer. He had lost a lot of fluid and his arm was causing him a great deal of pain. After a few moments he tensed his muscles to try to lift Jed but he could not.

"Jed I'm...I'm not in a good way I'm afraid." Christian looked down at Jed. "I'm sorry mate I can't lift you up. Climb up me."

Jed could see that Christian was struggling to keep them both anchored on. The walkway juddered sharply and Christian's grip loosened slightly from the metalwork. Jed saw that Christian was really struggling to continue holding both of their weight.

"Chris!"

"Yes mate?"

"Chris, if I climbed up you, do you think you'd be able to get *yourself* up the walkway?"

"Yes, yes I think so mate."

"Chris, are you *sure*?"

"Yes. Yes I'm pretty sure of it."

Jed looked up at Christian. "Chris?"

Christian looked down at Jed and could see tears rolling down his flushed cheeks. "Yes?"

"Take care of Hannah for me, would you?"

Christian's pupils dilated with fear, "What, what? What the fuck are you talking about mate? What are you thinking? We can make this mate. Come on, climb up. Quick. Please. Please Jed, climb up."

"You know we haven't got time mate. We can't both make it. You're smarter than me so you know it's true. I love you mate!"

"NO! NO! NO! CLIMB UP, NO. CLIMB UP YOU FUCKER!" Christian hooked tighter with his damaged arm and tried desperately in vein to lift them both with it.

Jed tried to pull himself free from Christian's grip but could not so he twisted his glove with his free hand and pulled the release for it.

"NO! NO! JED, NO! PLEASE!" Christians' eyes flooded with soot stained fluid and he could feel a fearful rage within himself trying to fight this impossibility of reason.

The glove snapped open, Jed looked past Christian and up towards where the sky would be, "Yes I know. I'm coming." With that, the glove failed and, a now flatly smiling Jed, fell quickly downwards dragging smoke with him like a stone dropped into a muddy lake. He quickly disappeared out of Christian's site and, in the efficiently engineered blink of a synthetically manufactured eye, he was gone.

"NO-O-O-O-O-O-O-O-O!" Christian thrashed out frantically with his now freed arm at where Jed had been, desperate to catch him, knowing all the while, that it was too late, knowing that his friend was gone. The weight that he felt in his heart would surely drag him down also as he clung to the walkway and wept uncontrollably. He looked up at his damaged arm and cursed it for failing him, failing his friend. For a moment he contemplated releasing his grip and joining his friend. But, in that same moment, he decided that this would have devalued Jed's sacrifice and dishonoured his memory. Christian took hold of the walkway with his good arm and, slowly and painfully, began to climb.

CHAPTER FOURTEEN

"The parting glass"

1

Silence filled the hall with unspoken expectation. Occasionally someone would cough or shuffle in their seat but then, realising how loudly this echoed, quickly stifled their cough or limited their shuffling. The large traditional wood and brick fascia'd interior was carpeted throughout. At the end of the hall Jed's coffin sat atop a wheeled platform adorned with a fantastic display of flowers and a hologram of him in full uniform standing next to the coffin *as was tradition.*

The Chief Officer walked in with his wife and, looking for a space to sit down, was greeted with unwelcome looks from the already seated Firefighters. He therefore walked towards the back and sat behind the rest of the congregation.

Over the sound system came a recording of the dulcet tones of Shaun Davey as he sang *The Parting Glass*. A song of forgiveness and understanding, of hope, apology and moving on. Katie sat at the front with Mother and his wife. Next to them sat Christian and Hannah. A tear rolled down Katie's puffy red cheeks and she lowered her head into her hand as she painfully reflected on the loss of her dear friend. Mother's wife squeezed his arm as his eyes began to well, the sadness of the song not helping to lessen his grief. Christian sat, simply staring at Jed's coffin, Hannah's hand rested in his.

A bearded comely looking vicar slowly walked solemnly from the back of the hall between the pews and then stood by Jed's coffin. He rested his hand on it then bowed his head for a moment. After a few seconds he smiled, raised his head and turned towards the lectern that was raised up on a few steps. As he stepped behind the lectern the music began to fade.

He ushered the congregation, who had all stood when he walked in, to "Please be seated". He smiled at the audience a respectful welcoming smile. "Dearly beloved we are gathered here today not to mourn the passing of a friend and colleague but to celebrate his life. Mourning is a very personal experience and how we deal with this is individual to us all. *We* are here today however to celebrate the deeds and work of Firefighter Jonathon Edwards, who I understand liked to be called Jed, so I shall, hereafter, refer to him as thus…..if you will indulge me." He looked over his glasses and smiled an almost Christmas card smile at those gathered. "The life of a man, or woman, is but a drop in the ocean of their full existence. The ripples that we cast out in *this* life however, touch the lives of all those that we meet and these ripples follow us as we move into the next phase of our *being*. Now I understand that those whom Jed affected were *so* touched as to imply that rather than those ripples being caused by the dropping of a pebble, his were more like the crashing of an asteroid into the sea." He indulged himself with another smile. He then spoke of the relationship between man and God and then read two psalms appropriate for the occasion. "Now Jed's friends and colleagues Shaun and Leslie wished to read something but before I hand you over to them I would like to finish with a short poem by the novelist Samuel Butler who lived in the nineteenth century." He coughed to clear his throat.

> *"I fall asleep in the full and certain hope*
> *That my slumber shall not be broken;*
> *And that though I be all-forgetting,*
> *Yet shall I not be forgotten,*
> *But continue that life in the thoughts and deeds*
> *Of those I loved."*

The vicar silently closed the book he was reading and placed his hands together for a moment, smiling. He then stood upright and beckoned Mother to come forward to say a few words.

Mother stood at the Lectern. He gulped and then concentrated on straightening his tie to try to calm his nerves. "I hope you will forgive me but I am not known for my public speaking. Nor am I famous for my writing. So with this in mind I hope that you will pardon me for having chosen to read the words of better writers than myself. The first is from Alexander Graham Bell."

'When one door closes, another opens; but we often look so long and so regretfully upon the closed door that we do not see the one that has opened for us.'

"It pleases me that this particular quote is from Alexander Bell as he was a scientist and inventor and would have appreciated the reasoning for this choice of words and that is that we must not forget that Jed's sacrifice was not in vein. His sacrifice had meaning and value. It allowed the survival of Christian. Let us not mourn the passing of our Brother so much that we forget our remaining Brother." Mother stretched out his hand down towards where Christian sat. Christian who sat with arm in sling tried to smile at Mother gratefully but a flat tear stained smile was all that he could muster. Mother nodded. "The other quote I would like to read to you is un-credited." He smiled, "I *also* stole this from the Uni-web."

'I always knew looking back on the tears would make me laugh, but I never knew looking back on the laughs would make me cry.'

Mother sighed deeply and composed himself for a moment. He bowed his head as he wiped away a tear from his eye and clenched his jaw tight to prevent himself from crying further. "The Fire Brigade has not lost a Firefighter for just under eighty years. Eighty years! I never expected to lose a Firefighter on my watch." Mother leaned against the lectern with both of his outstretched arms and looked to the floor. "I cannot bring him back and I struggle to come to terms with his loss." Mother sniffed away tears and stood upright almost at attention. "Jed was an excellent Firefighter. He was a decent man and an irreplaceable friend. The only solace I can take from this is that his actions prevented the loss of our friend Christian. I will never be able to show him how grateful I am for this nor be able to see his smile or hear his terrible jokes."

The audience was slightly lifted by soft chuckles and giggles at remembering his jokes and stories.

"Christian's survival is Jed's legacy and for that we should be eternally grateful. It was a far, far better thing that he did then than he had ever done. It was a far, far better resting place that he went to than he had ever known. Together at last, may he and Laura both now rest in peace." Mother paused for a moment, head still bowed, and then returned to his seat. His wife leaned into him and kissed him on the temple as he lowered his head forward in his seat.

Les now took his cue and stepped forward from the rear of the hall. Walking between the pews, he strode with confidence in a long black respectful dress complete with fascinator.

The Chief Officer looked around in discomfort. He leaned forward to the pew in front of him and tapped a man on his shoulder.

The man, Jerry, turned to the Chief Officer, "Yes?"

"Please don't tell me that's one of my Firefighters."

"Ok then Guv."

"What? Well, is he?"

"You just told me *not* to tell you Guv."

The Chief Officer sighed, "Ok, very good. *Is* that one of my Firefighters?"

"Yes Guv."

"Well does he always wear a dress?"

"No Guv."

"Oh, thank goodness for that."

"He says he can't find a female undress uniform that will fit him, but he *has* ordered a made to measure. Now is there anything else you wanna bother me with during this funeral?"

The Chief Officer sat back into his pew and smiled awkwardly at his wife.

Les tipped his fascinator slightly forward as he leaned against the lectern. "Jed is gone. Now I know that for some of us it will take longer to come to terms with than others but together we can get through this and I think that that's what he would have wanted. Jed fully embraced life and I think that that's what he would want of us now. Jed was a good Firefighter, a good husband. He was a very funny guy and I shared many laughs with him. I know that I have many things to look back on, many happy memories. I hope that you all will learn with me to not weep but to relish these moments, for in them Jed will continue to be with us, continue to live on." *Les paused for a moment standing upright, he cleared his throat. "Now one thing I do think was Jed's biggest failing though was that he was a complete arse."*

There was a murmuring chorus of uncertain disrespectful displeasure from the audience.

Les raised an elegantly black gloved hand to temper the crowd. "Now hold on one moment. Before you think me too harsh, let me give you some examples to explain what I mean." From within the top section of his dress he produced a small tablet. He put on some glasses that he'd had in his handbag, placed the tablet on the lectern, lowered his glasses and began to read. "Okay, so before you all judge me, hear me out. 'Exhibit A.' There was the time that he took Kevin's work-wear boots home after Kevin became a little bit too cocky, a little bit too quickly, having just joined the watch. He then proceeded to fill them with jelly and custard and set them in his fridge at home. He then brought said boots back and had placed them such that when Kevin finished testing his suit he placed his feet straight back into them and was covered in custard." Les looked over his glasses at the jury, 'Oh dear Kevin.' remarked Jed. 'You appear to have gotten yourself a trifle, *too* big, for your boots!"

The audience began a ripple of giggles from those that were hearing this tale for the first time and belly laughs from those that were there at the time of it happening.

The Chief Officer turned to his wife, "I can't believe that one of my Firefighters behaved like that. I shall have a word with their Officer in Charge."

Without turning her head and, in a disapproving tone, his wife replied, "Do I need to remind you Donald of all the *shit* you got up to when you were a Firefighter? Now keep quiet, I'm listening."

The Chief motioned to protest.

"Besides Donald, this is a funeral. You've lost one of your Firefighters. Please, can't you take your head out of your arse just this once?"

Jerry turned round and nodded to the Chief just to politely remind him that his actions and attitude were not going unnoticed.

Les overran for about twenty minutes as he continued to amuse all of those present with stories of jokes played *on* Jed and *by* him, funny recollections of occurrences at incidents or during nights out on the town. As the laughter began to subside, Les nodded to signal that he had ended his delivery. Bagpipes now began to play over the sound system. Amazing Grace. Les stepped down and walked to the front seats and beckoned those seated to stand and walk out before him. Christian, Hannah, Mother and his wife stood and walked out followed by the remaining congregation. Les waited a moment for Katie to stand to walk out but she did not. He stepped over and sat next to her. Silently, slightly numbed, she said nothing but simply rested her head on his shoulder.

2

Outside, though cold, the sky was a perfectly clear, cloudless, light blue. The funeral had finished and most of Jed's friends and colleagues had begun to depart so that they could head towards a nearby hotel where Les and Richie had organised a reception. Christian and Hannah sat together on a wooden patron-donated bench under a tree in the graveyard that overlooked the site where Jed had just been laid to rest. The temperature was low and the wind that blew through the graveyard chilled quickly through to the bone.

Christian stood, removed his jacket and placed it around Hannah's shoulders. He sat back down and placed his arm around her to keep her warm. She looked at him sideways. He noticed this and loosened his grip on her, "Oh sorry I was…"

"No, no that's fine. Sorry I don't mind." She smiled at him.

"Good lord Hannah how can you be so nice to me after…"

"After what?"

"Hannah, he died, I survived. How can you be so calm about it?"

"Because I'm calm about it, doesn't mean I'm not affected by it Chris." She lowered her eyes. "I will deal with this in my own way in my own time. I'm simply trying to be pragmatic about it. If I allow this to overtake me now I think it might just consume me."

"I'm sorry." Christian's eyes began to water and then he lowered his head into his hands as tears began to flow through his fingers. He tried to stifle the tears but he could not. "It's just, I…I started to climb. He was in trouble and, without thinking, I started to climb away from him before going back to help him. I just…"

"Oh my word Chris, how boringly Neuro-typical you are becoming."

Christian looked up from his hands, "What? How…what?"

Hannah raised her eyes, "Neuro Typical Chris. Oh please don't go getting all 'normal' on me. I was just beginning to like you."

Christian shook his head and then sniffed away a tear as he sat up, "Eh?"

"Human Chris. Human. You're becoming typically human. You climbed because your human instinct forced you to survive. It was your courage that overrode that instinct and allowed you to climb down to try to save him. Many would not have been so brave. I can't

273

blame you for your actions and, having read the initial reports on it, I don't believe anything you could have done could have saved…Jed. But I do thank you for trying. It was very brave. I understand why he spoke so highly of you." Hannah laid her hand onto Chris' and smiled.

Christian pulled her towards him and she rested her head on his shoulder.

They both sat silently for several minutes. Eventually Chris spoke, "Hannah."

"Yes?"

"I have been thinking of finding another name for myself. I don't like that the company have tagged me with this name and I wondered if you thought it would be appropriate for me to take Jed's name?"

Hannah paused for a moment. "His full name?"

"No, just Jed. As a middle name. In *honour* of him."

Hannah smiled again, "I think that's very sweet. Christian Jed Mann."

"Well, no, *actually* I wanted to drop Christian too. I like the name Martin."

"Really? Martin's nice. Any particular reason why?

"Actually no, well, no, I'm not sure. It just seems right somehow. I just like it."

"Well if that's what you want, it's okay with me. A robot by any other name, *you know*?"

Christian chuckled. Hannah waited a few more minutes. "Martin?"

Christian smiled at her, "Yes?"

"Do you think this will be the church that we shall get married in?"

Christian grinned at her directness. He thought to himself that perhaps he could get used to this honest form of discussion. He thought that maybe this Asperger's thing was a pretty good thing after all. "Jed asked me to look after you. He didn't mention getting married to you."

"Does that mean we're *not* getting married here then?"

"I didn't say that."

"Good." Hannah squeezed Christian's hand and rested her head lower onto his shoulder. She lifted her head up again quickly, "Oh sorry this doesn't hurt your arm does it?"

Christian smiled at her. "No, no that's fine. I've worked out how to turn off my pain receptors for the time being and my arm should have repaired itself within a couple more days anyway." After a pause he continued. "I guess if this place is good enough for Jed and Laura then it's good enough for us."

Christian looked up hearing a woman approaching from his left.

"You two coming? Me and Anna are waiting in the pod to give you a lift if you want it."

Hannah looked down at Les' dress.

"I know what you're thinking." Les smiled and struck a pose. "It's what he would have wanted."

"There're not many guys as big as you would look as good in that dress as you do Les."

"Thank-you Hannah."

Christian and Hannah stood. Arm in arm the three friends walked together to the waiting pod.

As they stood by the pod waiting for its doors to open, Hannah turned to Les and softly asked, "Les?"

"Yes Hannah?"

"Would you ever consider being a brides' maid?"

EPILOGUE

The main seat of fire had been dealt with leaving only a few hot spots for crews to deal with. Some smoke still poured from sections of the shopping mall but these were soon becoming replaced by steam as the smoke dissipated into the atmosphere due to crews making steady progress through the separate retail units. Two appliances were parked outside the front, one of which was the command pump. Two other appliances were parked at the rear of the mall due to the incident being large enough to warrant being sectorised. A bulky single-seater red pod pulled up, slightly away from the command pump and out stepped Assistant Divisional Officer Knight. Newly transferred into the London Brigade, but with several years under his belt, and a couple more bulging out over the top of it, he stood for a moment and surveyed the shopping mall before walking to the rear of his pod and retrieving his fire suit. Once donned, he strode haughtily towards the command pump. In his *previous* Brigade he considered himself very important due to the low number of A.D.O.'s there but, here in London, he was yet to learn that A.D.O.'s came fifteen to the dozen. As he reached the command pump he was greeted by Divisional Officer Riley and Assistant Chief Officer McCormick who both shook his hand and welcomed him.

"Hello." Said Mother, "My name is Shaun, Shaun riley, this is Nigel, Nigel McCormick."

"Hello." Shake. "I am A.D.O. Knight, Gavin Knight." Shake.

Knight stood slightly awkwardly having believed that *he* would be the highest ranking Officer on the fire ground and being slightly disappointed to discover that there were two higher ranking Officers already in attendance.

"Can I ask which of you has taken over this job then Guv's?"

Mother looked sideways at Nigel, smiled and looked back at Knight. Neither of us.

Knight flinched then asked, "So, sorry, have you both *just* arrived then?"

"No, no we've been here a while. We just came to see how things were. Excuse really just to have a little ride out."

Knight frowned. This was most irregular. Senior Officers arriving at a fire ground and not taking over? Were these two *incompetent*? Lazy? Arrogant? He huffed. "Well Guv's, do you not think we should take over command of this incident if we're here?"

"Knight, if we had thought it appropriate to take over this incident we would have done so, do you not think? Station Officer Martin Mann is in control of this incident, and when Station Officer Mann is in control of an incident, take it from us, you could do a lot worse than attend and observe, just to see how it *should* be done."

Knight leaned backwards slightly as if avoiding a flashover of condemnation. He was not used to being put in his place. In the smaller Brigade he'd come from he was considered a big cheese but here he seemed to be a small slice of cheese that had been left out and had begun to go off a little. He coughed and spluttered his protestations under his breath with a series of grunts and barks, but with no distinguishable words or meanings, so as to show his indignation but not be held accountable for any words he may have said.

As he stood for a moment deciding how best to walk away or move the conversation on without losing any more face, Station Officer Mann appeared from behind the command pump and walked past him towards Mother and Nigel. Martin took off his suit's glove and shook hands with them both.

"Hello guys, how long have you been here for?"

Nigel looked at Mother for confirmation, "Oh, about ten minutes maybe?"

Mother nodded agreement, "Yeah, about ten minutes I guess."

Martin smiled at Mother, "Oh, of course that nice café is not far from here is it, so no wonder you turned up."

Mother smirked his reply and rolled his eyes in acceptance of Martin's insight. "So, you coming to Nigel's retirement do tonight?"

"Hell yes, just to make sure you leave, you old Bugger." Martin slapped Nigel on his arm.

"Is Hannah coming?"

"Yes, she said she wouldn't miss it for the world. Kevin's coming too, although that may just be to show off his new pod." Martin shook his head towards the sky, "Since the company paid him out he thinks he's some kind of playboy."

"About time too. How many years did it take for them to cough up? Six?"

"No, he's literally just been paid out so, near on nigh seven." Martin huffed and looked away for a moment. "I can't believe no one has ever been convicted though." He rubbed his arm subconsciously remembering.

"Money talks Martin. *You* know how it is."

Martin nodded. "Oh Katie's coming. She found a baby sitter after all."

Nigel nodded, "Oh good, I'd like to catch up with Katie. I've not seen *her* in a while either. I didn't know she and Richie had a baby though. God I really should have made more time to get over to see you all."

"That's ok Nige' I know you've been busy leading up to retirement."

"Retirement? I think not. I *wish* it were retirement. No, she's got so many plans for me indoors, I think she's trying to kill me. By the sounds of it I'd be better off rebuilding the whole house than doing all the decorating she's got planned for me."

A.D.O. knight, who had been standing to one side of them, coughed to announce his presence.

Mother leaned round Martin, "Oh sorry, of course." He stretched out a hand towards him to include him in the group. "Martin, this is A.D.O. Knight, A.D.O. Knight this…"

Before he could finish his sentence a window at the front of one of the shopping units failed and hissed aggressively as smoke coughed out through the now-gaping hole in it. Martin turned away and gave some commands into his helmet. Without saying anything to the Officers he then turned and ran towards the shop to continue controlling operations.

Knight stood with both hands on his hips camply exaggerating his dismay. He then deliberately shook his head, turned to Mother, "Unbelievable! I have never seen such insubordination in all my life."

Mother glanced at Nigel and under his breath muttered, "Welcome to London."

Knight turned to face where Martin had run to, "Does that man not know the correct protocols for greeting an Officer as laid down in policy? Does he not know that…..OOHH, I've an idea to give him a piece of my mind. Remind him of what is actually stated in policy!"

Nigel put a hand up towards Knight, "Oh, are you sure you want to…"

Mother pulled Nigel's hand down to stop him from advising Knight. "Oh I don't know Nigel, perhaps A.D.O. Knight has a point."

Mother raised his brow and tilted his enquiring head to Nigel. Nigel saw the silly humour in Mother's point.

Nigel stifled a pre-retirement-jape giggle and straightened his expression. "You know what Knight, you should go talk to him. You go give him a piece of your mind, see just how much he thinks he knows about policy!"

Knight nodded a stern face and strode off to battle. Nigel hid his head behind Mother as he treated himself to the kind of giggling he had not enjoyed since he was a Firefighter. Mother *too* began to laugh.

As they both looked on at A.D.O. Knight trying to better educate Martin on the correct quoting and use of policy they could see him becoming more and more stooped where his shoulders clearly hung heavier and heavier in his suit. Mother and Nigel also bent further and further over as they became more and more amused the lower Knight became. Martin became more and more animated and was clearly taking no prisoners as he reeled off policies and facts verbatim after which he boldly exiled Knight from his incident ground.

As Knight walked back toward Nigel and Mother, Martin looked over to them to see Mother, who had needed to remove his helmet, wiping away a tear. Martin simply shook his head at them both for playing such an unpleasant prank on the new A.D.O.

Knight walked past them both as he returned to his pod. As he passed them he phlegmatically droned, "The man's like a bloody machine!"

At that, Mother was convinced that he was in danger of wetting himself as he turned from Knight and hid himself behind an also-laughing Nigel.

As Knight returned silently to his pod, Martin walked back towards the two Senior Officers Shaking his head and smiling. As he approached the two Officers, who were smirking like naughty school

281

boys, two Firefighters appeared from the other side of the command pump and approached him.

"Morning Guv' our Officer in charge doesn't need us at the moment so wondered if you needed any extra hands this side of the building." As Martin turned to face them, the Firefighter leaned back, "Captain Novis?"

Martin scrunched his face slightly. "Um, excuse me?"

"Sorry, it *is* Captain Novis, *isn't* it Sir?"

"Son, we don't *have* any captains in the Brigade. I'm a Station Officer and also, I'm not Novis I'm *Mann*. I think you have me mistaken young man." Martin smiled at him.

The Firefighter looked to the floor, "Oh, sorry Guv, yes of course. It's just that…well, I've got this old picture at home of a guy my Dad served with who he used to speak about a lot. You are the spitting image though Guv. It's uncanny Sir. Sorry for the confusion."

"That's quite alright young man, no need to apologise. So your Father was in the Brigade too?"

"No Sir, he was in the Royal Gurkhas, attached to the pioneers, but…" The Firefighter swallowed hard, "I'm afraid he, um…he died Sir, on Mars."

Martin's brow furrowed and he tilted an intrigued head, "Oh I'm sorry to hear that. The Pioneers, eh?"

"Yes, he was shot whilst out on patrol." The Firefighter stopped talking, obviously shaken by the memory of it.

"Well I'm sorry to hear that and I'm sorry for your loss. The Gurkhas are a brave bunch. Well, Anyway, I don't need you guys round here so you two can head back to your sector."

"Okay Guv." The two Firefighters turned and walked away. Just before they disappeared behind the appliance again, Martin called after them, "Hey son?"

The Firefighter turned, "Yes Guv?"

"What's your name?"

"Walker Sir. Firefighter Walker." He turned again to walk off.

"Son, sorry, one more thing."

"Yes Guv?"

"This Novis, what was his first name, do you know?

"Um, Matthew, um, no-no, Martin I think it was Guv. Yeah, it was Martin." The Firefighter nodded and both he and his colleague disappeared behind the appliance.

Christian froze for a moment open mouthed. Memories, that may or may not be his own, now began flooding back to him. He looked up to the heavens aware that somewhere above him a six and a half thousand kilometre wide ball of red dusty rock, that he may have once called home, tumbled through space. After a few minutes he snapped back to Earth to get on with his task at hand and, as he marched off to finish his work, he glanced once more up into the sky and simply mumbled "Bollocks."

Printed in Great Britain
by Amazon